THE L·O·S·T
C O L O N Y

BOOK NO.2
THE Red MENACE

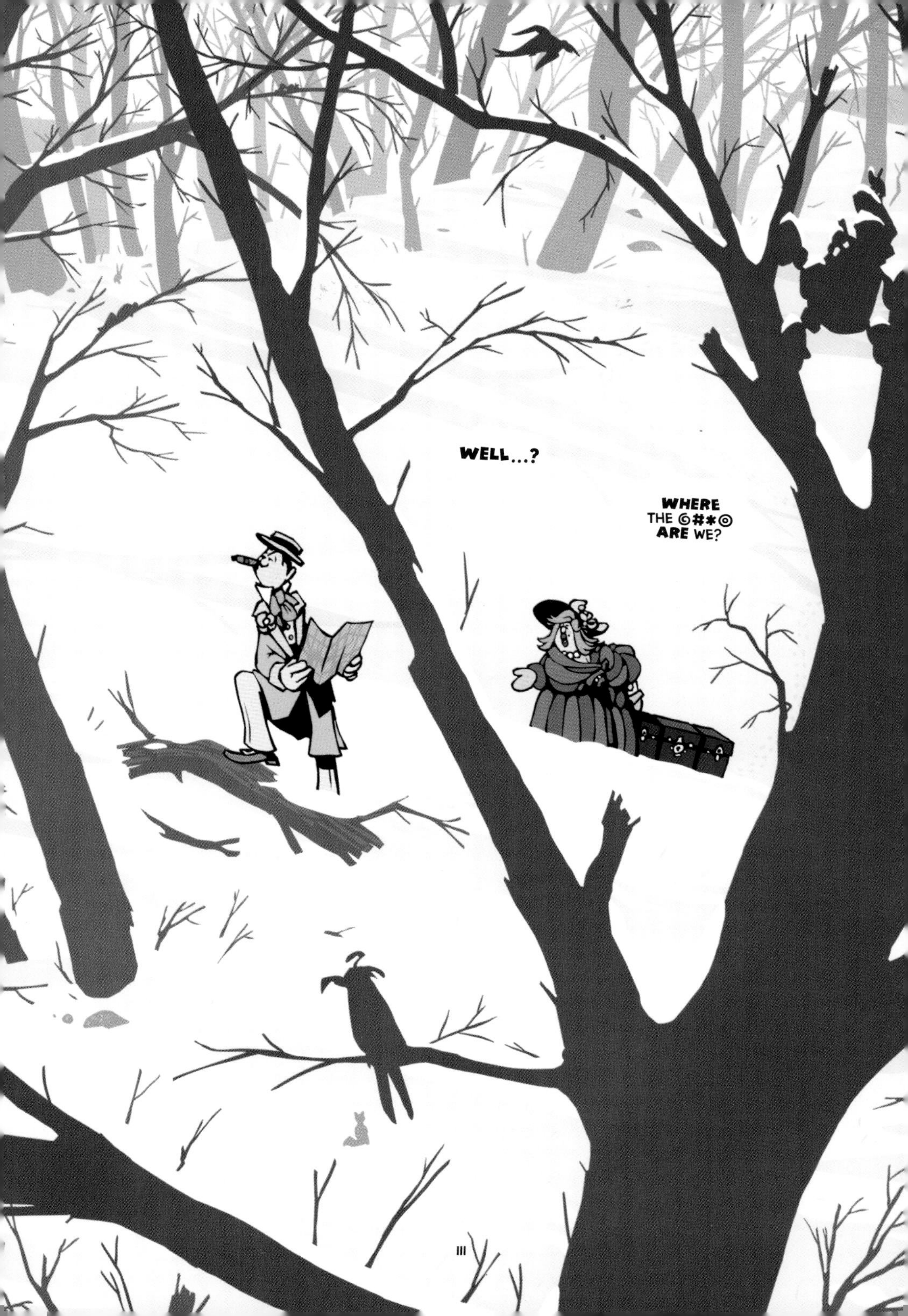
WELL...?
WHERE THE ©#*© ARE WE?

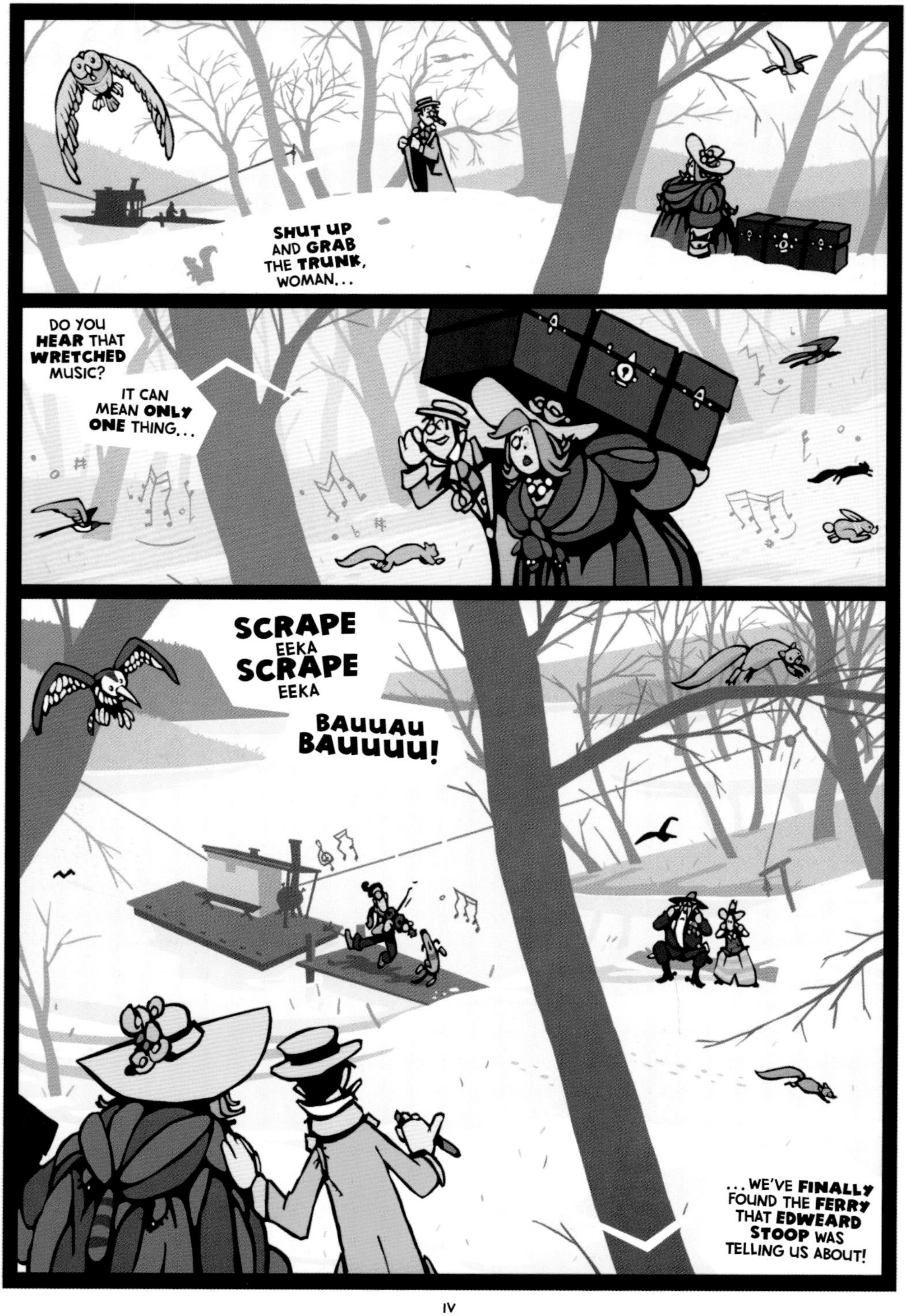
SHUT UP AND GRAB THE TRUNK, WOMAN...
DO YOU HEAR THAT WRETCHED MUSIC?
IT CAN MEAN ONLY ONE THING...
SCRAPE EEKA SCRAPE EEKA
BAUUAU BAUUUU!
...WE'VE FINALLY FOUND THE FERRY THAT EDWEARD STOOP WAS TELLING US ABOUT!

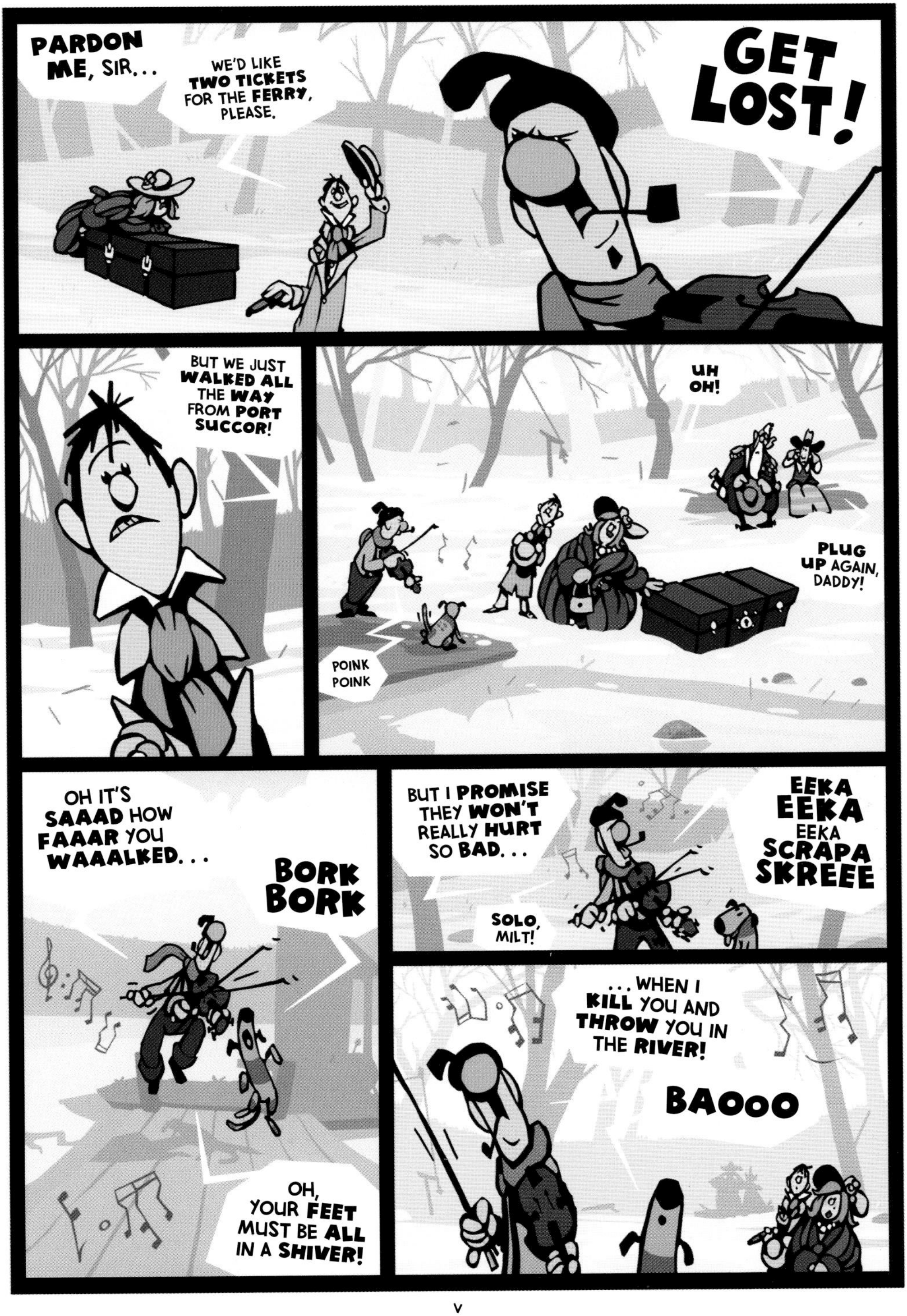
PARDON ME, SIR...
WE'D LIKE TWO TICKETS FOR THE FERRY, PLEASE.
GET LOST!
BUT WE JUST WALKED ALL THE WAY FROM PORT SUCCOR!
UH OH!
PLUG UP AGAIN, DADDY!
POINK POINK
OH IT'S SAAAD HOW FAAAR YOU WAAALKED...
BORK BORK
OH, YOUR FEET MUST BE ALL IN A SHIVER!
BUT I PROMISE THEY WON'T REALLY HURT SO BAD...
EEKA EEKA EEKA SCRAPA SKREEE
SOLO, MILT!
...WHEN I KILL YOU AND THROW YOU IN THE RIVER!
BAOOO

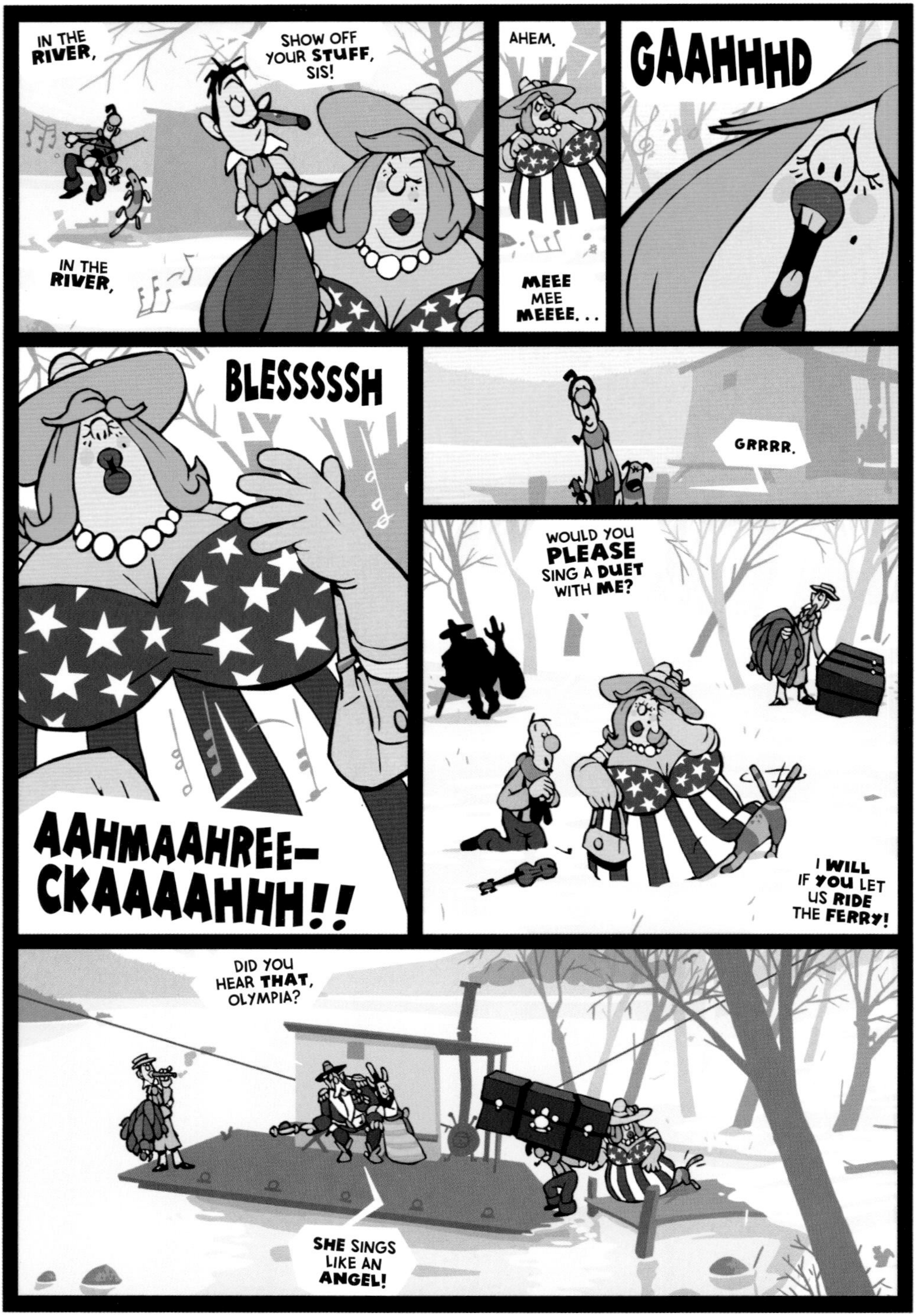

IN THE **RIVER**,
SHOW OFF YOUR **STUFF**, SIS!
IN THE **RIVER**,
AHEM.
MEEE MEE **MEEEE**. . .
GAAHHHD
BLESSSSSH
AAHMAAHREE-CKAAAAHHH!!
GRRRR.
WOULD YOU **PLEASE** SING A **DUET** WITH **ME**?
I **WILL** IF **YOU** LET US **RIDE** THE **FERRY**!
DID YOU HEAR **THAT**, OLYMPIA?
SHE SINGS LIKE AN **ANGEL**!

THE
L·O·S·T
COLONY

BOOK NO. 2

OF THE Red MENACE

ADMIT ONE
READER
BEGRUDGINGLY
NO. 2

DO NOT TRESPASS

Grady Klein

:01

First Second

NEW YORK & LONDON

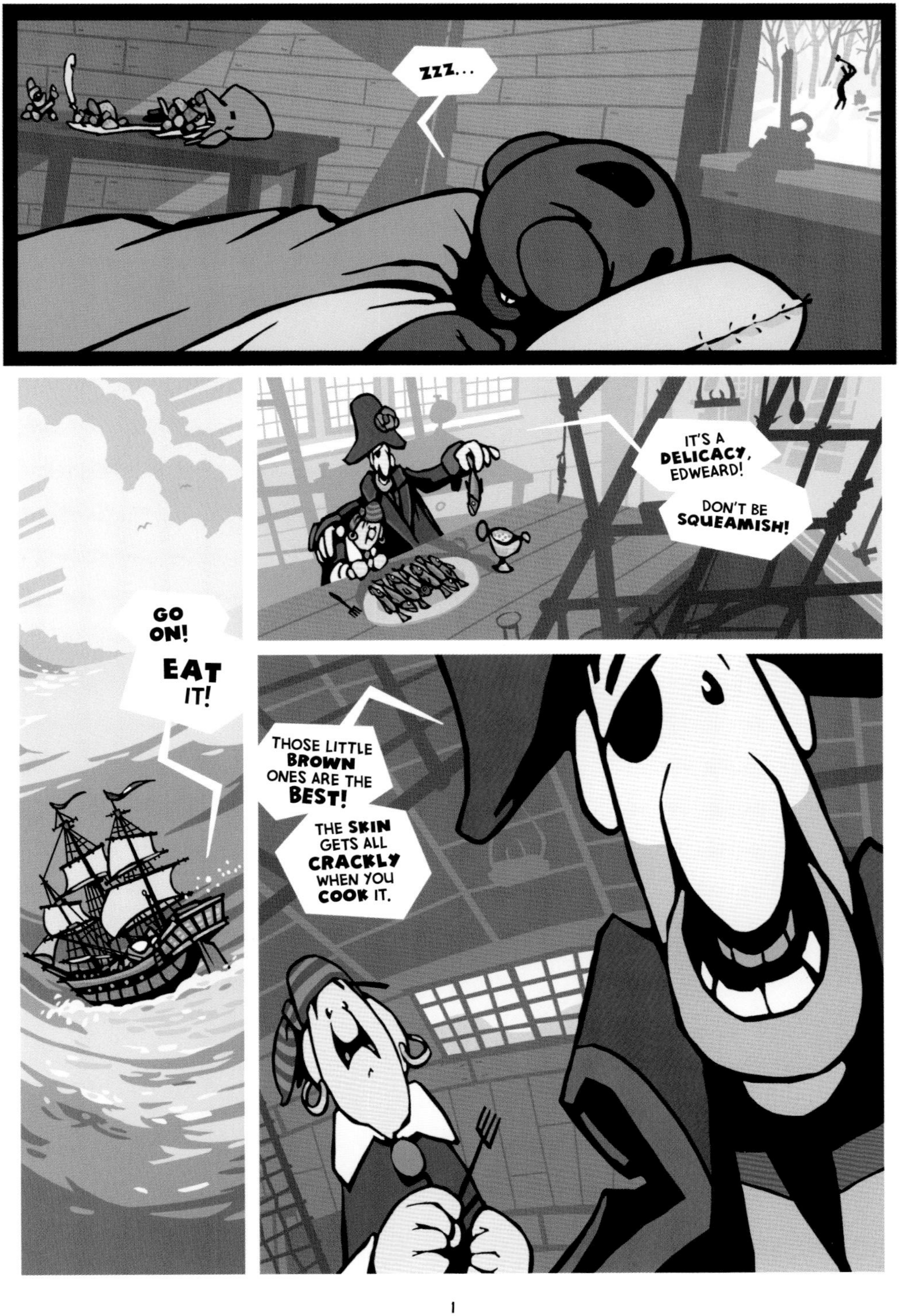
ZZZ...
GO ON!
EAT IT!
IT'S A DELICACY, EDWEARD!
DON'T BE SQUEAMISH!
THOSE LITTLE BROWN ONES ARE THE BEST!
THE SKIN GETS ALL CRACKLY WHEN YOU COOK IT.

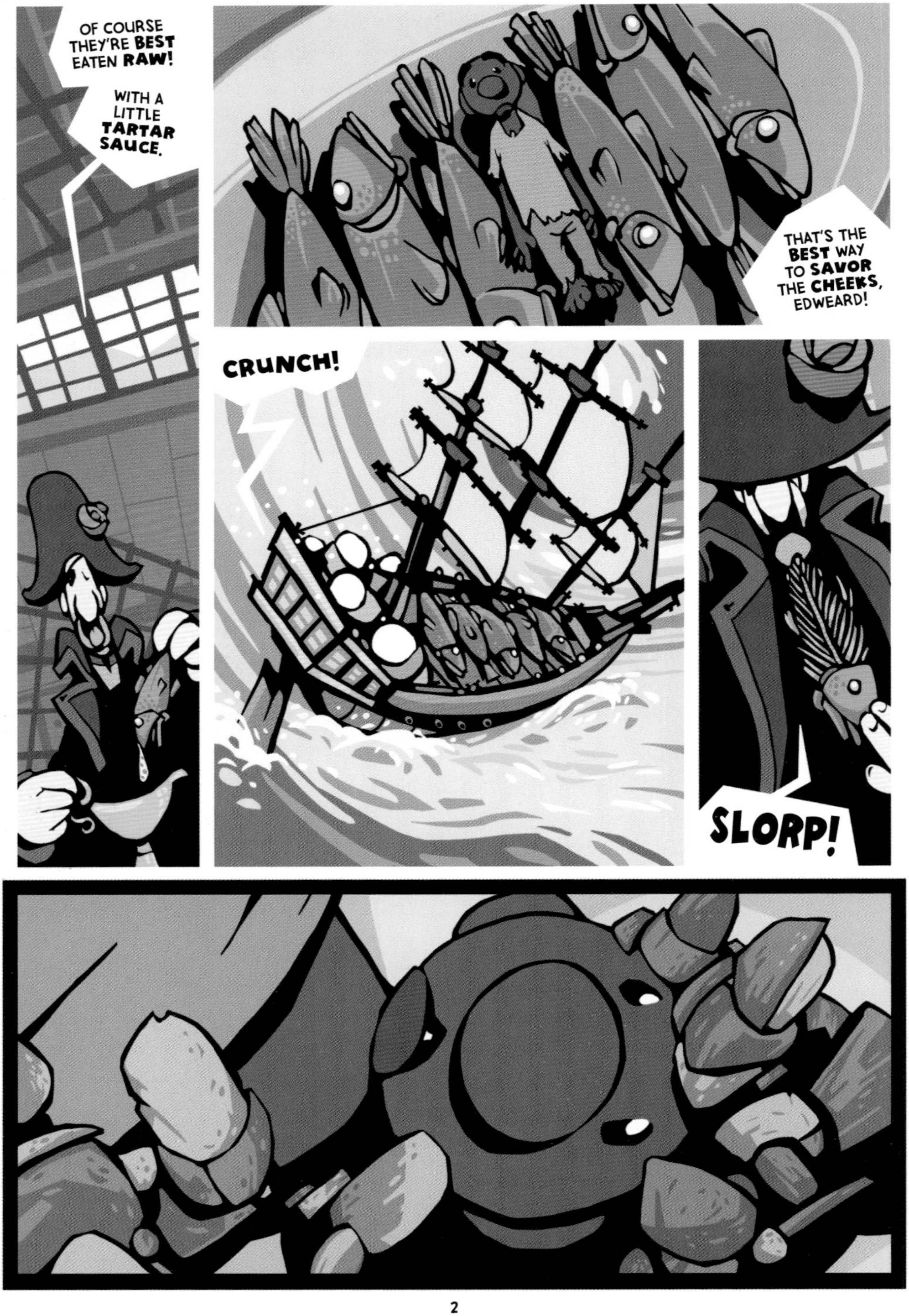
OF COURSE THEY'RE **BEST** EATEN **RAW!**
WITH A LITTLE **TARTAR SAUCE.**
THAT'S THE **BEST** WAY TO **SAVOR** THE **CHEEKS,** EDWEARD!
CRUNCH!
SLORP!

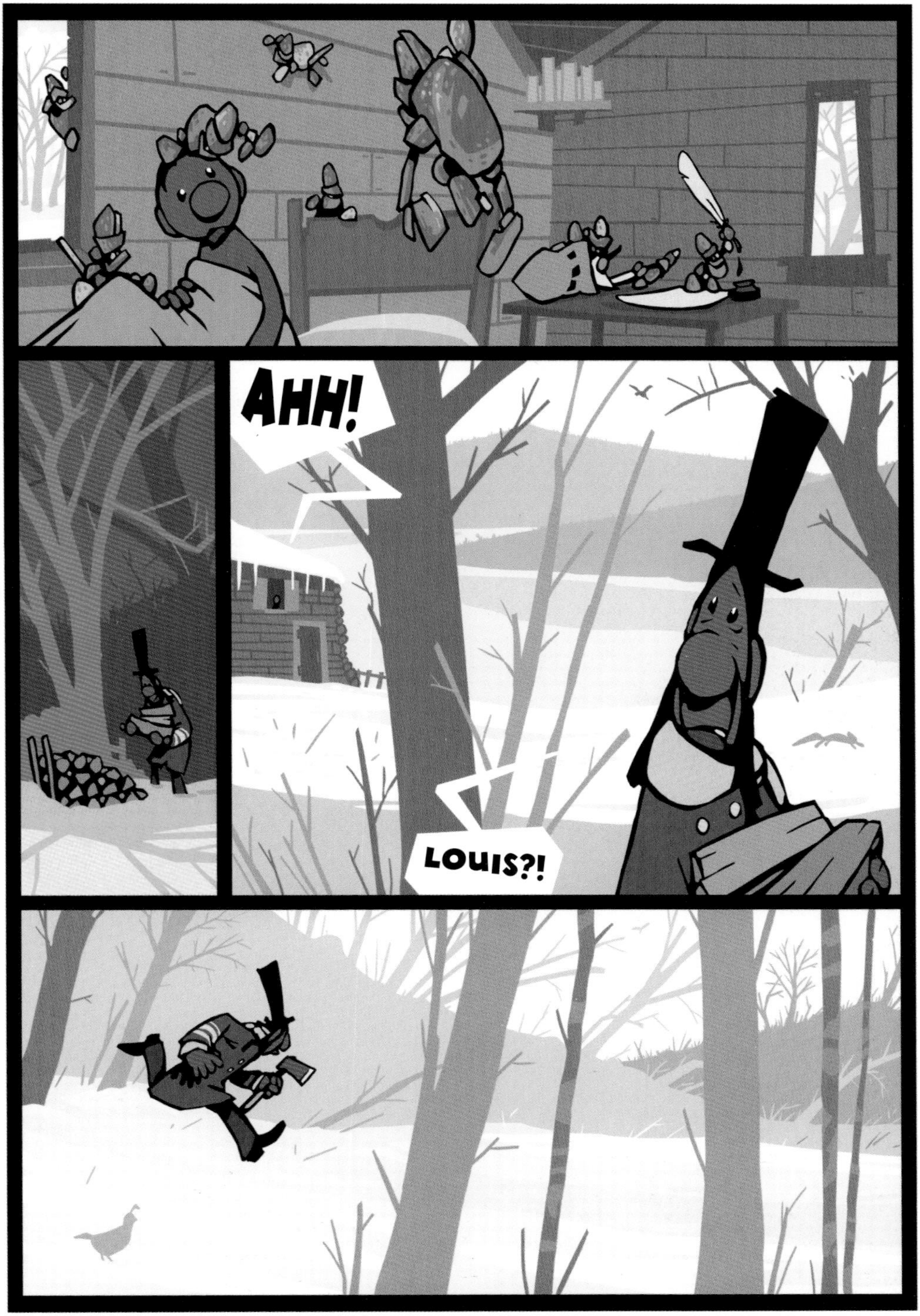
AHH!
LOUIS?!

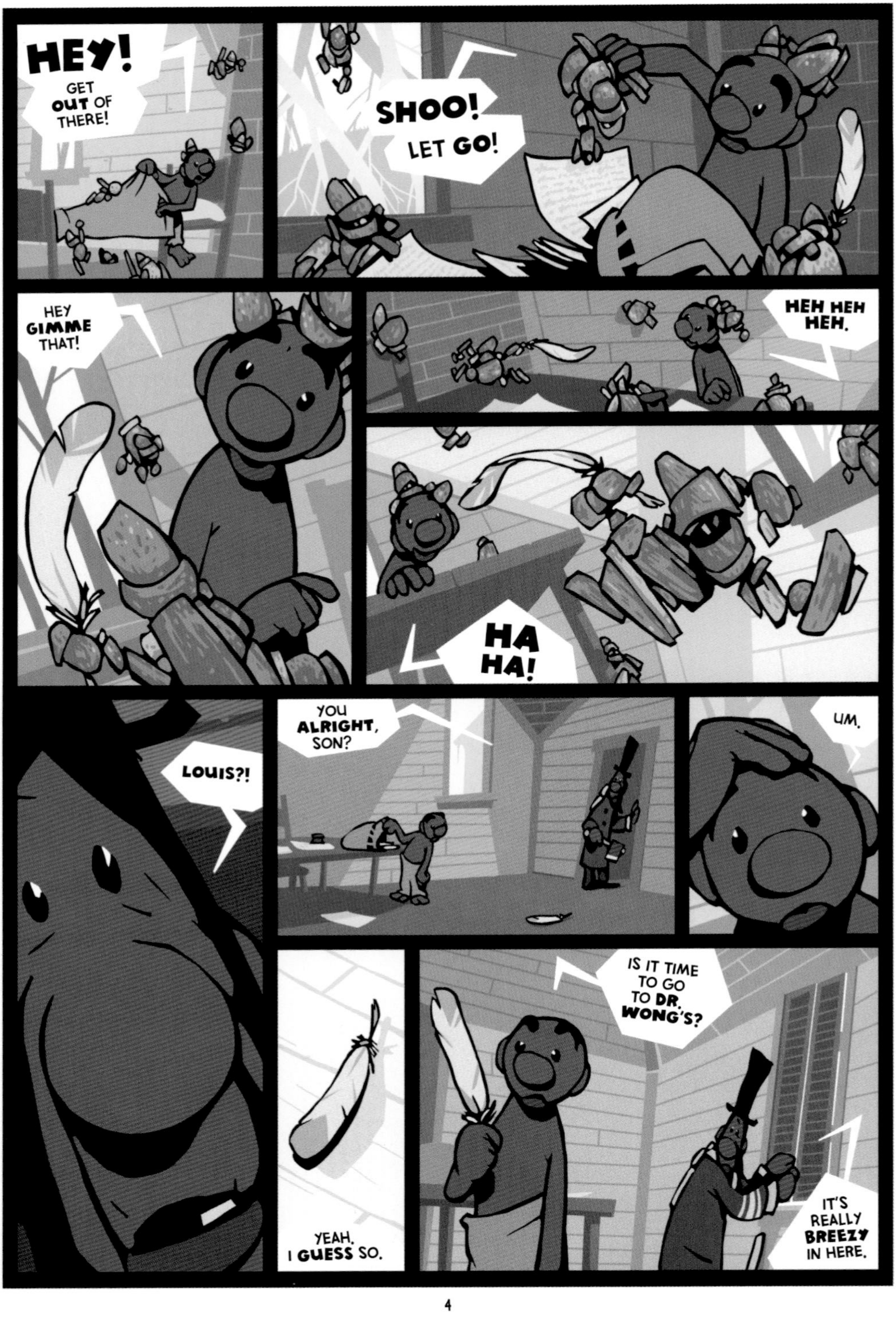
HEY! GET OUT OF THERE!
SHOO!
LET GO!
HEY GIMME THAT!
HEH HEH HEH.
HA HA!
LOUIS?!
YOU ALRIGHT, SON?
UM.
YEAH. I GUESS SO.
IS IT TIME TO GO TO DR. WONG'S?
IT'S REALLY BREEZY IN HERE.

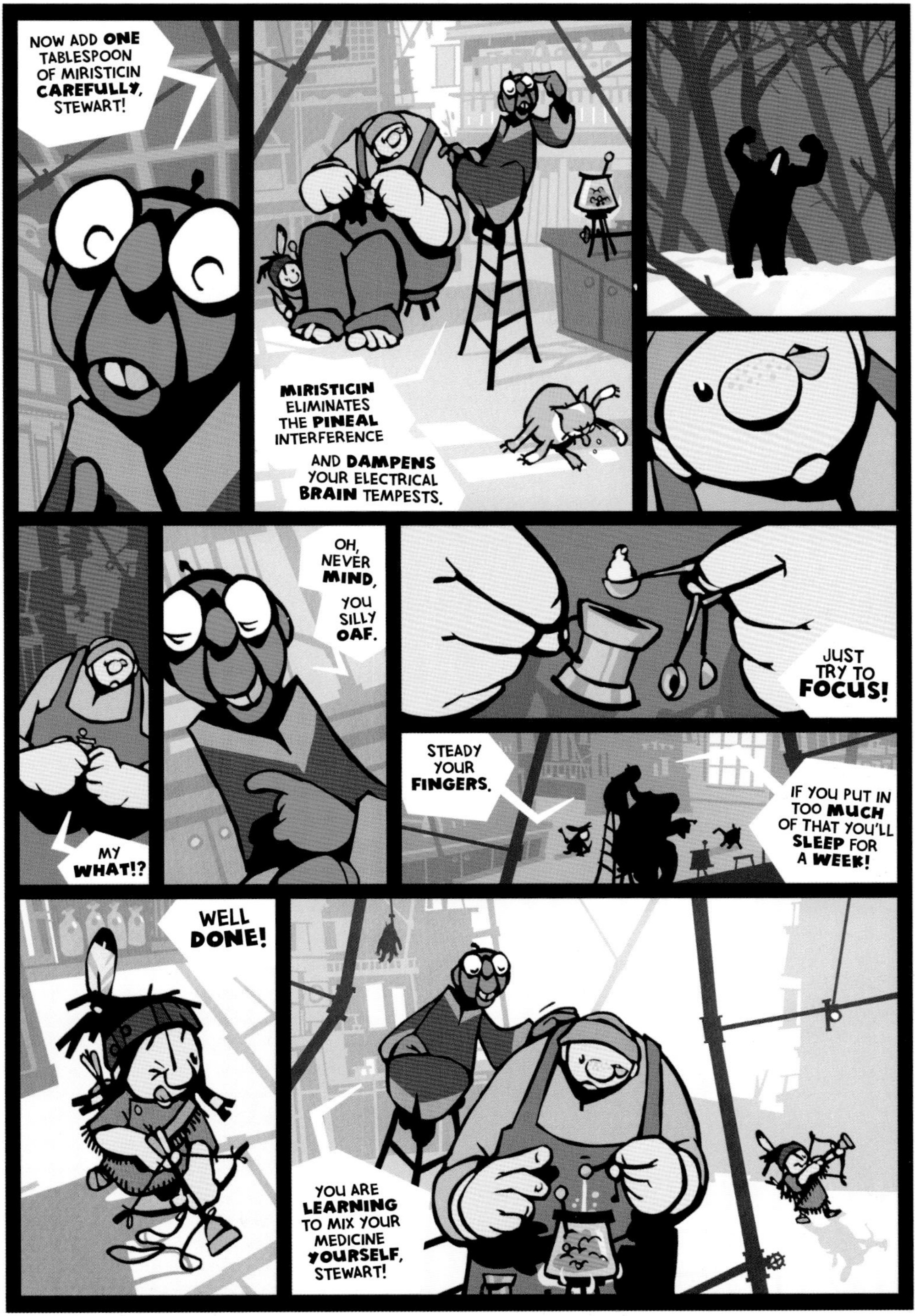

NOW ADD ONE TABLESPOON OF MIRISTICIN CAREFULLY, STEWART!
MIRISTICIN ELIMINATES THE PINEAL INTERFERENCE
AND DAMPENS YOUR ELECTRICAL BRAIN TEMPESTS.
MY WHAT!?
OH, NEVER MIND,
YOU SILLY OAF.
JUST TRY TO FOCUS!
STEADY YOUR FINGERS.
IF YOU PUT IN TOO MUCH OF THAT YOU'LL SLEEP FOR A WEEK!
WELL DONE!
YOU ARE LEARNING TO MIX YOUR MEDICINE YOURSELF, STEWART!

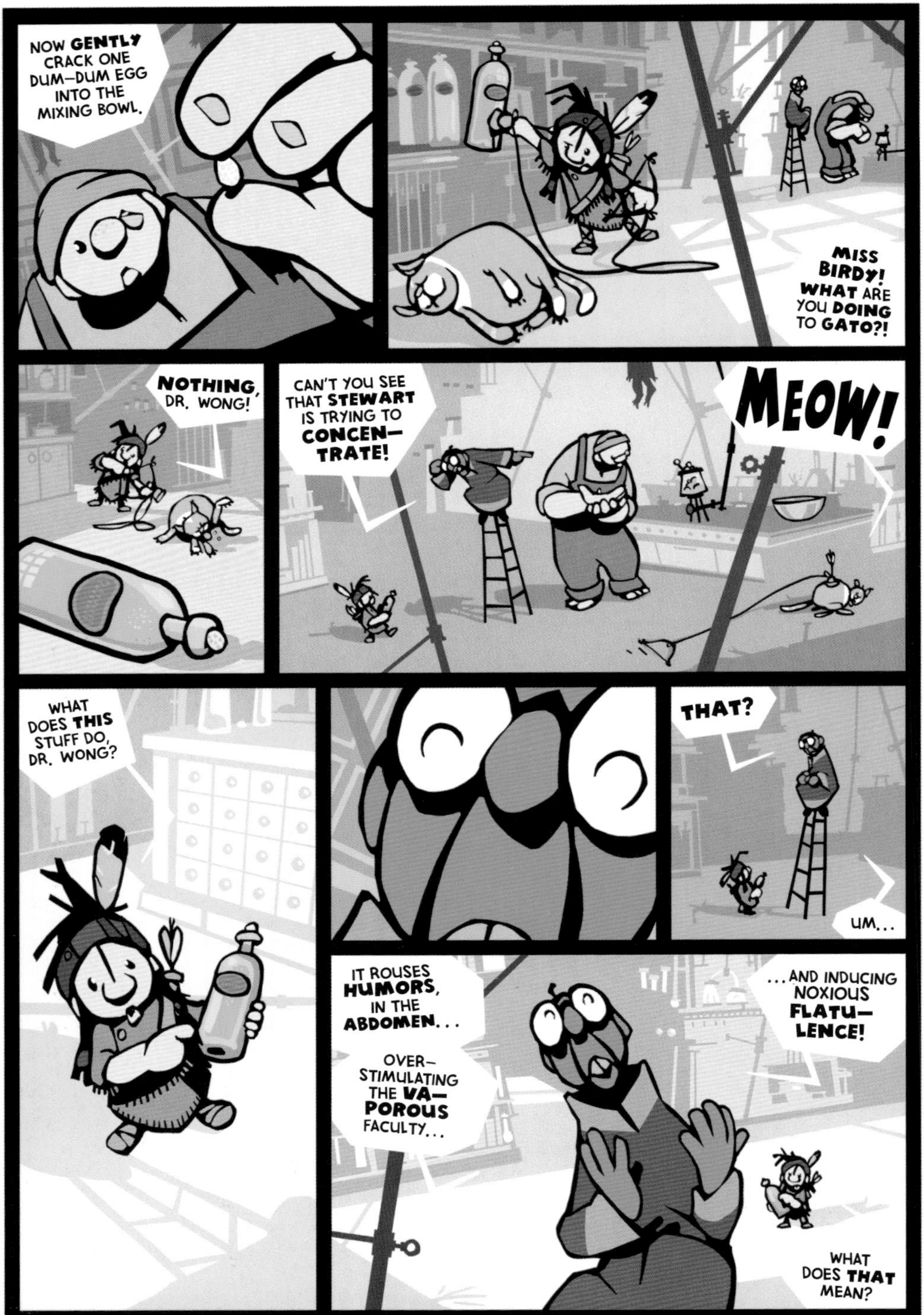
NOW GENTLY CRACK ONE DUM-DUM EGG INTO THE MIXING BOWL.
MISS BIRDY! WHAT ARE YOU DOING TO GATO?!
NOTHING, DR. WONG!
CAN'T YOU SEE THAT STEWART IS TRYING TO CONCEN-TRATE!
MEOW!
WHAT DOES THIS STUFF DO, DR. WONG?
THAT?
UM...
IT ROUSES HUMORS, IN THE ABDOMEN...
OVER-STIMULATING THE VA-POROUS FACULTY...
...AND INDUCING NOXIOUS FLATU-LENCE!
WHAT DOES THAT MEAN?

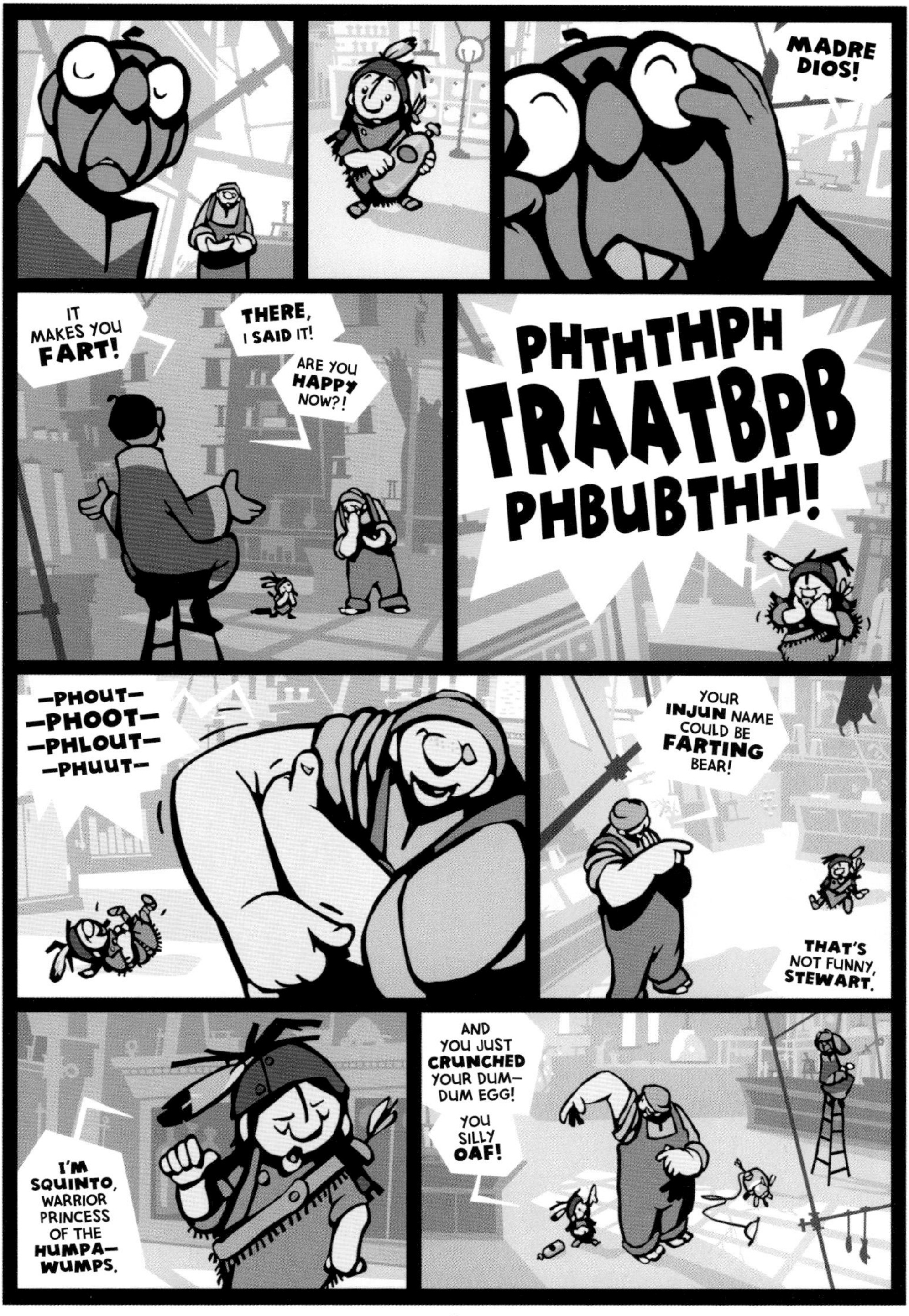
MADRE DIOS!
IT MAKES YOU FART!
THERE, I SAID IT!
ARE YOU HAPPY NOW?!
PHTHTHPH TRAATBPB PHBUBTHH!
—PHOUT— —PHOOT— —PHLOUT— —PHUUT—
YOUR INJUN NAME COULD BE FARTING BEAR!
THAT'S NOT FUNNY, STEWART.
I'M SQUINTO, WARRIOR PRINCESS OF THE HUMPA-WUMPS.
AND YOU JUST CRUNCHED YOUR DUM-DUM EGG!
YOU SILLY OAF!

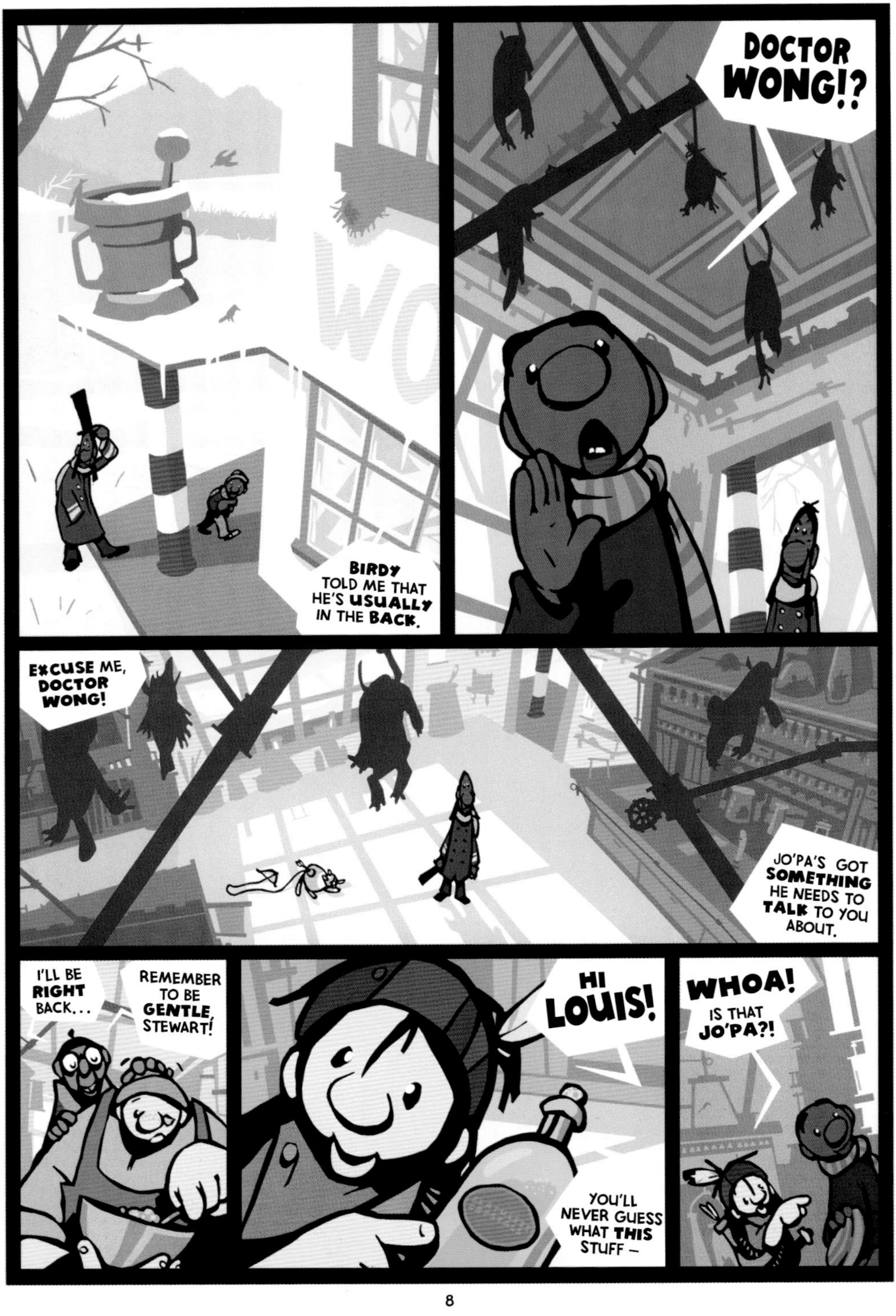
BIRDY TOLD ME THAT HE'S USUALLY IN THE BACK.
DOCTOR WONG!?
EXCUSE ME, DOCTOR WONG!
JO'PA'S GOT SOMETHING HE NEEDS TO TALK TO YOU ABOUT.
I'LL BE RIGHT BACK...
REMEMBER TO BE GENTLE, STEWART!
HI LOUIS!
YOU'LL NEVER GUESS WHAT THIS STUFF –
WHOA! IS THAT JO'PA?!

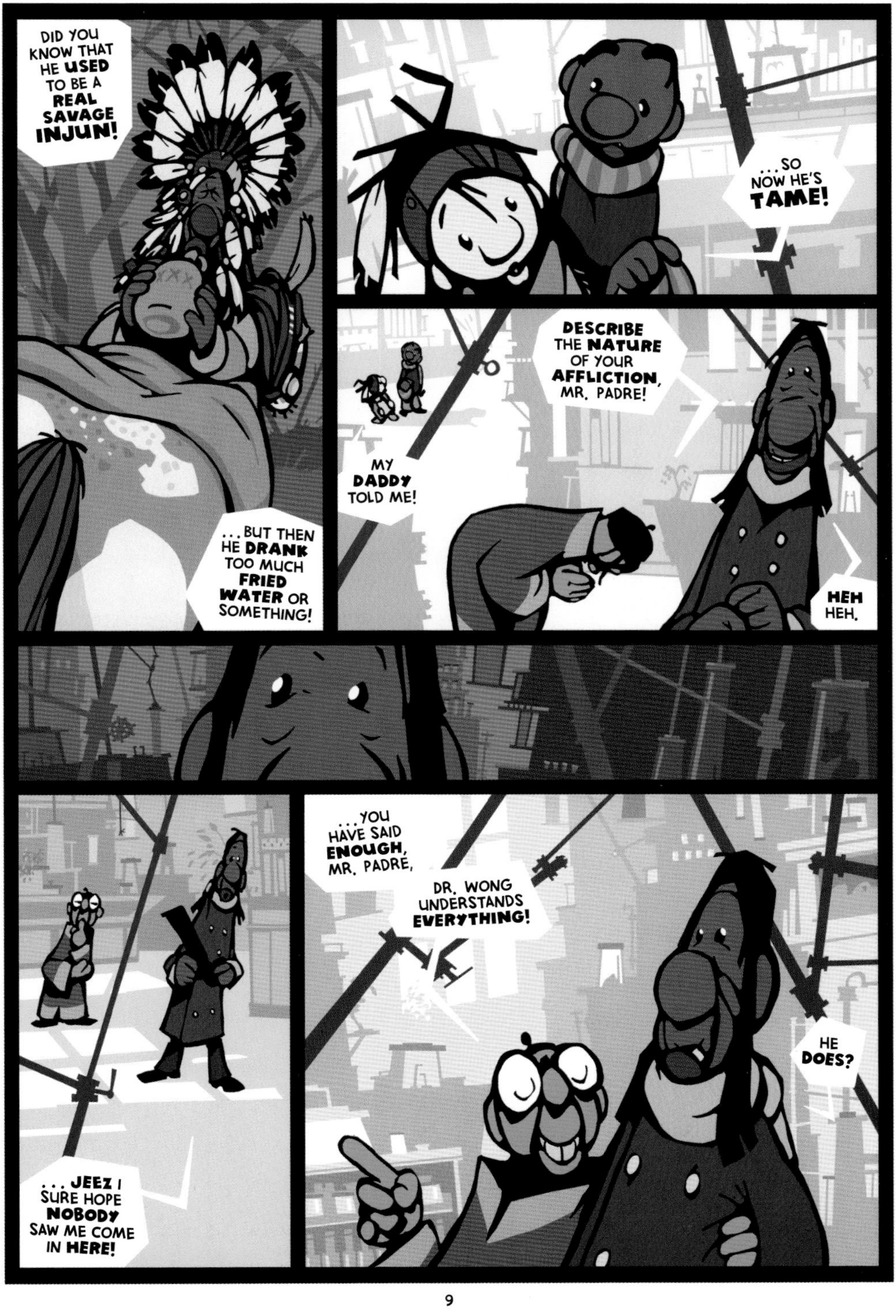
DID YOU KNOW THAT HE USED TO BE A REAL SAVAGE INJUN!
...BUT THEN HE DRANK TOO MUCH FRIED WATER OR SOMETHING!
...SO NOW HE'S TAME!
DESCRIBE THE NATURE OF YOUR AFFLICTION, MR. PADRE!
MY DADDY TOLD ME!
HEH HEH.
...JEEZ I SURE HOPE NOBODY SAW ME COME IN HERE!
...YOU HAVE SAID ENOUGH, MR. PADRE,
DR. WONG UNDERSTANDS EVERYTHING!
HE DOES?

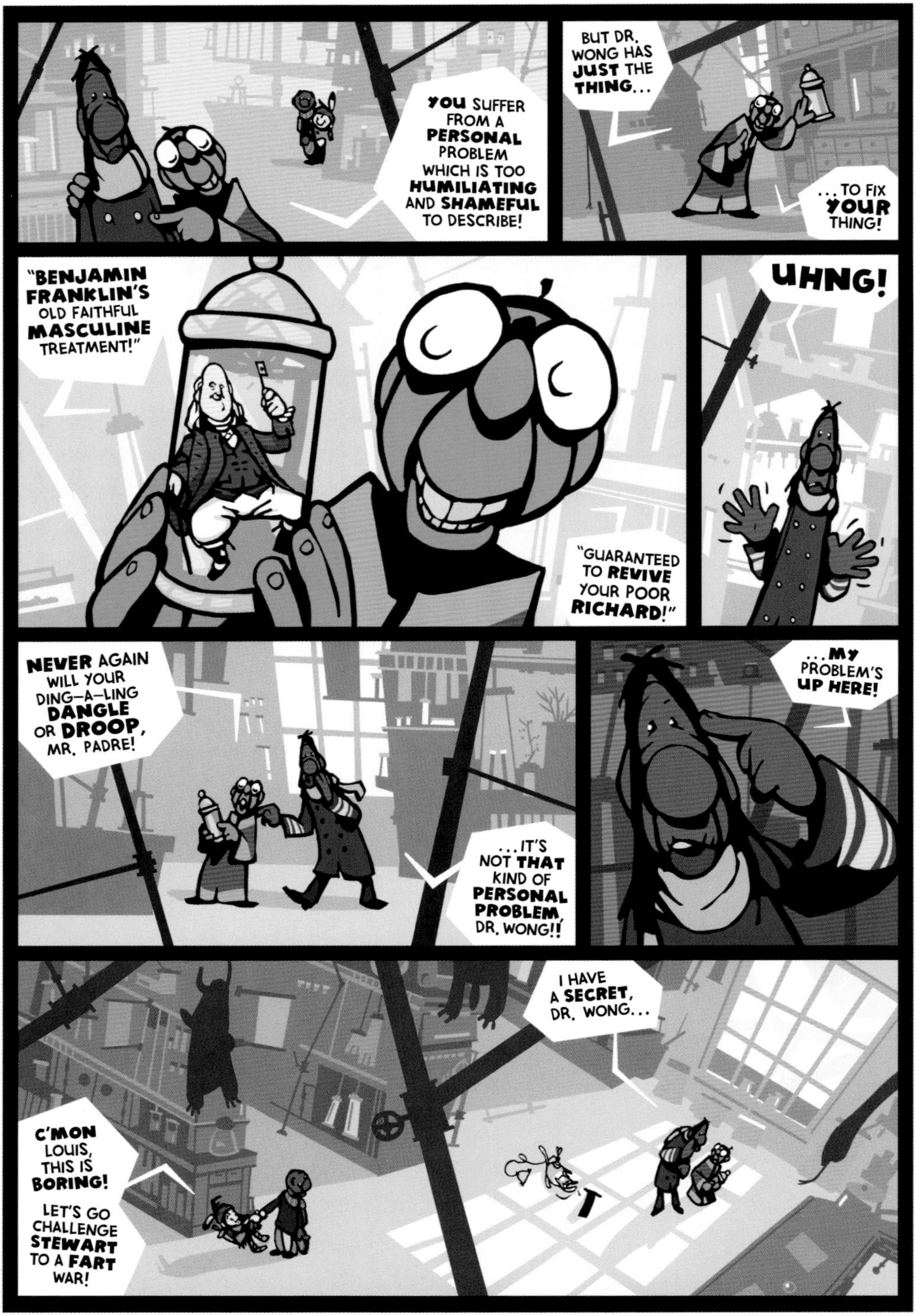

YOU SUFFER FROM A PERSONAL PROBLEM WHICH IS TOO HUMILIATING AND SHAMEFUL TO DESCRIBE!
BUT DR. WONG HAS JUST THE THING...
...TO FIX YOUR THING!
"BENJAMIN FRANKLIN'S OLD FAITHFUL MASCULINE TREATMENT!"
"GUARANTEED TO REVIVE YOUR POOR RICHARD!"
UHNG!
NEVER AGAIN WILL YOUR DING-A-LING DANGLE OR DROOP, MR. PADRE!
...IT'S NOT THAT KIND OF PERSONAL PROBLEM, DR. WONG!!
...MY PROBLEM'S UP HERE!
I HAVE A SECRET, DR. WONG...
C'MON LOUIS, THIS IS BORING!
LET'S GO CHALLENGE STEWART TO A FART WAR!

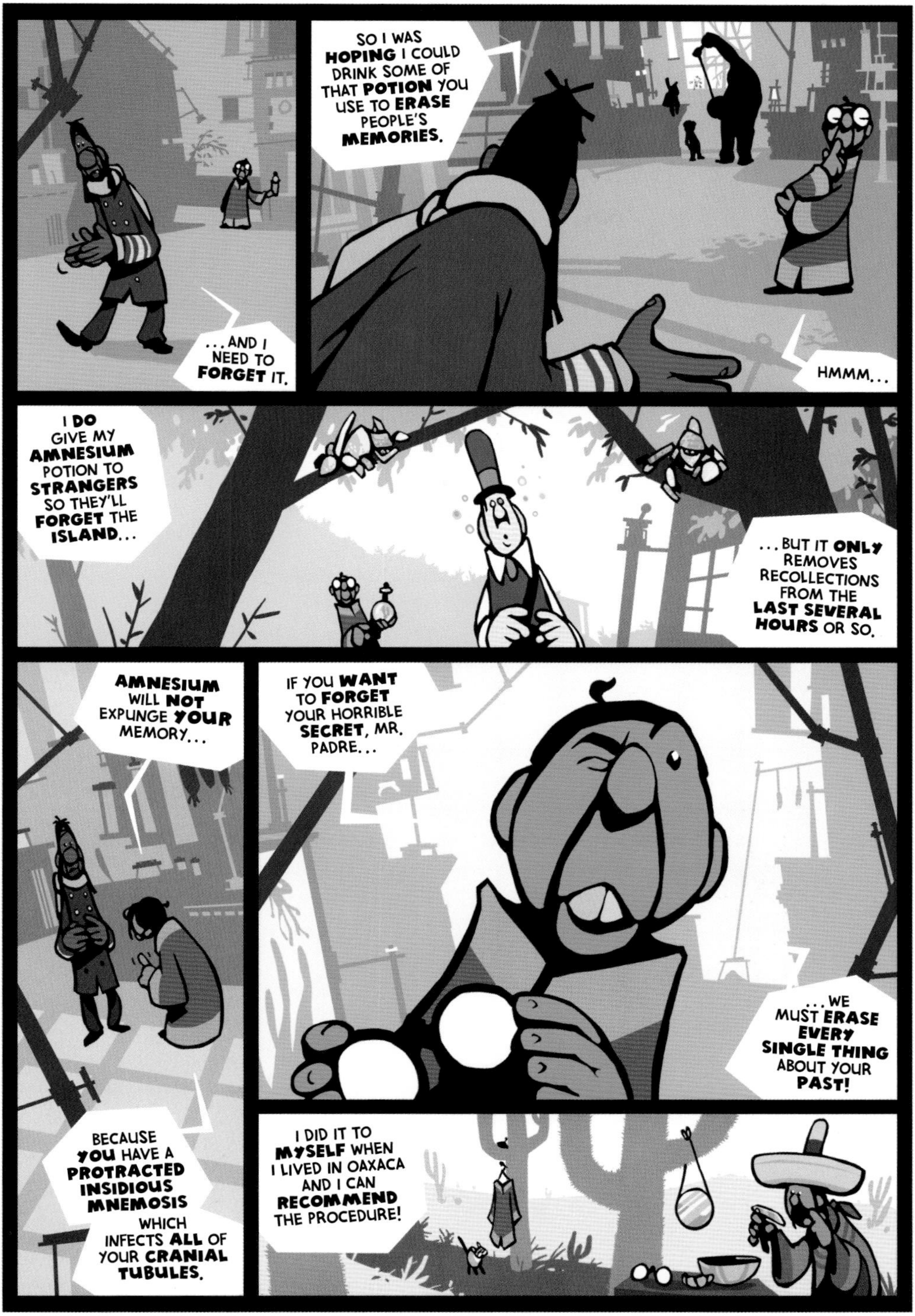
...AND I NEED TO FORGET IT.
SO I WAS HOPING I COULD DRINK SOME OF THAT POTION YOU USE TO ERASE PEOPLE'S MEMORIES.
HMMM...
I DO GIVE MY AMNESIUM POTION TO STRANGERS SO THEY'LL FORGET THE ISLAND...
...BUT IT ONLY REMOVES RECOLLECTIONS FROM THE LAST SEVERAL HOURS OR SO.
AMNESIUM WILL NOT EXPUNGE YOUR MEMORY...
IF YOU WANT TO FORGET YOUR HORRIBLE SECRET, MR. PADRE...
...WE MUST ERASE EVERY SINGLE THING ABOUT YOUR PAST!
BECAUSE YOU HAVE A PROTRACTED INSIDIOUS MNEMOSIS WHICH INFECTS ALL OF YOUR CRANIAL TUBULES.
I DID IT TO MYSELF WHEN I LIVED IN OAXACA AND I CAN RECOMMEND THE PROCEDURE!

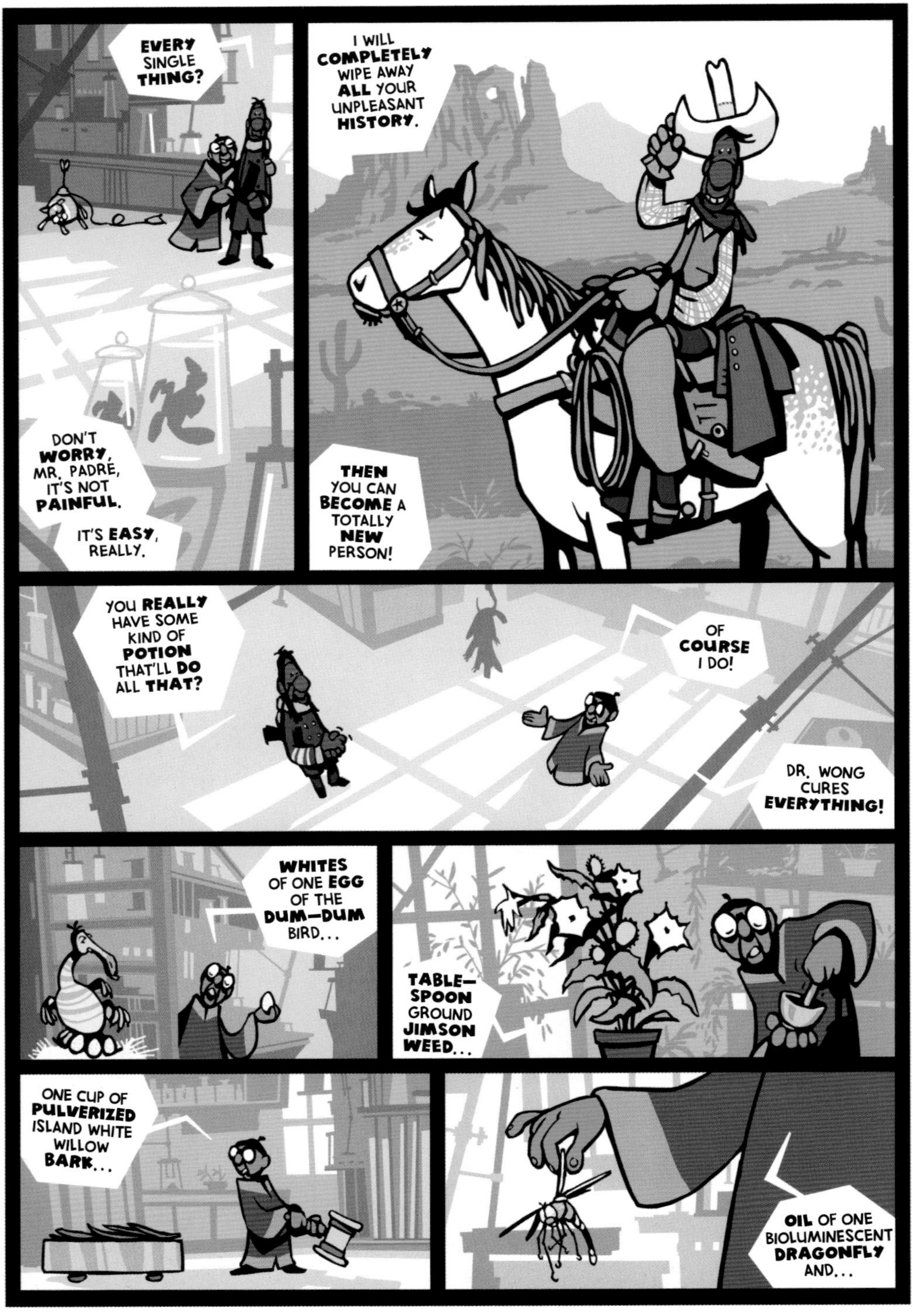
EVERY SINGLE THING?
I WILL COMPLETELY WIPE AWAY ALL YOUR UNPLEASANT HISTORY.
DON'T WORRY, MR. PADRE, IT'S NOT PAINFUL.
IT'S EASY, REALLY.
THEN YOU CAN BECOME A TOTALLY NEW PERSON!
YOU REALLY HAVE SOME KIND OF POTION THAT'LL DO ALL THAT?
OF COURSE I DO!
DR. WONG CURES EVERYTHING!
WHITES OF ONE EGG OF THE DUM-DUM BIRD...
TABLE-SPOON GROUND JIMSON WEED...
ONE CUP OF PULVERIZED ISLAND WHITE WILLOW BARK...
OIL OF ONE BIOLUMINESCENT DRAGONFLY AND...

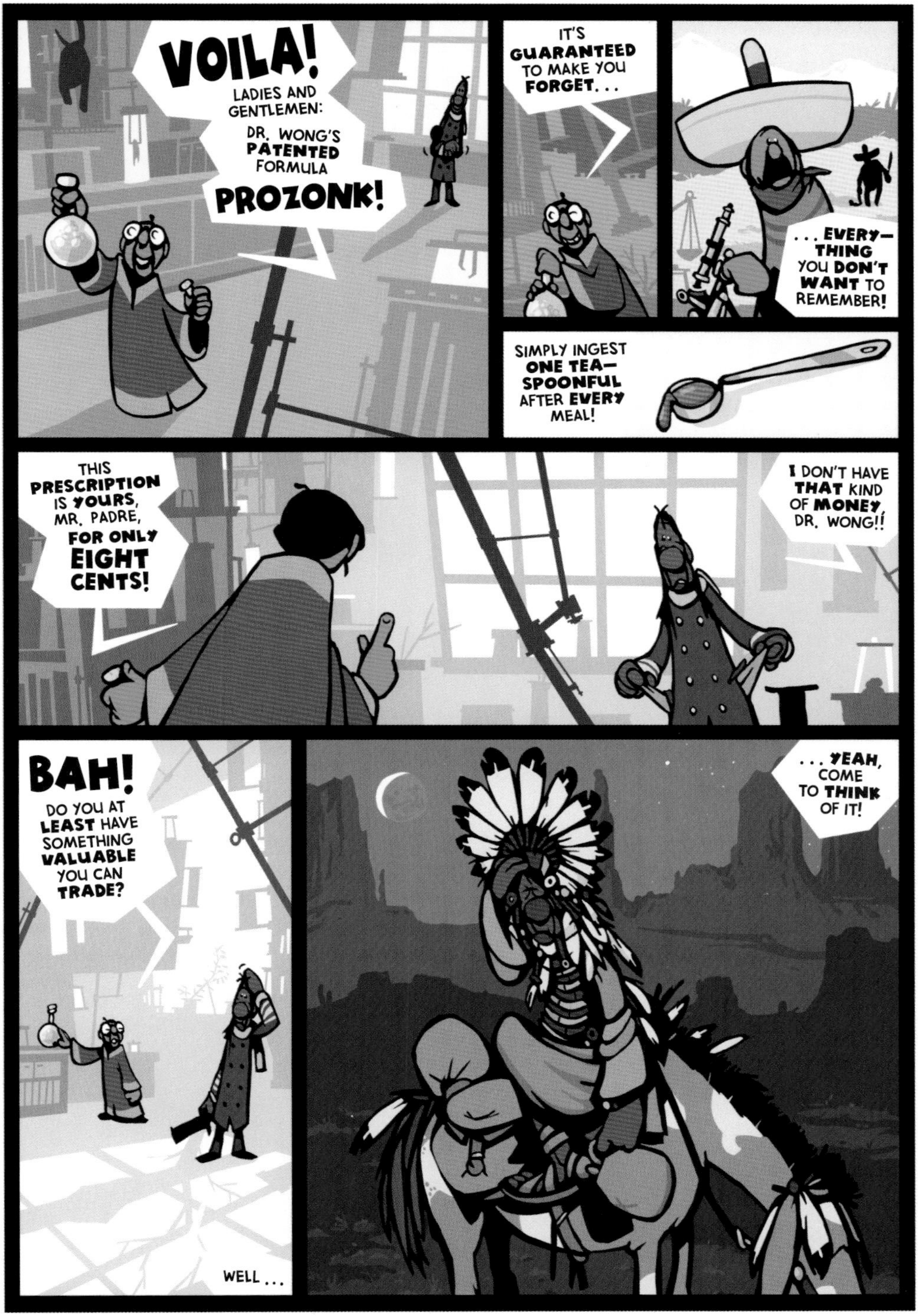
VOILA!
LADIES AND GENTLEMEN:
DR. WONG'S PATENTED FORMULA
PROZONK!
IT'S GUARANTEED TO MAKE YOU FORGET...
... EVERY-THING YOU DON'T WANT TO REMEMBER!
SIMPLY INGEST ONE TEA-SPOONFUL AFTER EVERY MEAL!
THIS PRESCRIPTION IS YOURS, MR. PADRE, FOR ONLY EIGHT CENTS!
I DON'T HAVE THAT KIND OF MONEY, DR. WONG!!
BAH!
DO YOU AT LEAST HAVE SOMETHING VALUABLE YOU CAN TRADE?
WELL...
... YEAH, COME TO THINK OF IT!

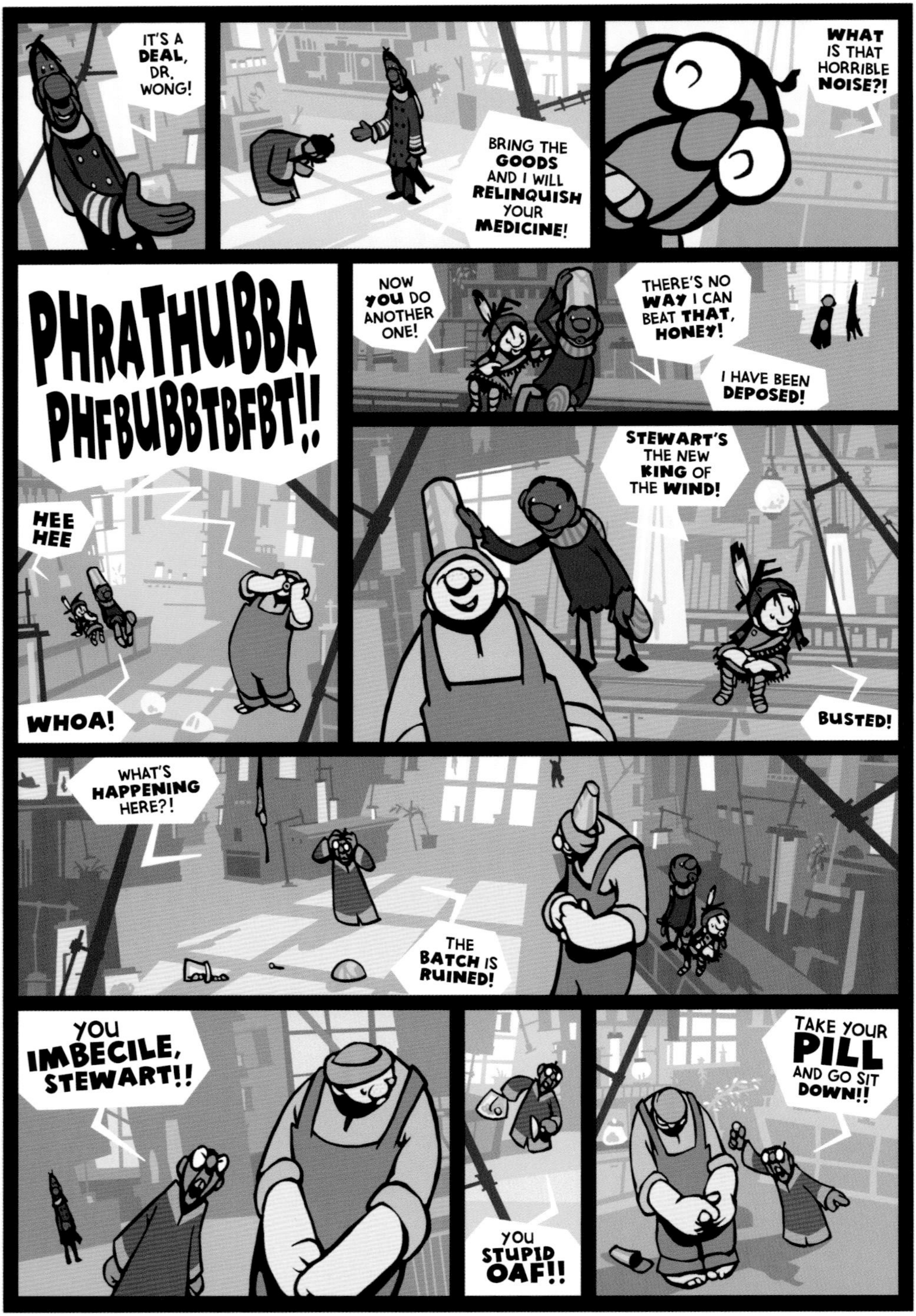
IT'S A DEAL, DR. WONG!
BRING THE GOODS AND I WILL RELINQUISH YOUR MEDICINE!
WHAT IS THAT HORRIBLE NOISE?!
PHRATHUBBA PHFBUBBTBFBT!!
HEE HEE
WHOA!
NOW YOU DO ANOTHER ONE!
THERE'S NO WAY I CAN BEAT THAT, HONEY!
I HAVE BEEN DEPOSED!
STEWART'S THE NEW KING OF THE WIND!
BUSTED!
WHAT'S HAPPENING HERE?!
THE BATCH IS RUINED!
YOU IMBECILE, STEWART!!
YOU STUPID OAF!!
TAKE YOUR PILL AND GO SIT DOWN!!

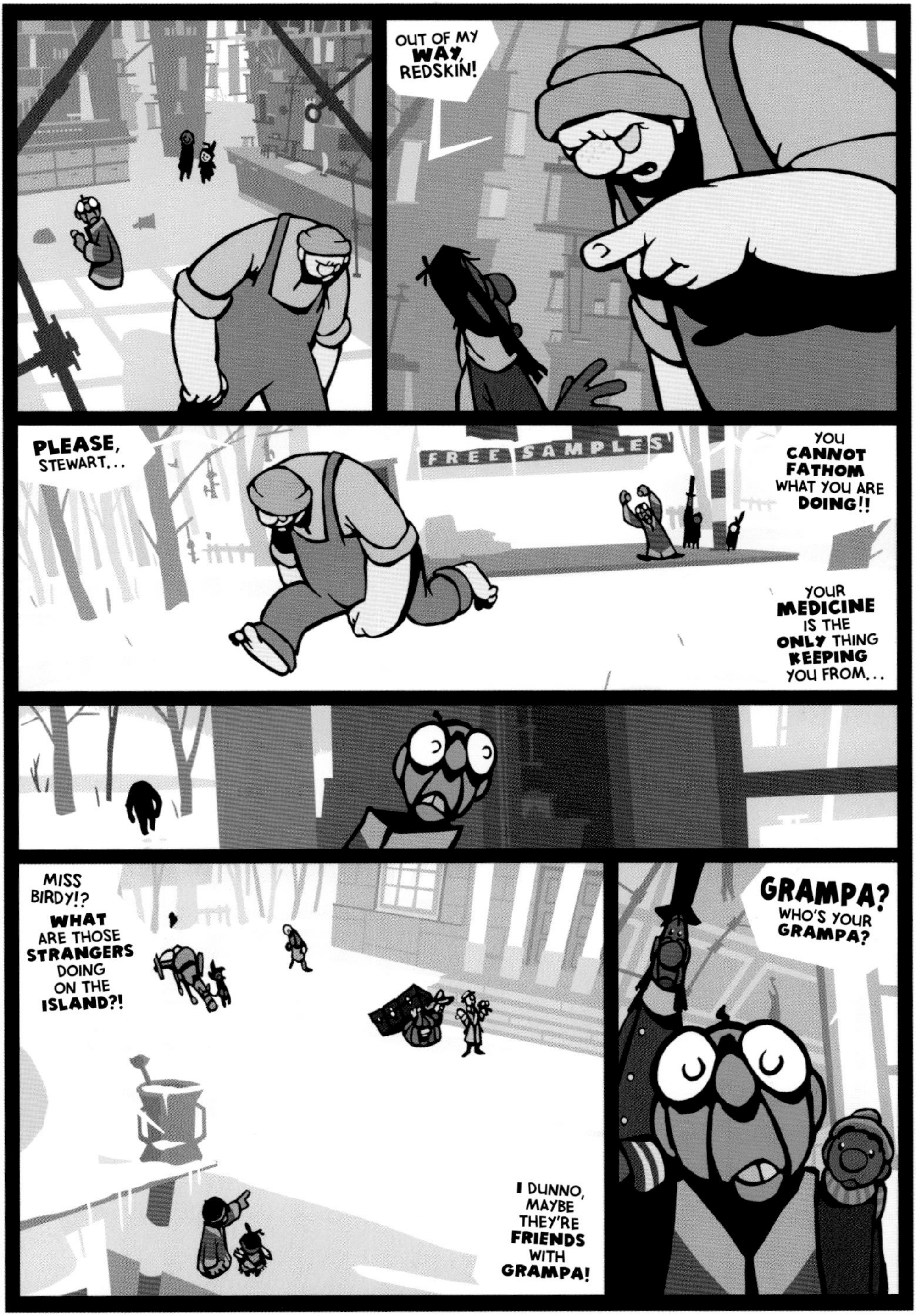

OUT OF MY WAY, REDSKIN!
PLEASE, STEWART...
YOU CANNOT FATHOM WHAT YOU ARE DOING!!
FREE SAMPLES
YOUR MEDICINE IS THE ONLY THING KEEPING YOU FROM...
MISS BIRDY!? WHAT ARE THOSE STRANGERS DOING ON THE ISLAND?!
I DUNNO, MAYBE THEY'RE FRIENDS WITH GRAMPA!
GRAMPA? WHO'S YOUR GRAMPA?

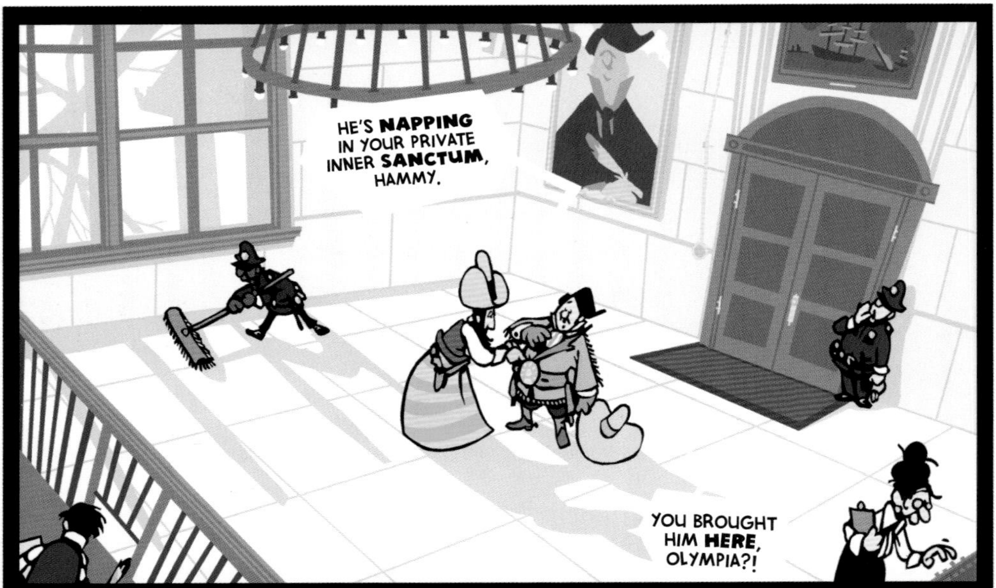
HE'S NAPPING IN YOUR PRIVATE INNER SANCTUM, HAMMY.
YOU BROUGHT HIM HERE, OLYMPIA?!

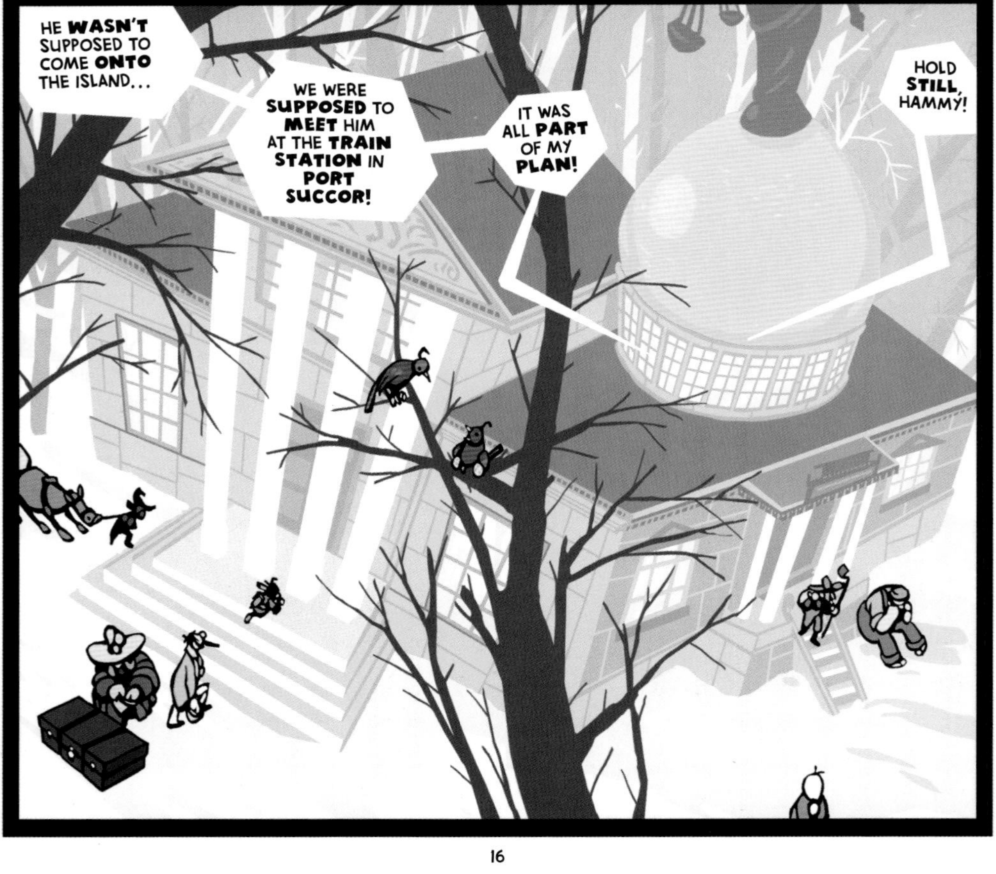
HE WASN'T SUPPOSED TO COME ONTO THE ISLAND...
WE WERE SUPPOSED TO MEET HIM AT THE TRAIN STATION IN PORT SUCCOR!
IT WAS ALL PART OF MY PLAN!
HOLD STILL, HAMMY!

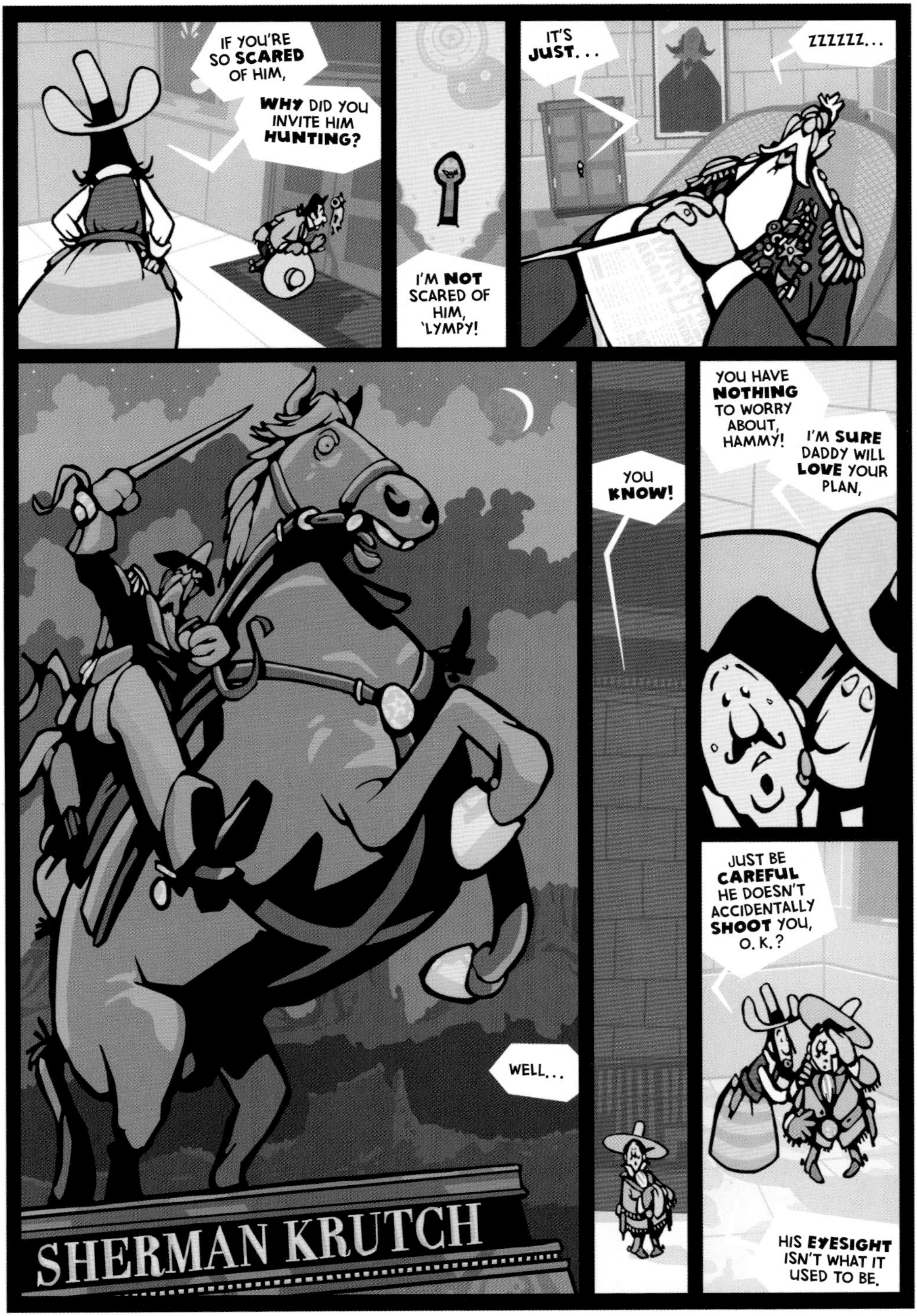
IF YOU'RE SO SCARED OF HIM,
WHY DID YOU INVITE HIM HUNTING?
I'M NOT SCARED OF HIM, 'LYMPY!
IT'S JUST...
ZZZZZZ...
SHERMAN KRUTCH
WELL...
YOU KNOW!
YOU HAVE NOTHING TO WORRY ABOUT, HAMMY!
I'M SURE DADDY WILL LOVE YOUR PLAN,
JUST BE CAREFUL HE DOESN'T ACCIDENTALLY SHOOT YOU, O.K.?
HIS EYESIGHT ISN'T WHAT IT USED TO BE.

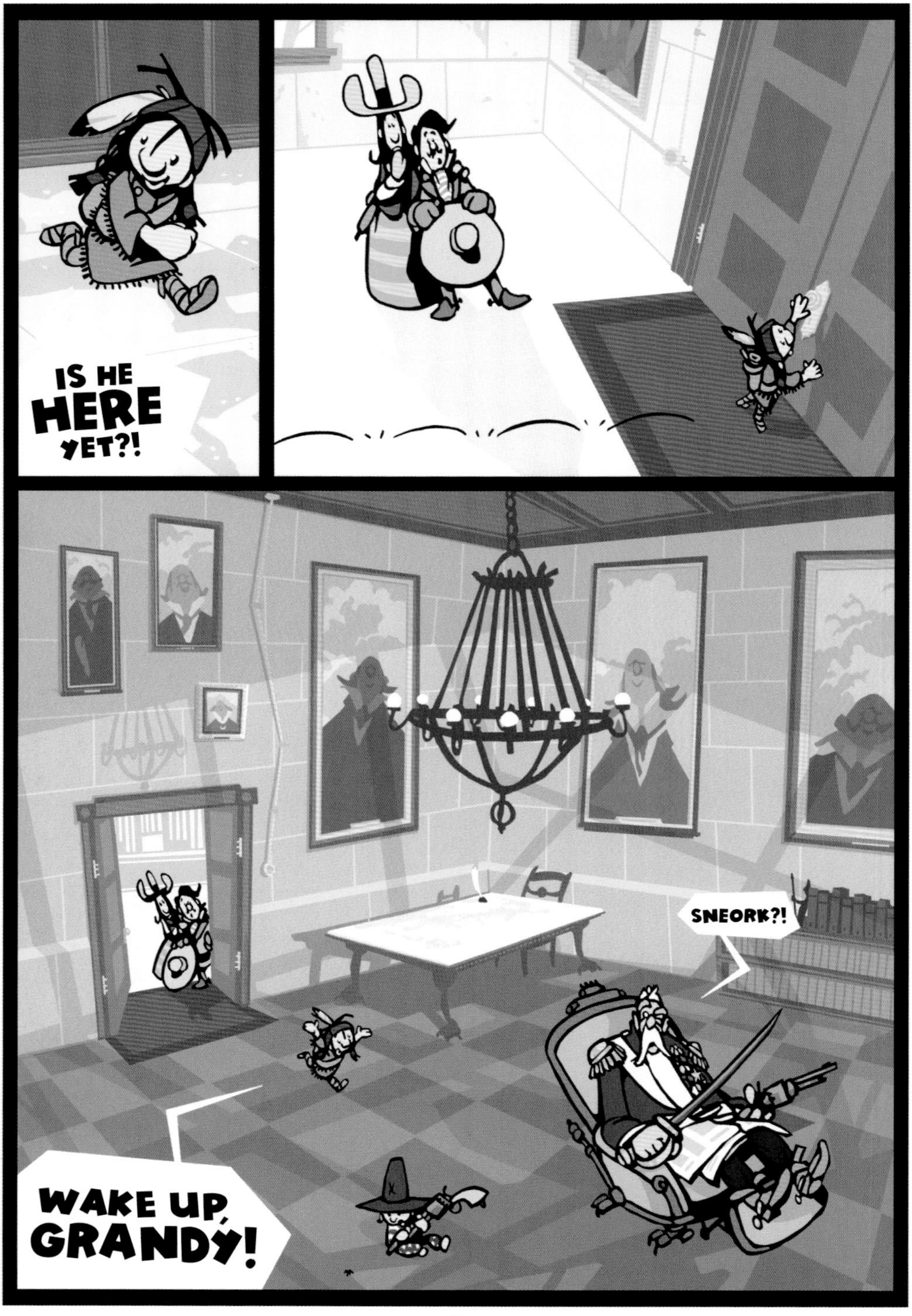
IS HE HERE YET?!
SNEORK?!
WAKE UP, GRANDY!

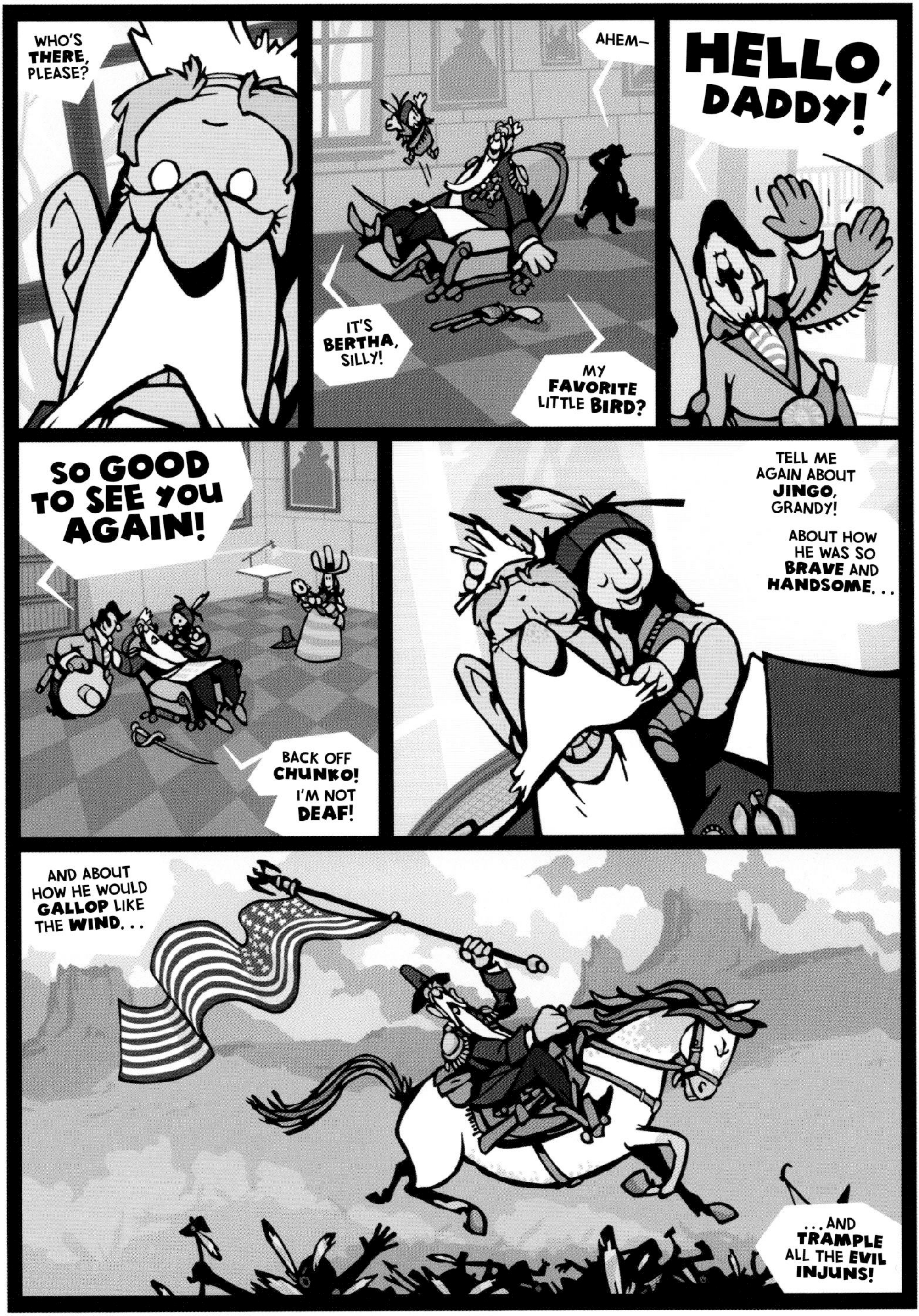
WHO'S THERE, PLEASE?
AHEM—
IT'S BERTHA, SILLY!
MY FAVORITE LITTLE BIRD?
HELLO, DADDY!
SO GOOD TO SEE YOU AGAIN!
BACK OFF CHUNKO! I'M NOT DEAF!
TELL ME AGAIN ABOUT JINGO, GRANDY!
ABOUT HOW HE WAS SO BRAVE AND HANDSOME...
AND ABOUT HOW HE WOULD GALLOP LIKE THE WIND...
...AND TRAMPLE ALL THE EVIL INJUNS!

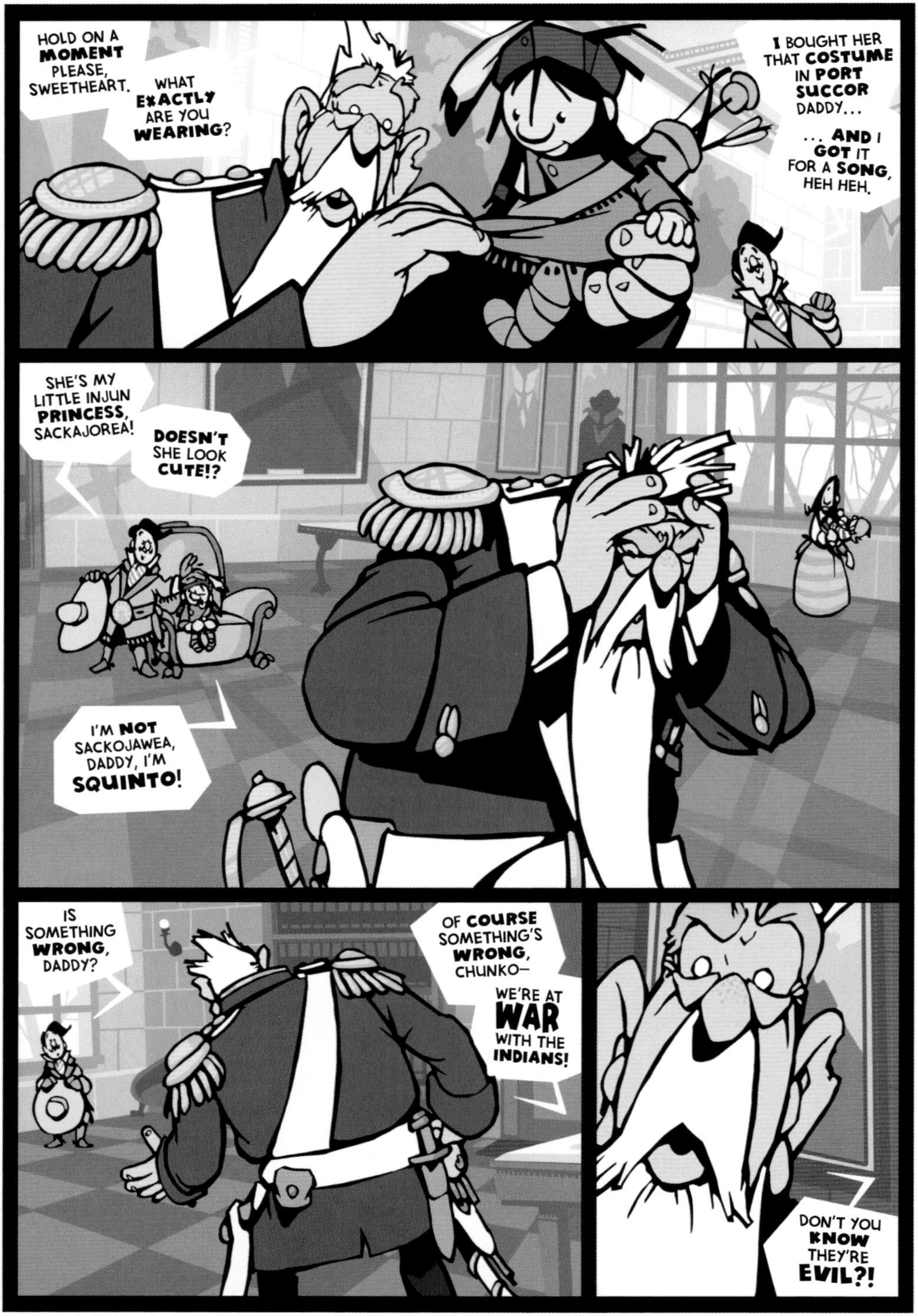
HOLD ON A MOMENT PLEASE, SWEETHEART.
WHAT EXACTLY ARE YOU WEARING?
I BOUGHT HER THAT COSTUME IN PORT SUCCOR DADDY...
... AND I GOT IT FOR A SONG, HEH HEH.
SHE'S MY LITTLE INJUN PRINCESS, SACKAJOREA!
DOESN'T SHE LOOK CUTE!?
I'M NOT SACKOJAWEA, DADDY, I'M SQUINTO!
IS SOMETHING WRONG, DADDY?
OF COURSE SOMETHING'S WRONG, CHUNKO–
WE'RE AT WAR WITH THE INDIANS!
DON'T YOU KNOW THEY'RE EVIL?!

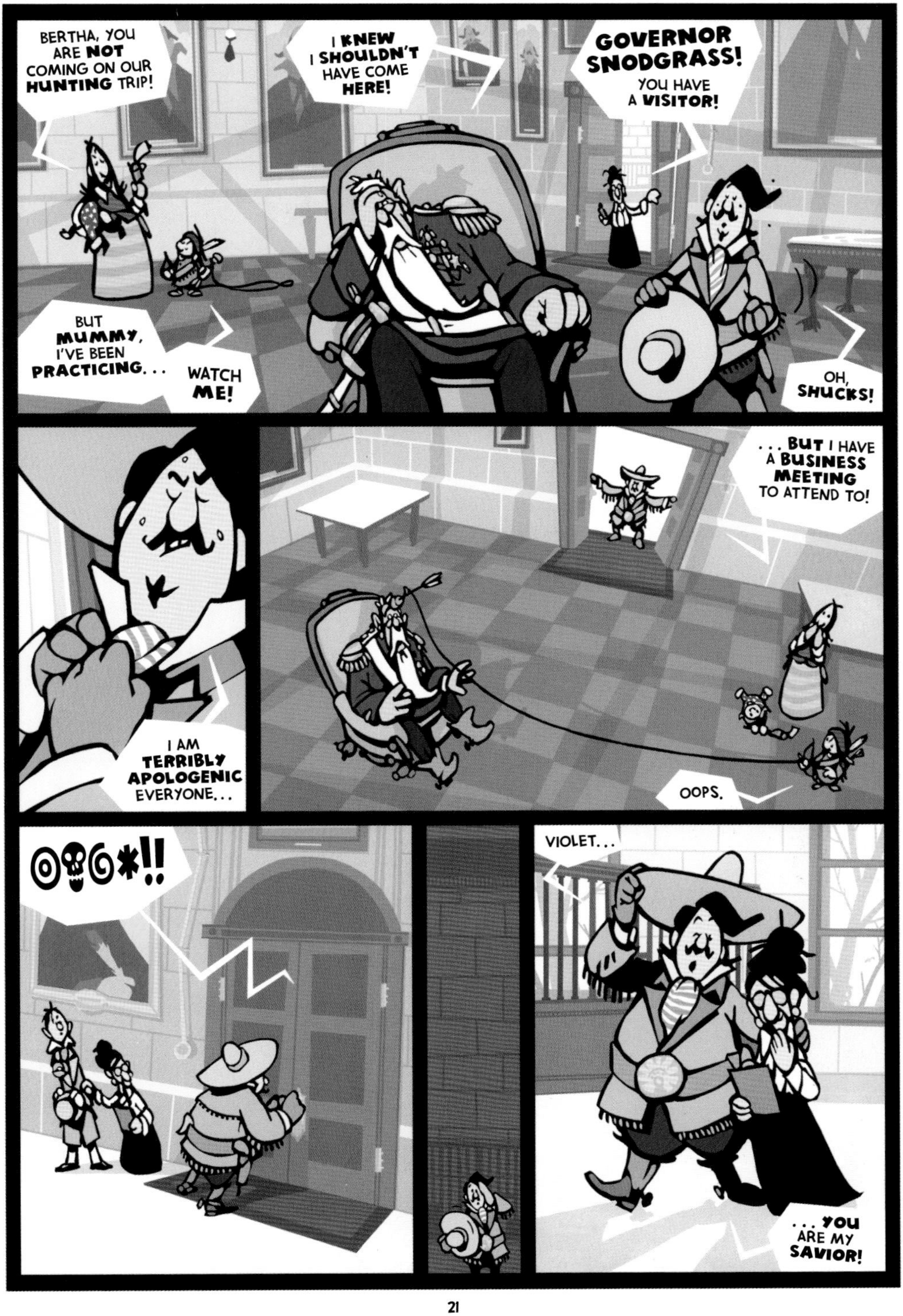

BERTHA, YOU ARE **NOT** COMING ON OUR **HUNTING** TRIP!
I **KNEW** I **SHOULDN'T** HAVE COME **HERE!**
GOVERNOR SNODGRASS! YOU HAVE A **VISITOR!**
BUT **MUMMY**, I'VE BEEN **PRACTICING**...
WATCH **ME!**
OH, **SHUCKS!**
I AM **TERRIBLY APOLOGENIC** EVERYONE...
...**BUT** I HAVE A **BUSINESS MEETING** TO ATTEND TO!
OOPS.
VIOLET...
...**YOU** ARE MY **SAVIOR!**

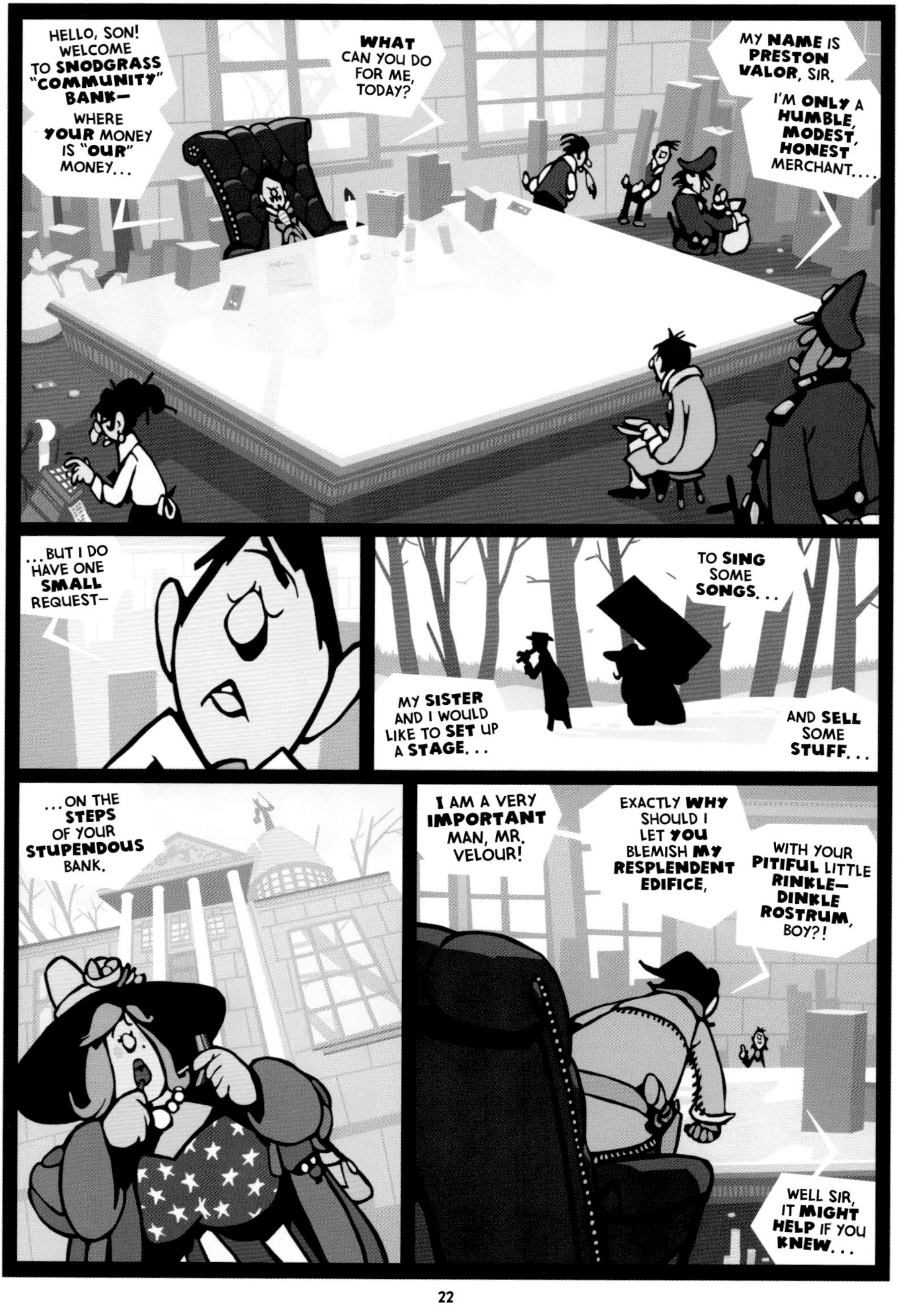
HELLO, SON! WELCOME TO SNODGRASS "COMMUNITY" BANK—
WHERE YOUR MONEY IS "OUR" MONEY...
WHAT CAN YOU DO FOR ME, TODAY?
MY NAME IS PRESTON VALOR, SIR.
I'M ONLY A HUMBLE, MODEST, HONEST MERCHANT....
...BUT I DO HAVE ONE SMALL REQUEST—
TO SING SOME SONGS...
MY SISTER AND I WOULD LIKE TO SET UP A STAGE...
AND SELL SOME STUFF...
...ON THE STEPS OF YOUR STUPENDOUS BANK.
I AM A VERY IMPORTANT MAN, MR. VELOUR!
EXACTLY WHY SHOULD I LET YOU BLEMISH MY RESPLENDENT EDIFICE,
WITH YOUR PITIFUL LITTLE RINKLE—DINKLE ROSTRUM, BOY?!
WELL SIR, IT MIGHT HELP IF YOU KNEW...

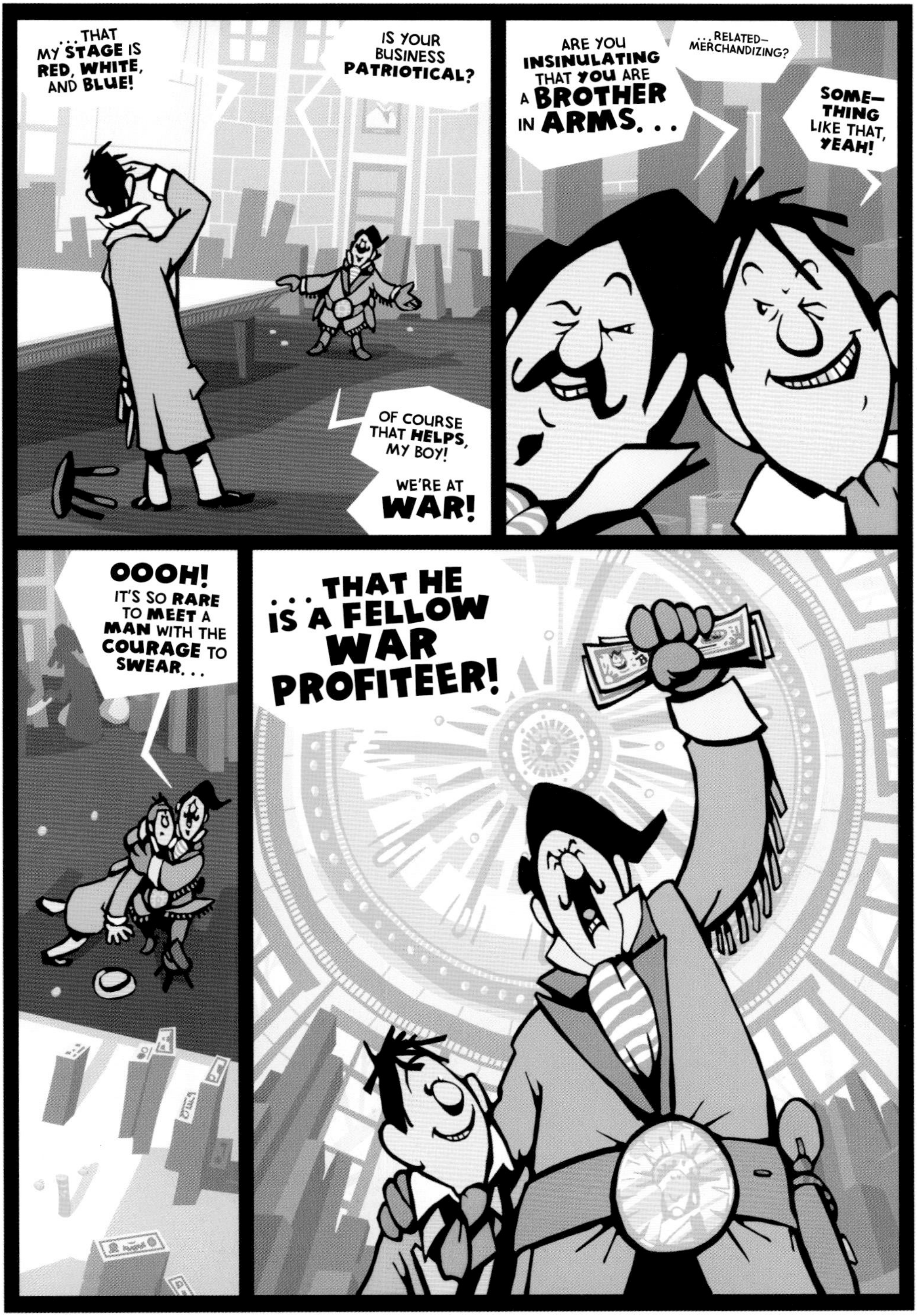
...THAT MY STAGE IS RED, WHITE, AND BLUE!
IS YOUR BUSINESS PATRIOTICAL?
OF COURSE THAT HELPS, MY BOY!
WE'RE AT WAR!
ARE YOU INSINULATING THAT YOU ARE A BROTHER IN ARMS...
...RELATED— MERCHANDIZING?
SOME— THING LIKE THAT, YEAH!
OOOH! IT'S SO RARE TO MEET A MAN WITH THE COURAGE TO SWEAR...
...THAT HE IS A FELLOW WAR PROFITEER!

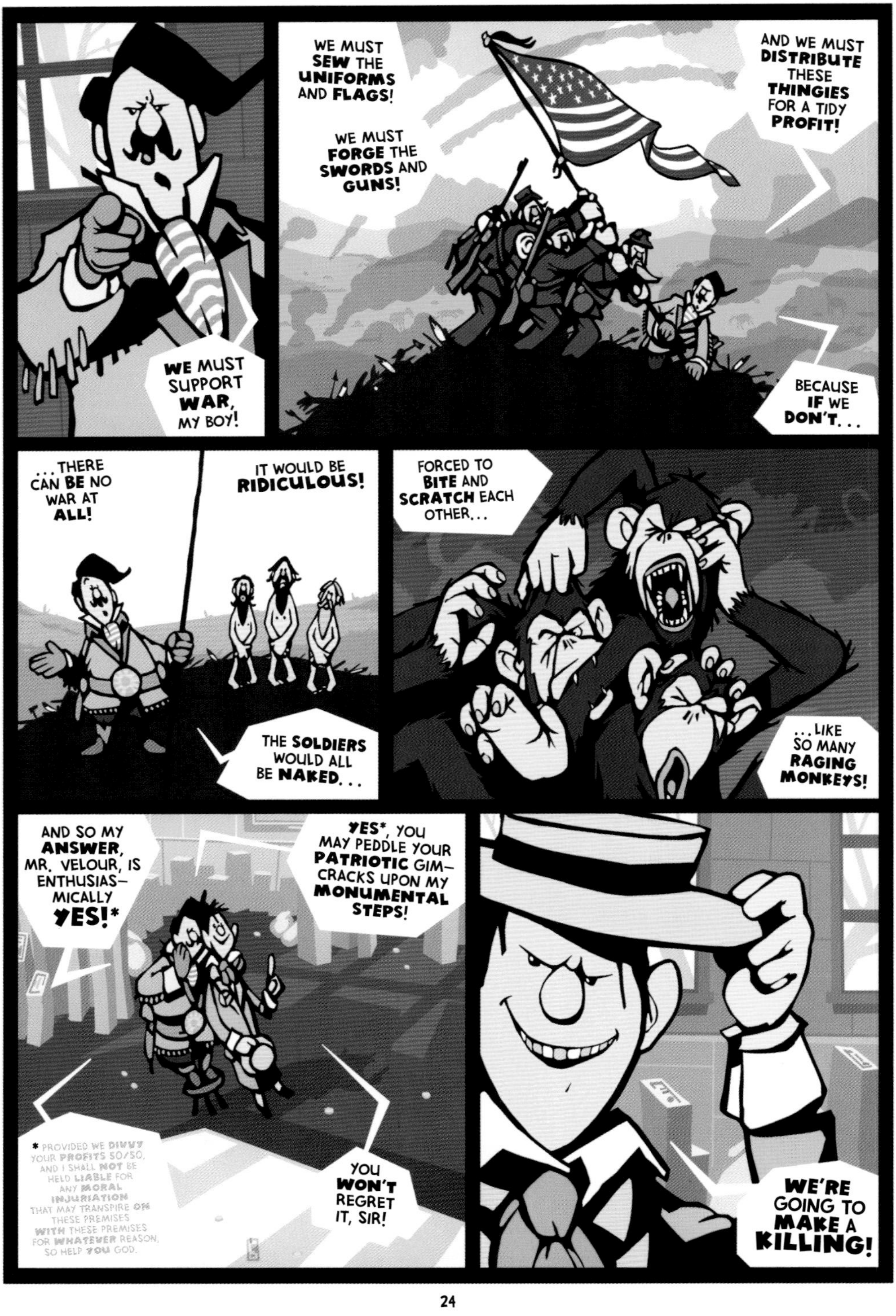
WE MUST SUPPORT WAR, MY BOY!
WE MUST SEW THE UNIFORMS AND FLAGS!
WE MUST FORGE THE SWORDS AND GUNS!
AND WE MUST DISTRIBUTE THESE THINGIES FOR A TIDY PROFIT!
BECAUSE IF WE DON'T...
...THERE CAN BE NO WAR AT ALL!
IT WOULD BE RIDICULOUS!
THE SOLDIERS WOULD ALL BE NAKED...
FORCED TO BITE AND SCRATCH EACH OTHER...
...LIKE SO MANY RAGING MONKEYS!
AND SO MY ANSWER, MR. VELOUR, IS ENTHUSIAS-MICALLY YES!*
YES*, YOU MAY PEDDLE YOUR PATRIOTIC GIM-CRACKS UPON MY MONUMENTAL STEPS!
* PROVIDED WE DIVVY YOUR PROFITS 50/50, AND I SHALL NOT BE HELD LIABLE FOR ANY MORAL INJURIATION THAT MAY TRANSPIRE ON THESE PREMISES WITH THESE PREMISES FOR WHATEVER REASON, SO HELP YOU GOD.
YOU WON'T REGRET IT, SIR!
WE'RE GOING TO MAKE A KILLING!

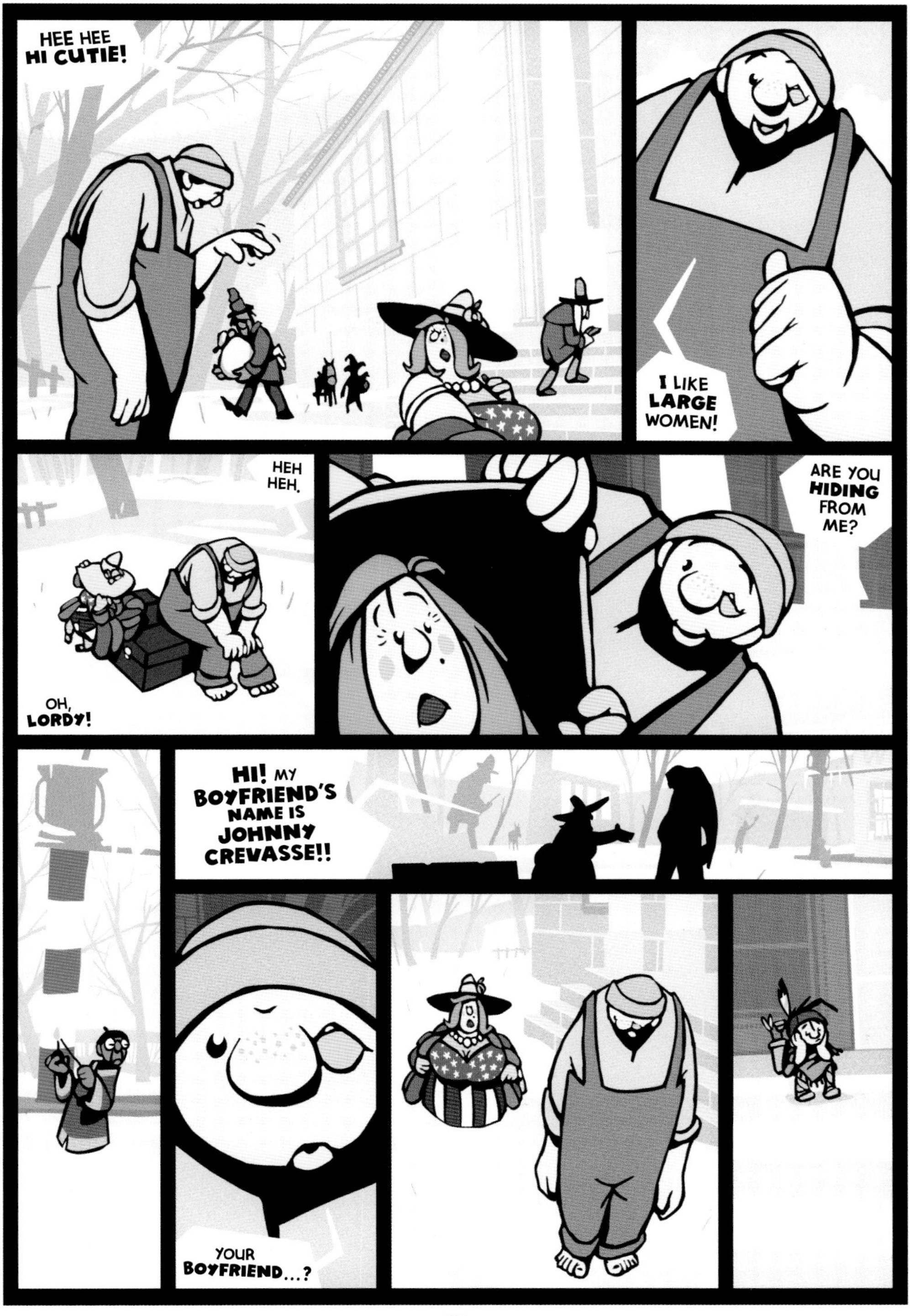
HEE HEE
HI CUTIE!
I LIKE LARGE WOMEN!
HEH HEH.
OH, LORDY!
ARE YOU HIDING FROM ME?
HI! MY BOYFRIEND'S NAME IS JOHNNY CREVASSE!!
YOUR BOYFRIEND...?

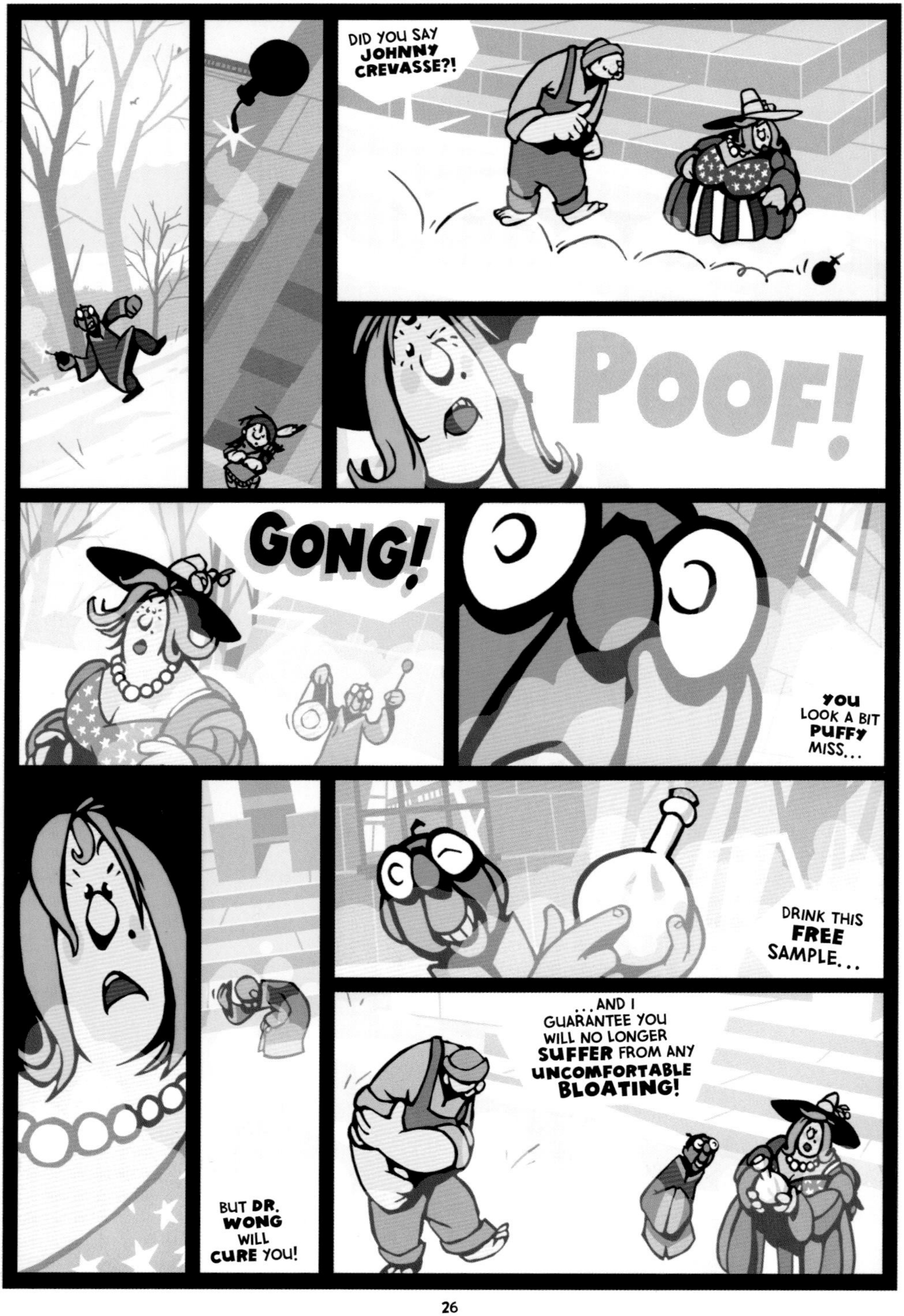
DID YOU SAY **JOHNNY CREVASSE?!**
POOF!
GONG!
YOU LOOK A BIT **PUFFY** MISS...
BUT **DR. WONG** WILL **CURE** YOU!
DRINK THIS **FREE** SAMPLE...
...AND I GUARANTEE YOU WILL NO LONGER **SUFFER** FROM ANY **UNCOMFORTABLE BLOATING!**

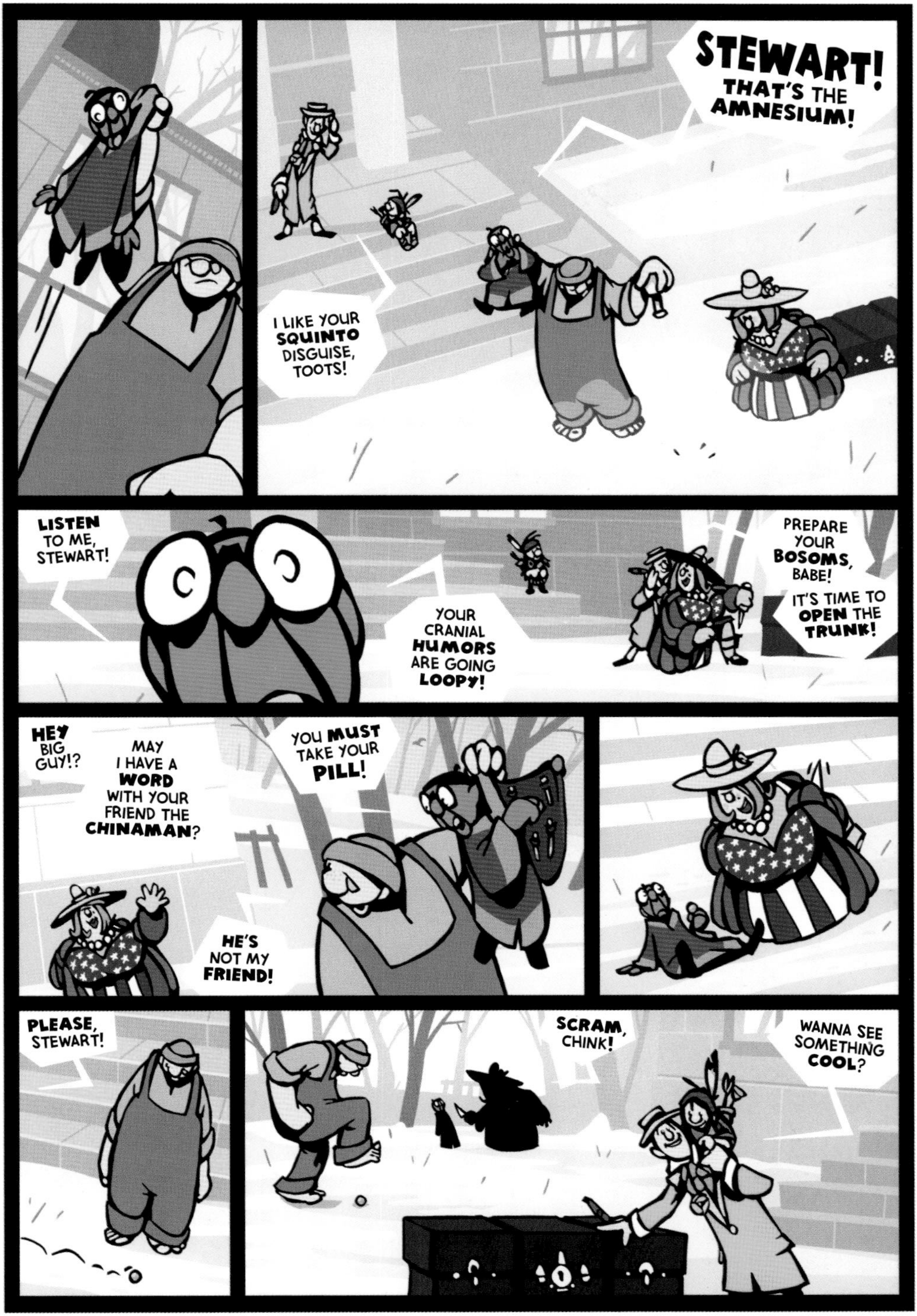
STEWART! THAT'S THE AMNESIUM!
I LIKE YOUR SQUINTO DISGUISE, TOOTS!
LISTEN TO ME, STEWART!
YOUR CRANIAL HUMORS ARE GOING LOOPY!
PREPARE YOUR BOSOMS, BABE!
IT'S TIME TO OPEN THE TRUNK!
HEY BIG GUY!?
MAY I HAVE A WORD WITH YOUR FRIEND THE CHINAMAN?
YOU MUST TAKE YOUR PILL!
HE'S NOT MY FRIEND!
PLEASE, STEWART!
SCRAM, CHINK!
WANNA SEE SOMETHING COOL?

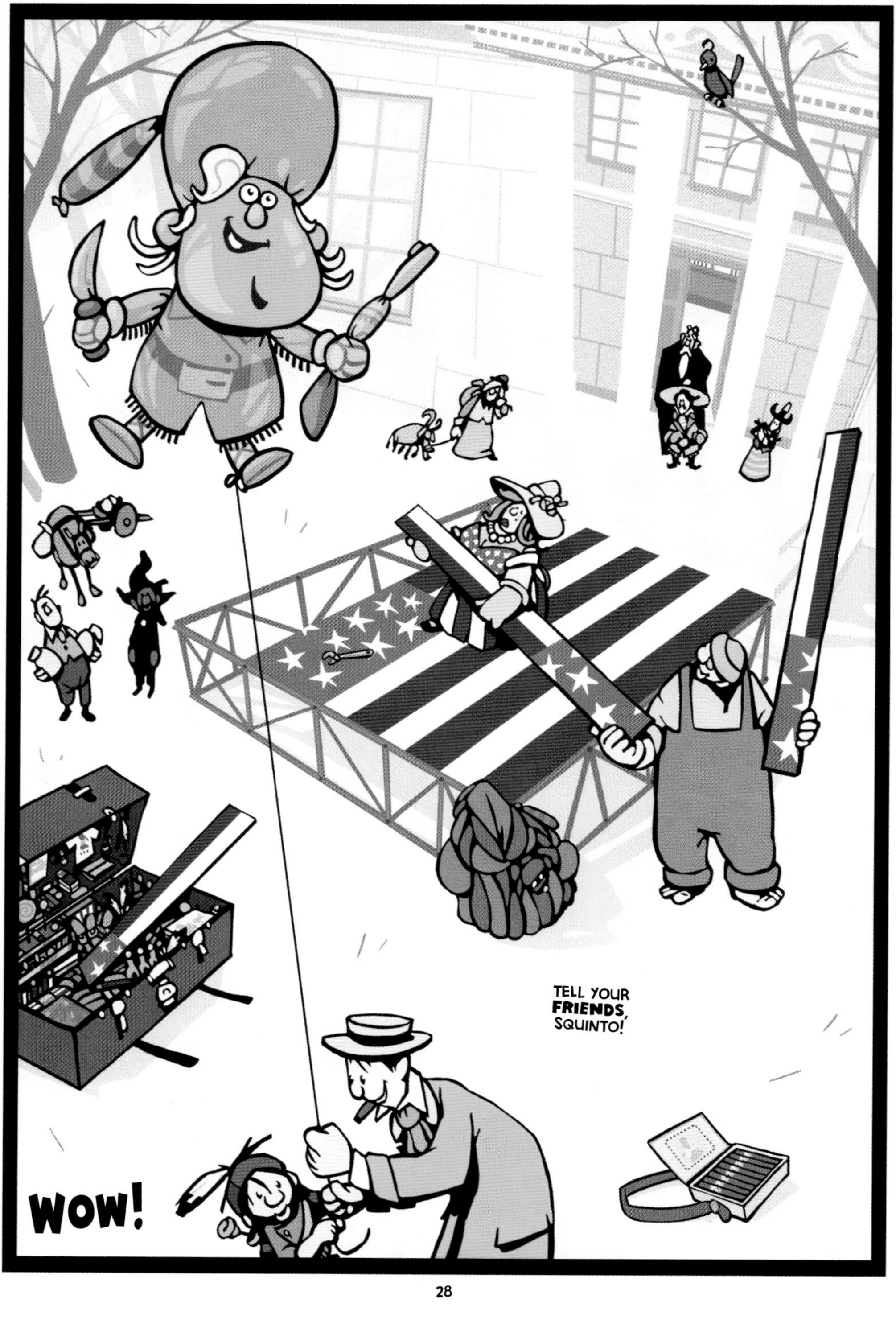
TELL YOUR FRIENDS, SQUINTO!
WOW!

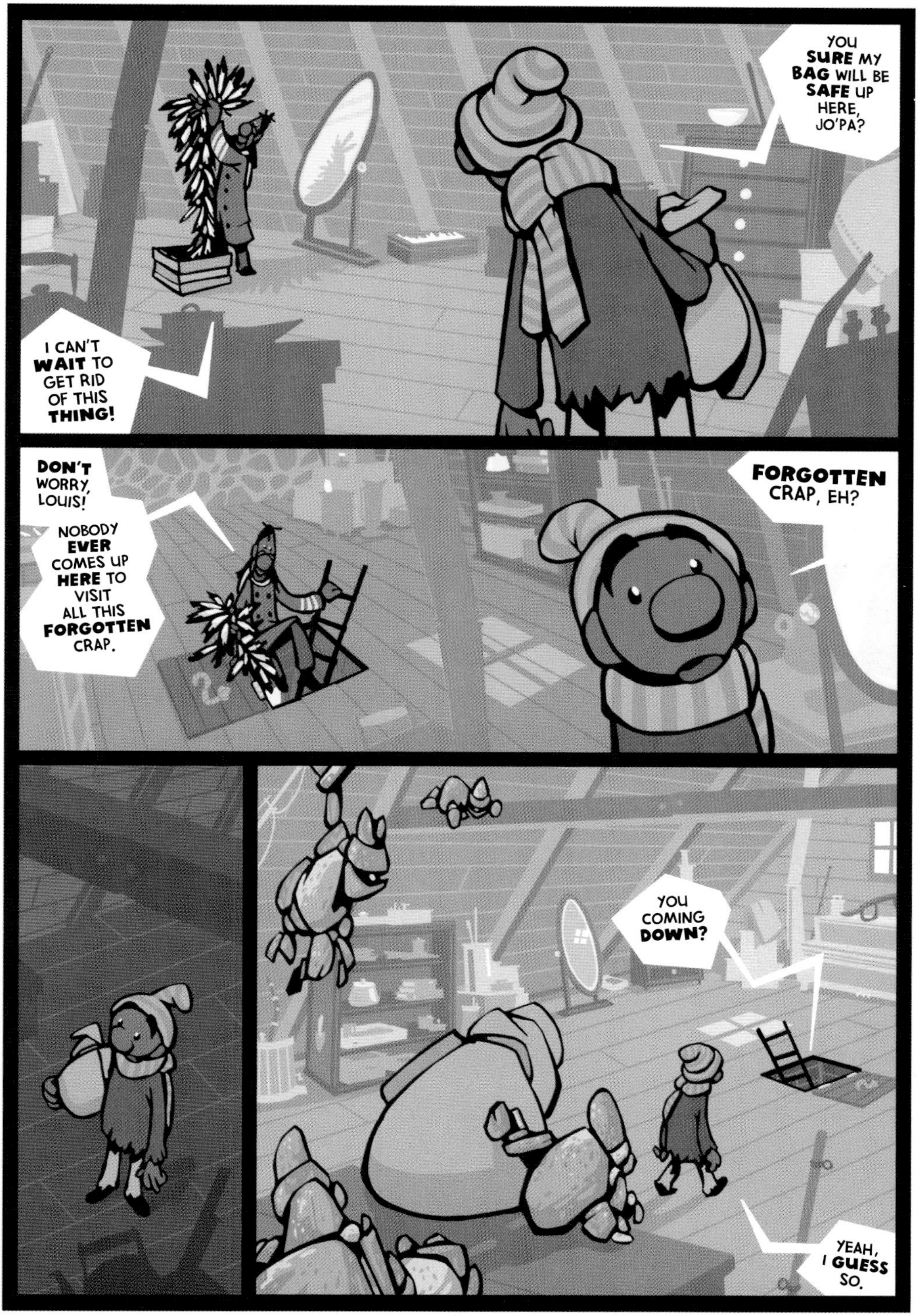

YOU SURE MY BAG WILL BE SAFE UP HERE, JO'PA?
I CAN'T WAIT TO GET RID OF THIS THING!
DON'T WORRY, LOUIS!
NOBODY EVER COMES UP HERE TO VISIT ALL THIS FORGOTTEN CRAP.
FORGOTTEN CRAP, EH?
YOU COMING DOWN?
YEAH, I GUESS SO.

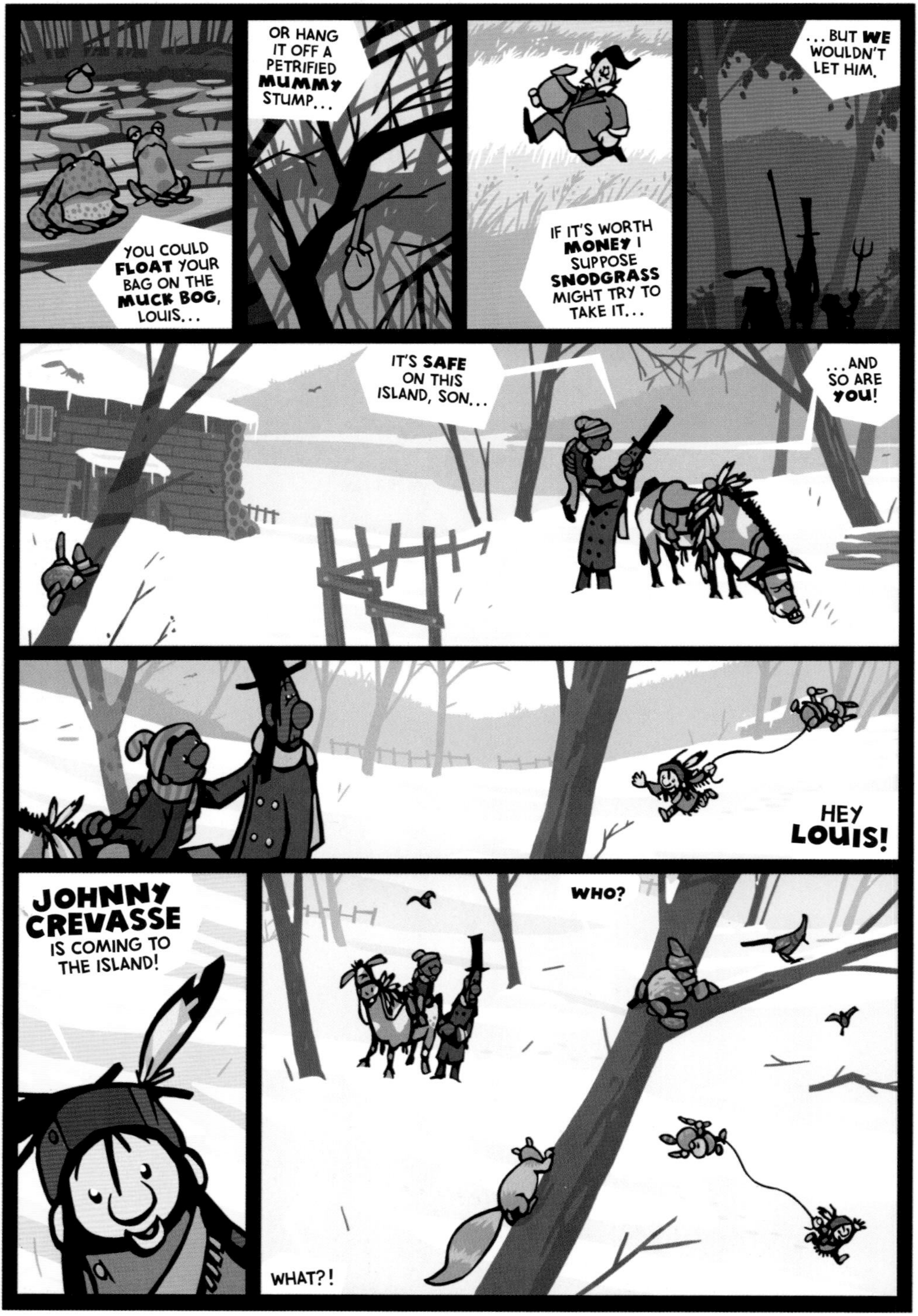
YOU COULD FLOAT YOUR BAG ON THE MUCK BOG, LOUIS...
OR HANG IT OFF A PETRIFIED MUMMY STUMP...
IF IT'S WORTH MONEY I SUPPOSE SNODGRASS MIGHT TRY TO TAKE IT...
...BUT WE WOULDN'T LET HIM.
IT'S SAFE ON THIS ISLAND, SON...
...AND SO ARE YOU!
HEY LOUIS!
JOHNNY CREVASSE IS COMING TO THE ISLAND!
WHO?
WHAT?!

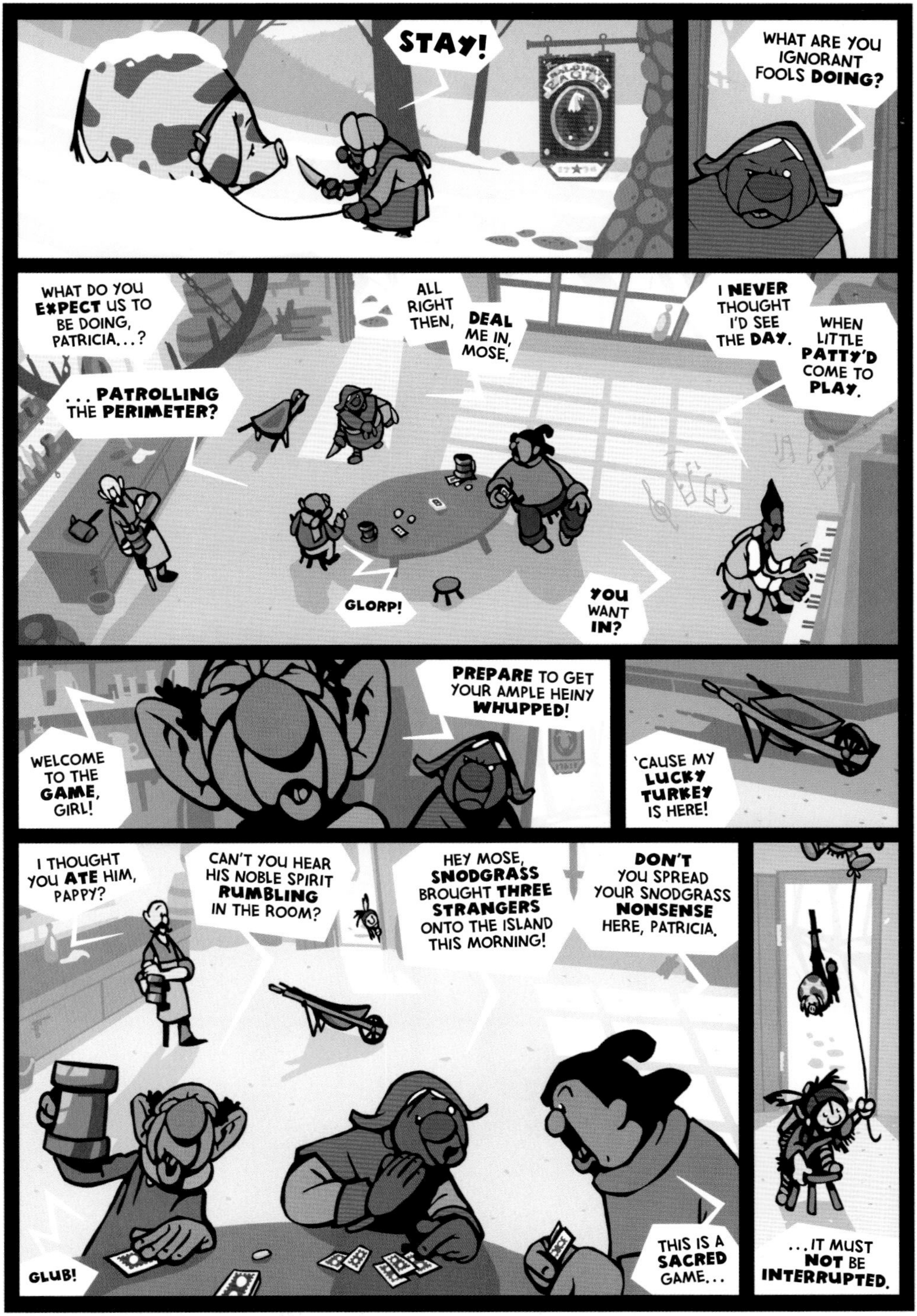
STAY!
WHAT ARE YOU IGNORANT FOOLS DOING?
WHAT DO YOU EXPECT US TO BE DOING, PATRICIA...?
...PATROLLING THE PERIMETER?
ALL RIGHT THEN, DEAL ME IN, MOSE.
GLORP!
I NEVER THOUGHT I'D SEE THE DAY.
WHEN LITTLE PATTY'D COME TO PLAY.
YOU WANT IN?
WELCOME TO THE GAME, GIRL!
PREPARE TO GET YOUR AMPLE HEINY WHUPPED!
'CAUSE MY LUCKY TURKEY IS HERE!
I THOUGHT YOU ATE HIM, PAPPY?
CAN'T YOU HEAR HIS NOBLE SPIRIT RUMBLING IN THE ROOM?
HEY MOSE, SNODGRASS BROUGHT THREE STRANGERS ONTO THE ISLAND THIS MORNING!
DON'T YOU SPREAD YOUR SNODGRASS NONSENSE HERE, PATRICIA.
GLUB!
THIS IS A SACRED GAME...
...IT MUST NOT BE INTERRUPTED.

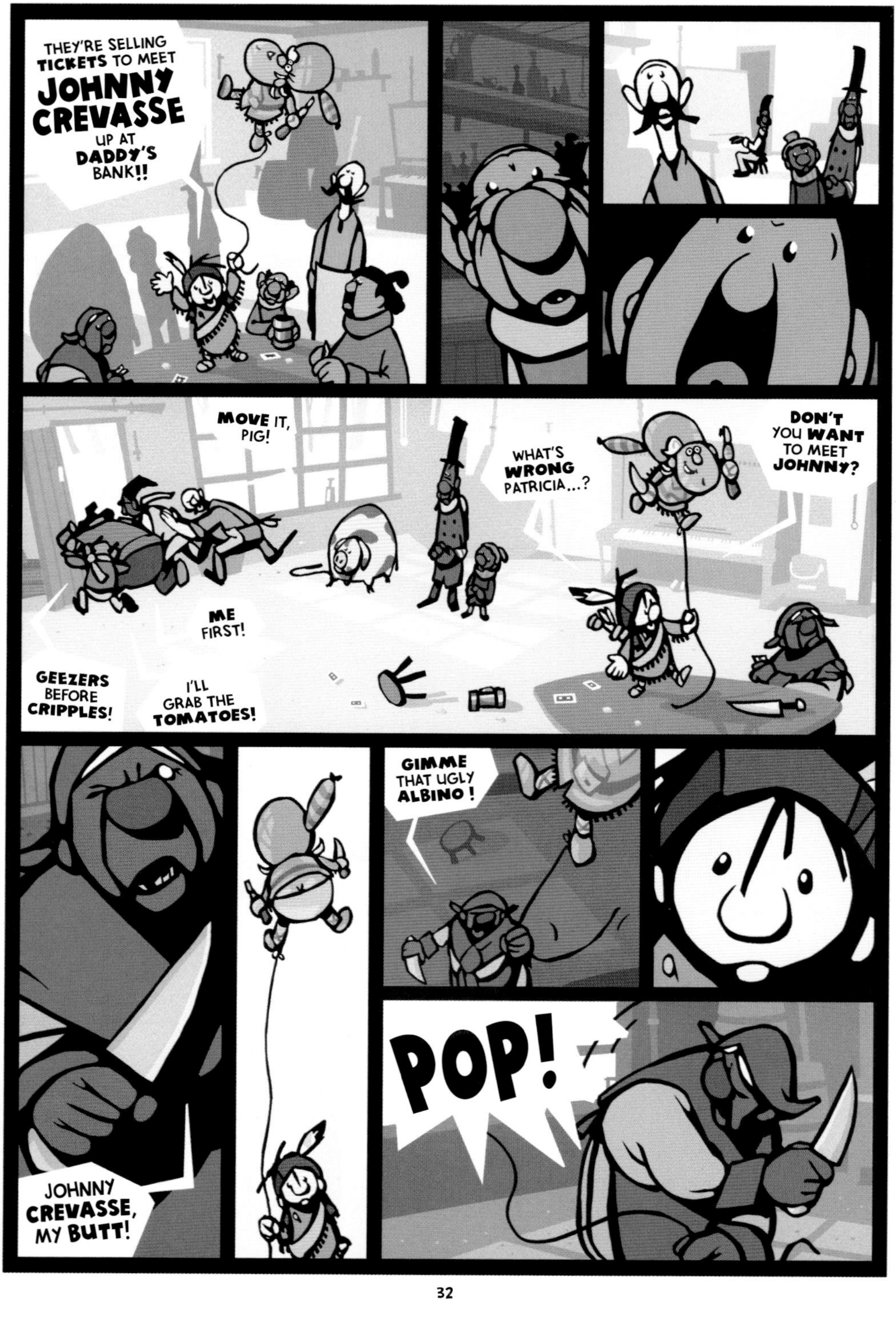

THEY'RE SELLING TICKETS TO MEET JOHNNY CREVASSE UP AT DADDY'S BANK!!
MOVE IT, PIG!
WHAT'S WRONG PATRICIA...?
DON'T YOU WANT TO MEET JOHNNY?
ME FIRST!
GEEZERS BEFORE CRIPPLES!
I'LL GRAB THE TOMATOES!
JOHNNY CREVASSE, MY BUTT!
GIMME THAT UGLY ALBINO!
POP!

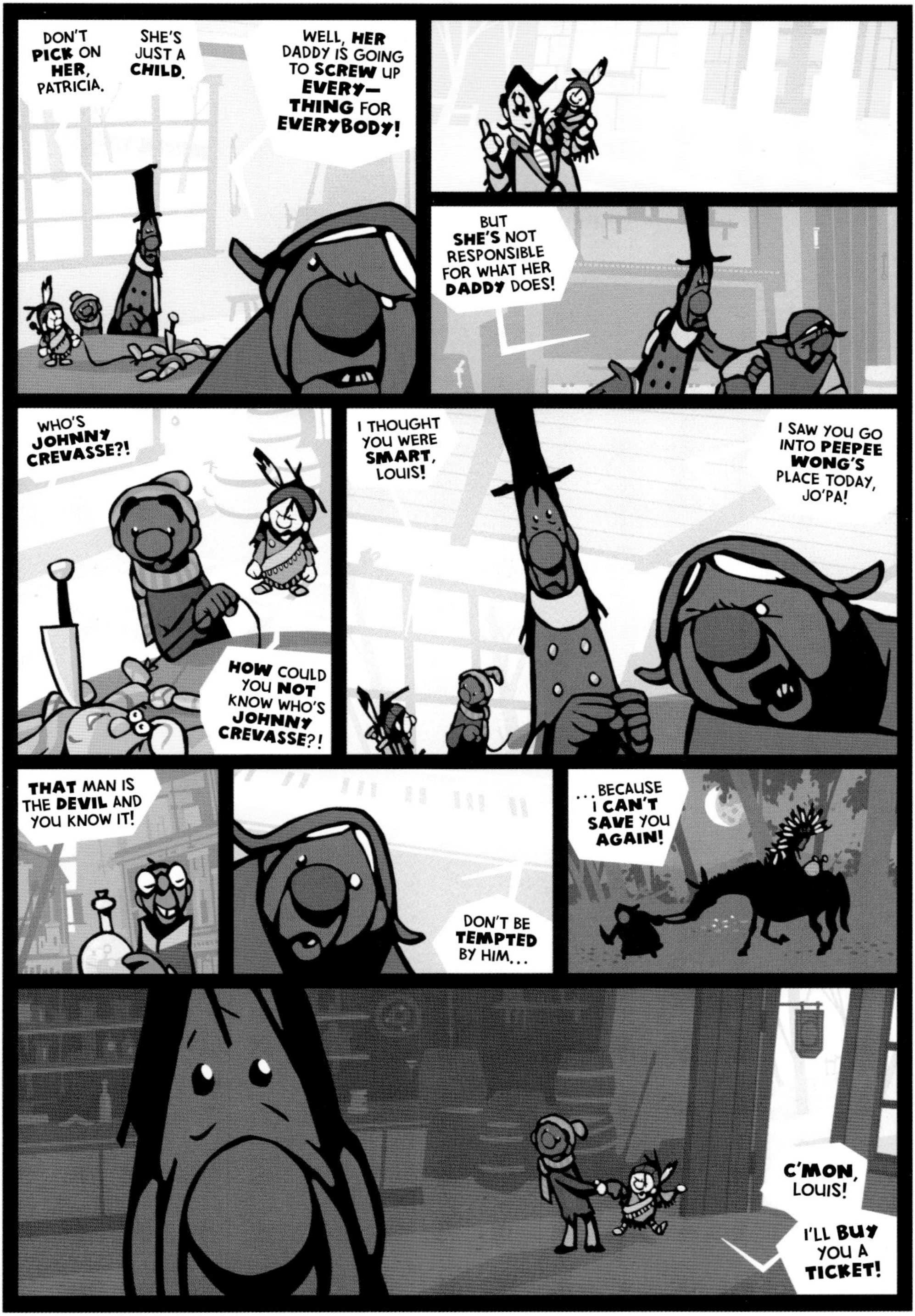
DON'T PICK ON HER, PATRICIA.
SHE'S JUST A CHILD.
WELL, HER DADDY IS GOING TO SCREW UP EVERY— THING FOR EVERYBODY!
BUT SHE'S NOT RESPONSIBLE FOR WHAT HER DADDY DOES!
WHO'S JOHNNY CREVASSE?!
HOW COULD YOU NOT KNOW WHO'S JOHNNY CREVASSE?!
I THOUGHT YOU WERE SMART, LOUIS!
I SAW YOU GO INTO PEEPEE WONG'S PLACE TODAY, JO'PA!
THAT MAN IS THE DEVIL AND YOU KNOW IT!
DON'T BE TEMPTED BY HIM...
...BECAUSE I CAN'T SAVE YOU AGAIN!
C'MON, LOUIS!
I'LL BUY YOU A TICKET!

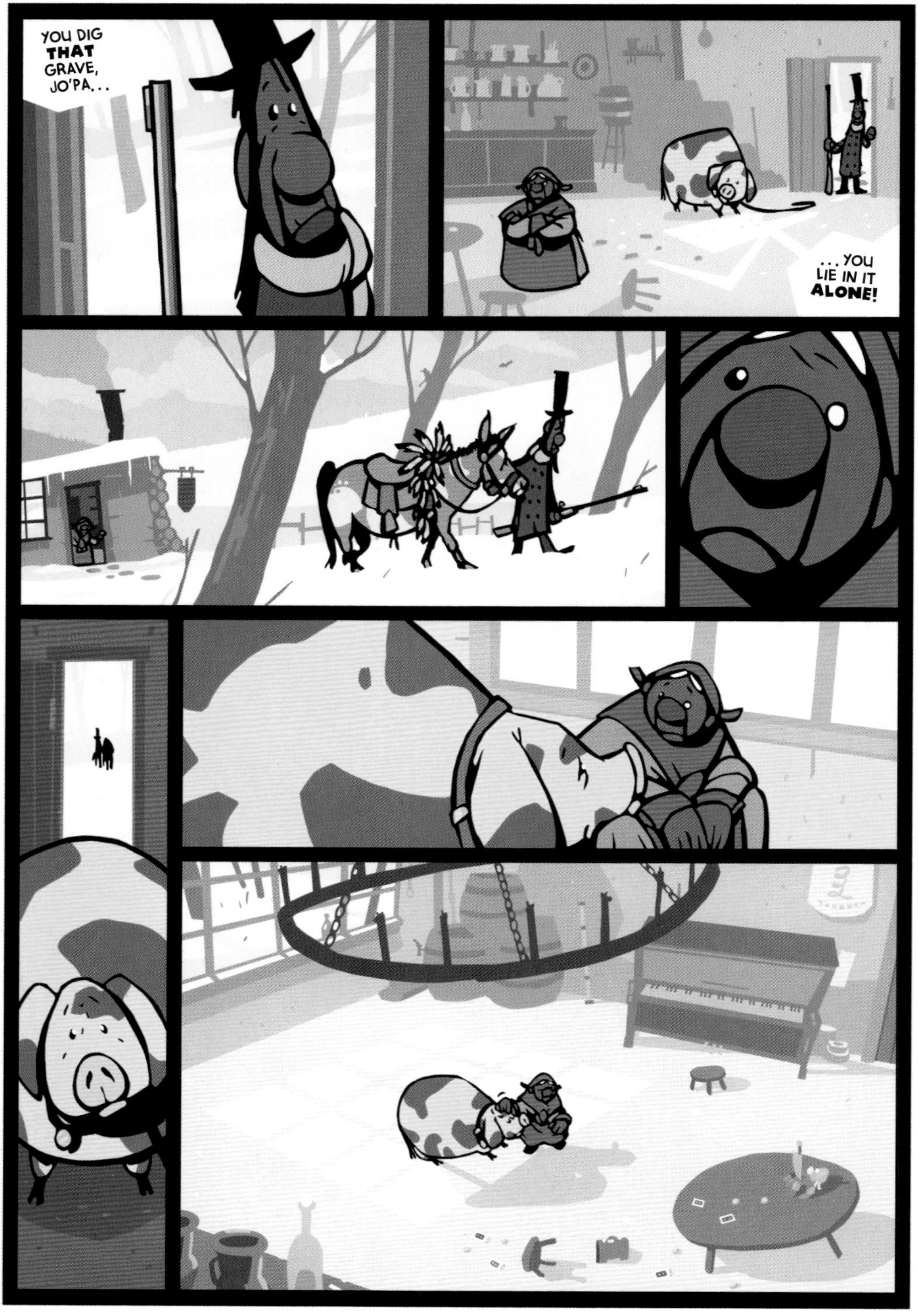
YOU DIG THAT GRAVE, JO'PA, . .
. . . YOU LIE IN IT ALONE!

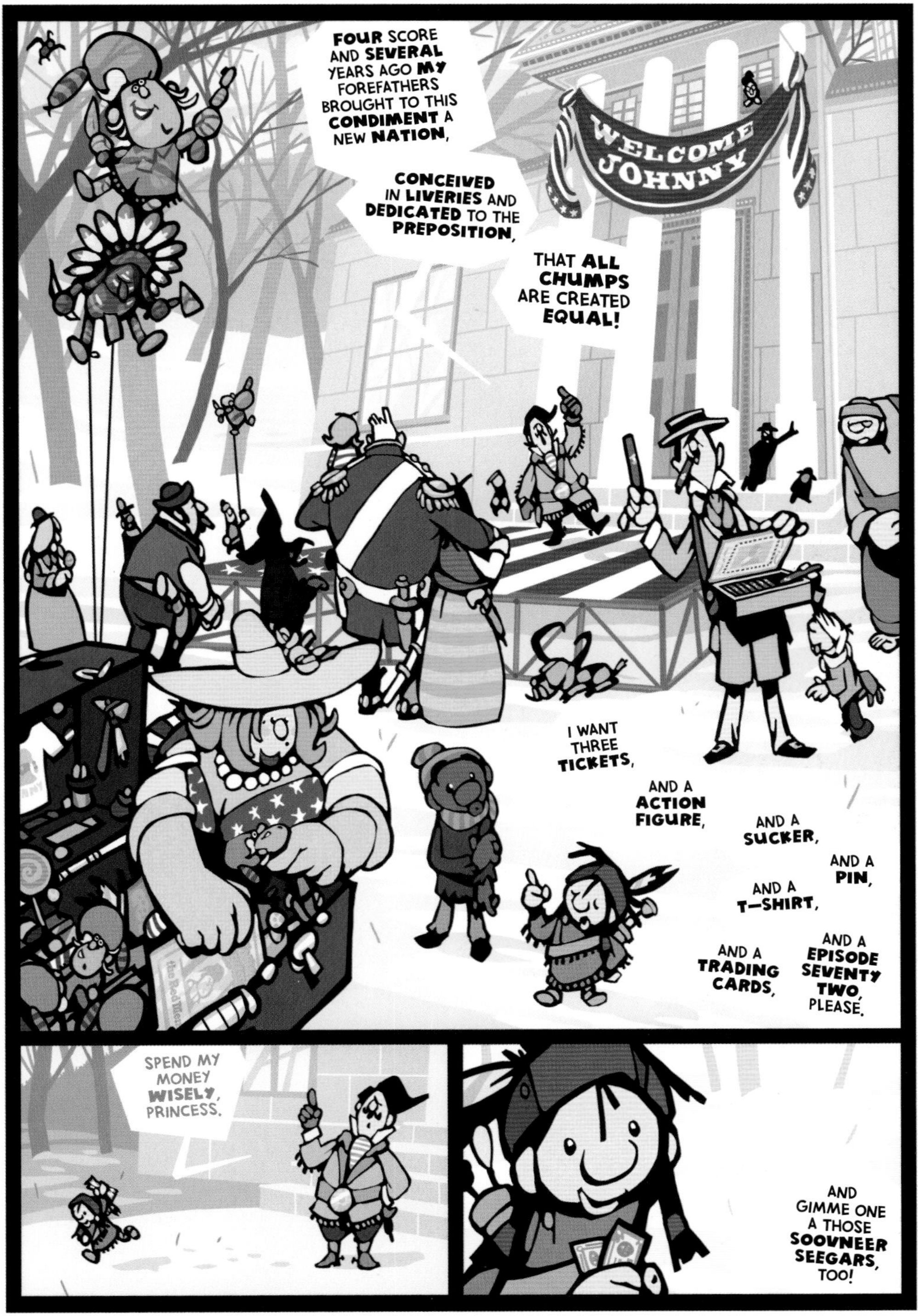
FOUR SCORE AND SEVERAL YEARS AGO MY FOREFATHERS BROUGHT TO THIS CONDIMENT A NEW NATION,
WELCOME JOHNNY
CONCEIVED IN LIVERIES AND DEDICATED TO THE PREPOSITION,
THAT ALL CHUMPS ARE CREATED EQUAL!
I WANT THREE TICKETS,
AND A ACTION FIGURE,
AND A SUCKER,
AND A PIN,
AND A T—SHIRT,
AND A TRADING CARDS,
AND A EPISODE SEVENTY TWO, PLEASE.
SPEND MY MONEY WISELY, PRINCESS.
AND GIMME ONE A THOSE SOOVNEER SEEGARS, TOO!

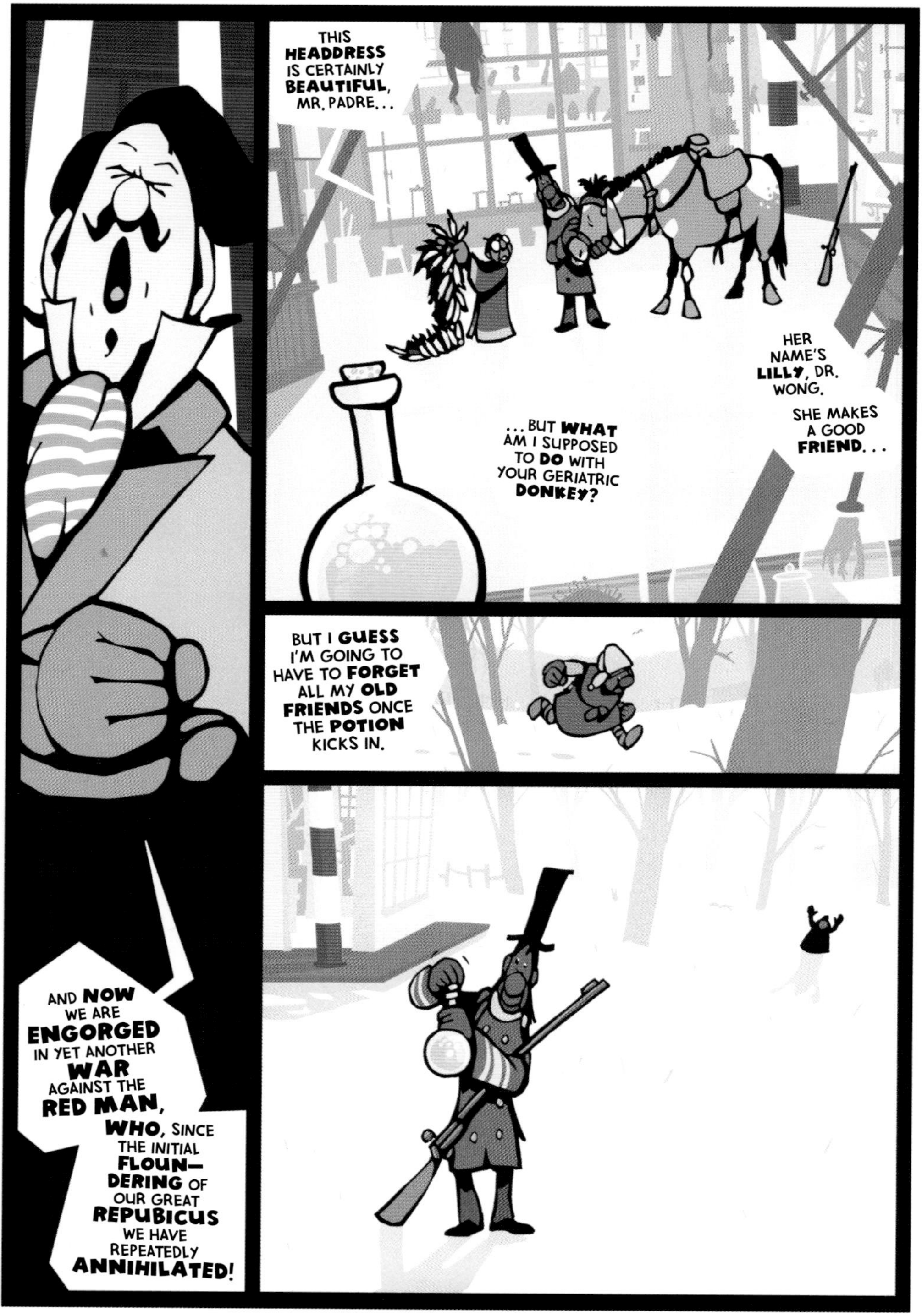

AND NOW WE ARE ENGORGED IN YET ANOTHER WAR AGAINST THE RED MAN, WHO, SINCE THE INITIAL FLOUN-DERING OF OUR GREAT REPUBICUS WE HAVE REPEATEDLY ANNIHILATED!
THIS HEADDRESS IS CERTAINLY BEAUTIFUL, MR. PADRE...
...BUT WHAT AM I SUPPOSED TO DO WITH YOUR GERIATRIC DONKEY?
HER NAME'S LILLY, DR. WONG.
SHE MAKES A GOOD FRIEND...
BUT I GUESS I'M GOING TO HAVE TO FORGET ALL MY OLD FRIENDS ONCE THE POTION KICKS IN.

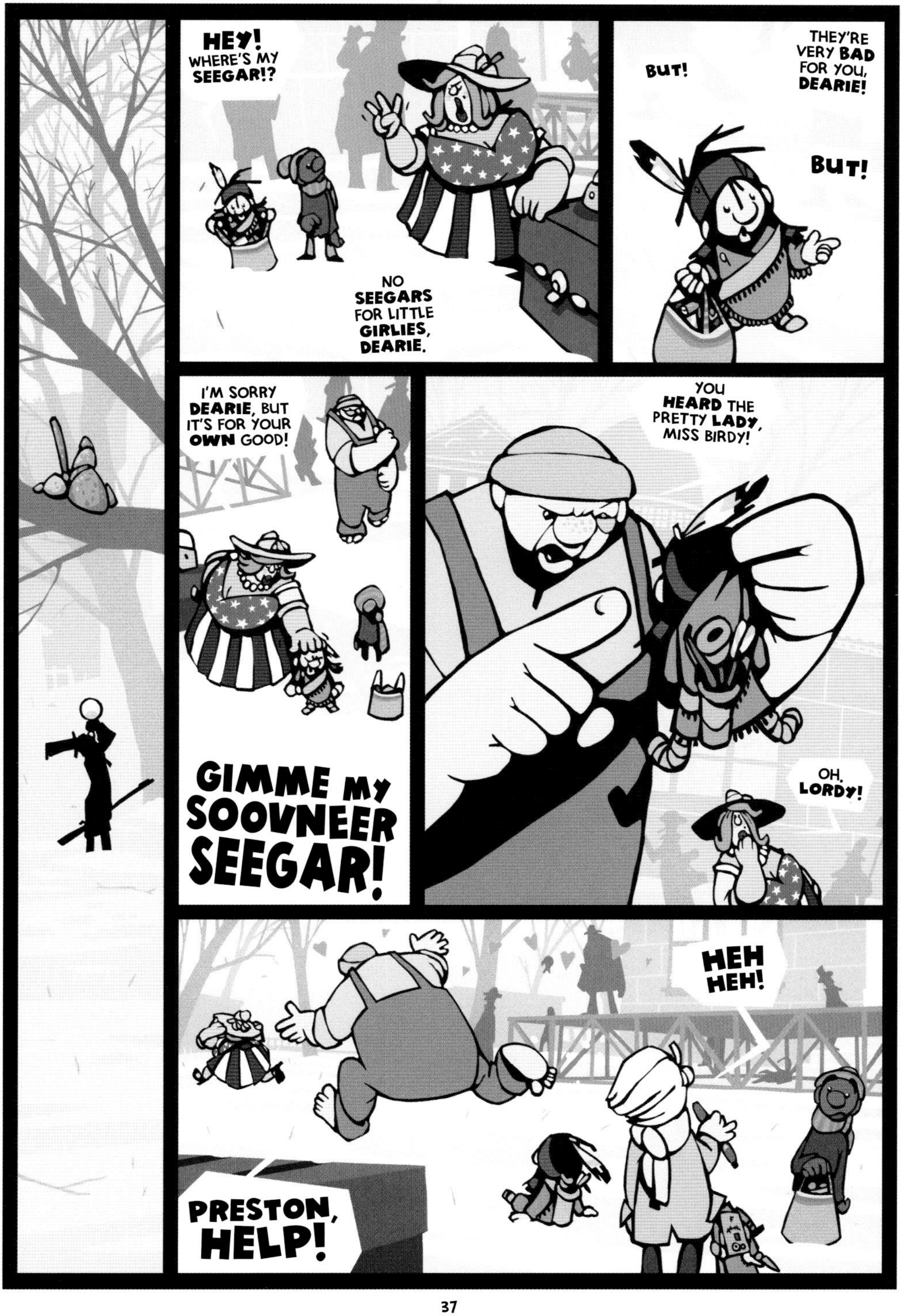

HEY! WHERE'S MY SEEGAR!?
NO SEEGARS FOR LITTLE GIRLIES, DEARIE.
BUT!
THEY'RE VERY BAD FOR YOU, DEARIE!
BUT!
I'M SORRY DEARIE, BUT IT'S FOR YOUR OWN GOOD!
GIMME MY SOOVNEER SEEGAR!
YOU HEARD THE PRETTY LADY, MISS BIRDY!
OH, LORDY!
HEH HEH!
PRESTON, HELP!

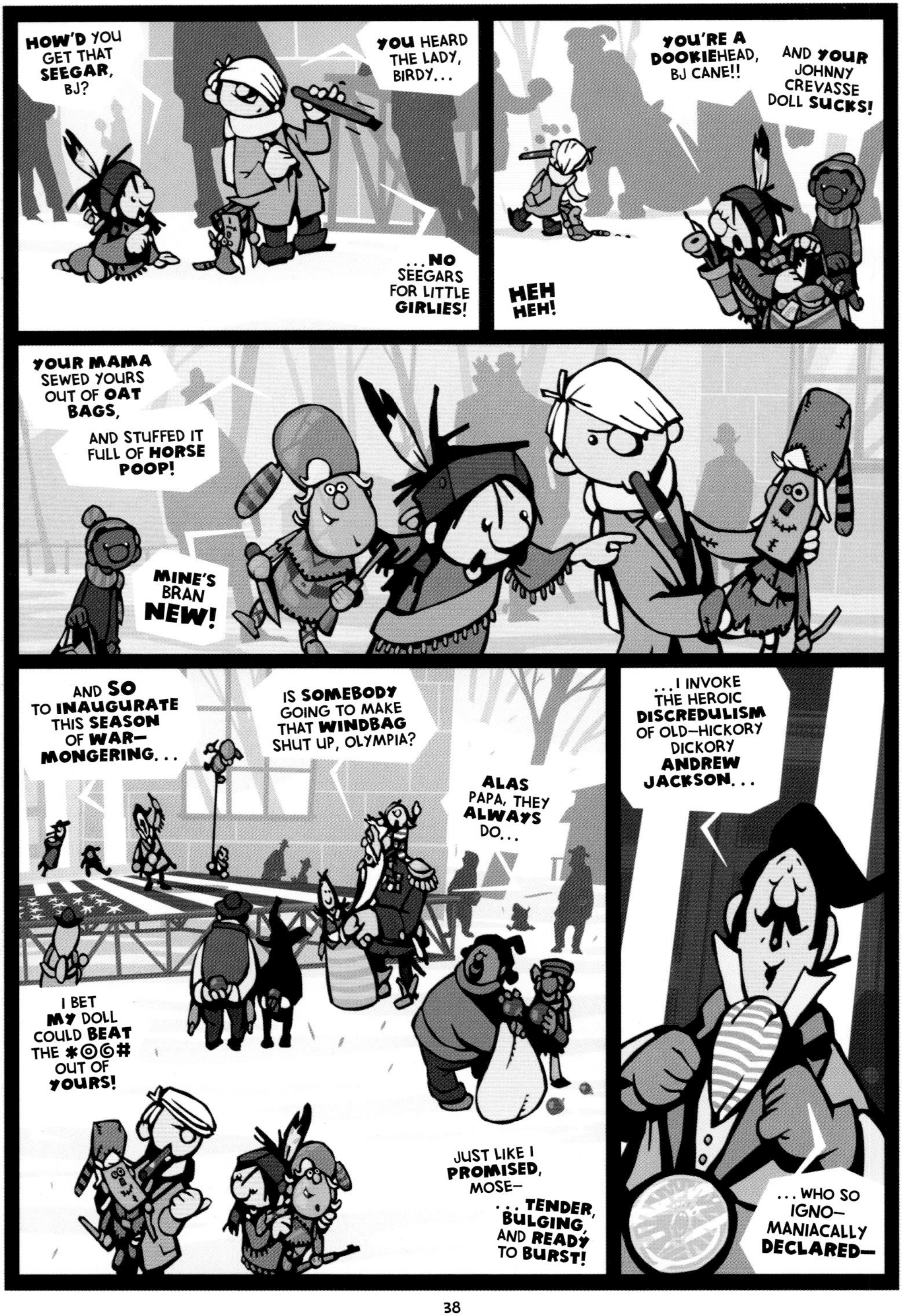
HOW'D YOU GET THAT SEEGAR, BJ?
YOU HEARD THE LADY, BIRDY...
...NO SEEGARS FOR LITTLE GIRLIES!
YOU'RE A DOOKIEHEAD, BJ CANE!!
AND YOUR JOHNNY CREVASSE DOLL SUCKS!
HEH HEH!
YOUR MAMA SEWED YOURS OUT OF OAT BAGS,
AND STUFFED IT FULL OF HORSE POOP!
MINE'S BRAN NEW!
AND SO TO INAUGURATE THIS SEASON OF WAR-MONGERING...
IS SOMEBODY GOING TO MAKE THAT WINDBAG SHUT UP, OLYMPIA?
ALAS PAPA, THEY ALWAYS DO...
I BET MY DOLL COULD BEAT THE *◎◎# OUT OF YOURS!
JUST LIKE I PROMISED, MOSE—
...TENDER, BULGING, AND READY TO BURST!
...I INVOKE THE HEROIC DISCREDULISM OF OLD-HICKORY DICKORY ANDREW JACKSON...
...WHO SO IGNO-MANIACALLY DECLARED—

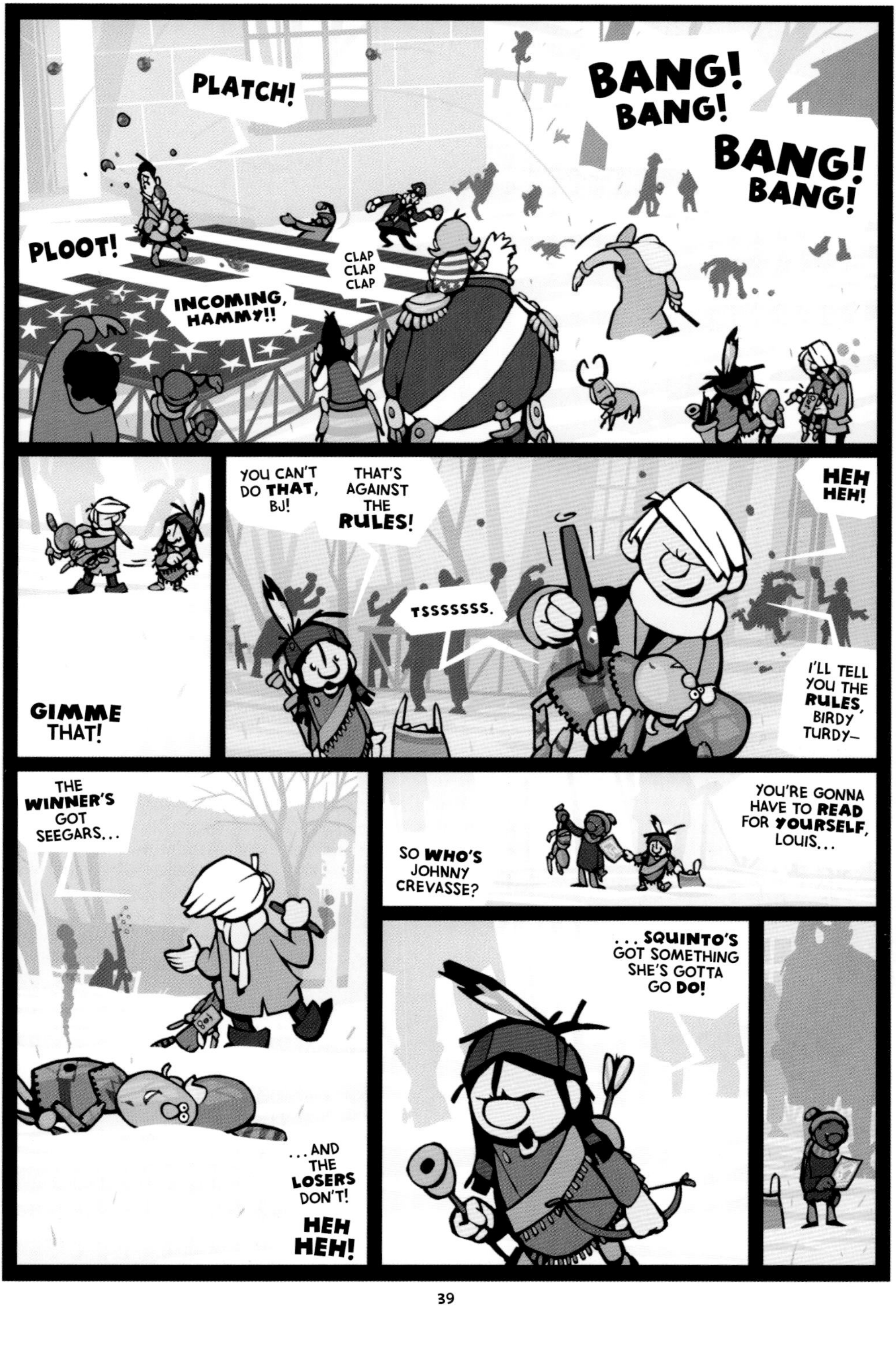
PLATCH!
BANG! BANG!
BANG! BANG!
PLOOT!
CLAP CLAP CLAP
INCOMING, HAMMY!!
GIMME THAT!
YOU CAN'T DO THAT, BJ!
THAT'S AGAINST THE RULES!
HEH HEH!
TSSSSSSS.
I'LL TELL YOU THE RULES, BIRDY TURDY—
THE WINNER'S GOT SEEGARS...
...AND THE LOSERS DON'T!
HEH HEH!
SO WHO'S JOHNNY CREVASSE?
YOU'RE GONNA HAVE TO READ FOR YOURSELF, LOUIS...
...SQUINTO'S GOT SOMETHING SHE'S GOTTA GO DO!

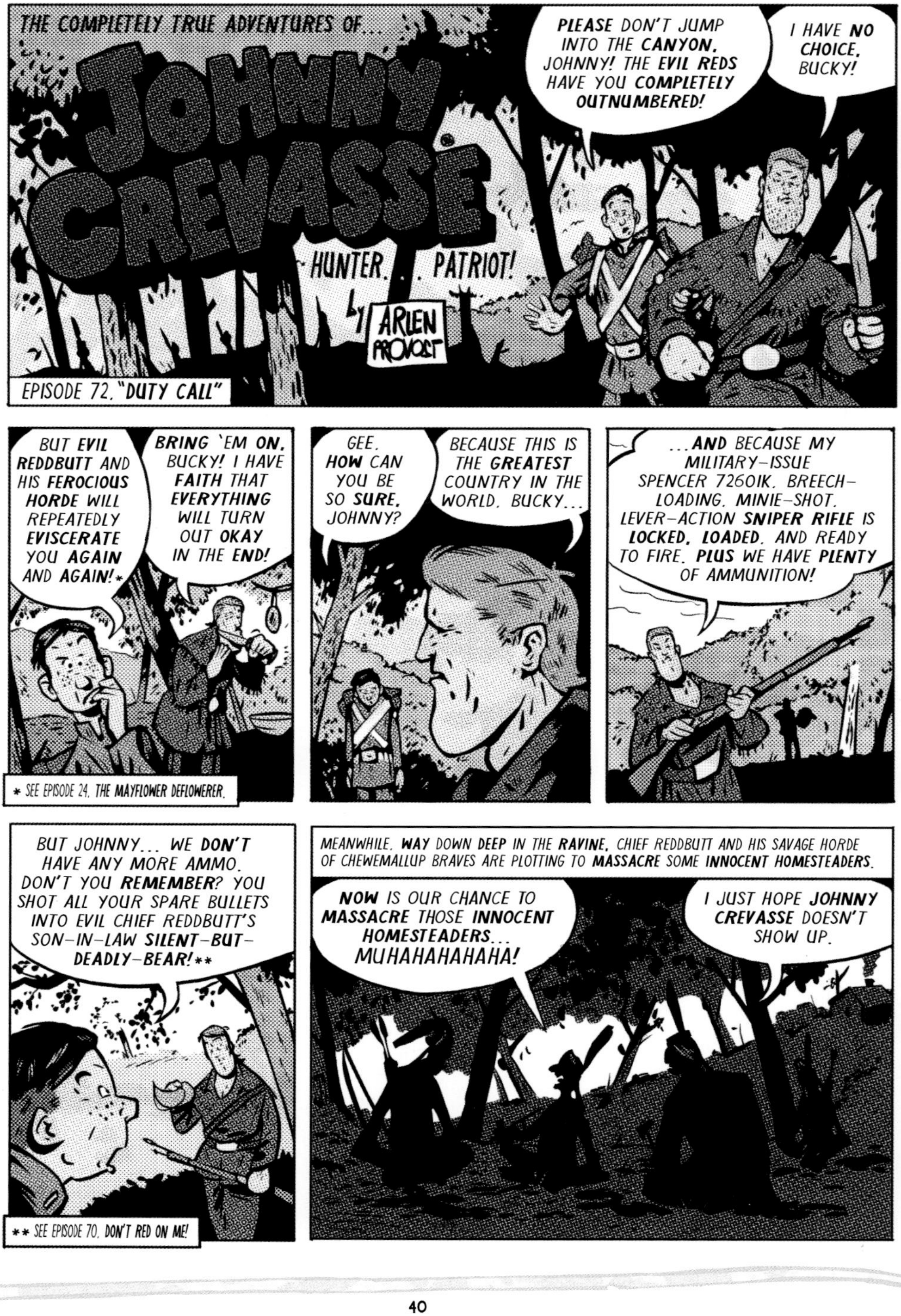
THE COMPLETELY TRUE ADVENTURES OF...
JOHNNY CREVASSÉ
HUNTER. PATRIOT!
by ARLEN PROVOST
PLEASE DON'T JUMP INTO THE CANYON, JOHNNY! THE EVIL REDS HAVE YOU COMPLETELY OUTNUMBERED!
I HAVE NO CHOICE, BUCKY!
EPISODE 72, "DUTY CALL"
BUT EVIL REDDBUTT AND HIS FEROCIOUS HORDE WILL REPEATEDLY EVISCERATE YOU AGAIN AND AGAIN!*
BRING 'EM ON, BUCKY! I HAVE FAITH THAT EVERYTHING WILL TURN OUT OKAY IN THE END!
* SEE EPISODE 24, THE MAYFLOWER DEFLOWERER.
GEE. HOW CAN YOU BE SO SURE, JOHNNY?
BECAUSE THIS IS THE GREATEST COUNTRY IN THE WORLD, BUCKY...
...AND BECAUSE MY MILITARY-ISSUE SPENCER 7260IK, BREECH-LOADING, MINIE-SHOT, LEVER-ACTION SNIPER RIFLE IS LOCKED, LOADED, AND READY TO FIRE. PLUS WE HAVE PLENTY OF AMMUNITION!
BUT JOHNNY... WE DON'T HAVE ANY MORE AMMO. DON'T YOU REMEMBER? YOU SHOT ALL YOUR SPARE BULLETS INTO EVIL CHIEF REDDBUTT'S SON-IN-LAW SILENT-BUT-DEADLY-BEAR!**
** SEE EPISODE 70, DON'T RED ON ME!
MEANWHILE, WAY DOWN DEEP IN THE RAVINE, CHIEF REDDBUTT AND HIS SAVAGE HORDE OF CHEWEMALLUP BRAVES ARE PLOTTING TO MASSACRE SOME INNOCENT HOMESTEADERS.
NOW IS OUR CHANCE TO MASSACRE THOSE INNOCENT HOMESTEADERS... MUHAHAHAHAHA!
I JUST HOPE JOHNNY CREVASSE DOESN'T SHOW UP.

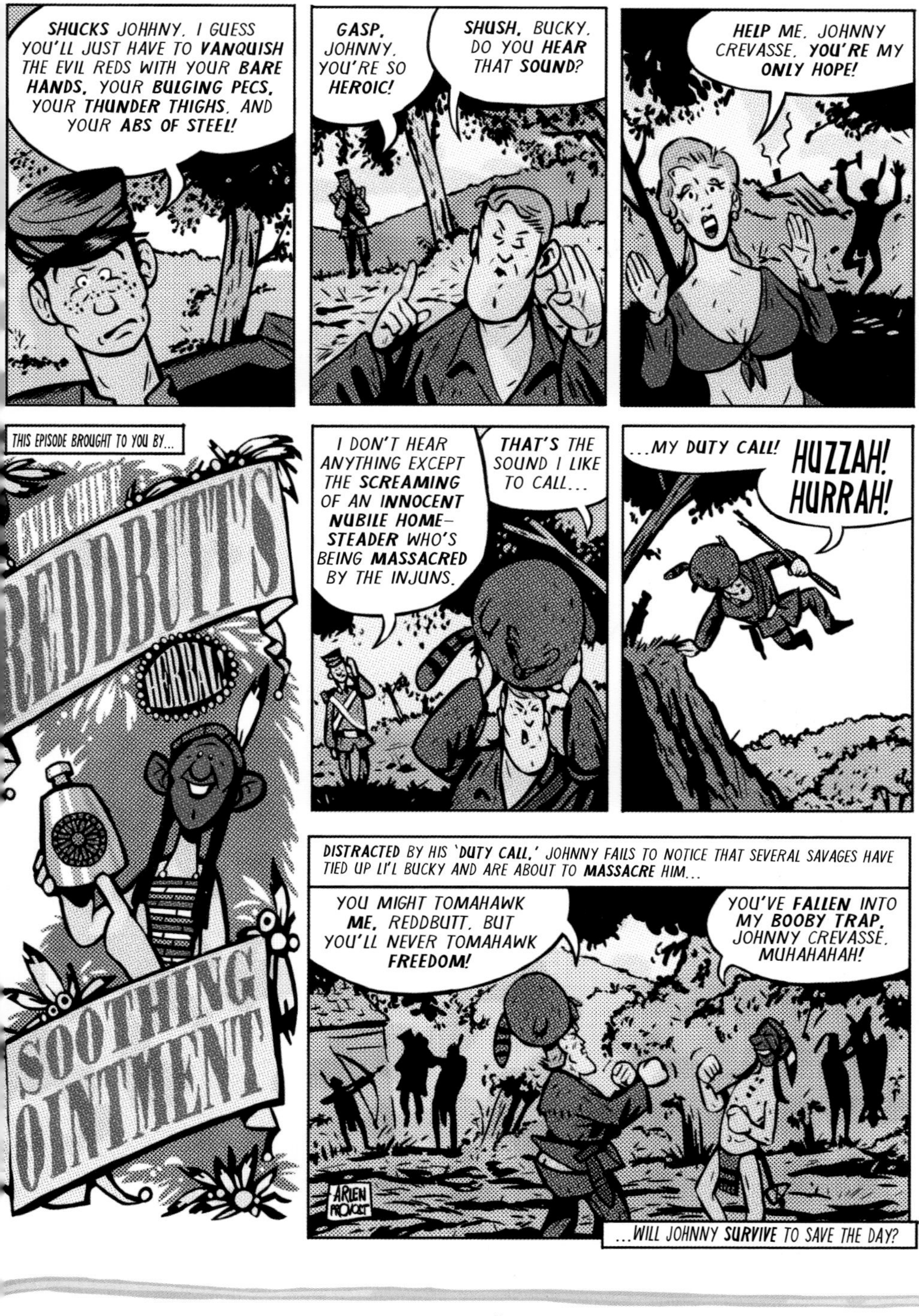

SHUCKS JOHNNY, I GUESS YOU'LL JUST HAVE TO VANQUISH THE EVIL REDS WITH YOUR BARE HANDS, YOUR BULGING PECS, YOUR THUNDER THIGHS, AND YOUR ABS OF STEEL!
GASP, JOHNNY, YOU'RE SO HEROIC!
SHUSH, BUCKY, DO YOU HEAR THAT SOUND?
HELP ME, JOHNNY CREVASSE, YOU'RE MY ONLY HOPE!
THIS EPISODE BROUGHT TO YOU BY...
EVIL CHIEF REDDBUTT'S HERBAL SOOTHING OINTMENT
I DON'T HEAR ANYTHING EXCEPT THE SCREAMING OF AN INNOCENT NUBILE HOME-STEADER WHO'S BEING MASSACRED BY THE INJUNS.
THAT'S THE SOUND I LIKE TO CALL...
...MY DUTY CALL!
HUZZAH! HURRAH!
DISTRACTED BY HIS 'DUTY CALL,' JOHNNY FAILS TO NOTICE THAT SEVERAL SAVAGES HAVE TIED UP LI'L BUCKY AND ARE ABOUT TO MASSACRE HIM...
YOU MIGHT TOMAHAWK ME, REDDBUTT, BUT YOU'LL NEVER TOMAHAWK FREEDOM!
YOU'VE FALLEN INTO MY BOOBY TRAP, JOHNNY CREVASSE, MUHAHAHAH!
ARLEN PROVOST
...WILL JOHNNY SURVIVE TO SAVE THE DAY?

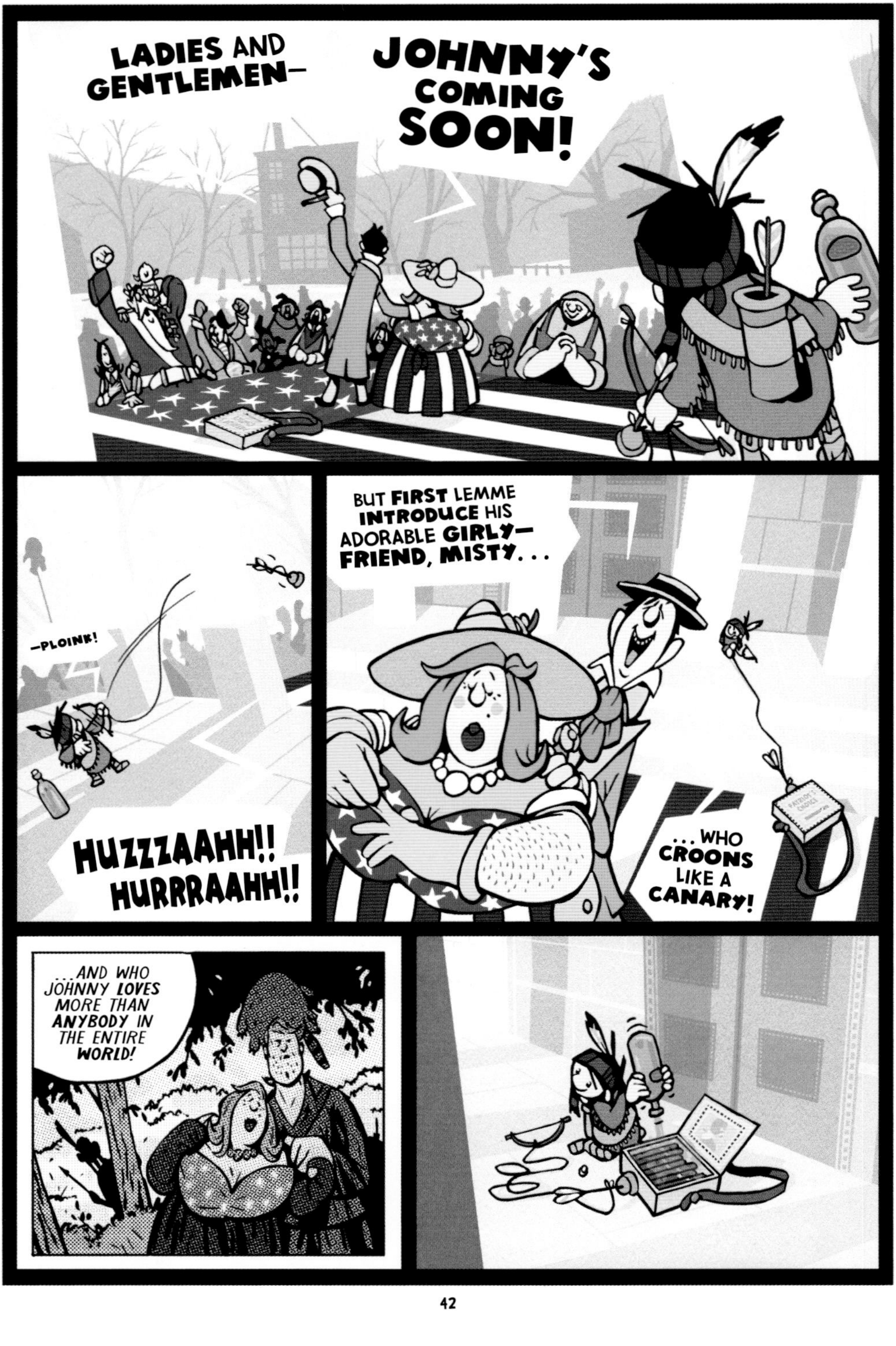
LADIES AND GENTLEMEN—
JOHNNY'S COMING SOON!
—PLOINK!
HUZZZAAHH!! HURRRAAHH!!
BUT FIRST LEMME INTRODUCE HIS ADORABLE GIRLY—FRIEND, MISTY. . .
. . . WHO CROONS LIKE A CANARY!
. . . AND WHO JOHNNY LOVES MORE THAN ANYBODY IN THE ENTIRE WORLD!

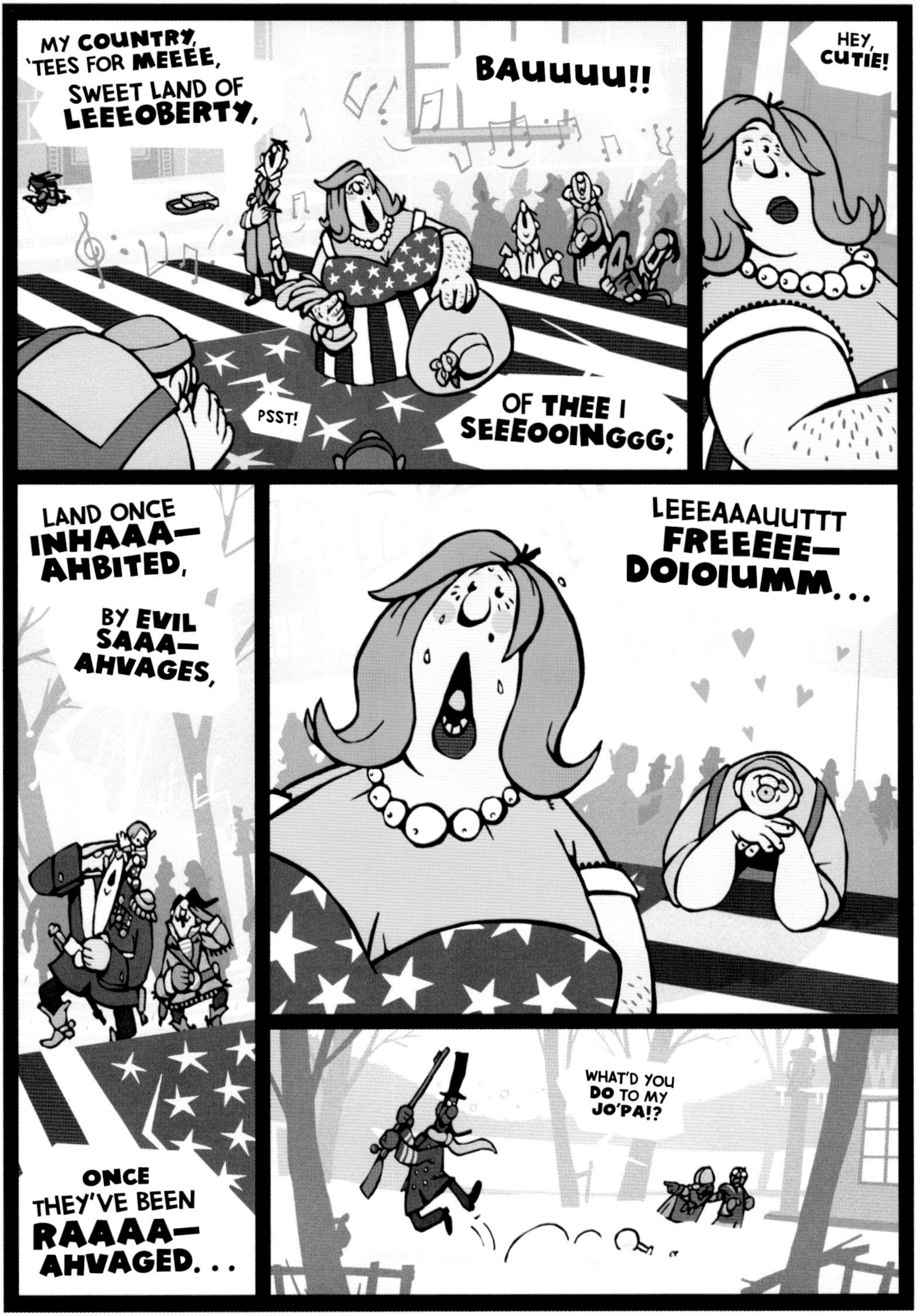
MY COUNTRY, 'TEES FOR MEEEE,
SWEET LAND OF LEEEOBERTY,
BAUUUU!!
PSST!
OF THEE I SEEEOOINGGG;
HEY, CUTIE!
LAND ONCE INHAAA-AHBITED,
BY EVIL SAAA-AHVAGES,
LEEEAAAUUTTT FREEEEE-DOIOIUMM...
ONCE THEY'VE BEEN RAAAA-AHVAGED...
WHAT'D YOU DO TO MY JO'PA!?

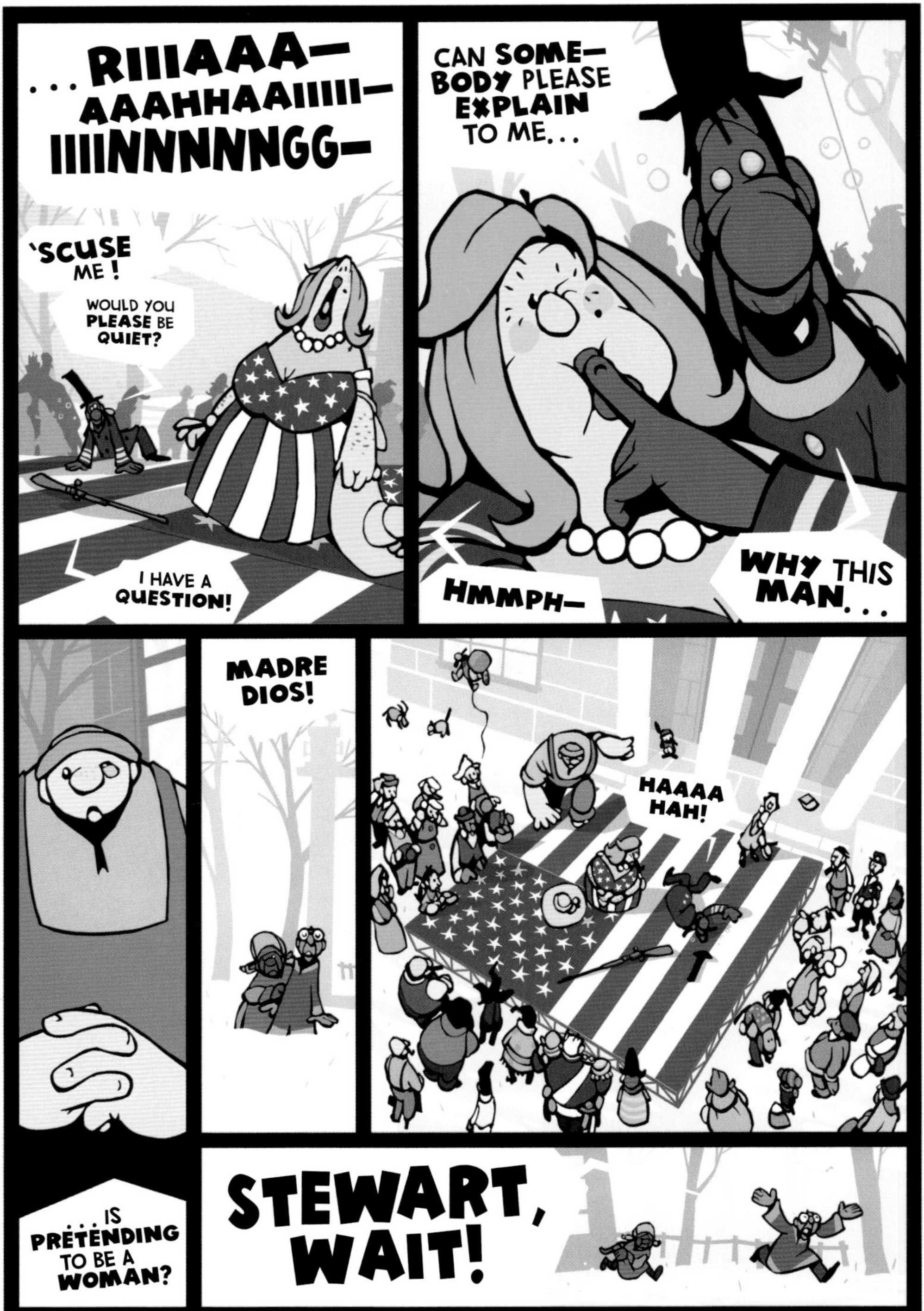

. . . RIIIAAA—AAAHHAAIIIII—IIIIINNNNNNGG—
'SCUSE ME!
WOULD YOU PLEASE BE QUIET?
I HAVE A QUESTION!
CAN SOMEBODY PLEASE EXPLAIN TO ME. . .
HMMPH—
WHY THIS MAN. . .
MADRE DIOS!
HAAAA HAH!
. . . IS PRETENDING TO BE A WOMAN?
STEWART, WAIT!

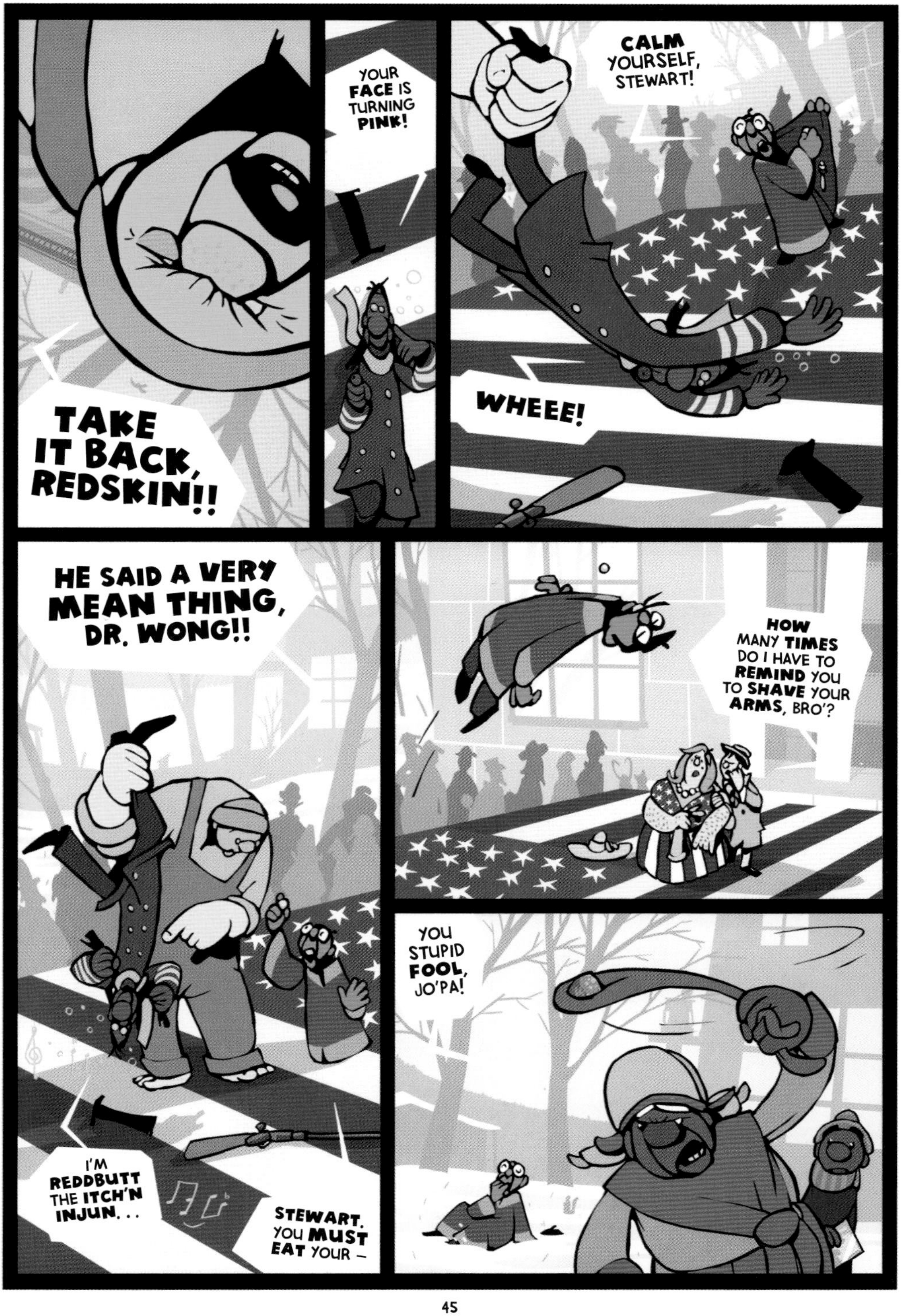
TAKE IT BACK, REDSKIN!!
YOUR FACE IS TURNING PINK!
CALM YOURSELF, STEWART!
WHEEE!
HE SAID A VERY MEAN THING, DR. WONG!!
I'M REDDBUTT THE ITCH'N INJUN. . .
STEWART, YOU MUST EAT YOUR –
HOW MANY TIMES DO I HAVE TO REMIND YOU TO SHAVE YOUR ARMS, BRO'?
YOU STUPID FOOL, JO'PA!

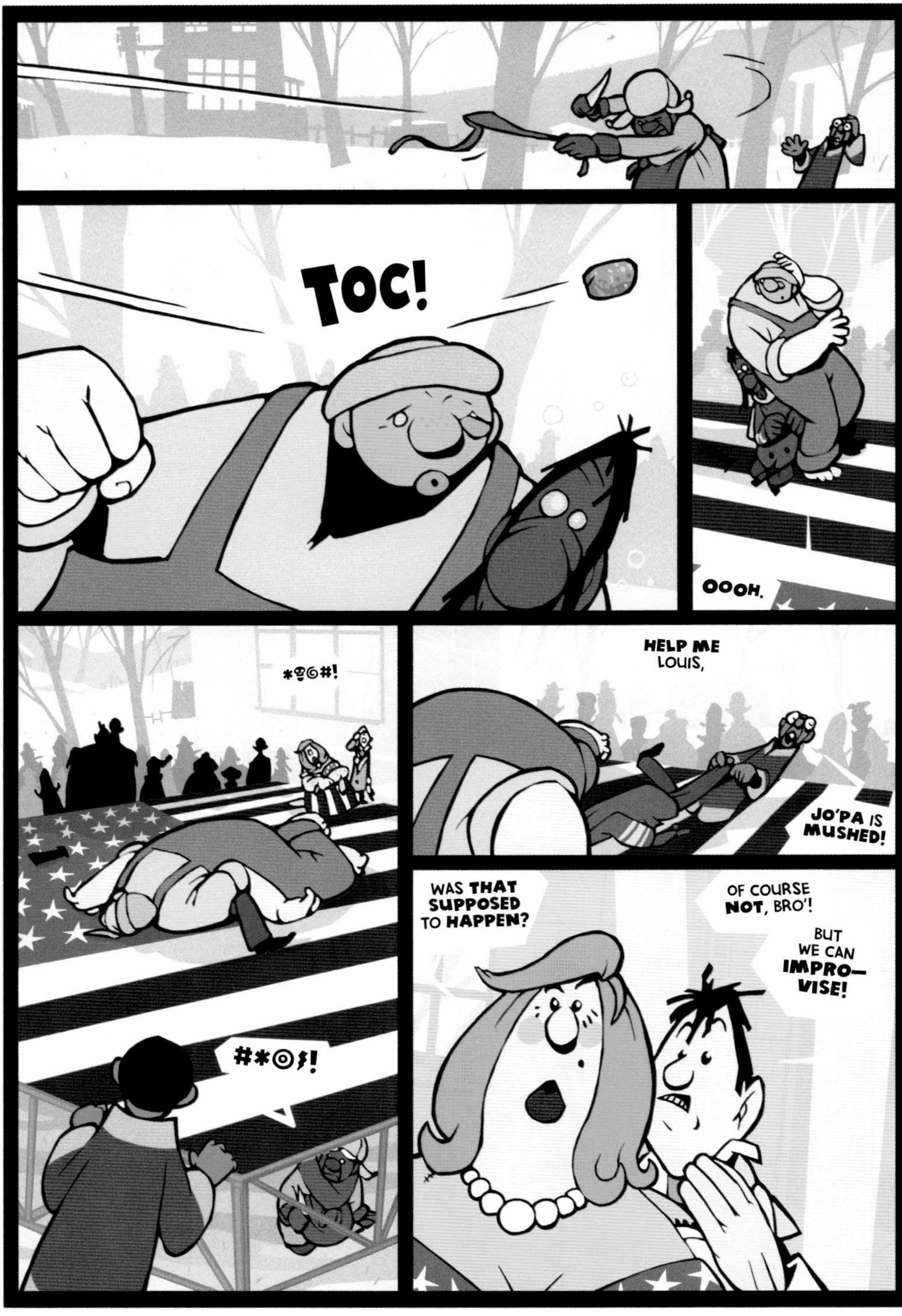
TOC!
OOOH.
*☠@#!
#*◎ϟ!
HELP ME LOUIS,
JO'PA IS MUSHED!
WAS THAT SUPPOSED TO HAPPEN?
OF COURSE NOT, BRO'!
BUT WE CAN IMPRO-VISE!

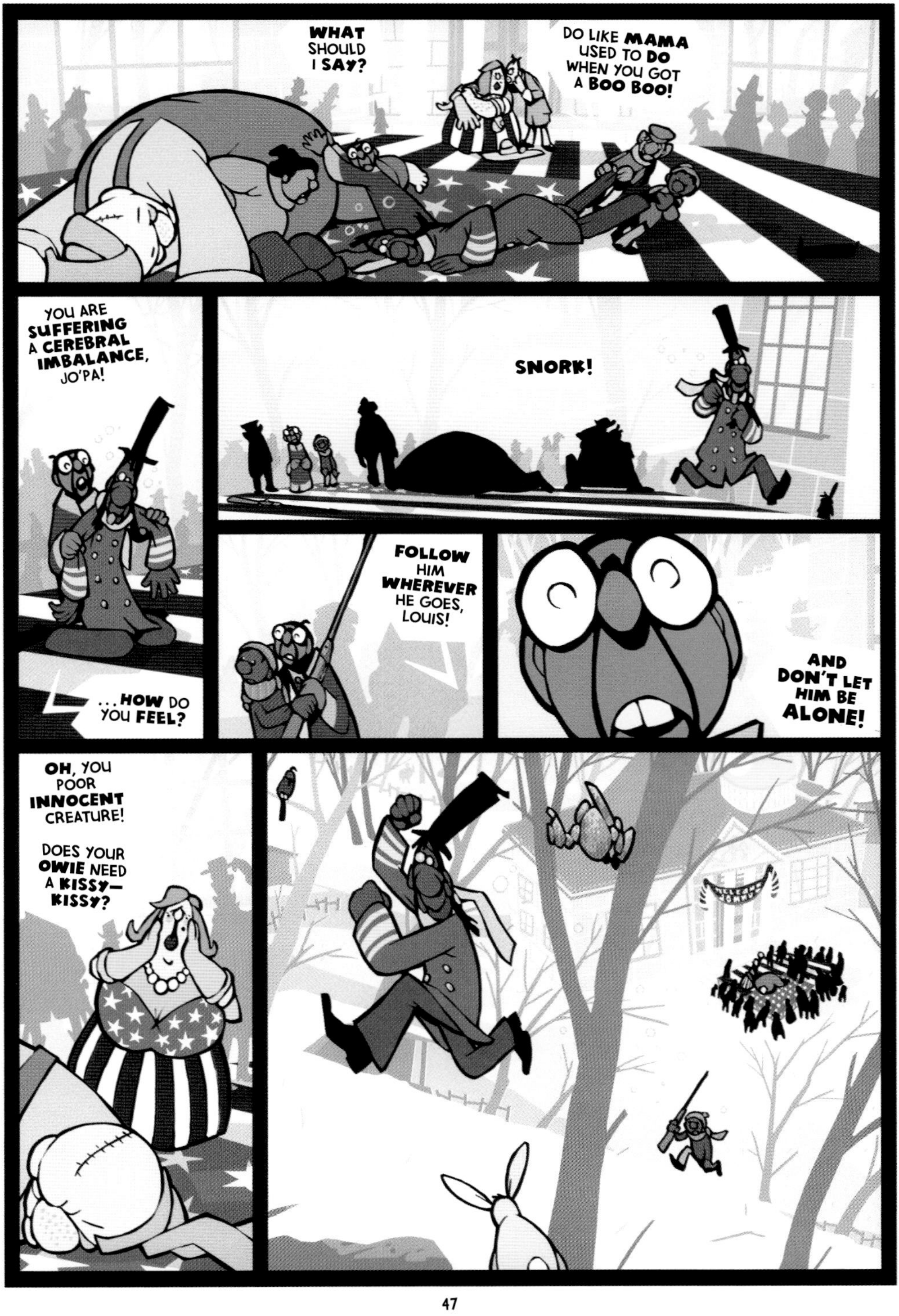
WHAT SHOULD I SAY?
DO LIKE MAMA USED TO DO WHEN YOU GOT A BOO BOO!
YOU ARE SUFFERING A CEREBRAL IMBALANCE, JO'PA!
...HOW DO YOU FEEL?
SNORK!
FOLLOW HIM WHEREVER HE GOES, LOUIS!
AND DON'T LET HIM BE ALONE!
OH, YOU POOR INNOCENT CREATURE!
DOES YOUR OWIE NEED A KISSY-KISSY?

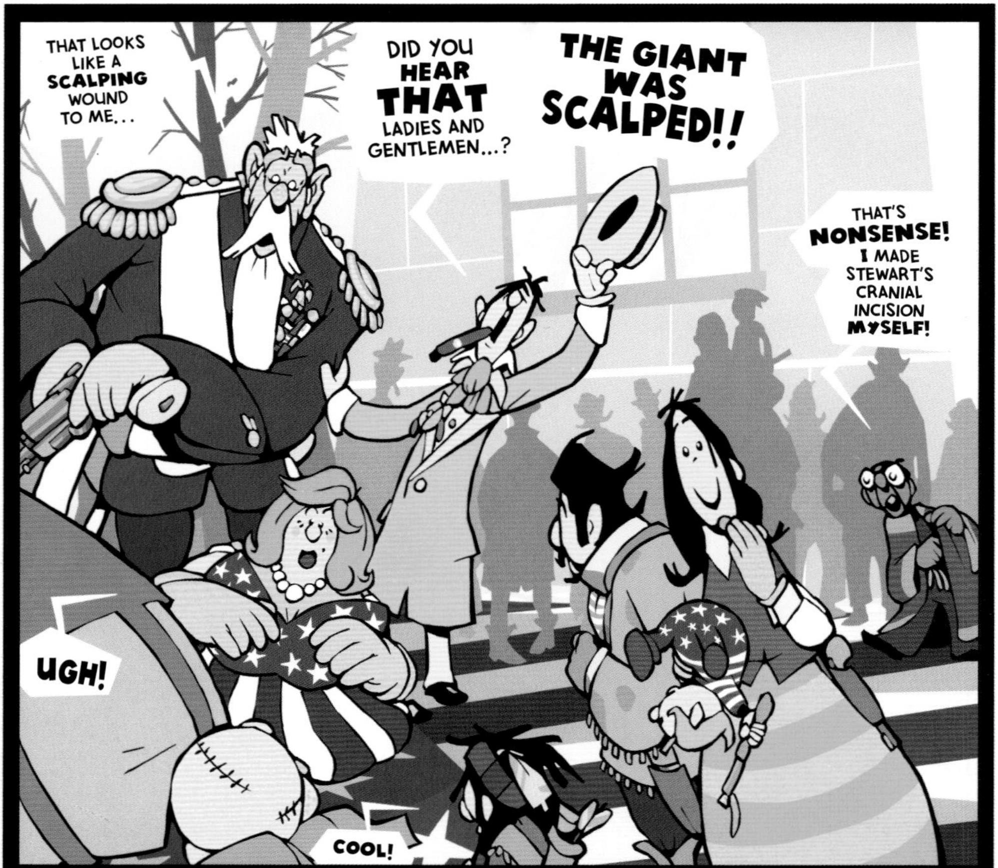
THAT LOOKS LIKE A SCALPING WOUND TO ME...
DID YOU HEAR THAT LADIES AND GENTLEMEN...?
THE GIANT WAS SCALPED!!
THAT'S NONSENSE! I MADE STEWART'S CRANIAL INCISION MYSELF!
UGH!
COOL!

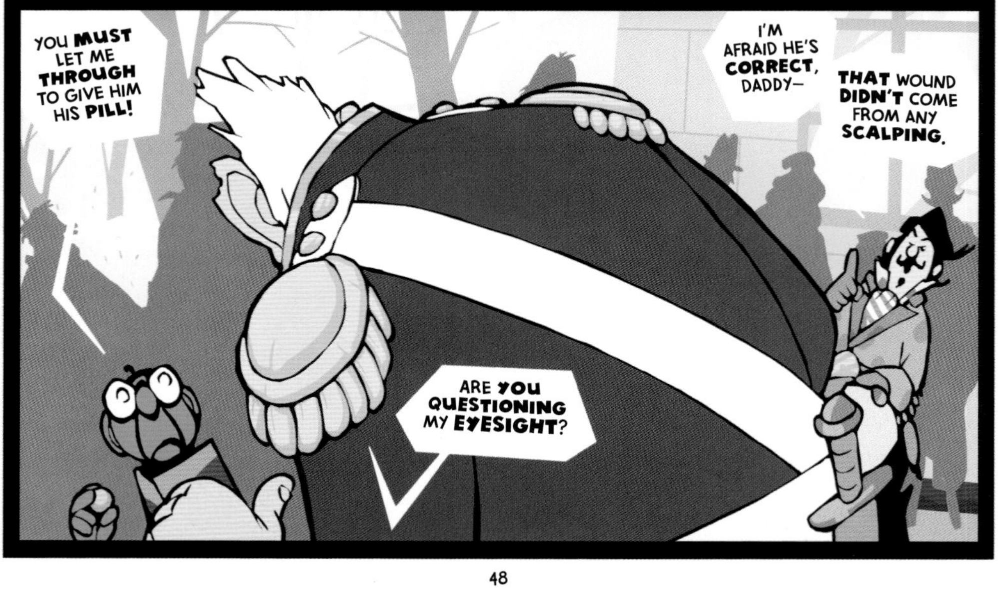
YOU MUST LET ME THROUGH TO GIVE HIM HIS PILL!
I'M AFRAID HE'S CORRECT, DADDY—
THAT WOUND DIDN'T COME FROM ANY SCALPING.
ARE YOU QUESTIONING MY EYESIGHT?

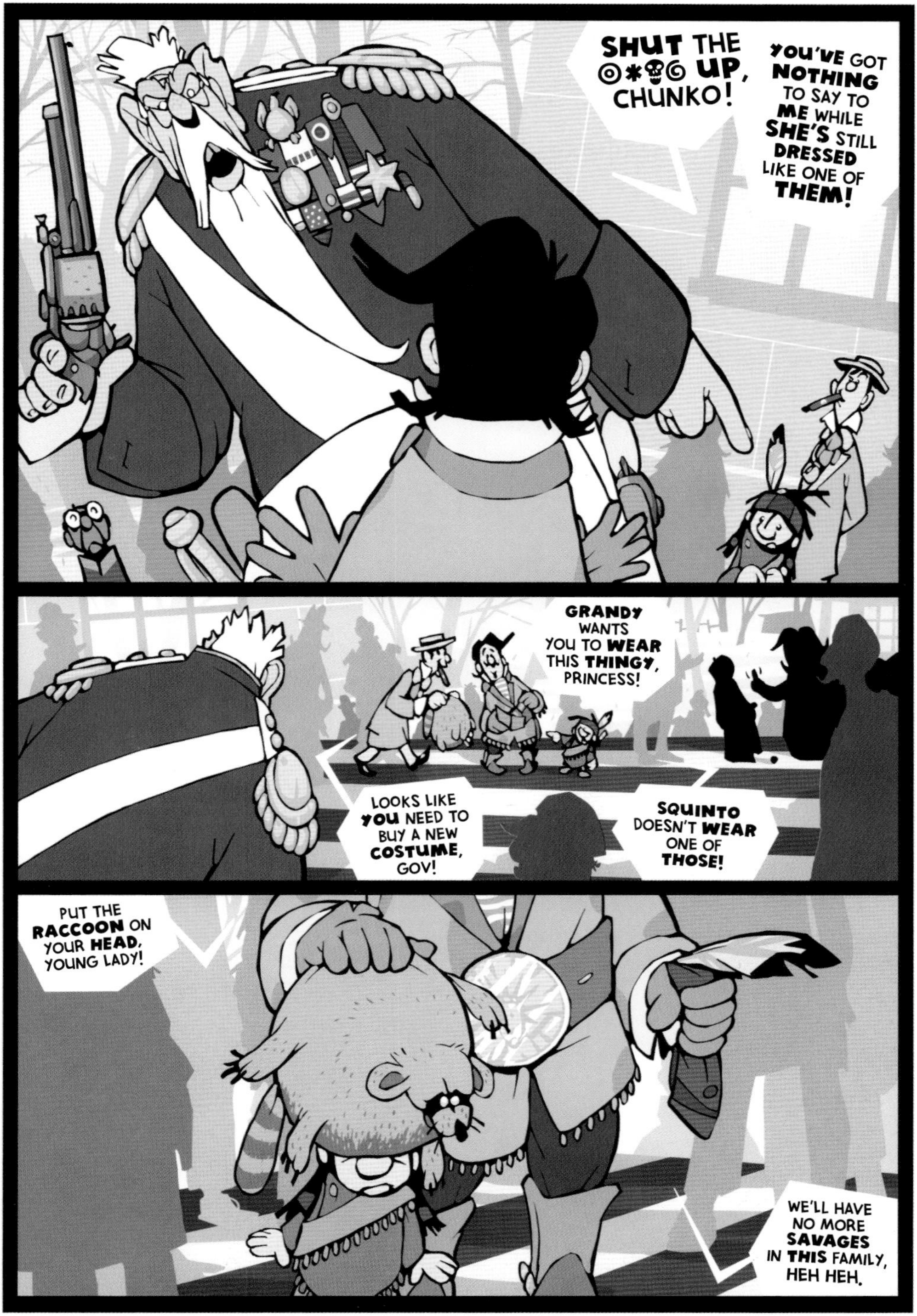
SHUT THE @*☠@ UP, CHUNKO!
YOU'VE GOT NOTHING TO SAY TO ME WHILE SHE'S STILL DRESSED LIKE ONE OF THEM!
GRANDY WANTS YOU TO WEAR THIS THINGY, PRINCESS!
LOOKS LIKE YOU NEED TO BUY A NEW COSTUME, GOV!
SQUINTO DOESN'T WEAR ONE OF THOSE!
PUT THE RACCOON ON YOUR HEAD, YOUNG LADY!
WE'LL HAVE NO MORE SAVAGES IN THIS FAMILY, HEH HEH.

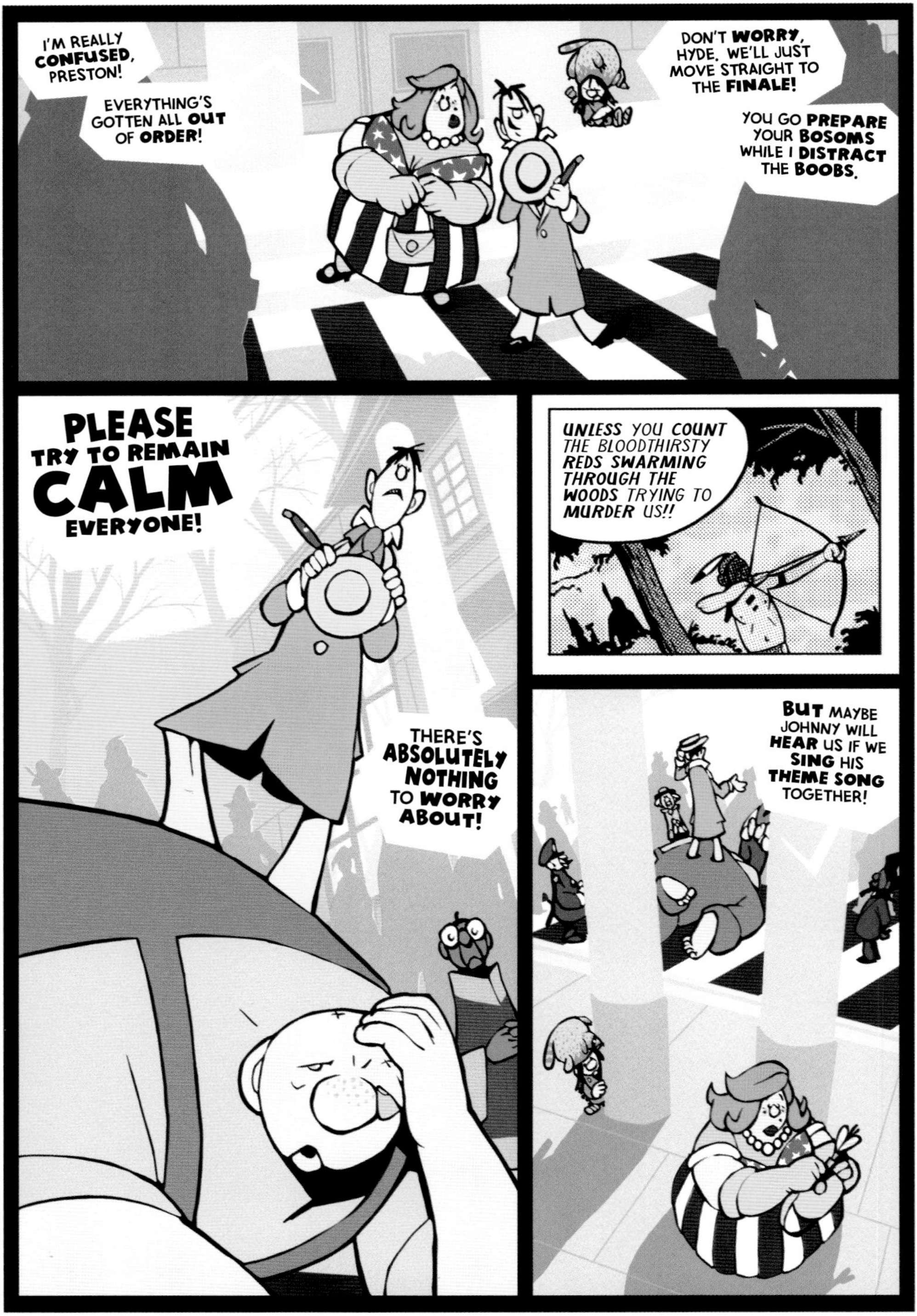

I'M REALLY **CONFUSED**, PRESTON!
EVERYTHING'S GOTTEN ALL **OUT** OF **ORDER**!
DON'T **WORRY**, HYDE. WE'LL JUST MOVE STRAIGHT TO THE **FINALE**!
YOU GO **PREPARE** YOUR **BOSOMS** WHILE I **DISTRACT** THE **BOOBS**.
PLEASE TRY TO REMAIN CALM EVERYONE!
THERE'S **ABSOLUTELY NOTHING** TO **WORRY ABOUT**!
UNLESS *YOU* ***COUNT*** *THE BLOODTHIRSTY* ***REDS SWARMING THROUGH THE WOODS*** *TRYING TO* ***MURDER*** *US!!*
BUT MAYBE JOHNNY WILL **HEAR** US IF WE **SING** HIS **THEME SONG** TOGETHER!

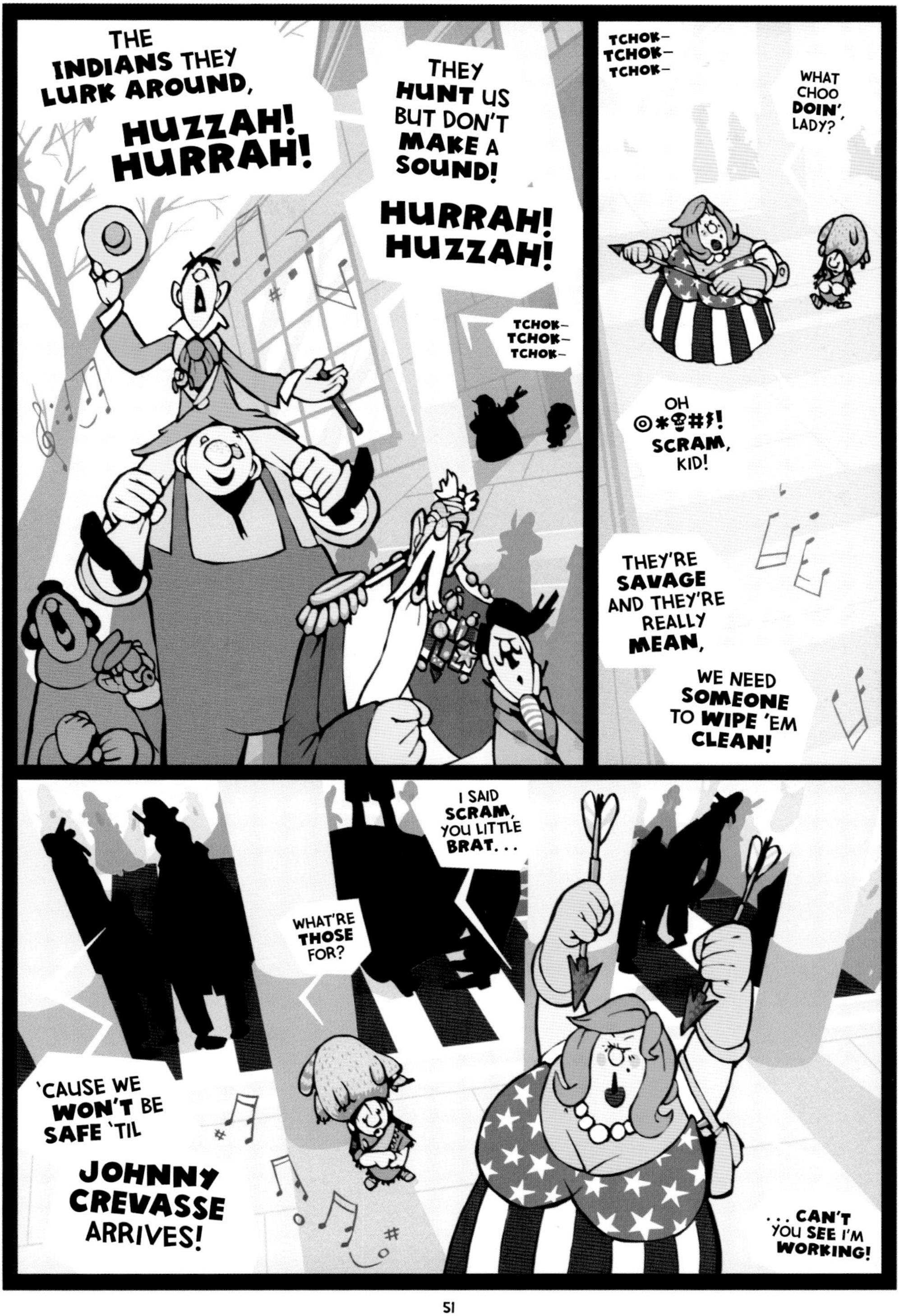

THE INDIANS THEY LURK AROUND,
HUZZAH! HURRAH!
THEY HUNT US BUT DON'T MAKE A SOUND!
HURRAH! HUZZAH!
TCHOK- TCHOK- TCHOK-
TCHOK- TCHOK- TCHOK-
WHAT CHOO DOIN', LADY?
OH ◎✱💀#⚡! SCRAM, KID!
THEY'RE SAVAGE AND THEY'RE REALLY MEAN,
WE NEED SOMEONE TO WIPE 'EM CLEAN!
I SAID SCRAM, YOU LITTLE BRAT...
WHAT'RE THOSE FOR?
'CAUSE WE WON'T BE SAFE 'TIL
JOHNNY CREVASSE ARRIVES!
...CAN'T YOU SEE I'M WORKING!

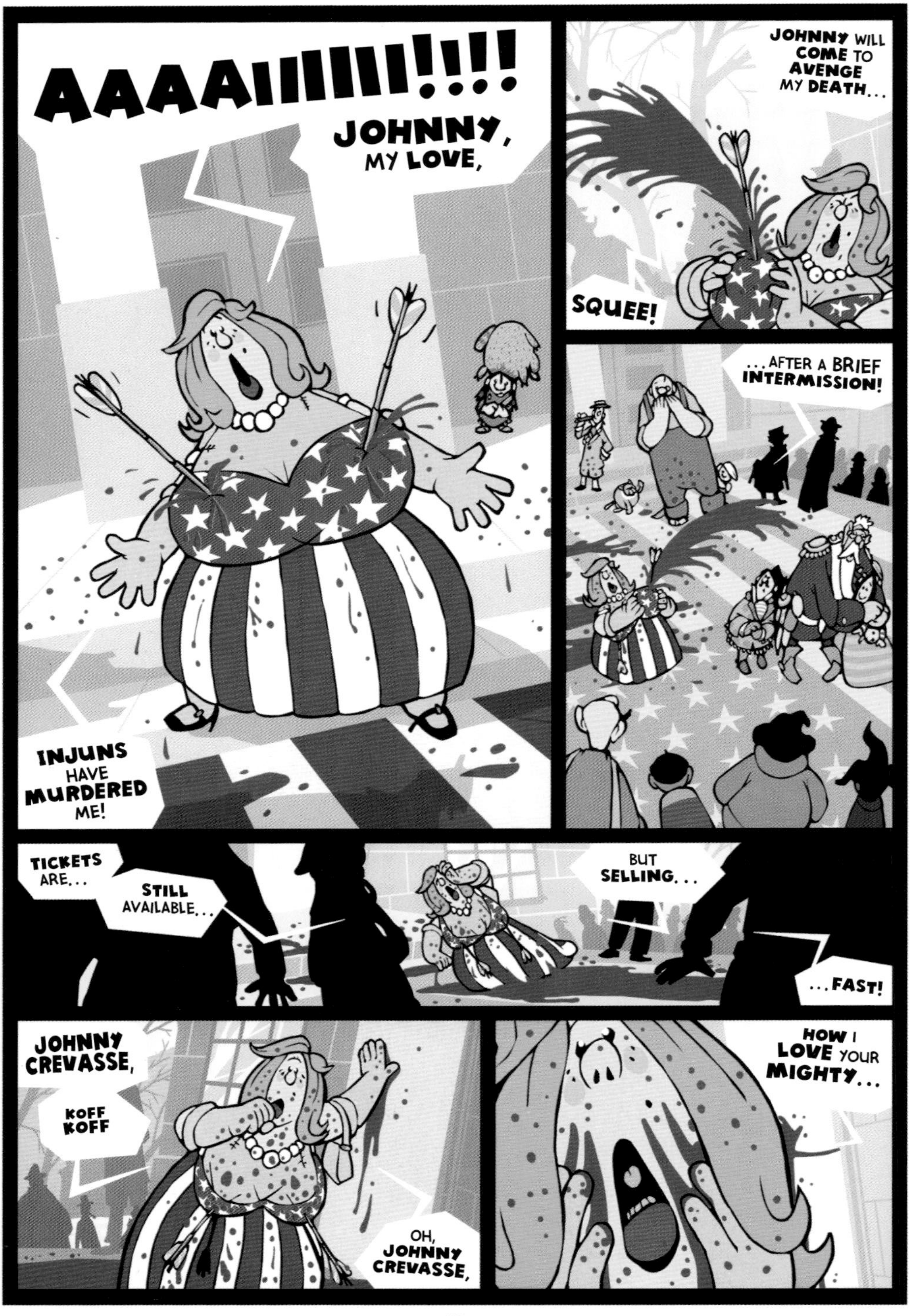
AAAAIIIIIII!!!!
JOHNNY, MY LOVE,
INJUNS HAVE MURDERED ME!
JOHNNY WILL COME TO AVENGE MY DEATH...
SQUEE!
...AFTER A BRIEF INTERMISSION!
TICKETS ARE...
STILL AVAILABLE...
BUT SELLING...
...FAST!
JOHNNY CREVASSE,
KOFF KOFF
OH, JOHNNY CREVASSE,
HOW I LOVE YOUR MIGHTY...

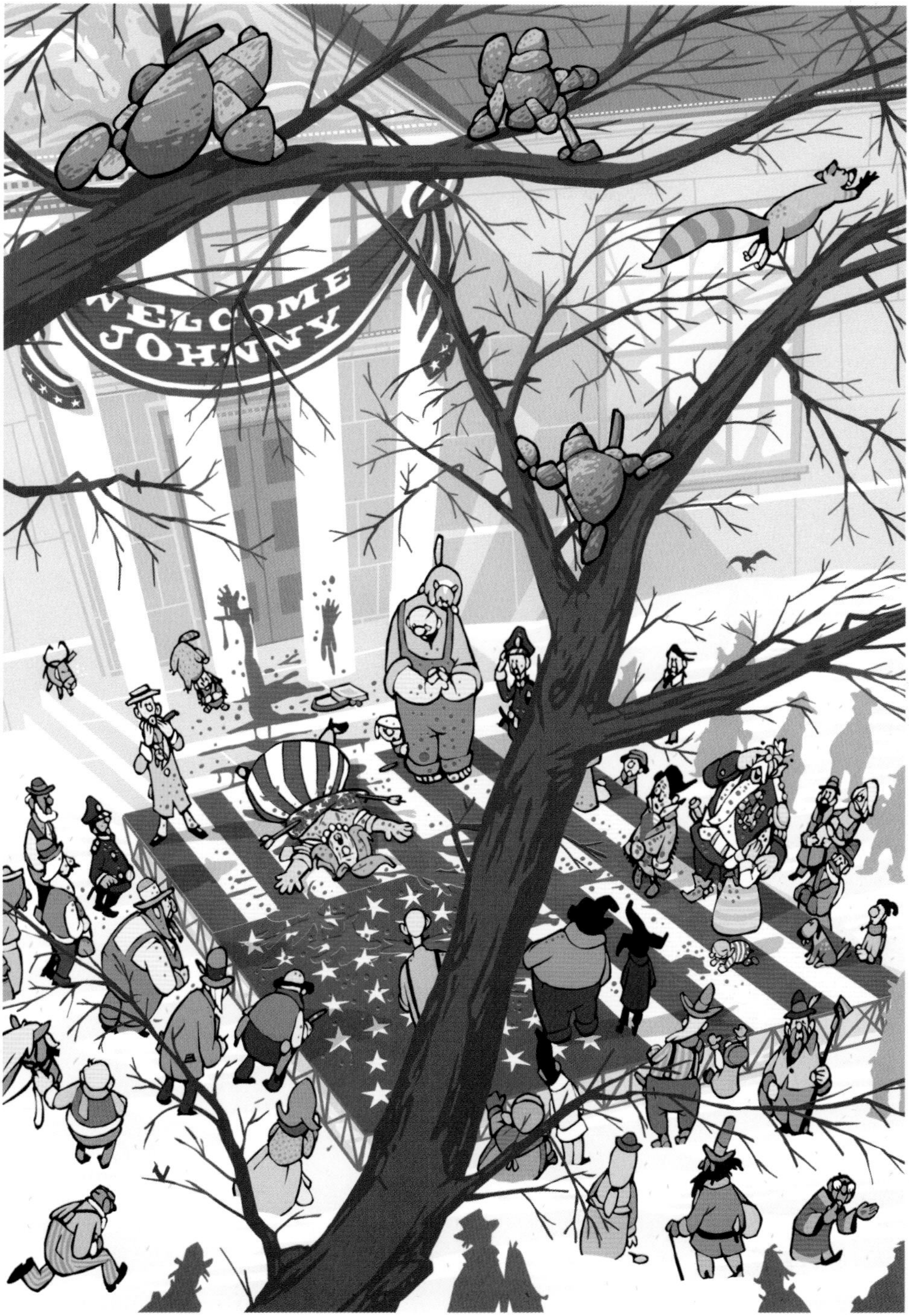
WELCOME
JOHNNY

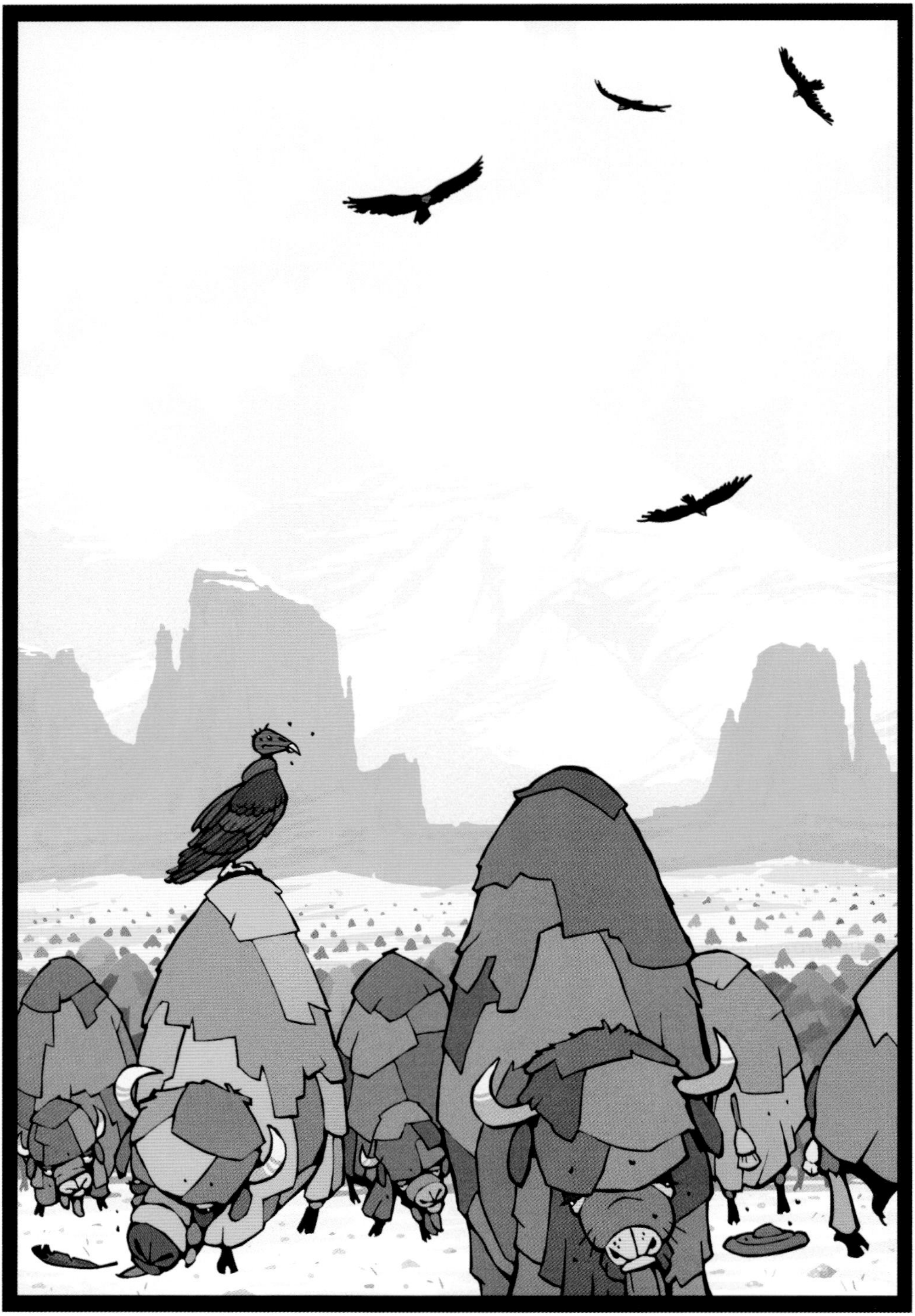

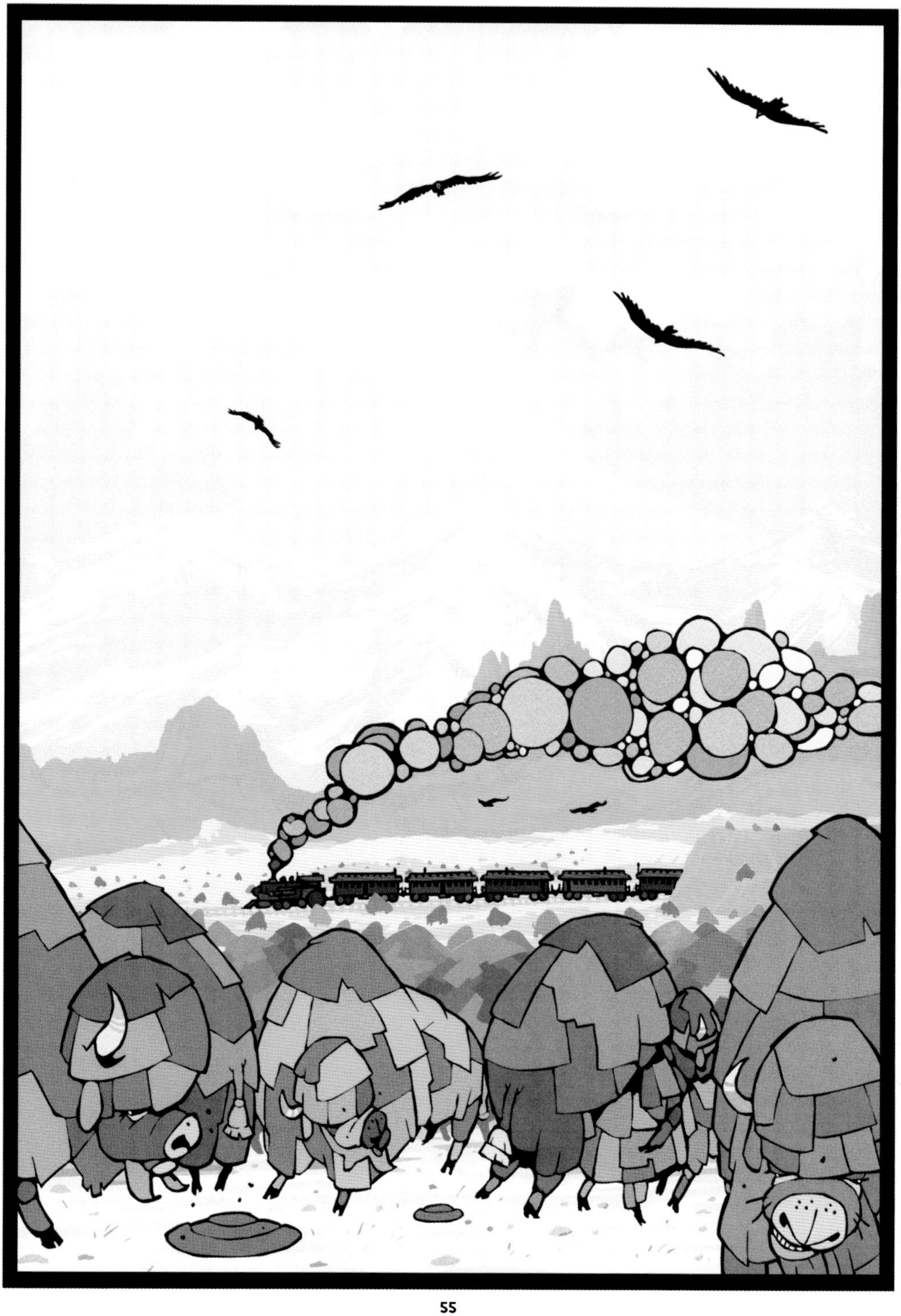

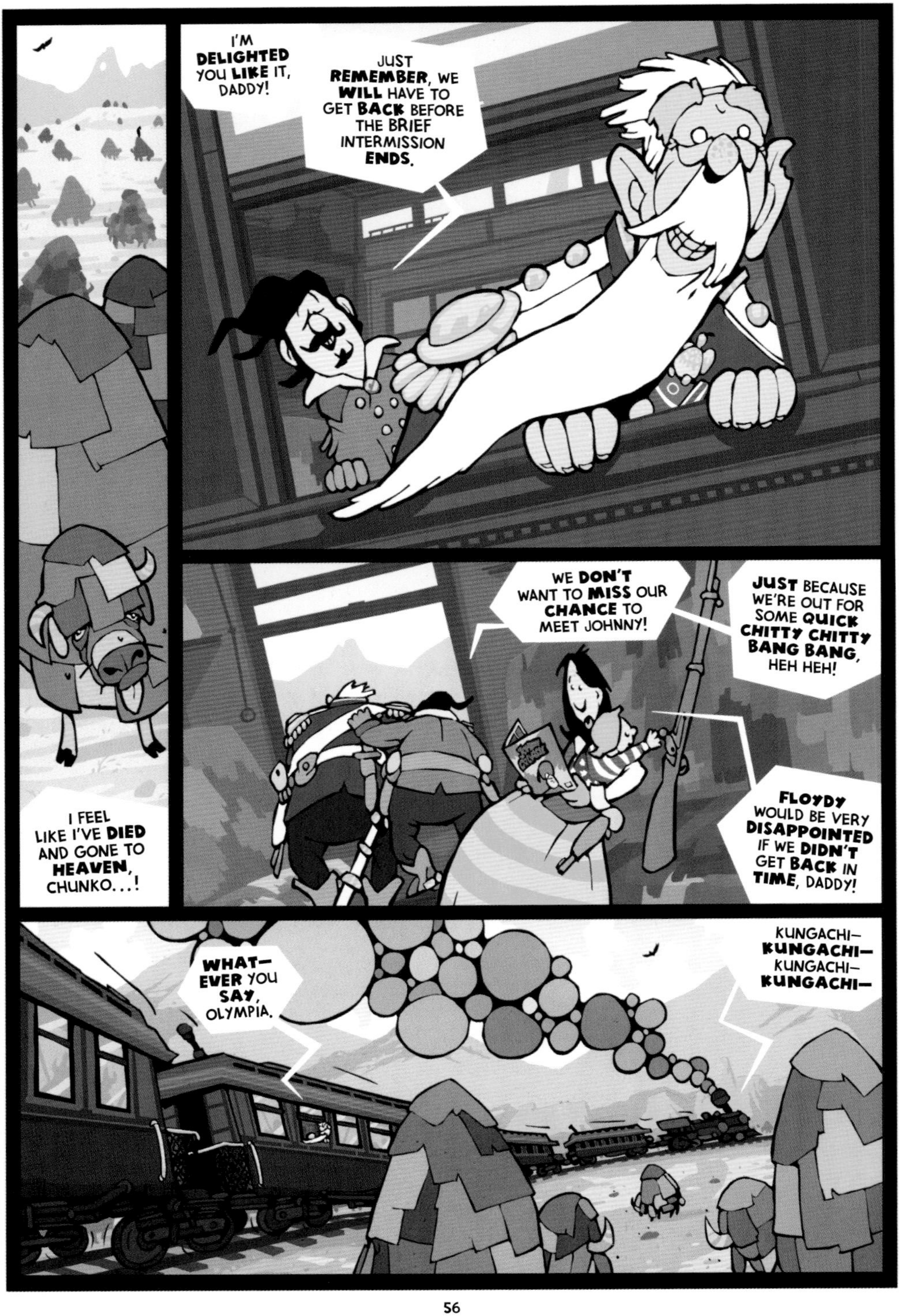
I'M DELIGHTED YOU LIKE IT, DADDY!
JUST REMEMBER, WE WILL HAVE TO GET BACK BEFORE THE BRIEF INTERMISSION ENDS.
I FEEL LIKE I'VE DIED AND GONE TO HEAVEN, CHUNKO...!
WE DON'T WANT TO MISS OUR CHANCE TO MEET JOHNNY!
JUST BECAUSE WE'RE OUT FOR SOME QUICK CHITTY CHITTY BANG BANG, HEH HEH!
FLOYDY WOULD BE VERY DISAPPOINTED IF WE DIDN'T GET BACK IN TIME, DADDY!
WHAT-EVER YOU SAY, OLYMPIA.
KUNGACHI-KUNGACHI-KUNGACHI-KUNGACHI-

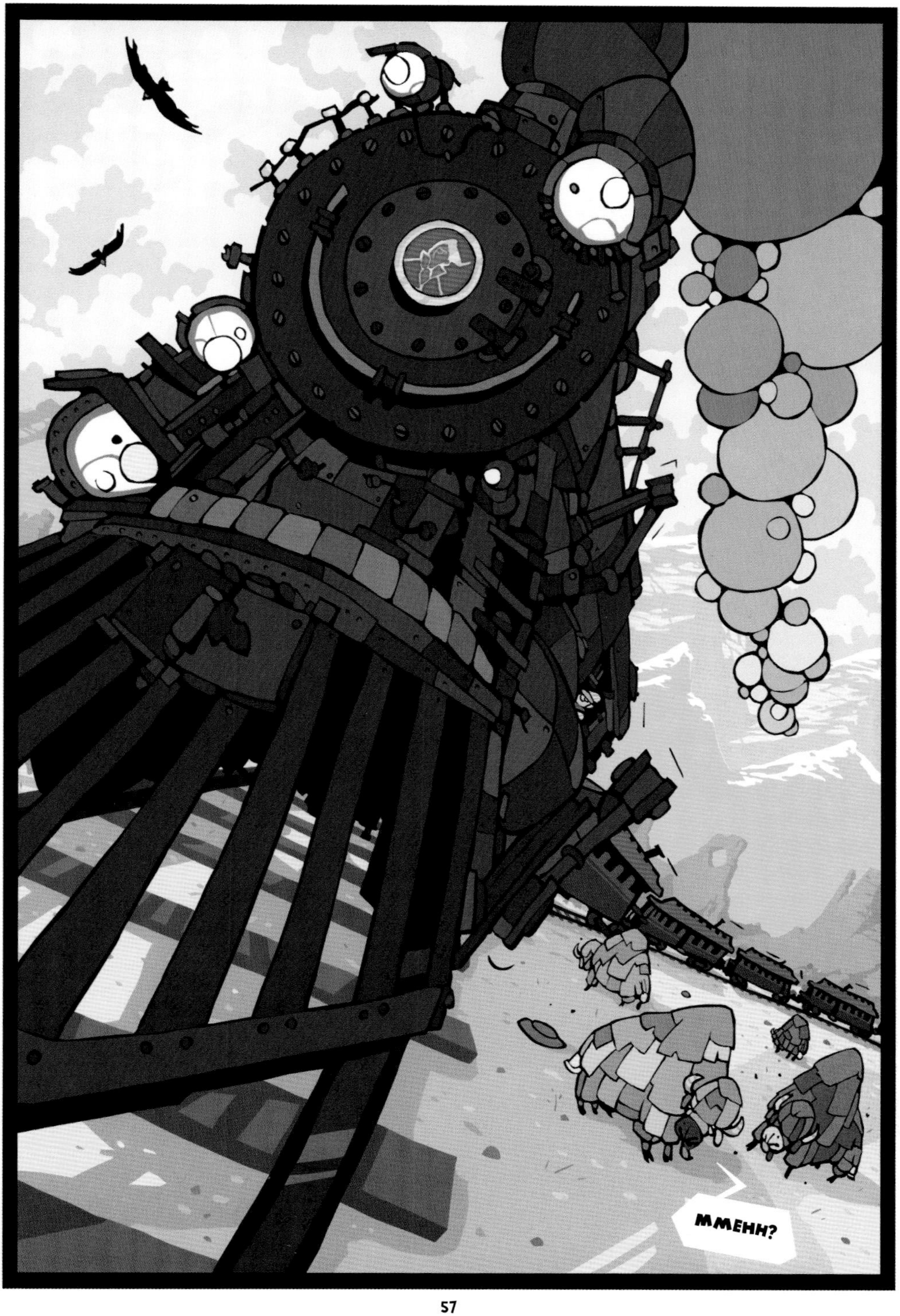
MMEHH?

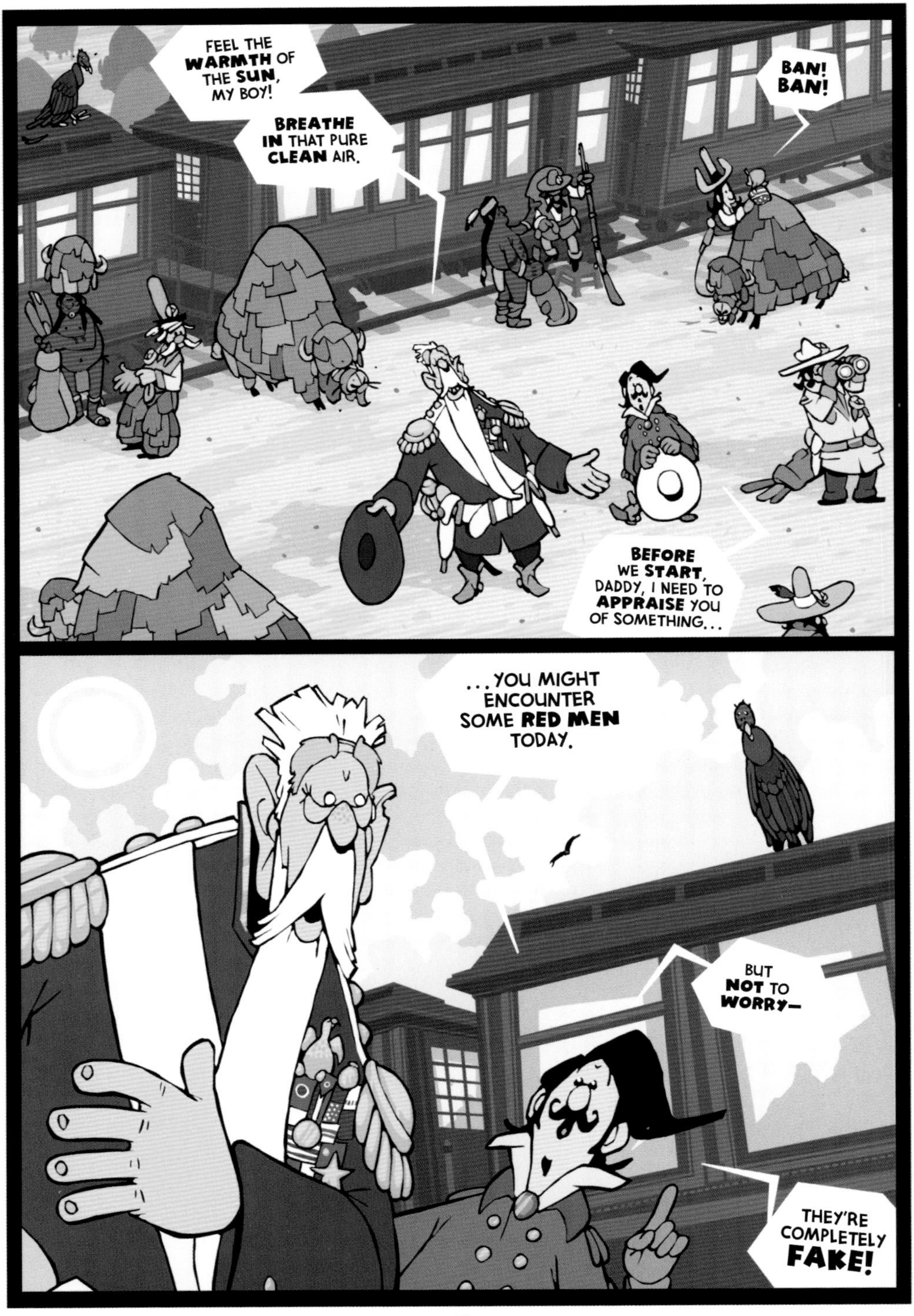
FEEL THE **WARMTH** OF THE **SUN**, MY BOY!
BREATHE IN THAT PURE **CLEAN** AIR.
BAN! BAN!
BEFORE WE **START**, DADDY, I NEED TO **APPRAISE** YOU OF SOMETHING...
...YOU MIGHT ENCOUNTER SOME **RED MEN** TODAY.
BUT **NOT** TO **WORRY**—
THEY'RE COMPLETELY **FAKE!**

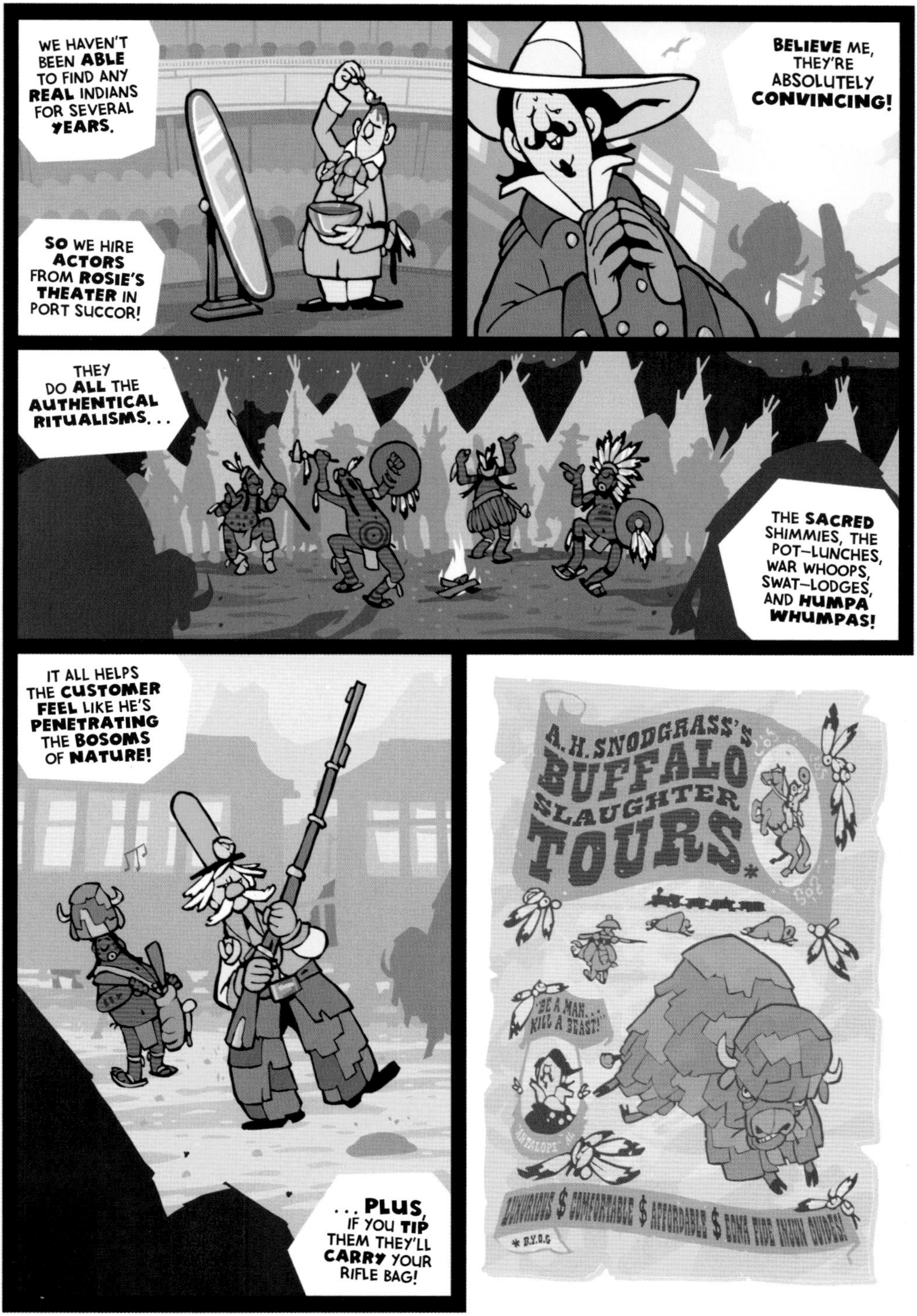
WE HAVEN'T BEEN ABLE TO FIND ANY REAL INDIANS FOR SEVERAL YEARS.
SO WE HIRE ACTORS FROM ROSIE'S THEATER IN PORT SUCCOR!
BELIEVE ME, THEY'RE ABSOLUTELY CONVINCING!
THEY DO ALL THE AUTHENTICAL RITUALISMS...
THE SACRED SHIMMIES, THE POT-LUNCHES, WAR WHOOPS, SWAT-LODGES, AND HUMPA WHUMPAS!
IT ALL HELPS THE CUSTOMER FEEL LIKE HE'S PENETRATING THE BOSOMS OF NATURE!
...PLUS, IF YOU TIP THEM THEY'LL CARRY YOUR RIFLE BAG!
A. H. SNODGRASS'S BUFFALO SLAUGHTER TOURS.*
"BE A MAN... KILL A BEAST!"
LUXURIOUS $ COMFORTABLE $ AFFORDABLE $ BONA FIDE INJUN GUIDES!
* B.Y.O.G

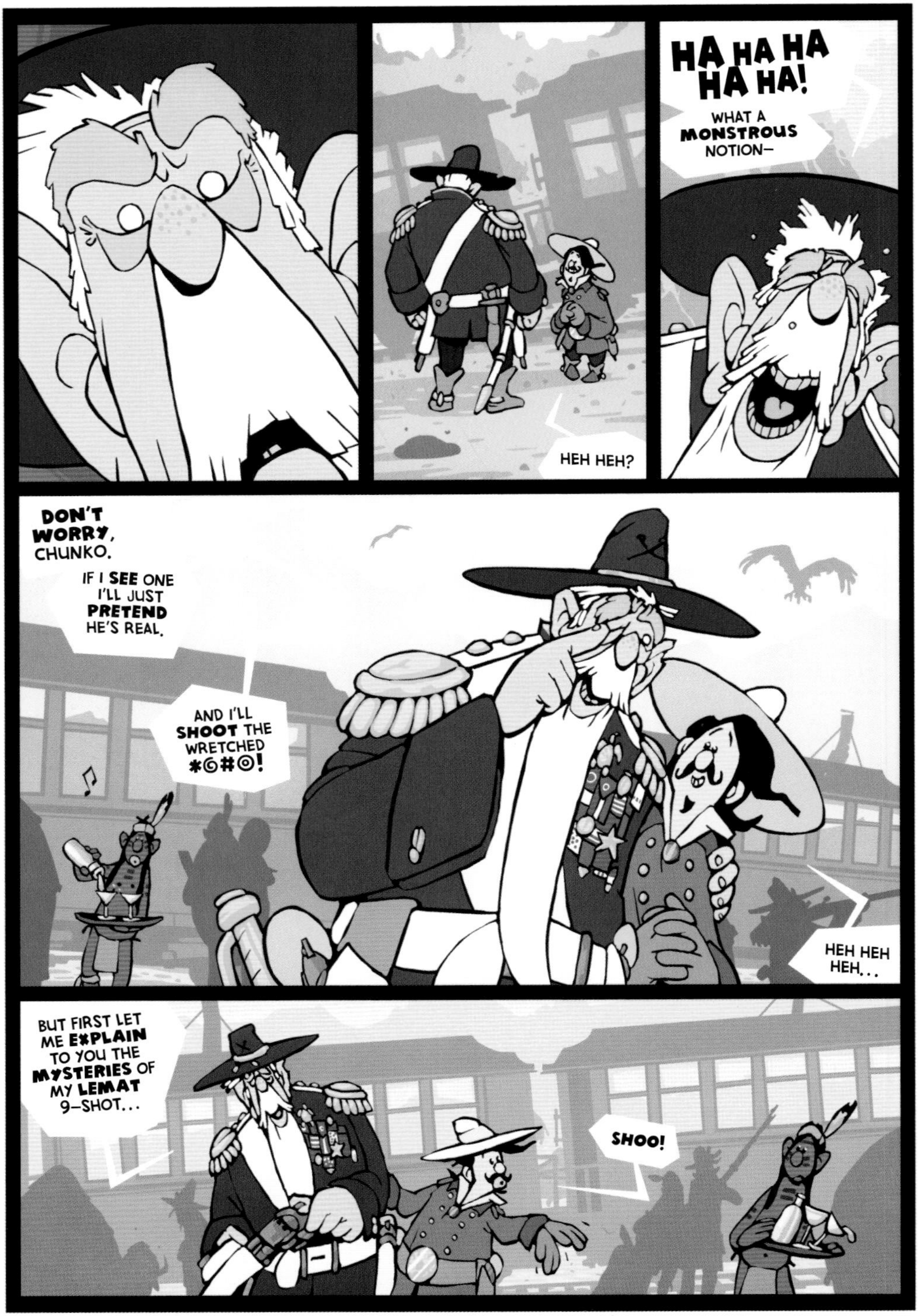
HA HA HA HA HA!
WHAT A MONSTROUS NOTION—
HEH HEH?
DON'T WORRY, CHUNKO.
IF I SEE ONE I'LL JUST PRETEND HE'S REAL.
AND I'LL SHOOT THE WRETCHED *@#@!
HEH HEH HEH...
BUT FIRST LET ME EXPLAIN TO YOU THE MYSTERIES OF MY LEMAT 9-SHOT...
SHOO!

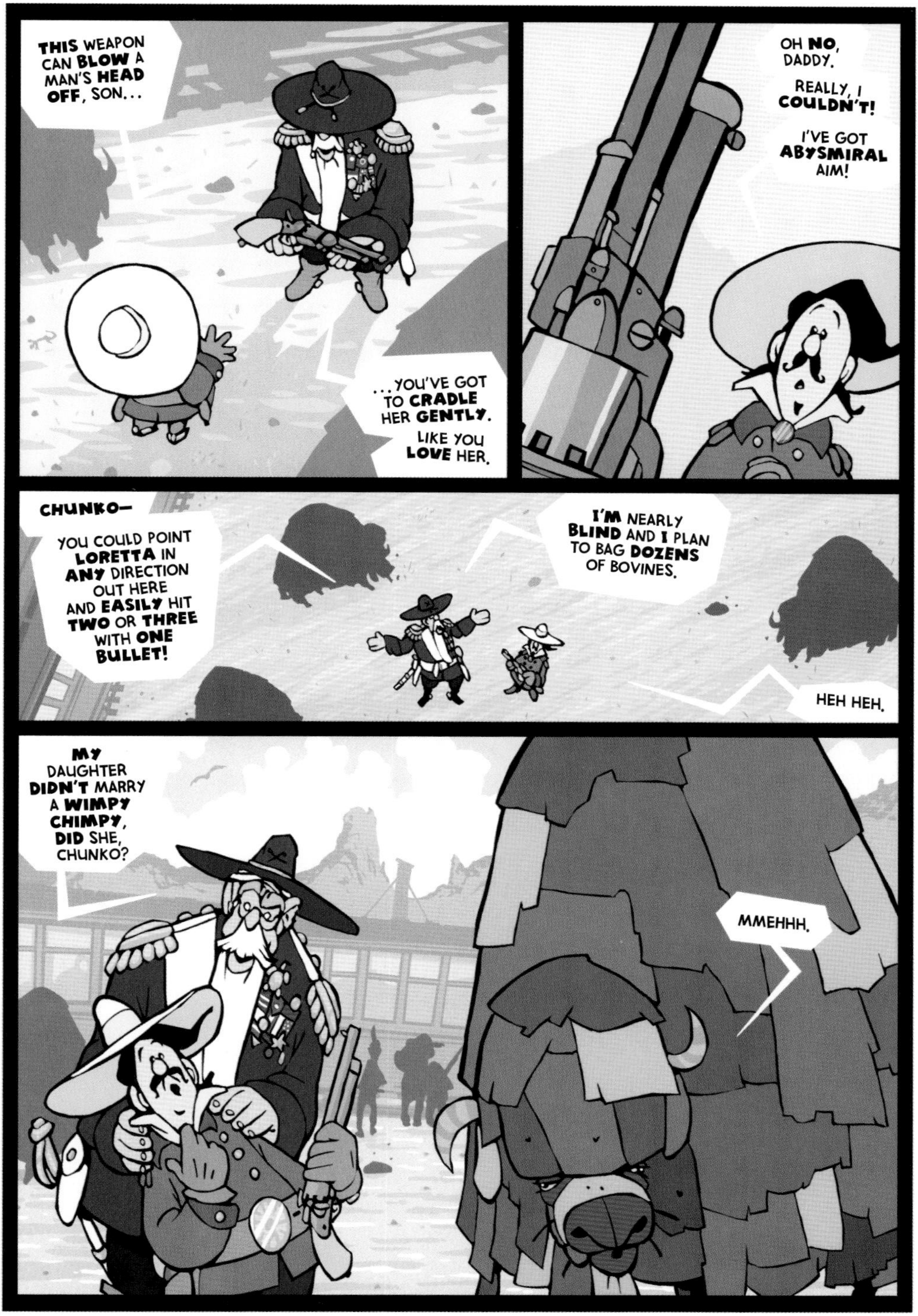
THIS WEAPON CAN BLOW A MAN'S HEAD OFF, SON...
...YOU'VE GOT TO CRADLE HER GENTLY.
LIKE YOU LOVE HER.
OH NO, DADDY.
REALLY, I COULDN'T!
I'VE GOT ABYSMIRAL AIM!
CHUNKO—
YOU COULD POINT LORETTA IN ANY DIRECTION OUT HERE AND EASILY HIT TWO OR THREE WITH ONE BULLET!
I'M NEARLY BLIND AND I PLAN TO BAG DOZENS OF BOVINES.
HEH HEH.
MY DAUGHTER DIDN'T MARRY A WIMPY CHIMPY, DID SHE, CHUNKO?
MMEHHH.

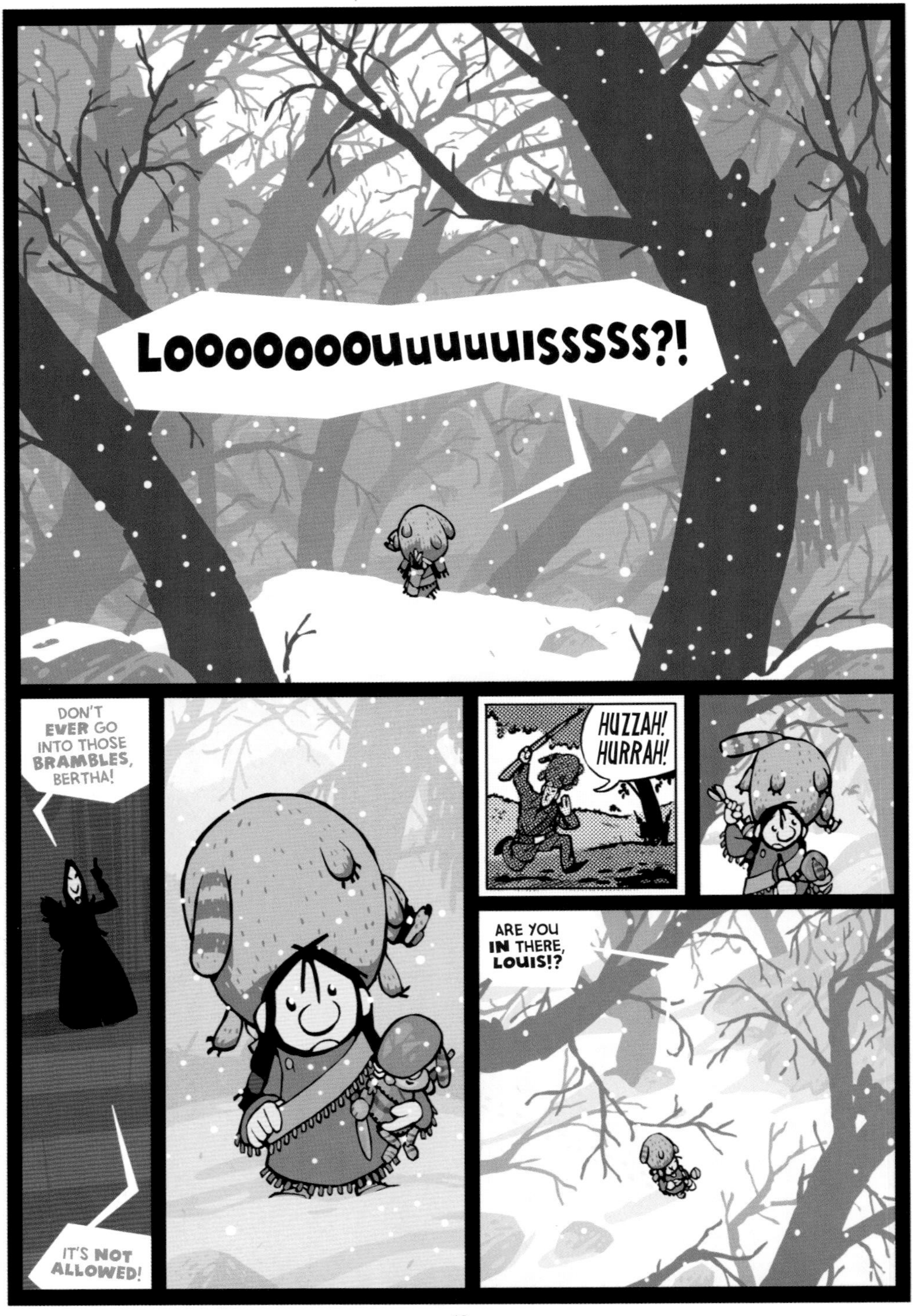
LOOOOOOOUUUUUISSSSS?!
DON'T EVER GO INTO THOSE BRAMBLES, BERTHA!
IT'S NOT ALLOWED!
HUZZAH! HURRAH!
ARE YOU IN THERE, LOUIS!?

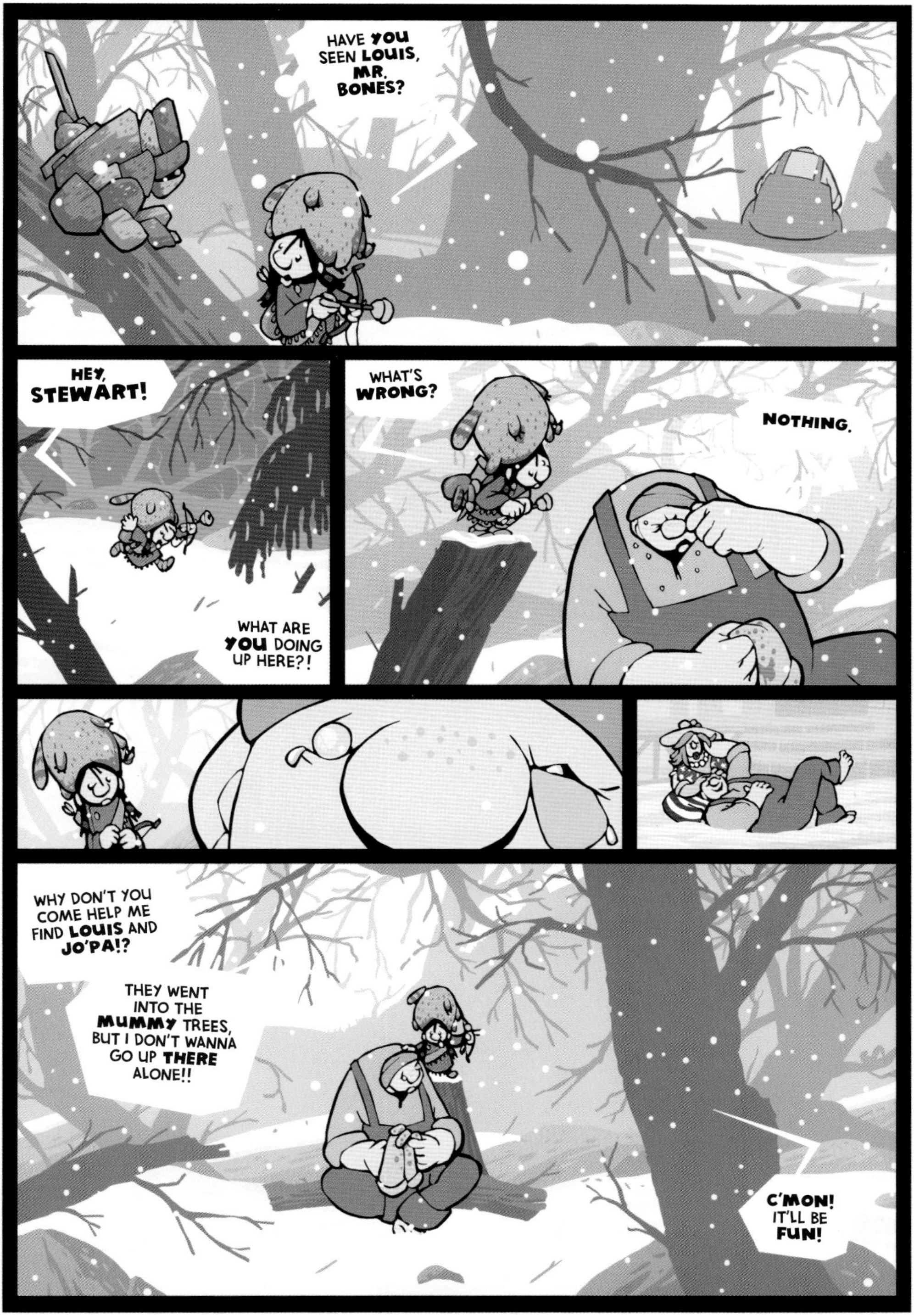
HAVE YOU SEEN LOUIS, MR. BONES?
HEY, STEWART!
WHAT ARE YOU DOING UP HERE?!
WHAT'S WRONG?
NOTHING.
WHY DON'T YOU COME HELP ME FIND LOUIS AND JO'PA!?
THEY WENT INTO THE MUMMY TREES, BUT I DON'T WANNA GO UP THERE ALONE!!
C'MON! IT'LL BE FUN!

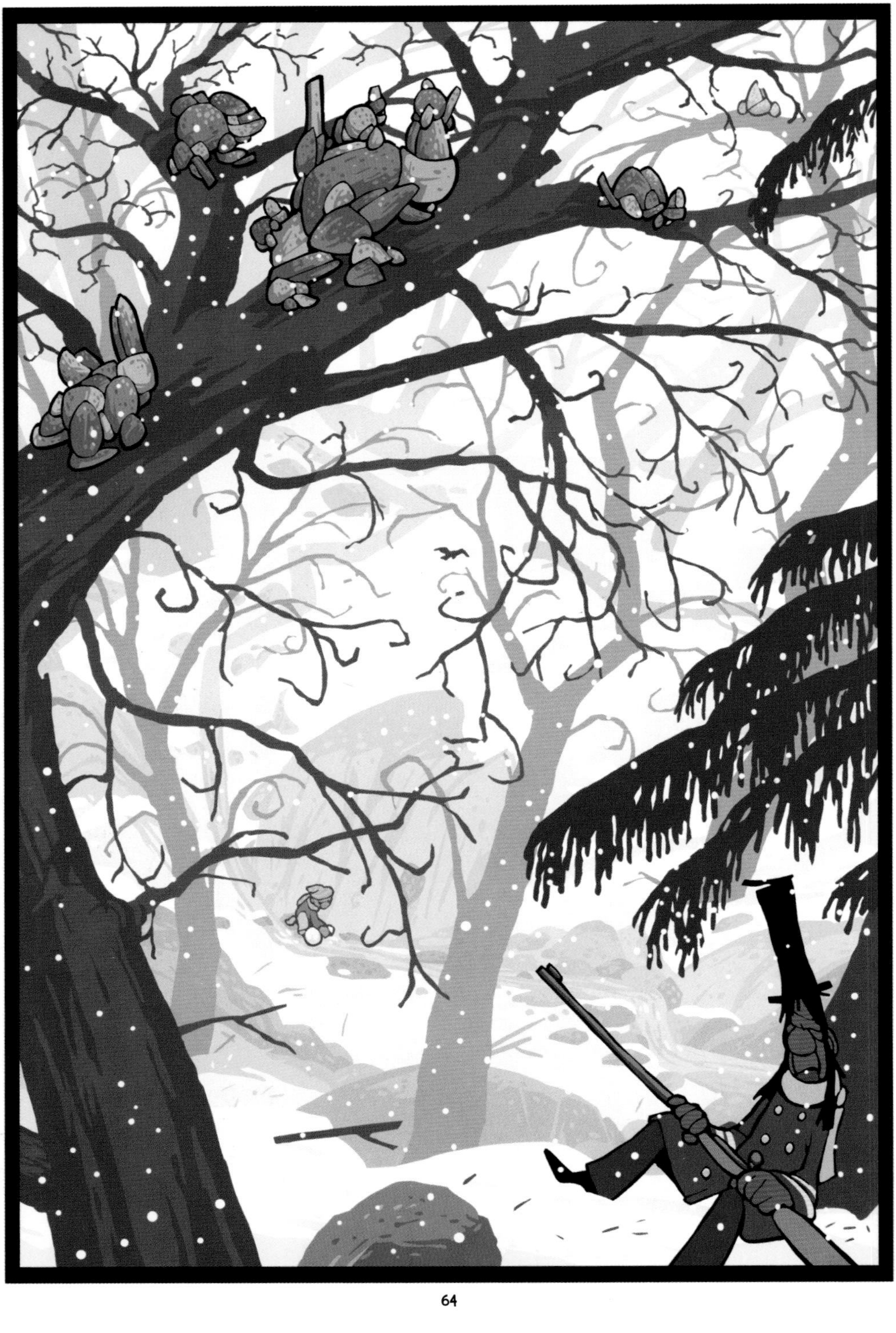

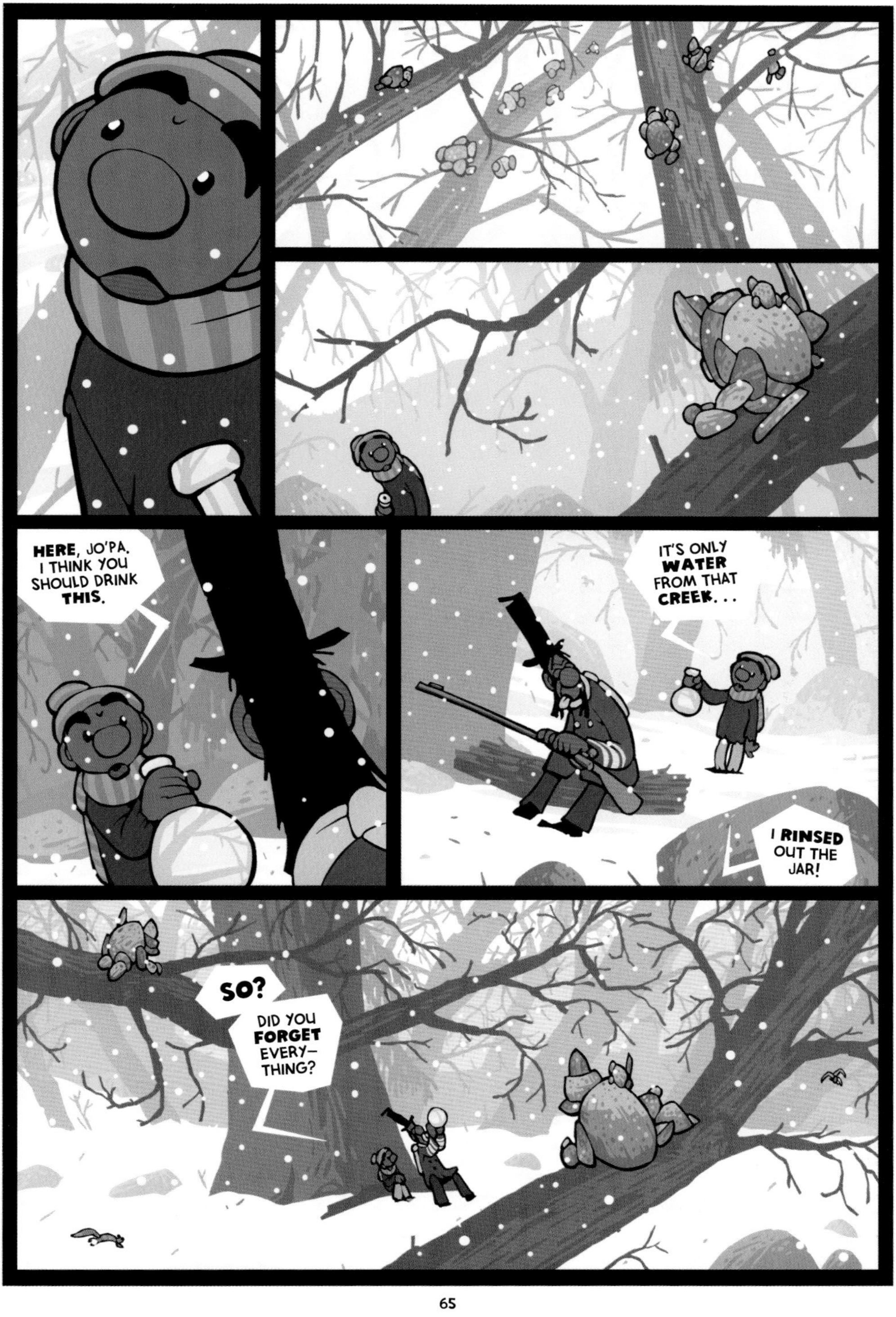

HERE, JO'PA. I THINK YOU SHOULD DRINK **THIS**.
IT'S ONLY **WATER** FROM THAT **CREEK**. . .
I **RINSED** OUT THE JAR!
SO?
DID YOU **FORGET** EVERY-THING?

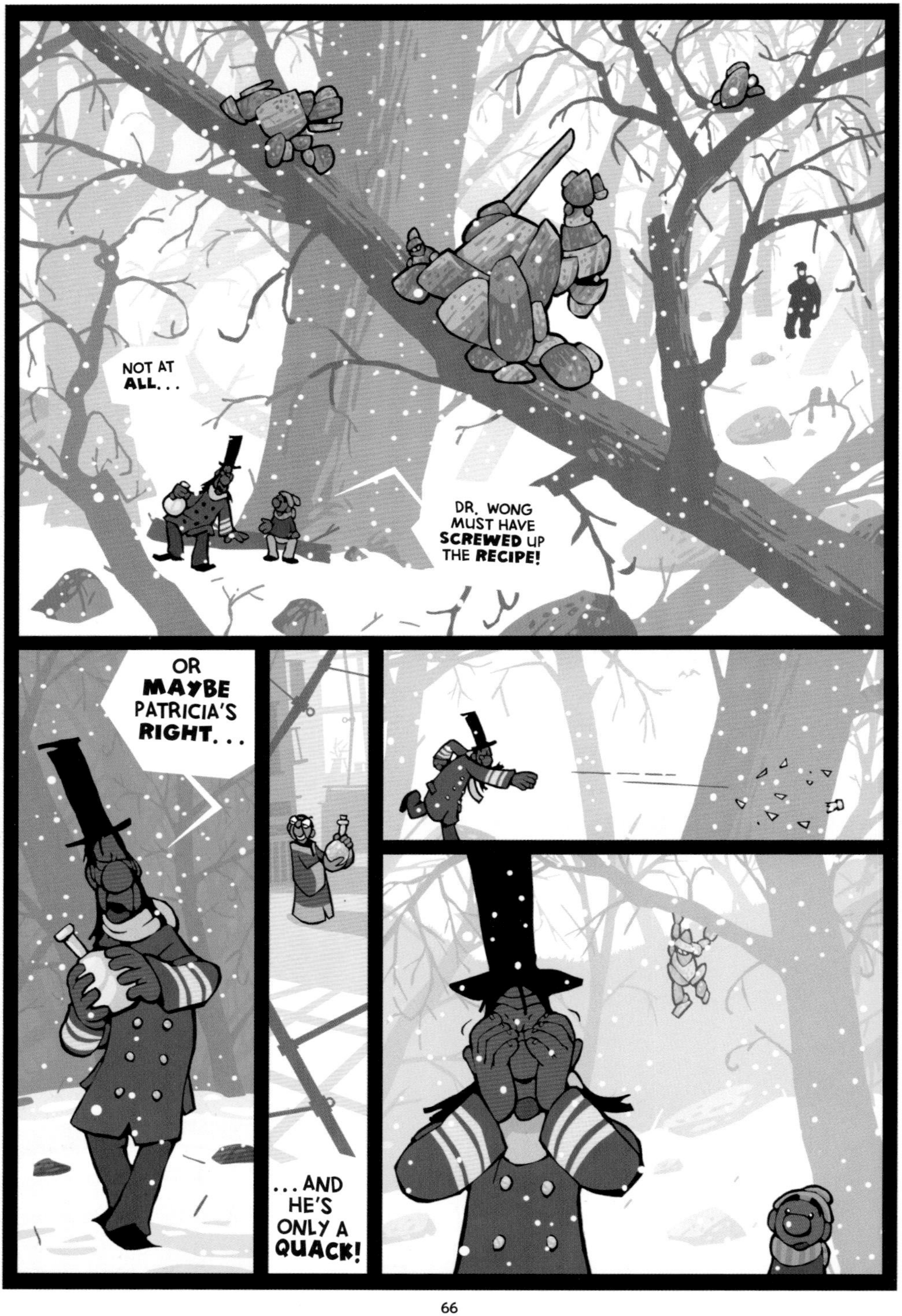
NOT AT ALL...
DR. WONG MUST HAVE SCREWED UP THE RECIPE!
OR MAYBE PATRICIA'S RIGHT...
...AND HE'S ONLY A QUACK!

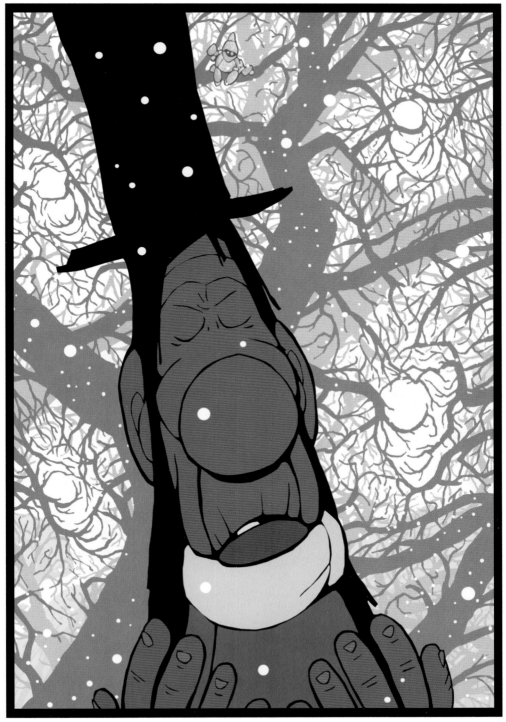

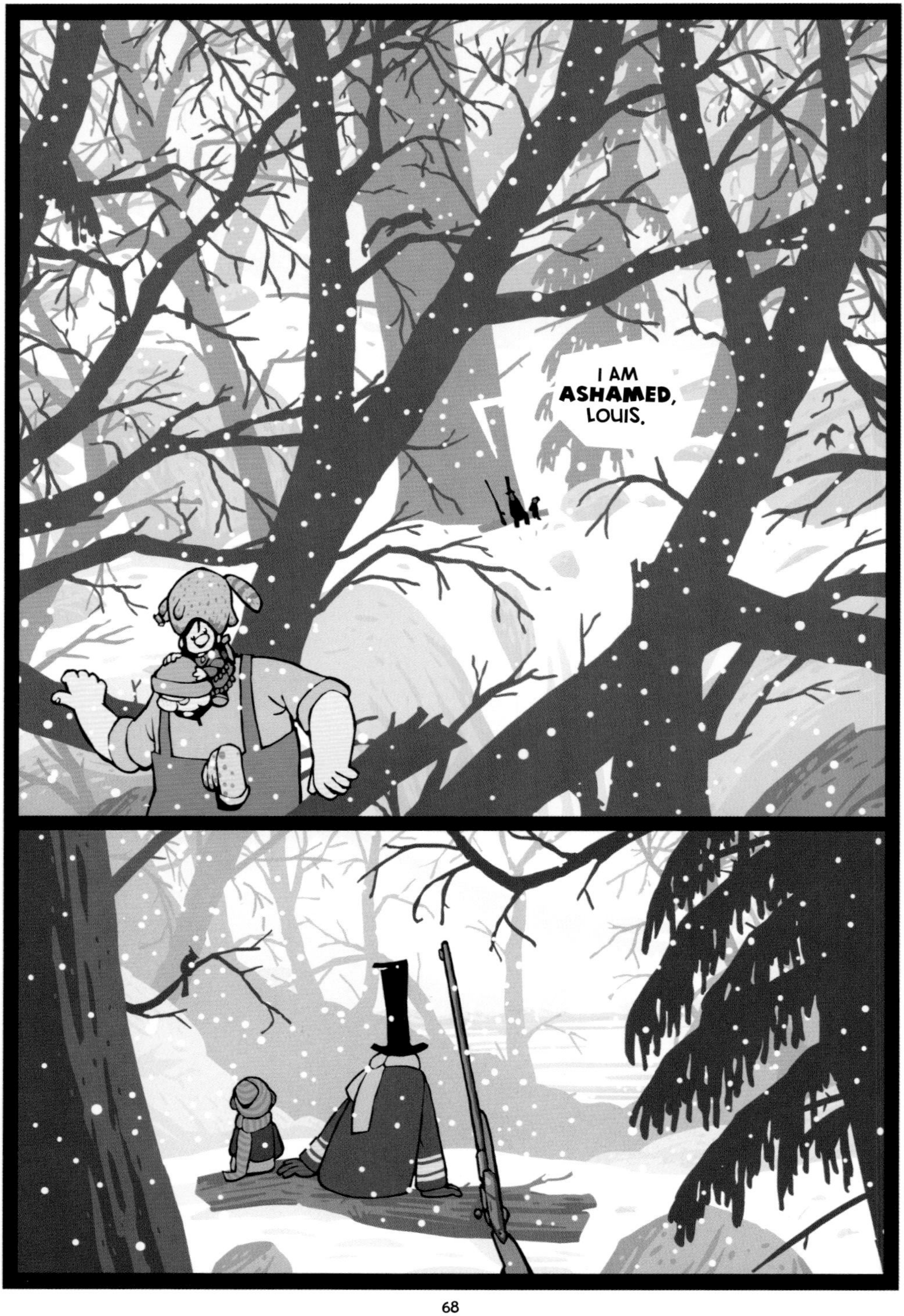
I AM ASHAMED, LOUIS.

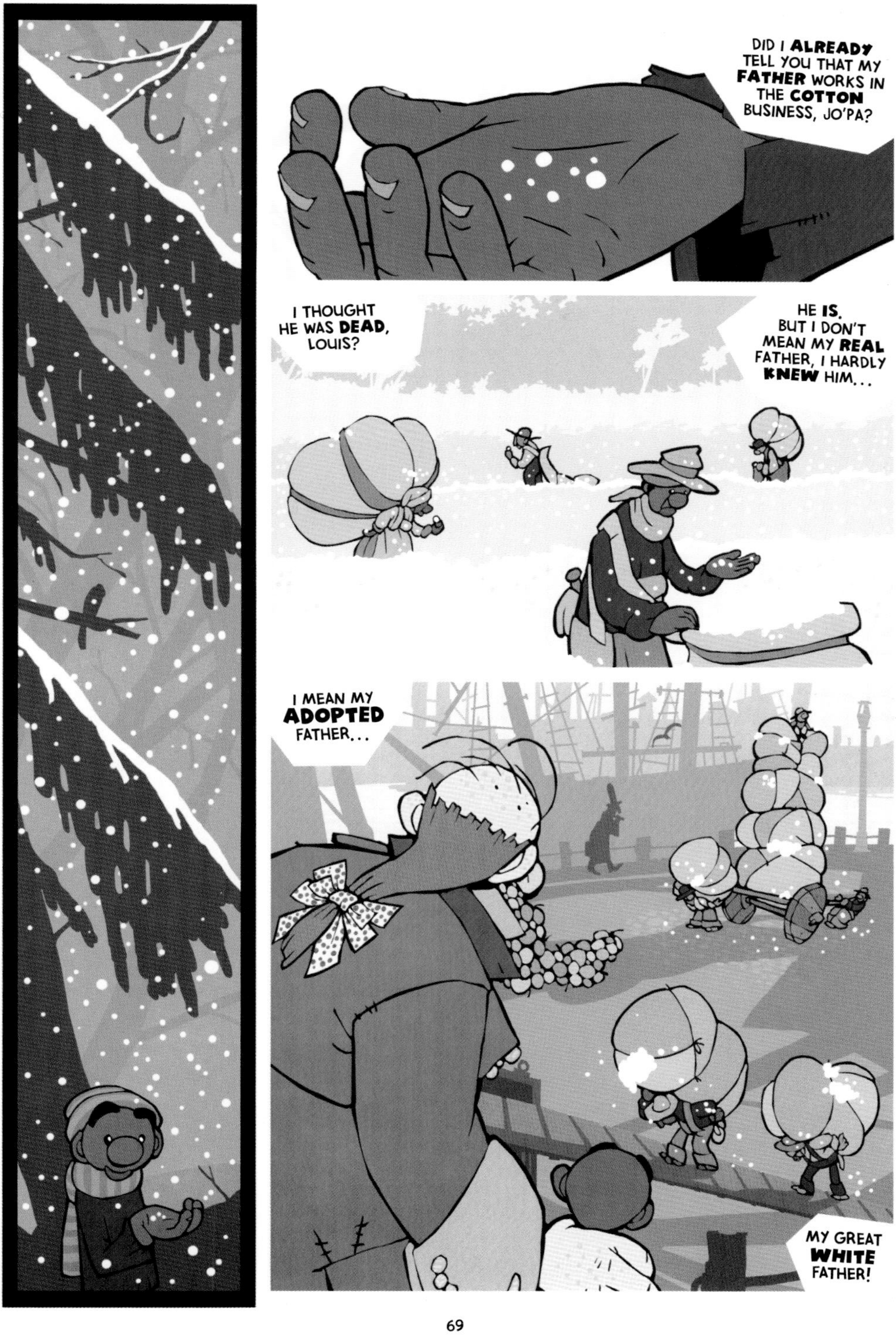

DID I ALREADY TELL YOU THAT MY FATHER WORKS IN THE COTTON BUSINESS, JO'PA?
I THOUGHT HE WAS DEAD, LOUIS?
HE IS. BUT I DON'T MEAN MY REAL FATHER, I HARDLY KNEW HIM...
I MEAN MY ADOPTED FATHER...
MY GREAT WHITE FATHER!

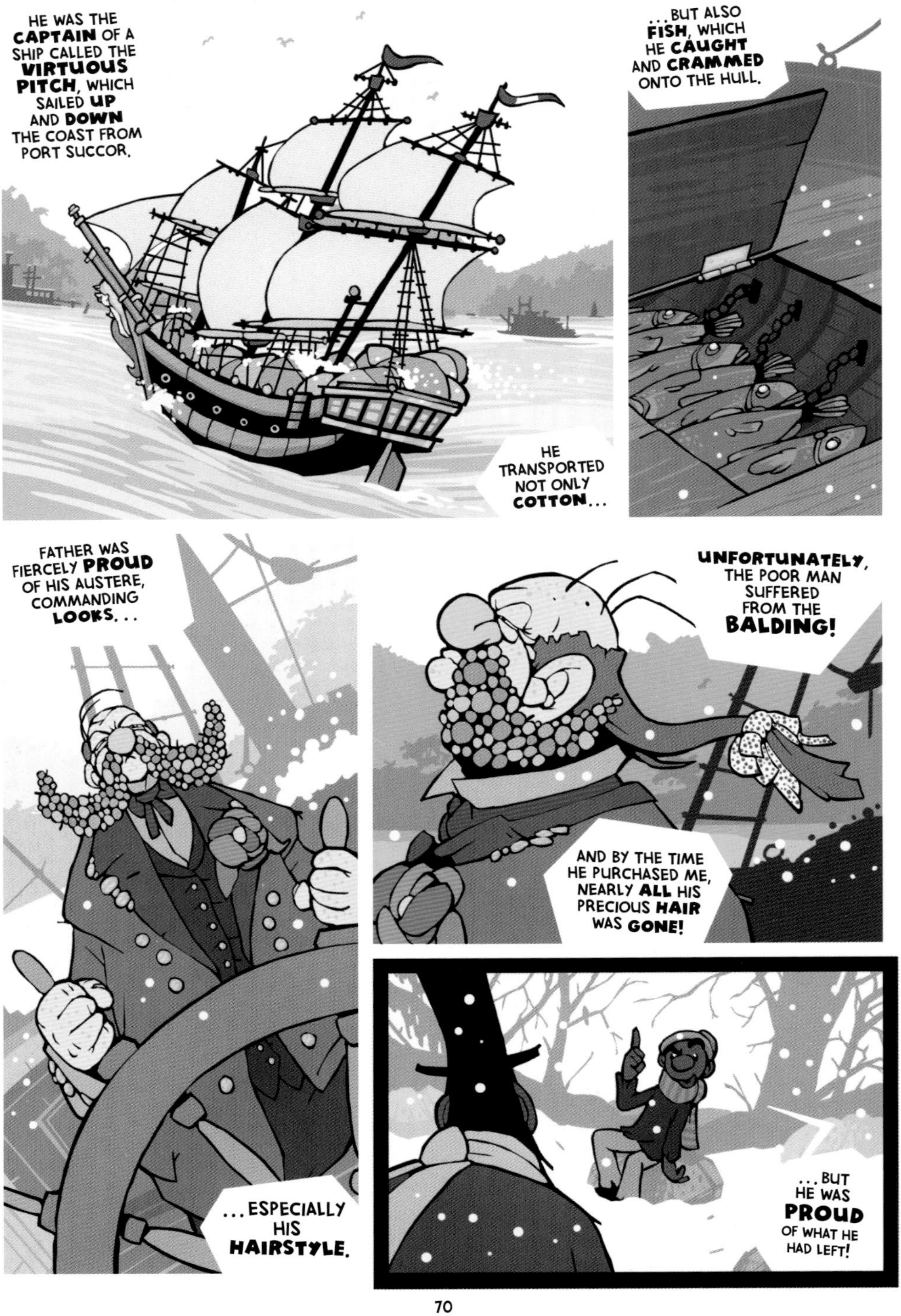
HE WAS THE CAPTAIN OF A SHIP CALLED THE VIRTUOUS PITCH, WHICH SAILED UP AND DOWN THE COAST FROM PORT SUCCOR.
HE TRANSPORTED NOT ONLY COTTON...
...BUT ALSO FISH, WHICH HE CAUGHT AND CRAMMED ONTO THE HULL.
FATHER WAS FIERCELY PROUD OF HIS AUSTERE, COMMANDING LOOKS...
...ESPECIALLY HIS HAIRSTYLE.
UNFORTUNATELY, THE POOR MAN SUFFERED FROM THE BALDING!
AND BY THE TIME HE PURCHASED ME, NEARLY ALL HIS PRECIOUS HAIR WAS GONE!
...BUT HE WAS PROUD OF WHAT HE HAD LEFT!

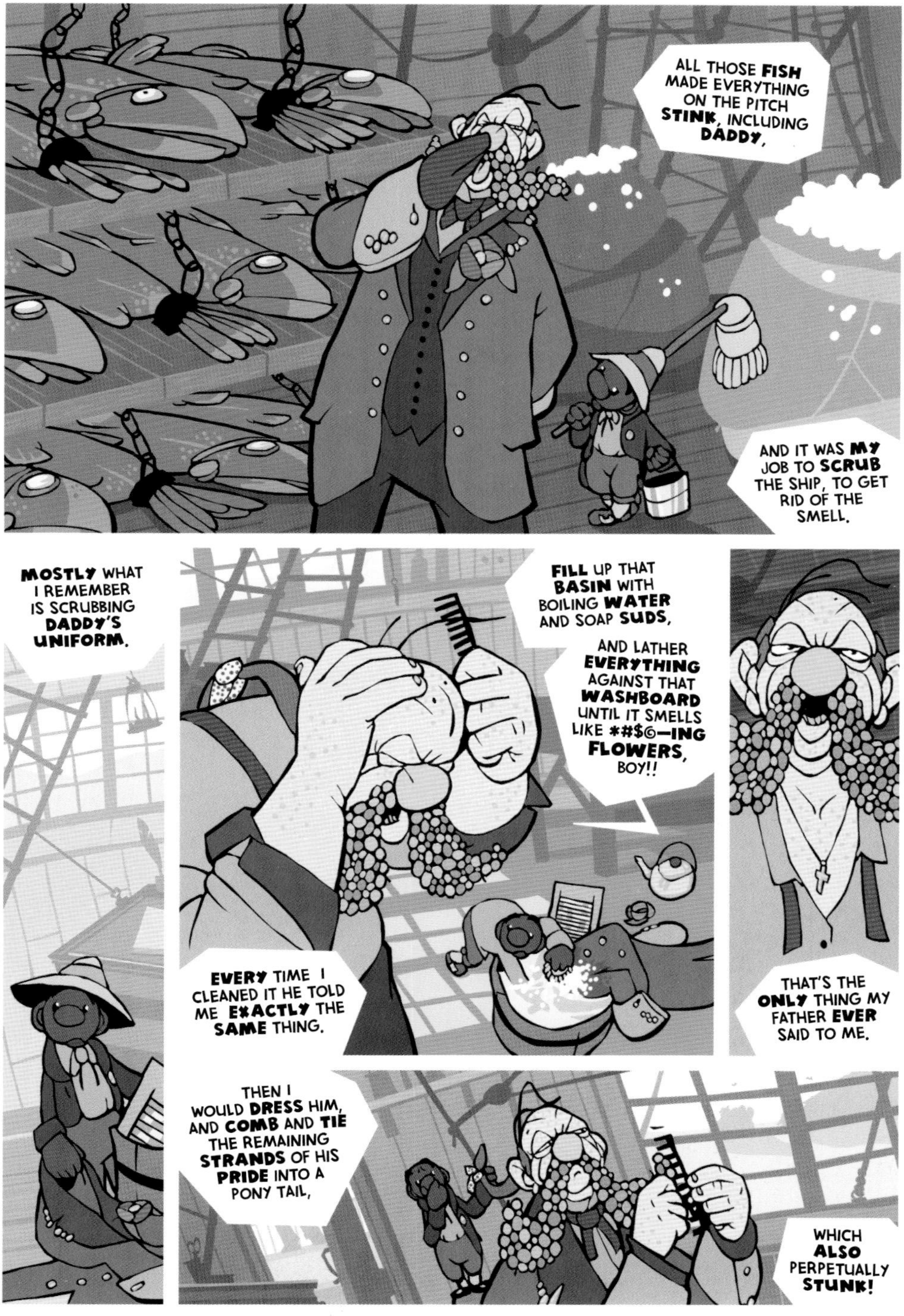

ALL THOSE FISH MADE EVERYTHING ON THE PITCH STINK, INCLUDING DADDY,
AND IT WAS MY JOB TO SCRUB THE SHIP, TO GET RID OF THE SMELL.
MOSTLY WHAT I REMEMBER IS SCRUBBING DADDY'S UNIFORM.
FILL UP THAT BASIN WITH BOILING WATER AND SOAP SUDS,
AND LATHER EVERYTHING AGAINST THAT WASHBOARD UNTIL IT SMELLS LIKE *#$@—ING FLOWERS, BOY!!
EVERY TIME I CLEANED IT HE TOLD ME EXACTLY THE SAME THING.
THAT'S THE ONLY THING MY FATHER EVER SAID TO ME.
THEN I WOULD DRESS HIM, AND COMB AND TIE THE REMAINING STRANDS OF HIS PRIDE INTO A PONY TAIL,
WHICH ALSO PERPETUALLY STUNK!

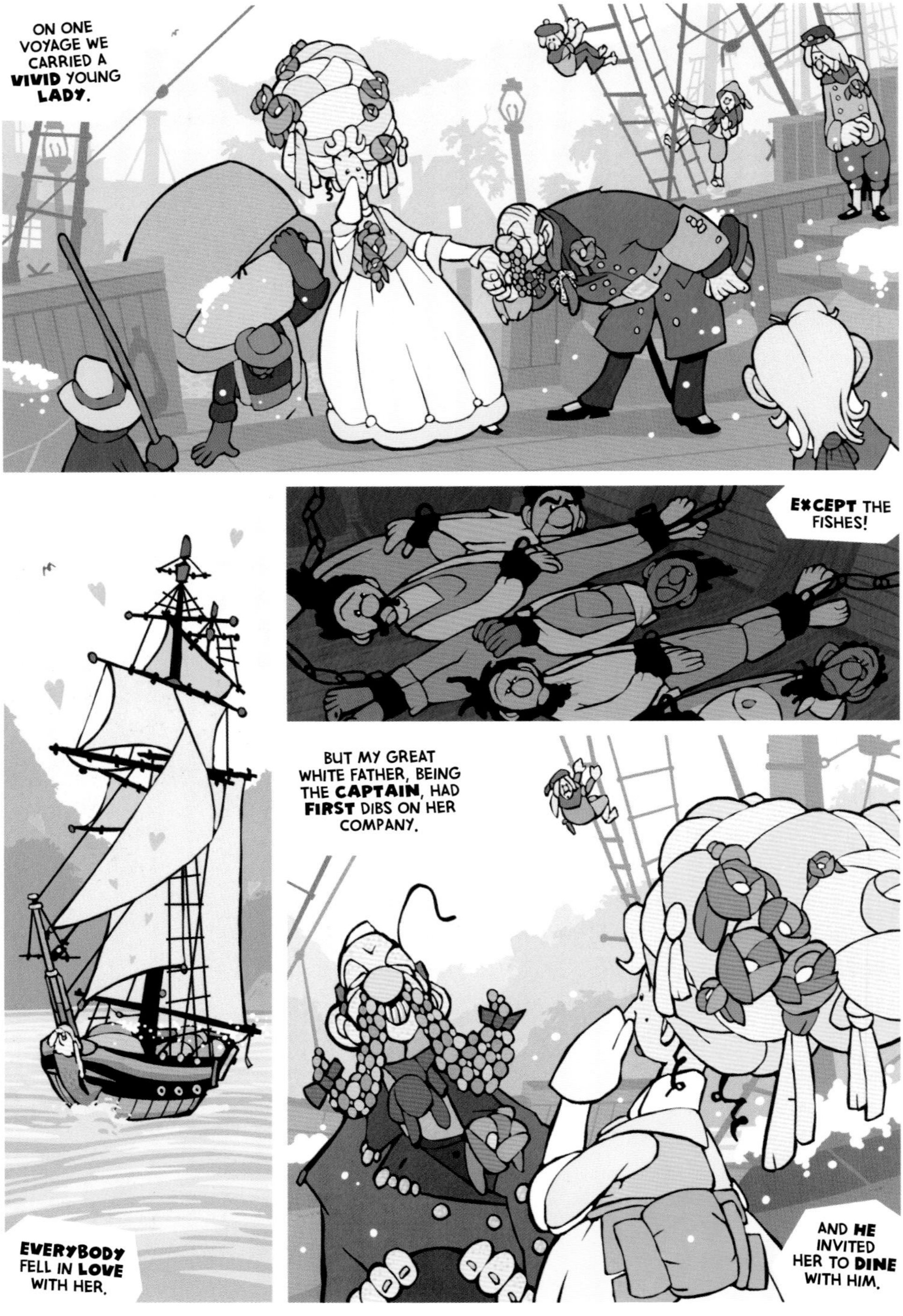
ON ONE VOYAGE WE CARRIED A VIVID YOUNG LADY.
EVERYBODY FELL IN LOVE WITH HER.
EXCEPT THE FISHES!
BUT MY GREAT WHITE FATHER, BEING THE CAPTAIN, HAD FIRST DIBS ON HER COMPANY.
AND HE INVITED HER TO DINE WITH HIM.

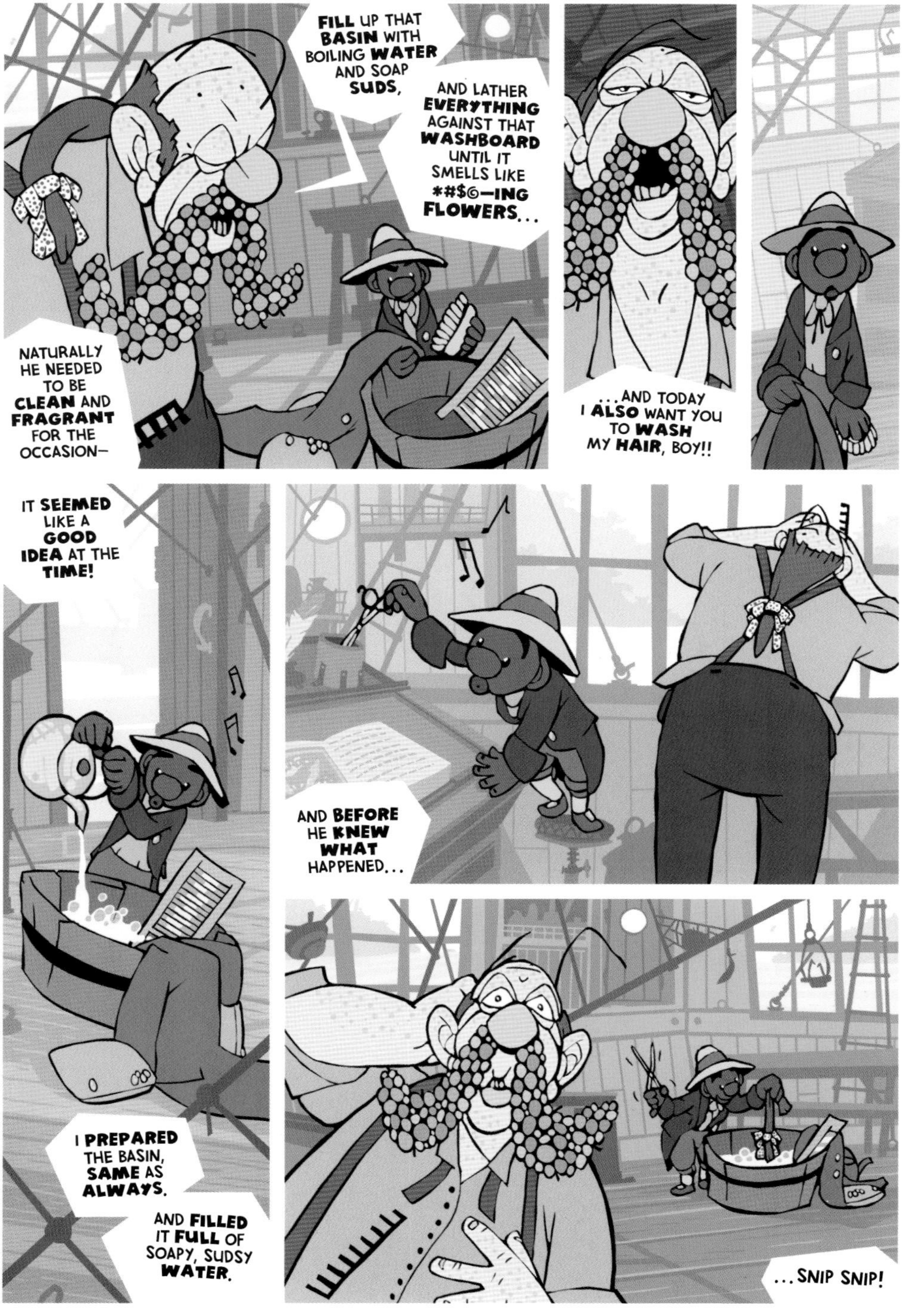
FILL UP THAT BASIN WITH BOILING WATER AND SOAP SUDS,
AND LATHER EVERYTHING AGAINST THAT WASHBOARD UNTIL IT SMELLS LIKE *#$©—ING FLOWERS...
NATURALLY HE NEEDED TO BE CLEAN AND FRAGRANT FOR THE OCCASION—
...AND TODAY I ALSO WANT YOU TO WASH MY HAIR, BOY!!
IT SEEMED LIKE A GOOD IDEA AT THE TIME!
I PREPARED THE BASIN, SAME AS ALWAYS.
AND FILLED IT FULL OF SOAPY, SUDSY WATER.
AND BEFORE HE KNEW WHAT HAPPENED...
...SNIP SNIP!

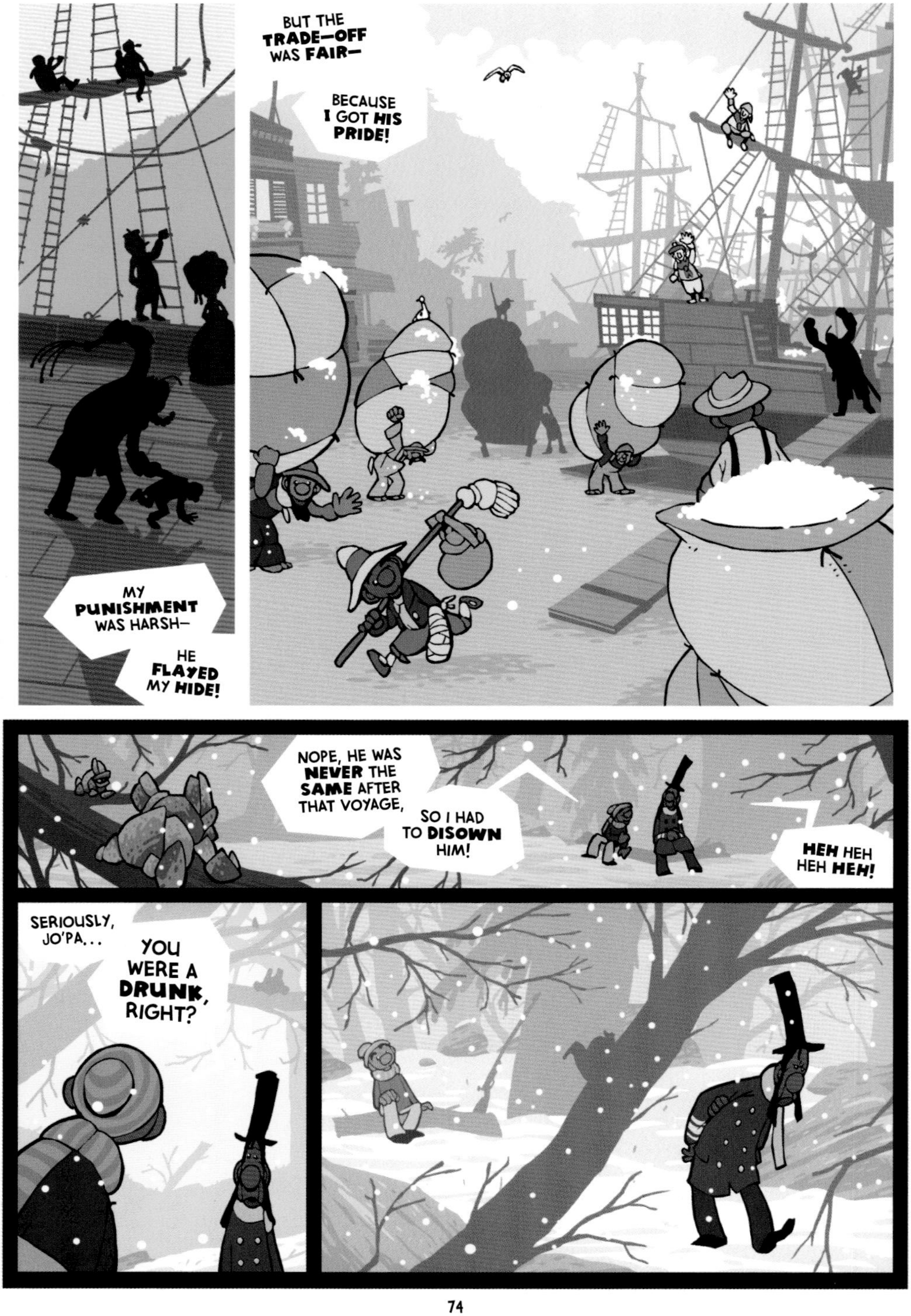
MY PUNISHMENT WAS HARSH—
HE FLAYED MY HIDE!
BUT THE TRADE—OFF WAS FAIR—
BECAUSE I GOT HIS PRIDE!
NOPE, HE WAS NEVER THE SAME AFTER THAT VOYAGE,
SO I HAD TO DISOWN HIM!
HEH HEH HEH HEH!
SERIOUSLY, JO'PA. . .
YOU WERE A DRUNK, RIGHT?

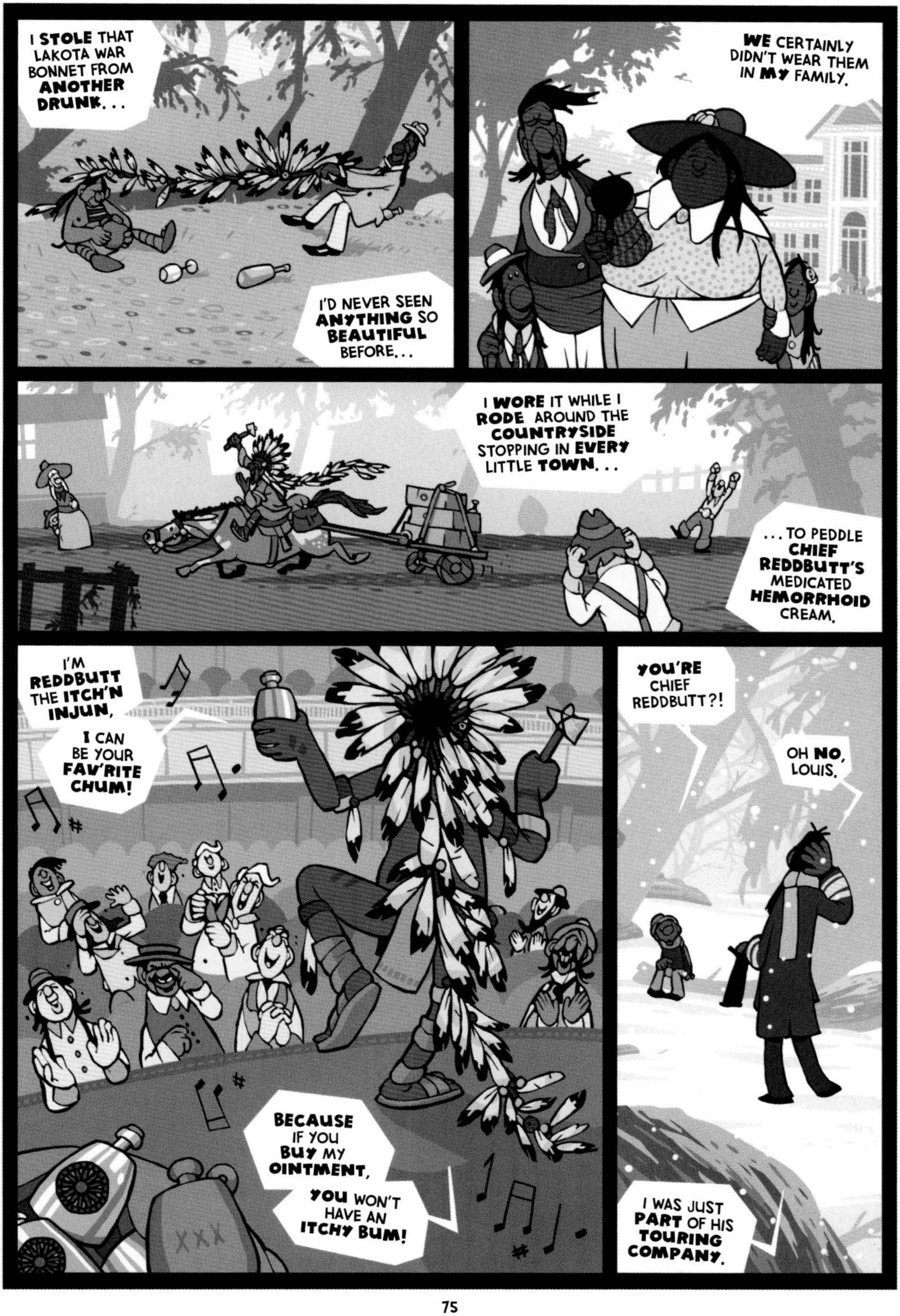
I STOLE THAT LAKOTA WAR BONNET FROM ANOTHER DRUNK...
I'D NEVER SEEN ANYTHING SO BEAUTIFUL BEFORE...
WE CERTAINLY DIDN'T WEAR THEM IN MY FAMILY.
I WORE IT WHILE I RODE AROUND THE COUNTRYSIDE STOPPING IN EVERY LITTLE TOWN...
...TO PEDDLE CHIEF REDDBUTT'S MEDICATED HEMORRHOID CREAM.
I'M REDDBUTT THE ITCH'N INJUN,
I CAN BE YOUR FAV'RITE CHUM!
BECAUSE IF YOU BUY MY OINTMENT,
YOU WON'T HAVE AN ITCHY BUM!
YOU'RE CHIEF REDDBUTT?!
OH NO, LOUIS.
I WAS JUST PART OF HIS TOURING COMPANY.

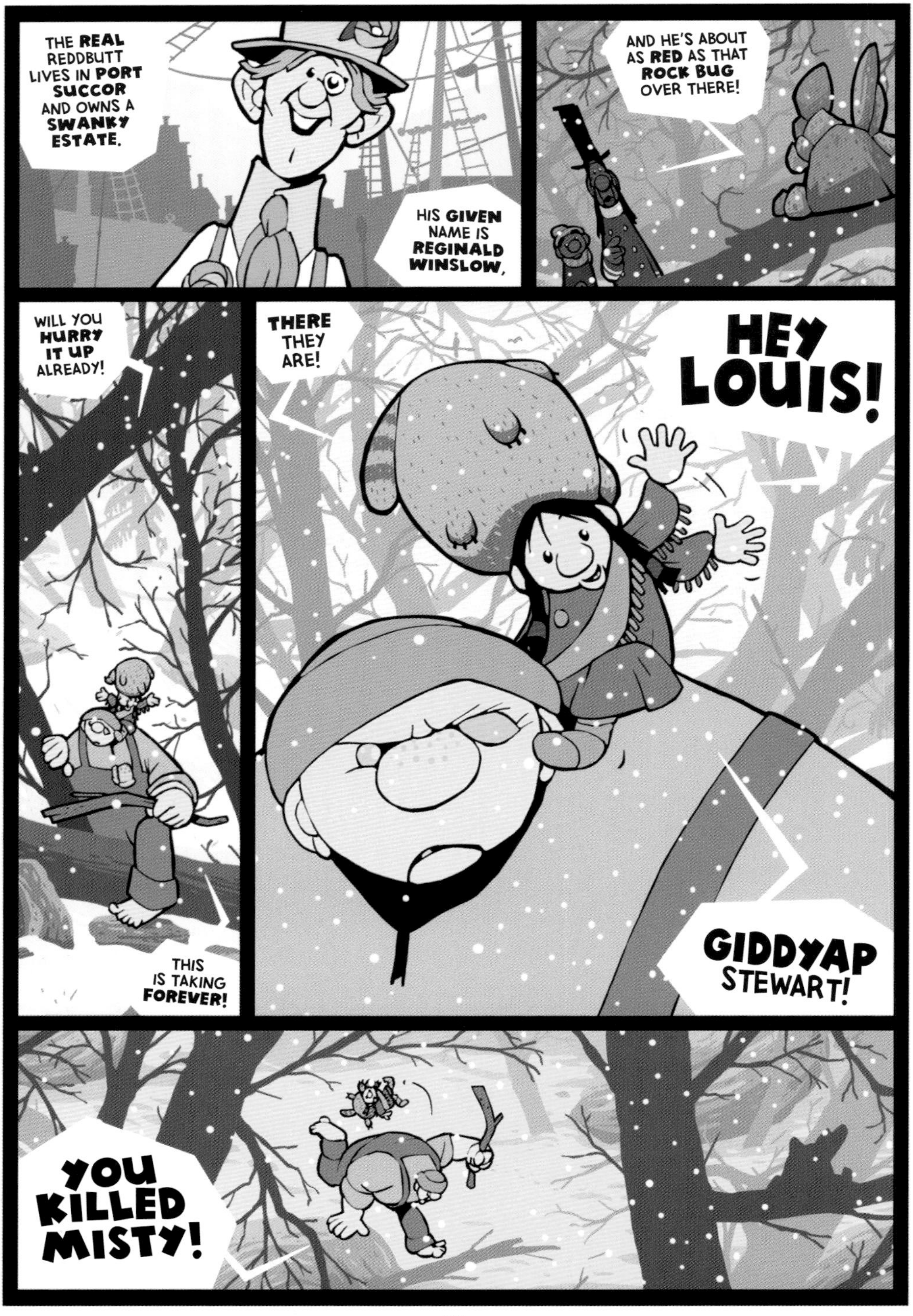
THE REAL REDDBUTT LIVES IN PORT SUCCOR AND OWNS A SWANKY ESTATE.
HIS GIVEN NAME IS REGINALD WINSLOW,
AND HE'S ABOUT AS RED AS THAT ROCK BUG OVER THERE!
WILL YOU HURRY IT UP ALREADY!
THIS IS TAKING FOREVER!
THERE THEY ARE!
HEY LOUIS!
GIDDYAP STEWART!
YOU KILLED MISTY!

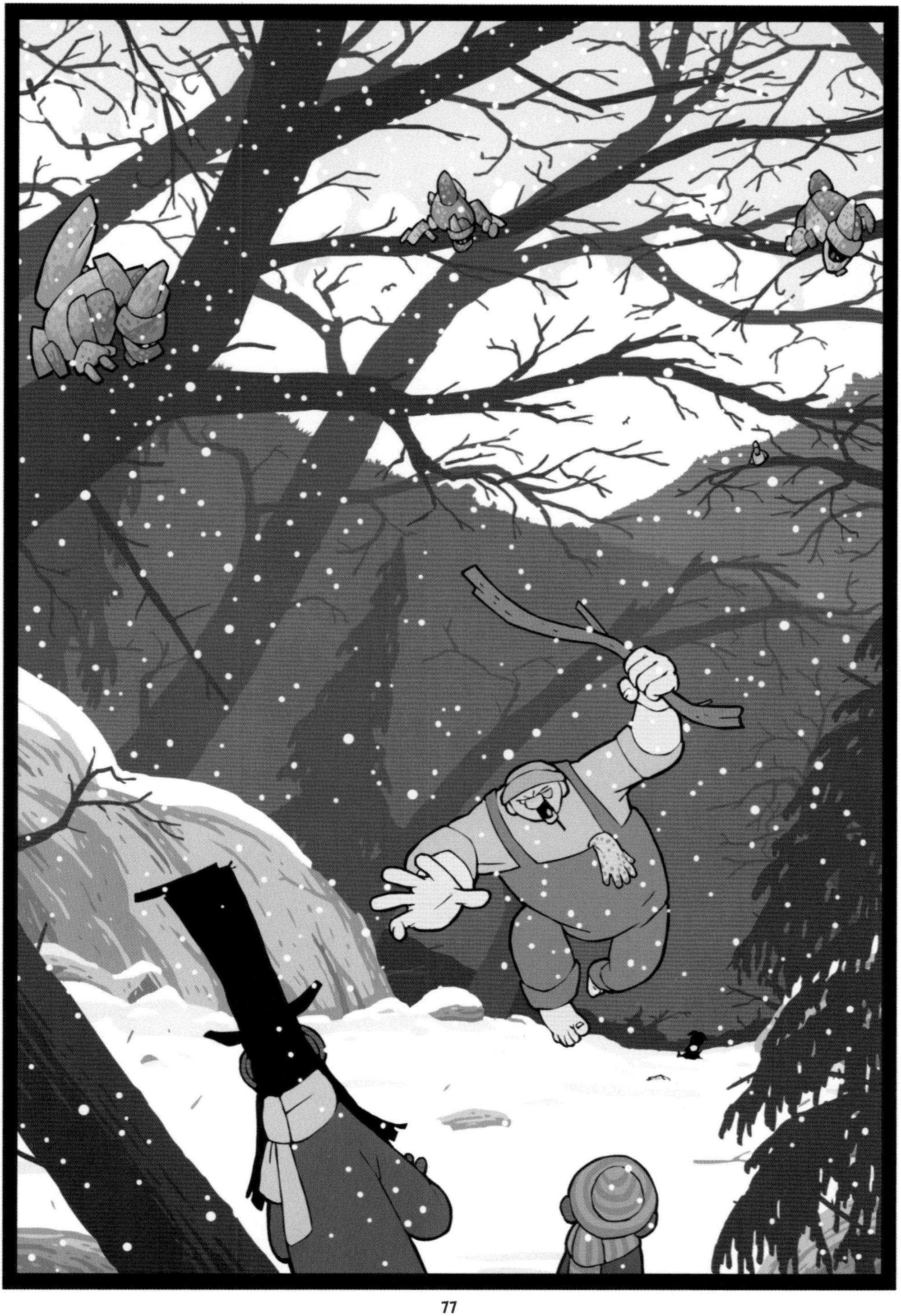

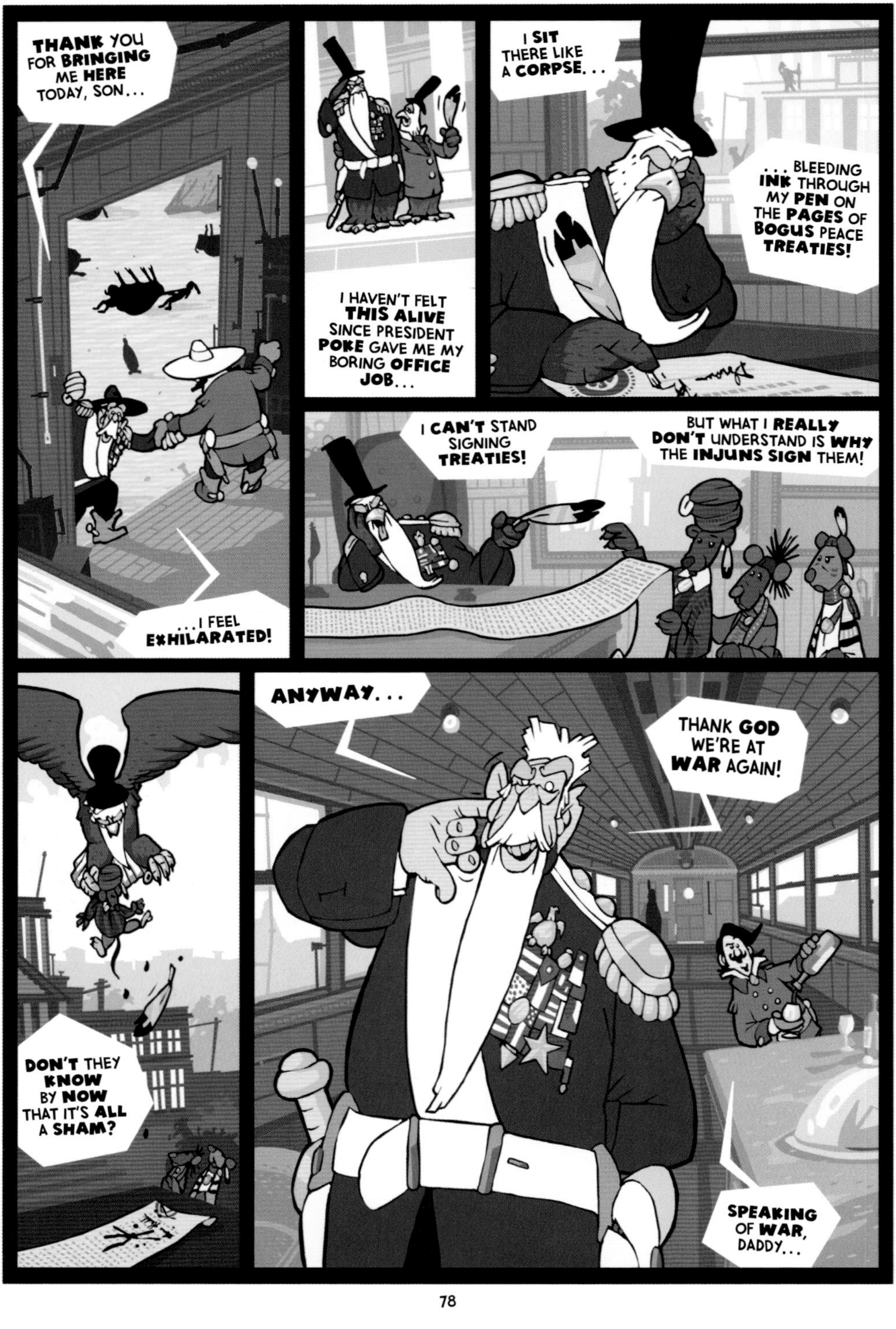

THANK YOU FOR BRINGING ME HERE TODAY, SON...
...I FEEL EXHILARATED!
I HAVEN'T FELT THIS ALIVE SINCE PRESIDENT POKE GAVE ME MY BORING OFFICE JOB...
I SIT THERE LIKE A CORPSE...
...BLEEDING INK THROUGH MY PEN ON THE PAGES OF BOGUS PEACE TREATIES!
I CAN'T STAND SIGNING TREATIES!
BUT WHAT I REALLY DON'T UNDERSTAND IS WHY THE INJUNS SIGN THEM!
DON'T THEY KNOW BY NOW THAT IT'S ALL A SHAM?
ANYWAY...
THANK GOD WE'RE AT WAR AGAIN!
SPEAKING OF WAR, DADDY...

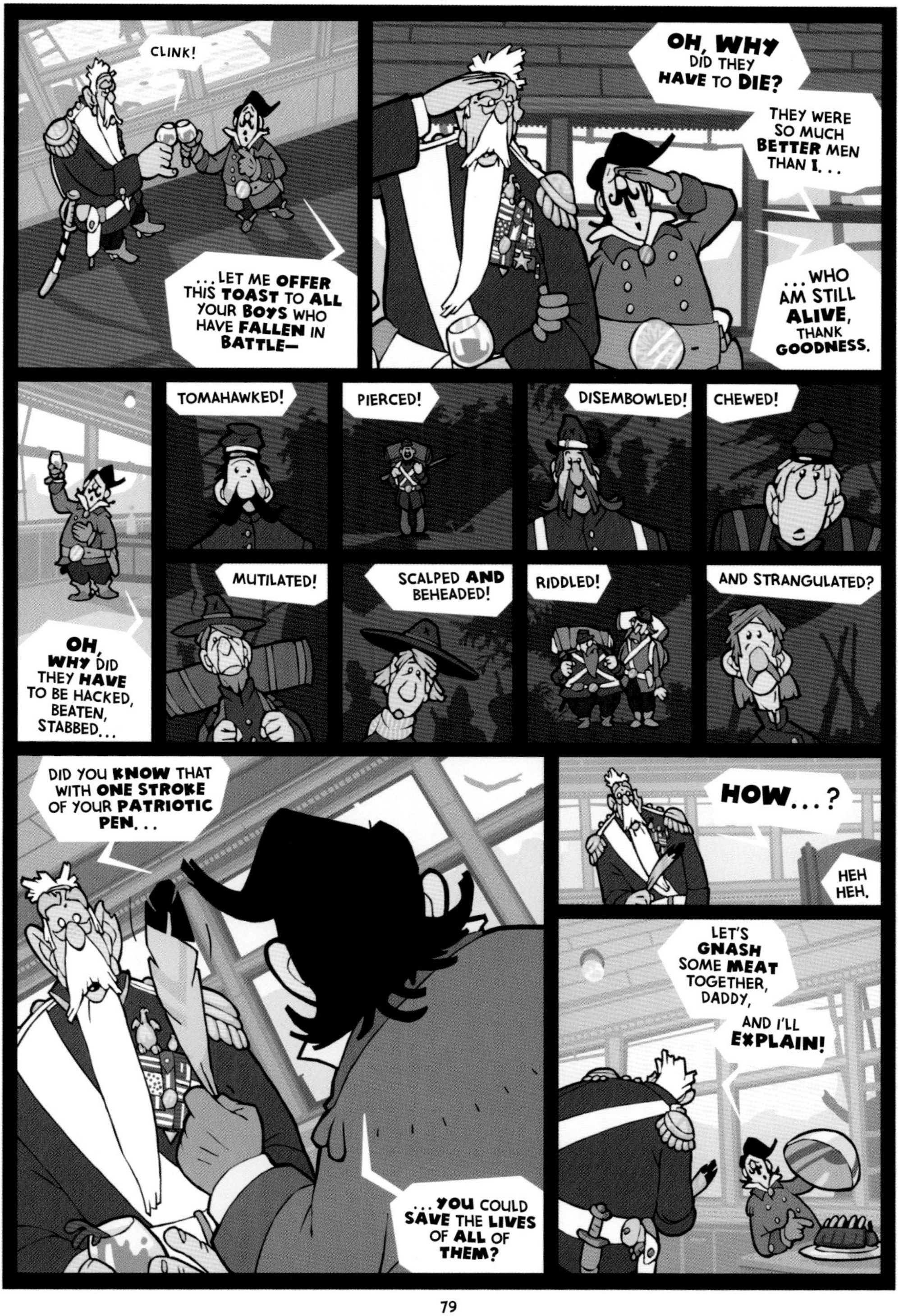
CLINK!
...LET ME OFFER THIS TOAST TO ALL YOUR BOYS WHO HAVE FALLEN IN BATTLE—
OH, WHY DID THEY HAVE TO DIE?
THEY WERE SO MUCH BETTER MEN THAN I...
...WHO AM STILL ALIVE, THANK GOODNESS.
OH, WHY DID THEY HAVE TO BE HACKED, BEATEN, STABBED...
TOMAHAWKED!
PIERCED!
DISEMBOWLED!
CHEWED!
MUTILATED!
SCALPED AND BEHEADED!
RIDDLED!
AND STRANGULATED?
DID YOU KNOW THAT WITH ONE STROKE OF YOUR PATRIOTIC PEN...
...YOU COULD SAVE THE LIVES OF ALL OF THEM?
HOW...?
HEH HEH.
LET'S GNASH SOME MEAT TOGETHER, DADDY,
AND I'LL EXPLAIN!

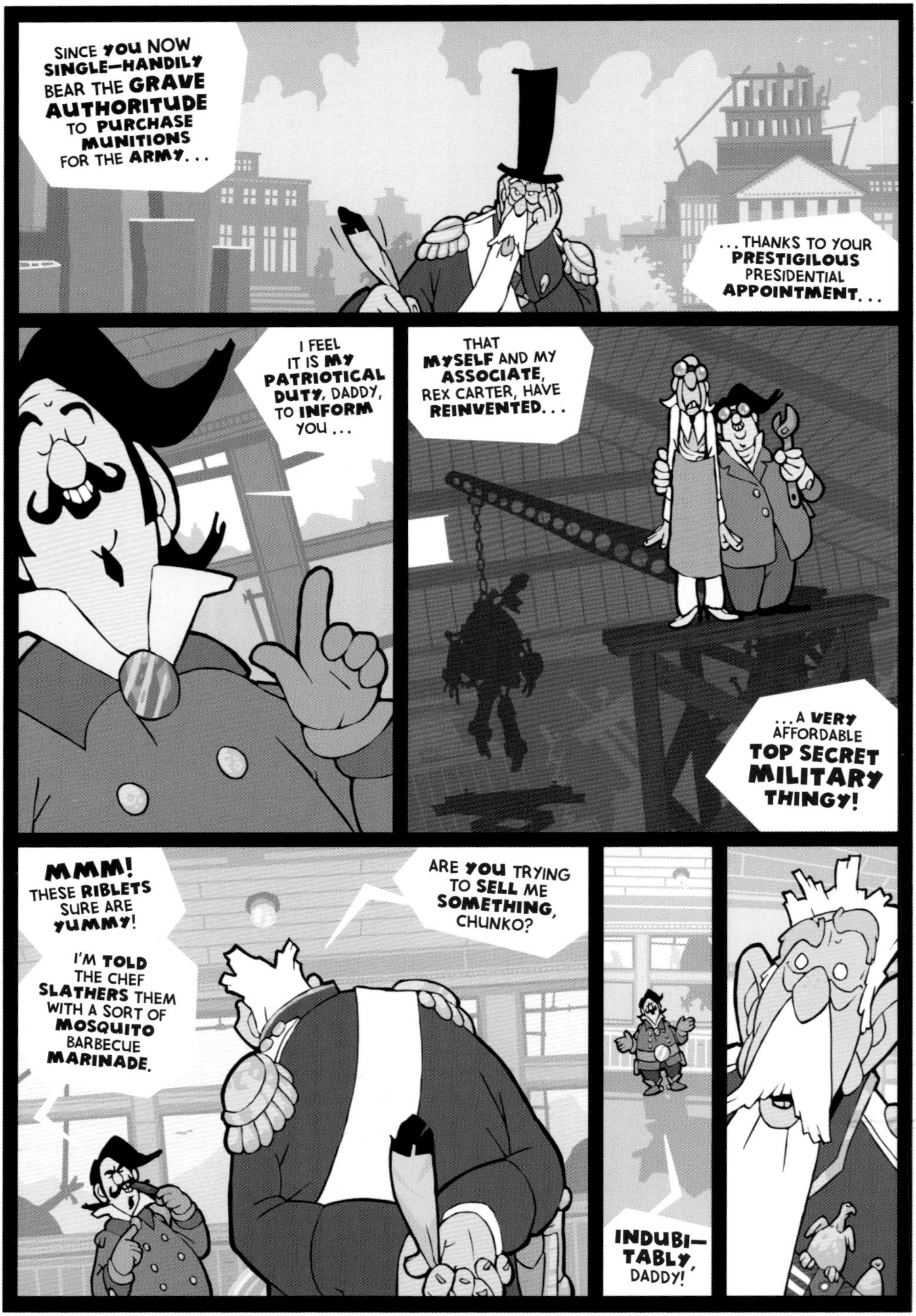

SINCE YOU NOW SINGLE-HANDILY BEAR THE GRAVE AUTHORITUDE TO PURCHASE MUNITIONS FOR THE ARMY...
...THANKS TO YOUR PRESTIGILOUS PRESIDENTIAL APPOINTMENT...
I FEEL IT IS MY PATRIOTICAL DUTY, DADDY, TO INFORM YOU...
THAT MYSELF AND MY ASSOCIATE, REX CARTER, HAVE REINVENTED...
...A VERY AFFORDABLE TOP SECRET MILITARY THINGY!
MMM! THESE RIBLETS SURE ARE YUMMY!
I'M TOLD THE CHEF SLATHERS THEM WITH A SORT OF MOSQUITO BARBECUE MARINADE.
ARE YOU TRYING TO SELL ME SOMETHING, CHUNKO?
INDUBI-TABLY, DADDY!

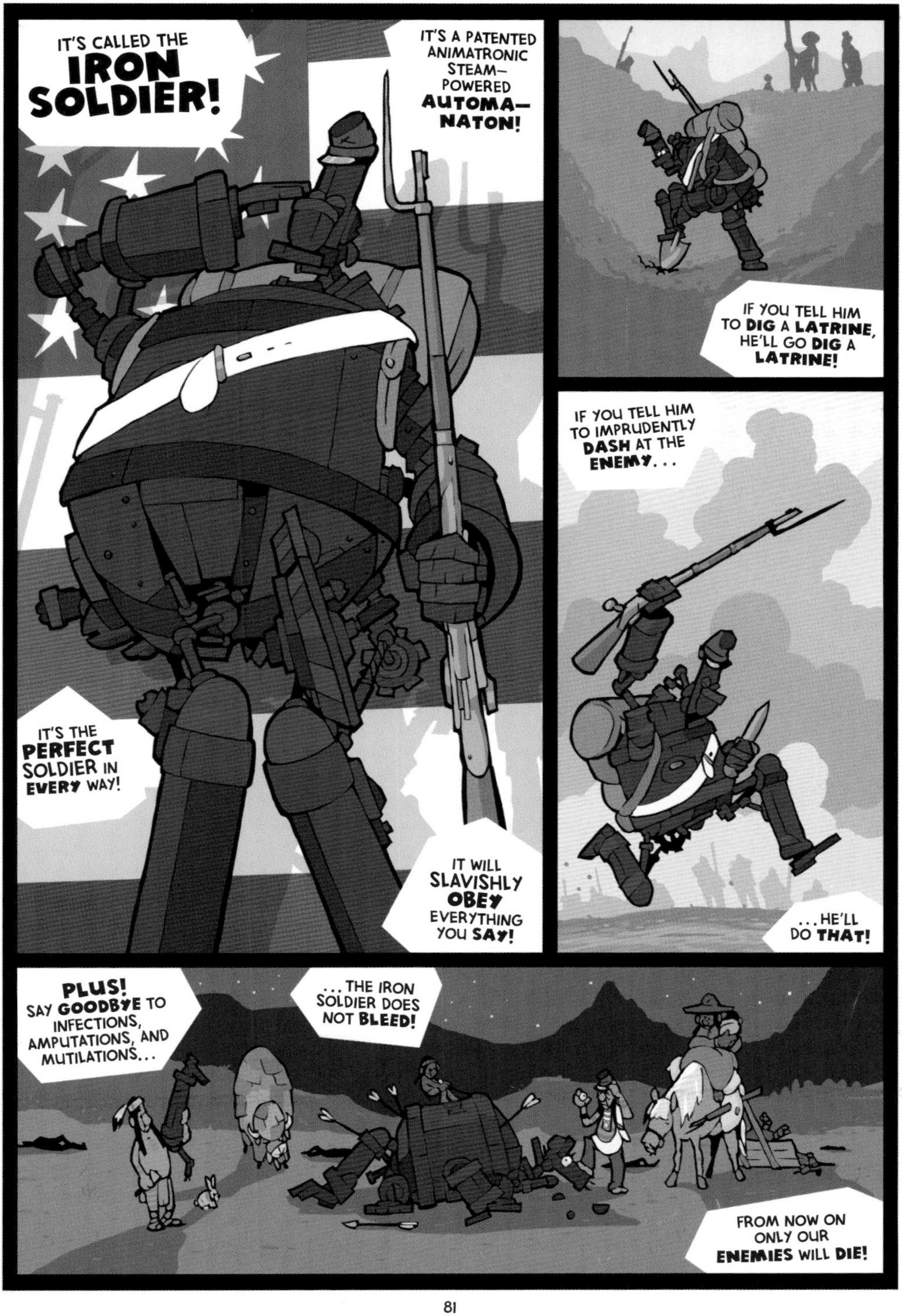
IT'S CALLED THE IRON SOLDIER!
IT'S A PATENTED ANIMATRONIC STEAM-POWERED AUTOMA-NATON!
IT'S THE PERFECT SOLDIER IN EVERY WAY!
IT WILL SLAVISHLY OBEY EVERYTHING YOU SAY!
IF YOU TELL HIM TO DIG A LATRINE, HE'LL GO DIG A LATRINE!
IF YOU TELL HIM TO IMPRUDENTLY DASH AT THE ENEMY...
...HE'LL DO THAT!
PLUS! SAY GOODBYE TO INFECTIONS, AMPUTATIONS, AND MUTILATIONS...
...THE IRON SOLDIER DOES NOT BLEED!
FROM NOW ON ONLY OUR ENEMIES WILL DIE!

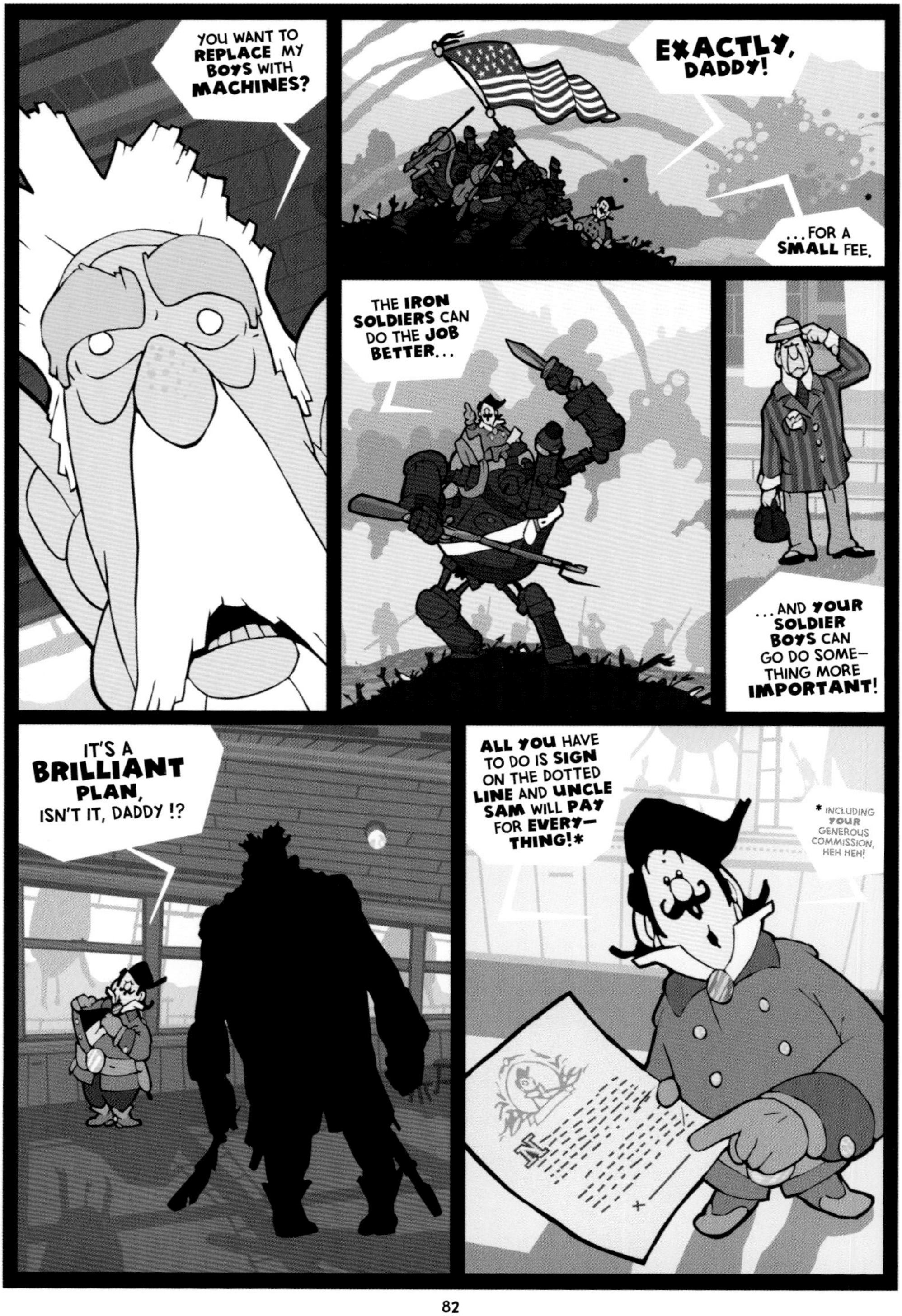
YOU WANT TO REPLACE MY BOYS WITH MACHINES?
EXACTLY, DADDY!
...FOR A SMALL FEE.
THE IRON SOLDIERS CAN DO THE JOB BETTER...
...AND YOUR SOLDIER BOYS CAN GO DO SOME-THING MORE IMPORTANT!
IT'S A BRILLIANT PLAN, ISN'T IT, DADDY !?
ALL YOU HAVE TO DO IS SIGN ON THE DOTTED LINE AND UNCLE SAM WILL PAY FOR EVERY-THING!*
* INCLUDING YOUR GENEROUS COMMISSION, HEH HEH!

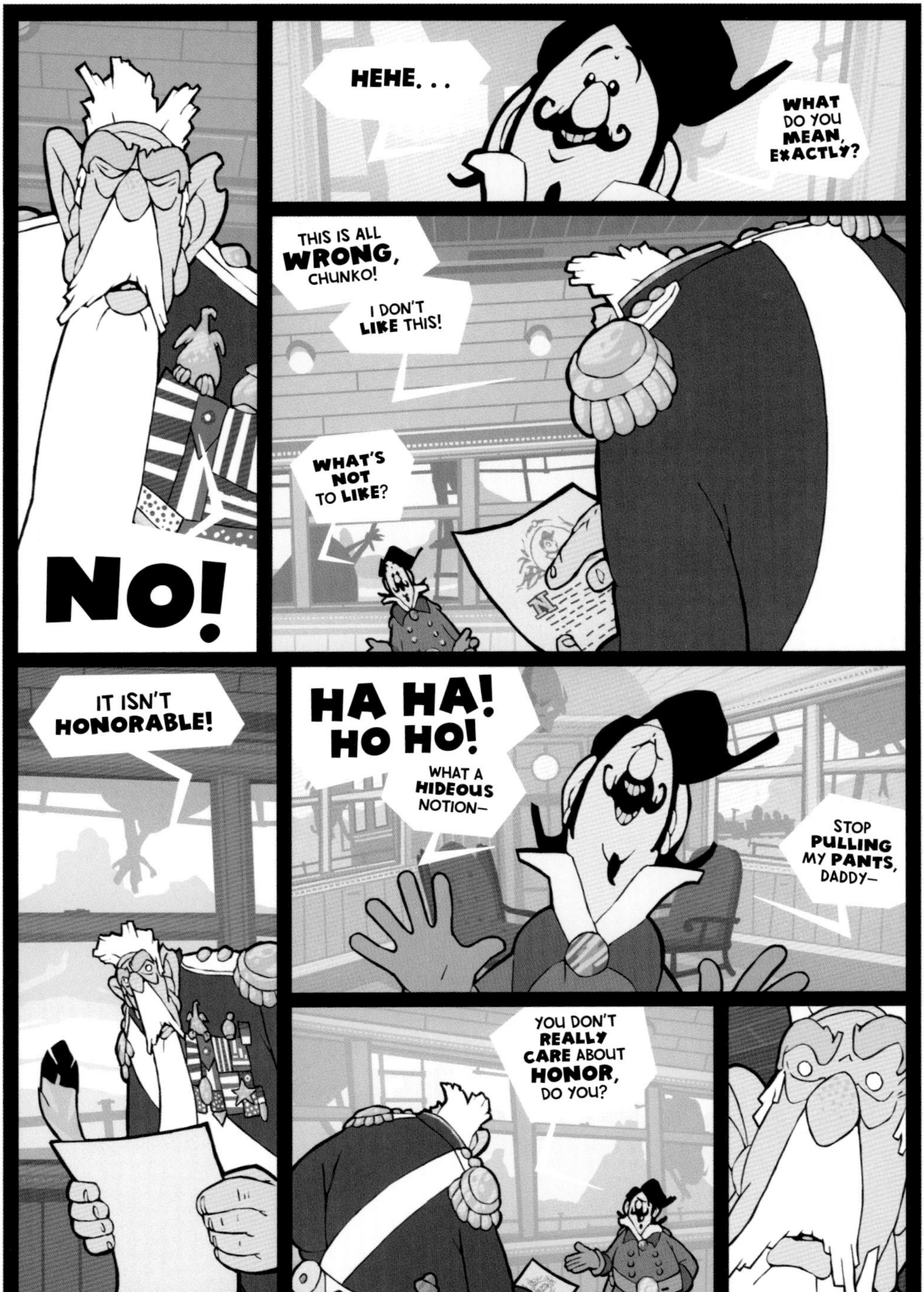
HEHE...
WHAT DO YOU MEAN, EXACTLY?
NO!
THIS IS ALL WRONG, CHUNKO!
I DON'T LIKE THIS!
WHAT'S NOT TO LIKE?
IT ISN'T HONORABLE!
HA HA! HO HO!
WHAT A HIDEOUS NOTION—
STOP PULLING MY PANTS, DADDY—
YOU DON'T REALLY CARE ABOUT HONOR, DO YOU?

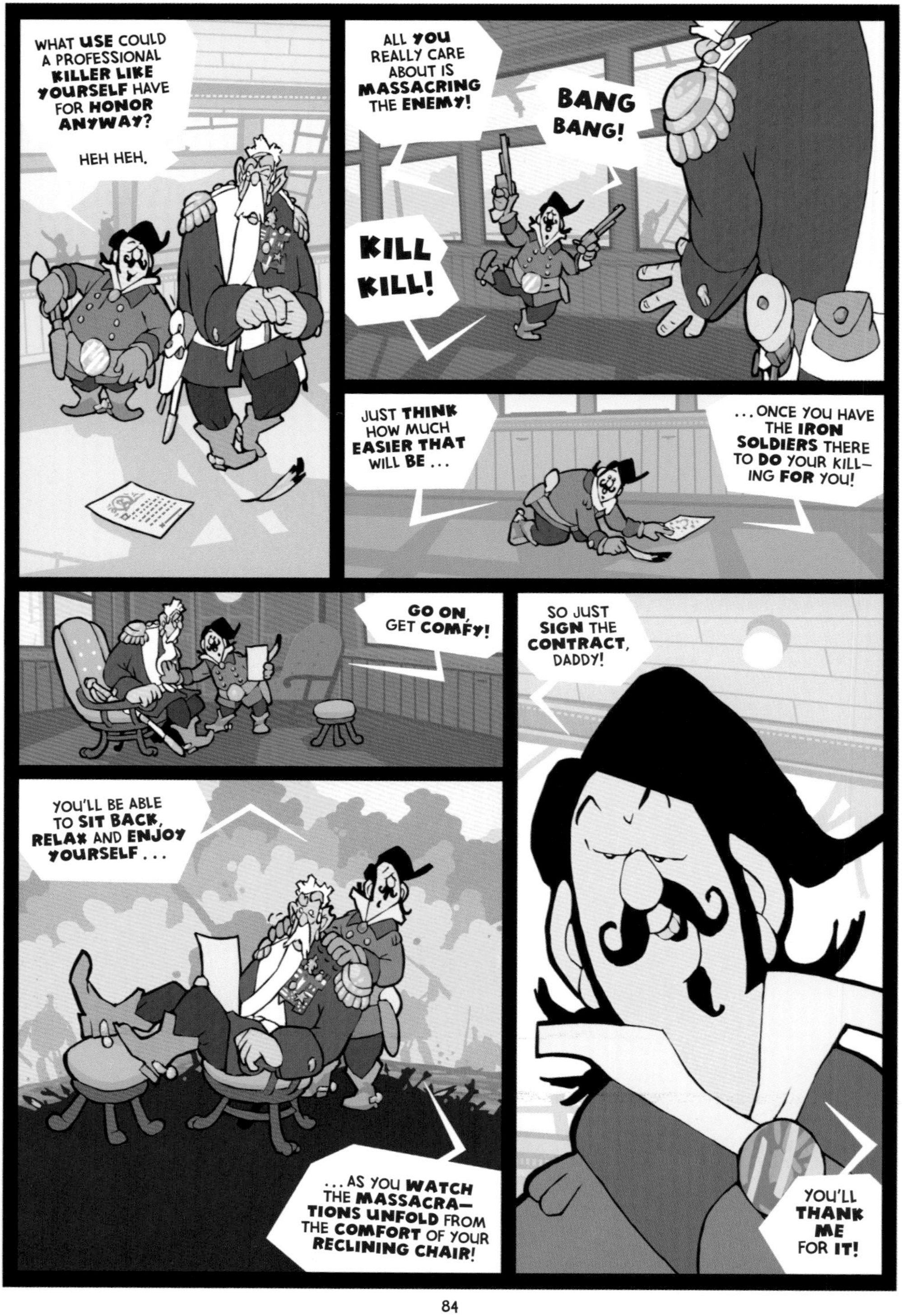
WHAT USE COULD A PROFESSIONAL KILLER LIKE YOURSELF HAVE FOR HONOR ANYWAY?
HEH HEH.
ALL YOU REALLY CARE ABOUT IS MASSACRING THE ENEMY!
BANG BANG!
KILL KILL!
JUST THINK HOW MUCH EASIER THAT WILL BE . . .
. . . ONCE YOU HAVE THE IRON SOLDIERS THERE TO DO YOUR KILL-ING FOR YOU!
GO ON, GET COMFY!
YOU'LL BE ABLE TO SIT BACK, RELAX AND ENJOY YOURSELF . . .
. . . AS YOU WATCH THE MASSACRA-TIONS UNFOLD FROM THE COMFORT OF YOUR RECLINING CHAIR!
SO JUST SIGN THE CONTRACT, DADDY!
YOU'LL THANK ME FOR IT!

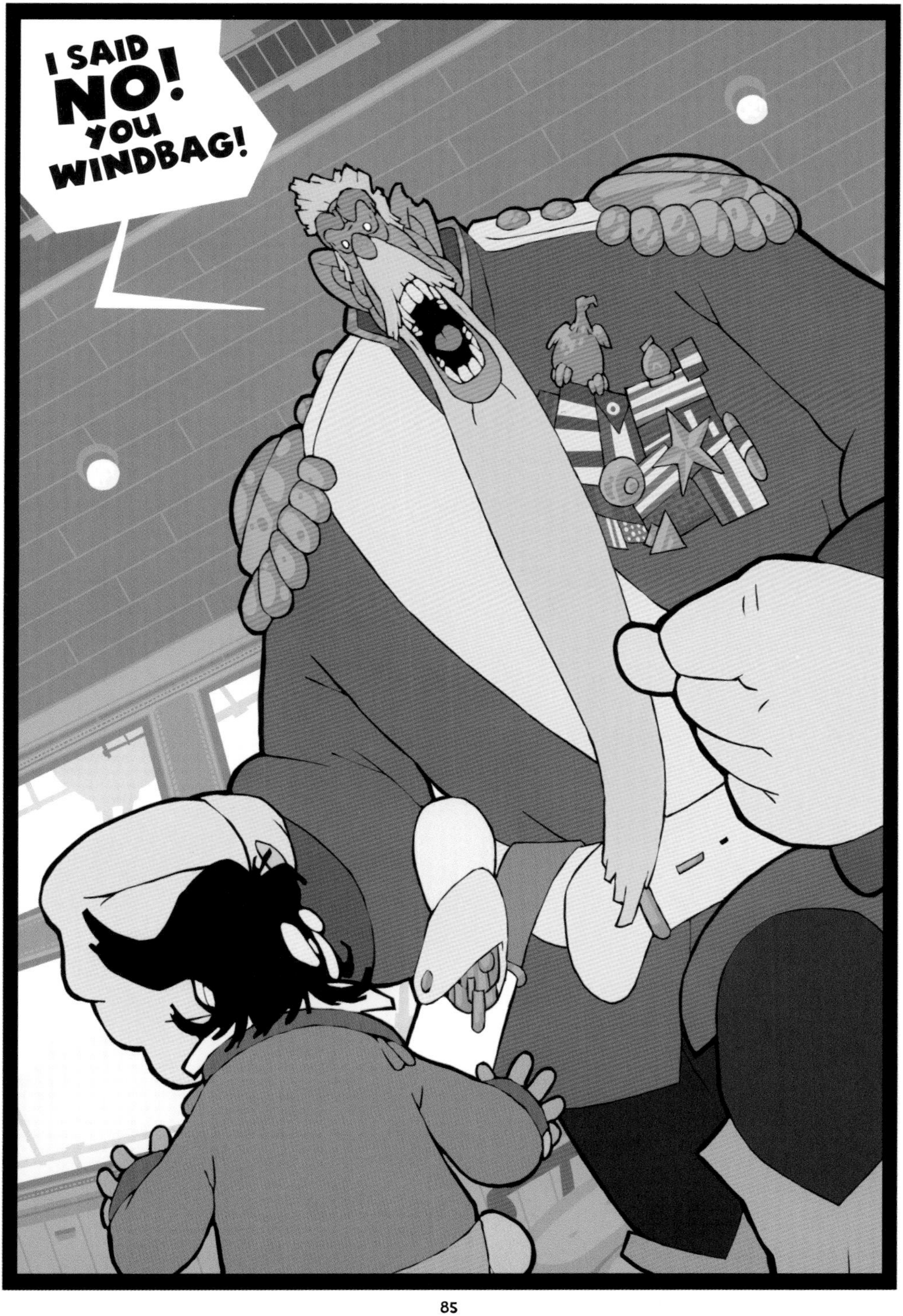
I SAID NO! YOU WINDBAG!

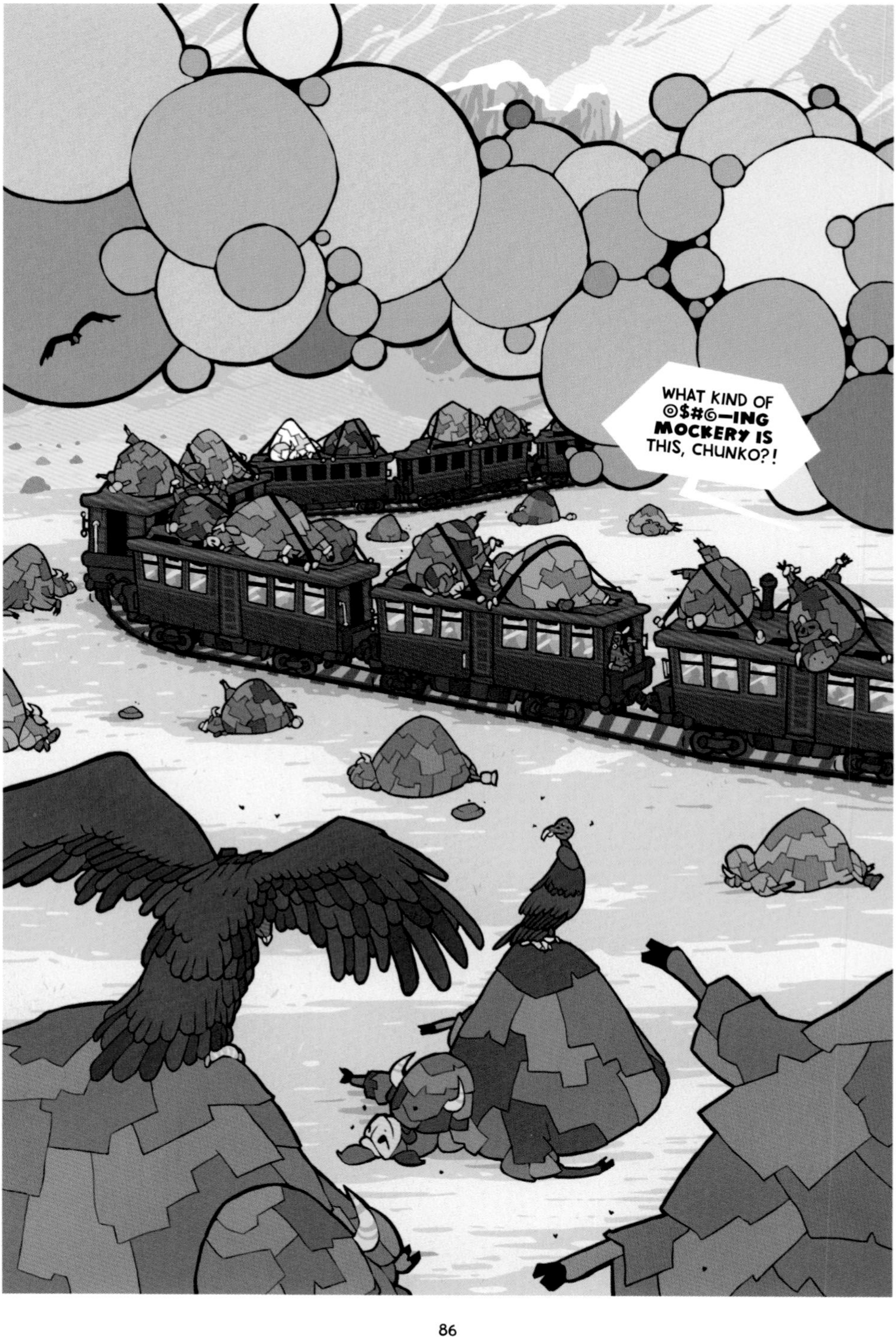
WHAT KIND OF ©$#Ⓖ—ING MOCKERY IS THIS, CHUNKO?!

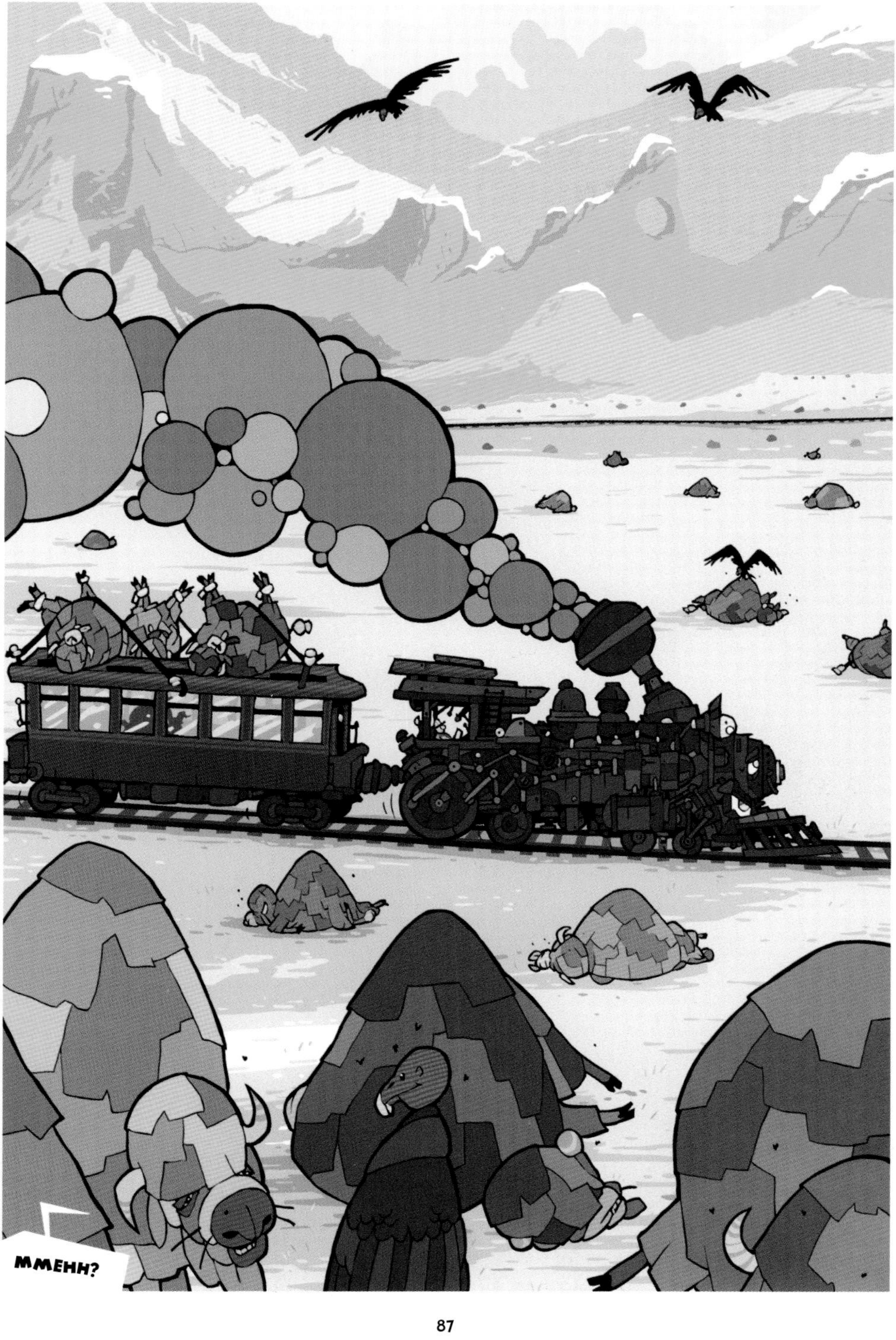
MMENH?

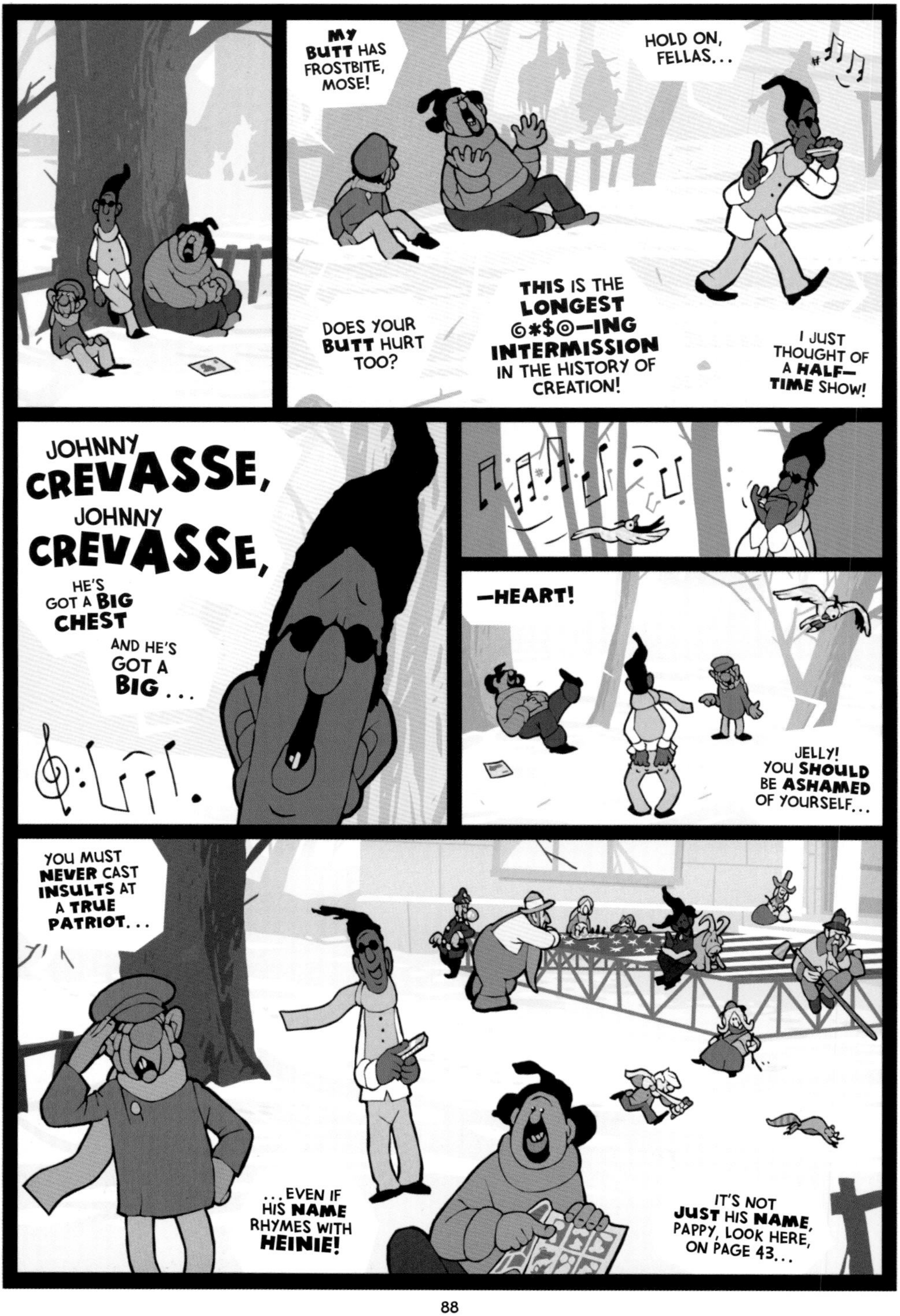
MY BUTT HAS FROSTBITE, MOSE!
HOLD ON, FELLAS...
DOES YOUR BUTT HURT TOO?
THIS IS THE LONGEST ⑥*$⊚-ING INTERMISSION IN THE HISTORY OF CREATION!
I JUST THOUGHT OF A HALF-TIME SHOW!
JOHNNY CREVASSE,
JOHNNY CREVASSE,
HE'S GOT A BIG CHEST
AND HE'S GOT A BIG...
-HEART!
JELLY! YOU SHOULD BE ASHAMED OF YOURSELF...
YOU MUST NEVER CAST INSULTS AT A TRUE PATRIOT...
...EVEN IF HIS NAME RHYMES WITH HEINIE!
IT'S NOT JUST HIS NAME, PAPPY, LOOK HERE, ON PAGE 43...

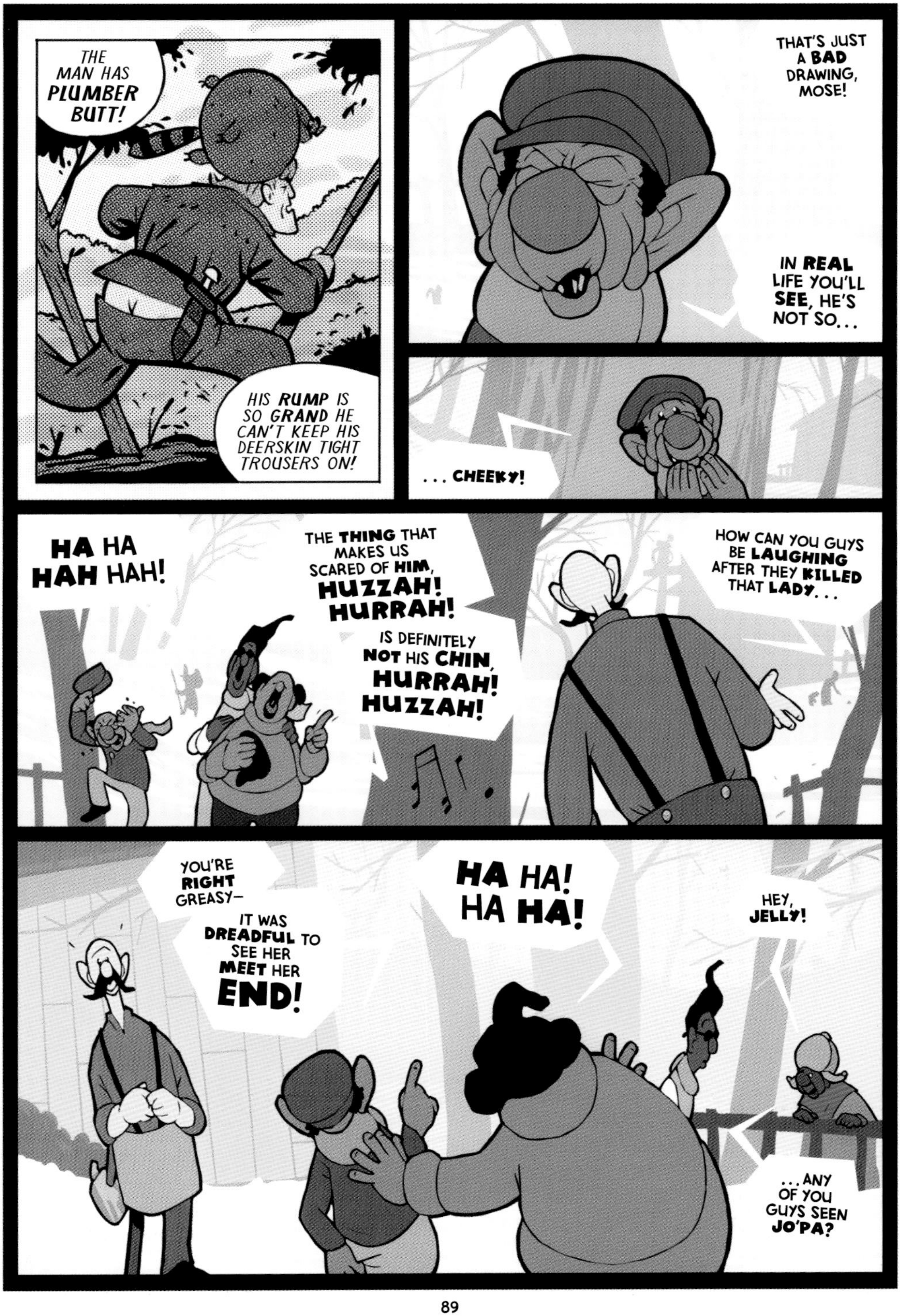
THE MAN HAS PLUMBER BUTT!
HIS RUMP IS SO GRAND HE CAN'T KEEP HIS DEERSKIN TIGHT TROUSERS ON!
THAT'S JUST A BAD DRAWING, MOSE!
IN REAL LIFE YOU'LL SEE, HE'S NOT SO...
...CHEEKY!
HA HA HAH HAH!
THE THING THAT MAKES US SCARED OF HIM, HUZZAH! HURRAH!
IS DEFINITELY NOT HIS CHIN, HURRAH! HUZZAH!
HOW CAN YOU GUYS BE LAUGHING AFTER THEY KILLED THAT LADY...
YOU'RE RIGHT GREASY—
IT WAS DREADFUL TO SEE HER MEET HER END!
HA HA! HA HA!
HEY, JELLY!
...ANY OF YOU GUYS SEEN JO'PA?

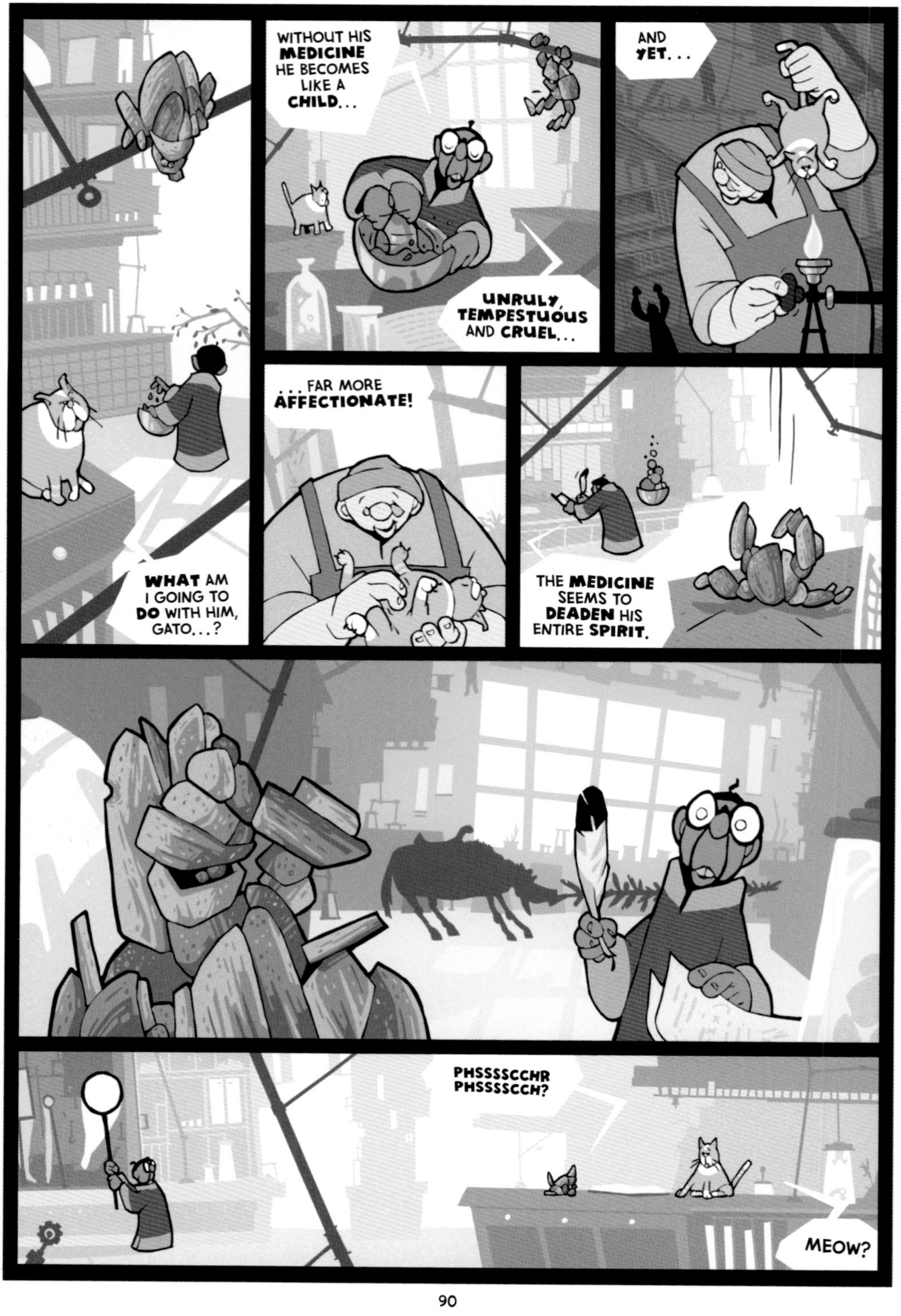
WHAT AM I GOING TO DO WITH HIM, GATO. . .?
WITHOUT HIS MEDICINE HE BECOMES LIKE A CHILD. . .
UNRULY, TEMPESTUOUS AND CRUEL. . .
AND YET. . .
. . . FAR MORE AFFECTIONATE!
THE MEDICINE SEEMS TO DEADEN HIS ENTIRE SPIRIT.
PHSSSSCCHR PHSSSSCCH?
MEOW?

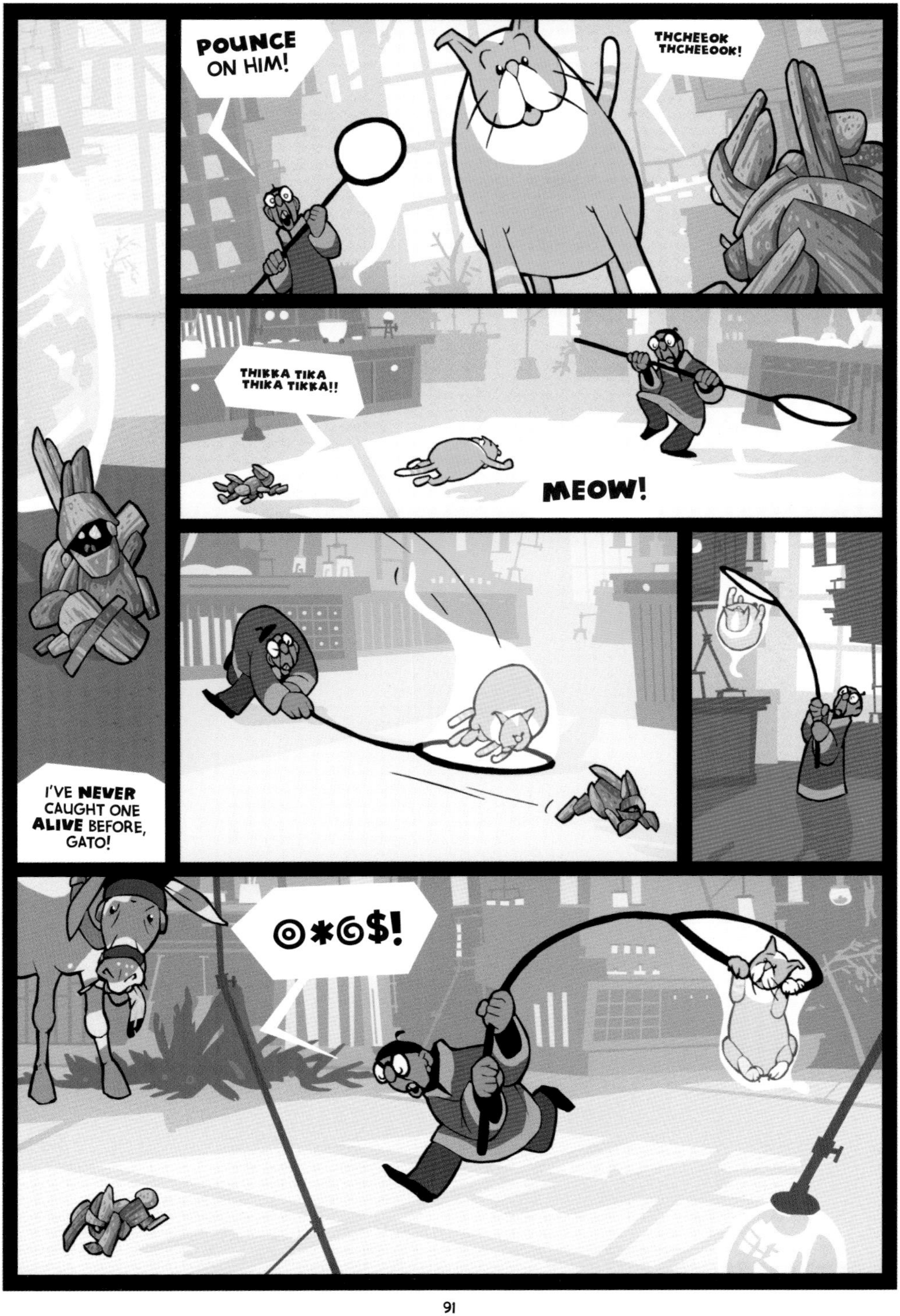
POUNCE ON HIM!
THCHEEOK THCHEEOOK!
THIKKA TIKA THIKA TIKKA!!
MEOW!
I'VE NEVER CAUGHT ONE ALIVE BEFORE, GATO!
@*6$!

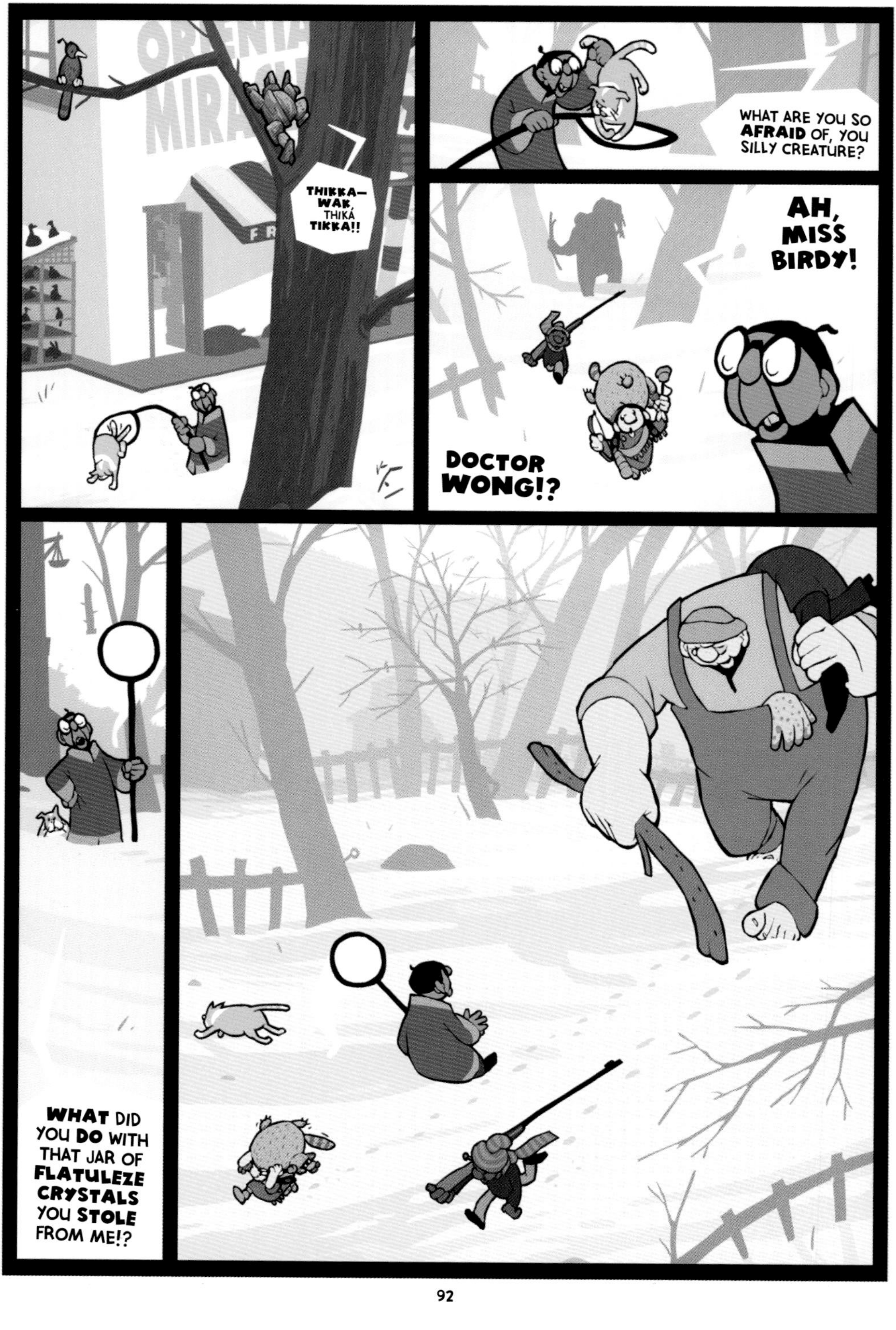
THIKKA-WAK, THIKÁ TIKKA!!
WHAT ARE YOU SO AFRAID OF, YOU SILLY CREATURE?
AH, MISS BIRDY!
DOCTOR WONG!?
WHAT DID YOU DO WITH THAT JAR OF FLATULEZE CRYSTALS YOU STOLE FROM ME!?

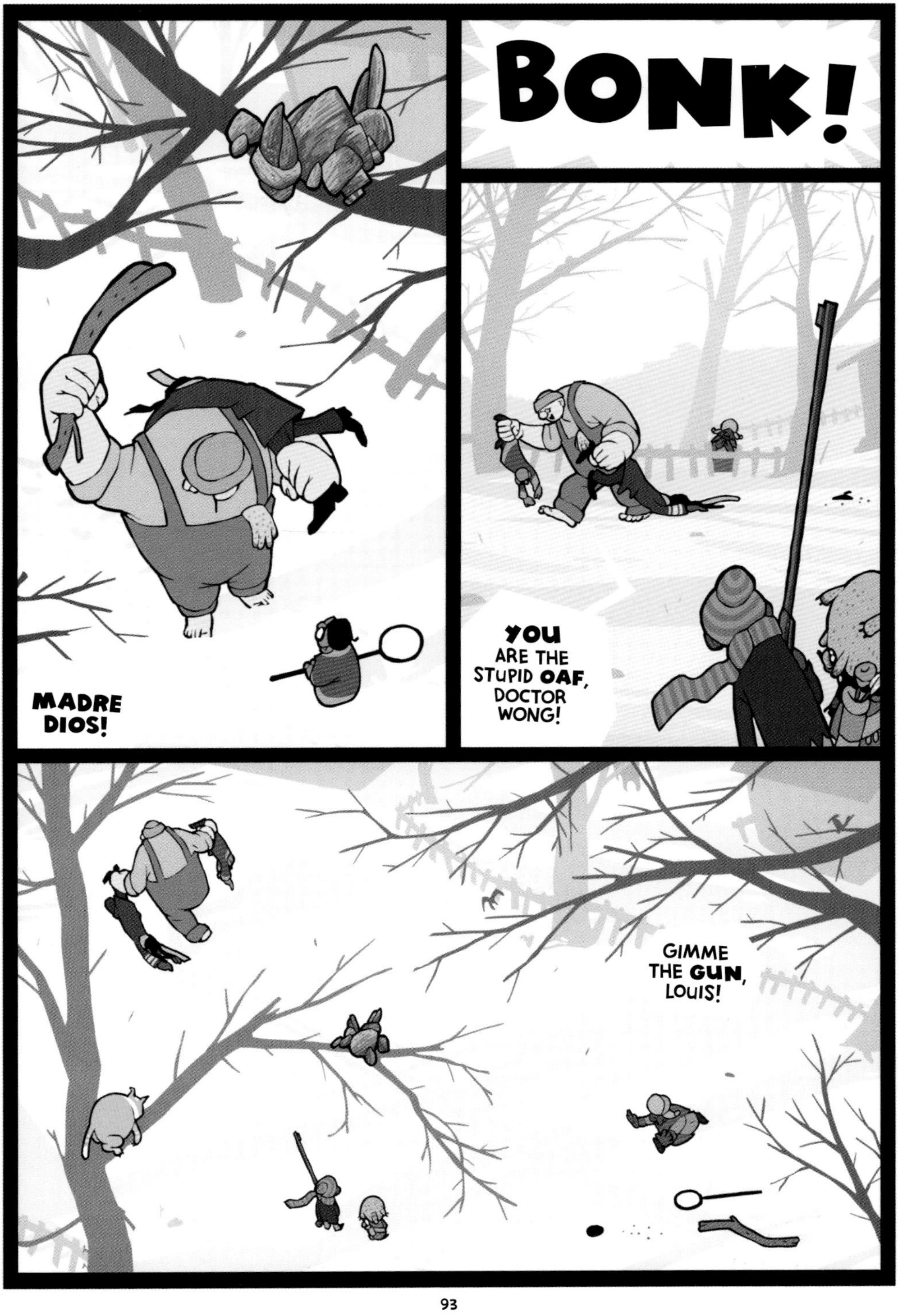
BONK!
MADRE DIOS!
YOU ARE THE STUPID OAF, DOCTOR WONG!
GIMME THE GUN, LOUIS!

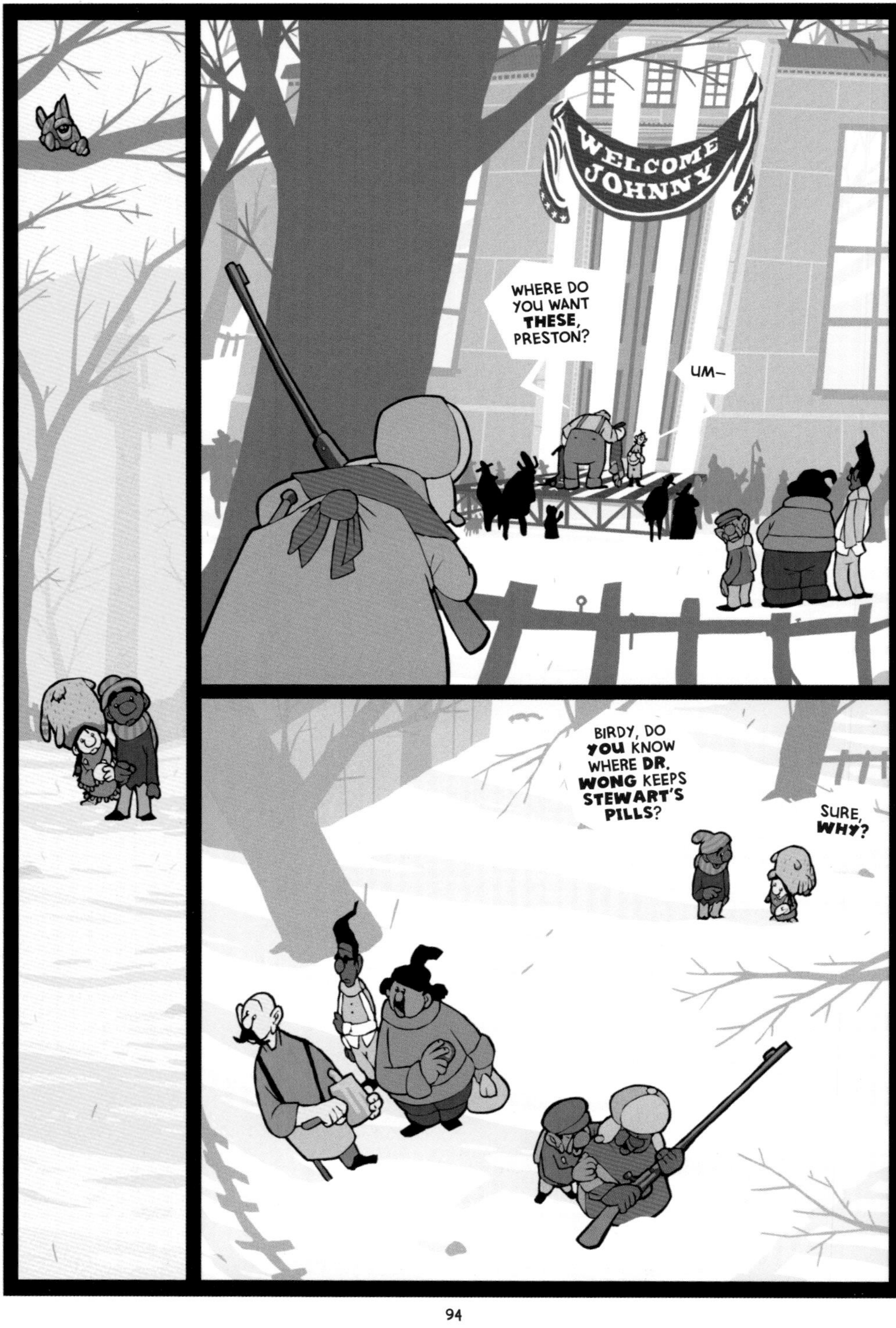
WELCOME JOHNNY
WHERE DO YOU WANT **THESE**, PRESTON?
UM–
BIRDY, DO **YOU** KNOW WHERE **DR. WONG** KEEPS **STEWART'S PILLS**?
SURE, **WHY**?

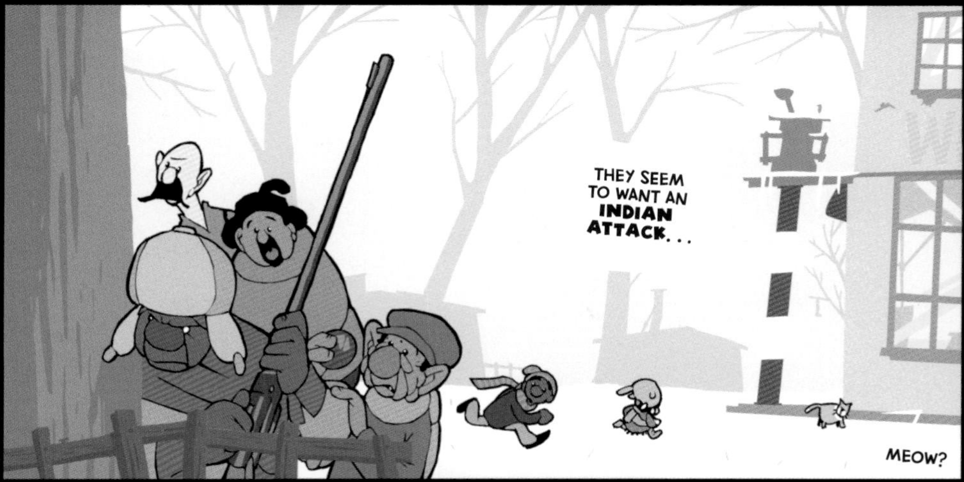
THEY SEEM TO WANT AN INDIAN ATTACK...
MEOW?

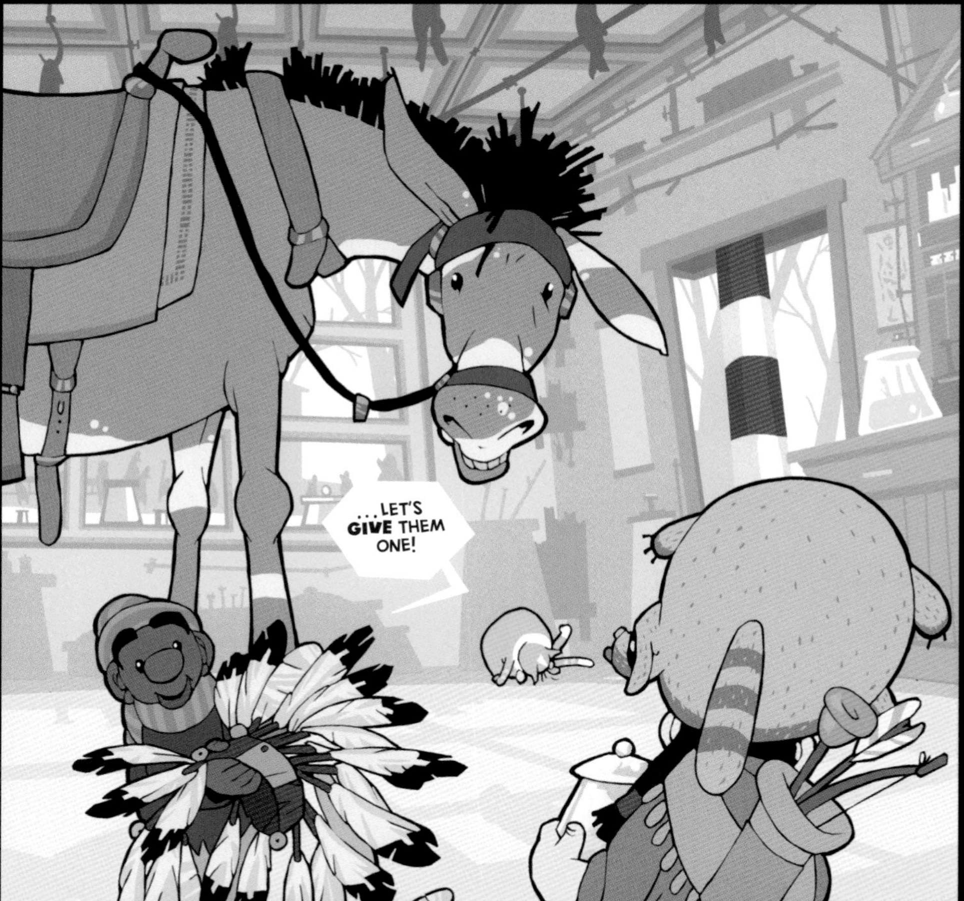
...LET'S GIVE THEM ONE!

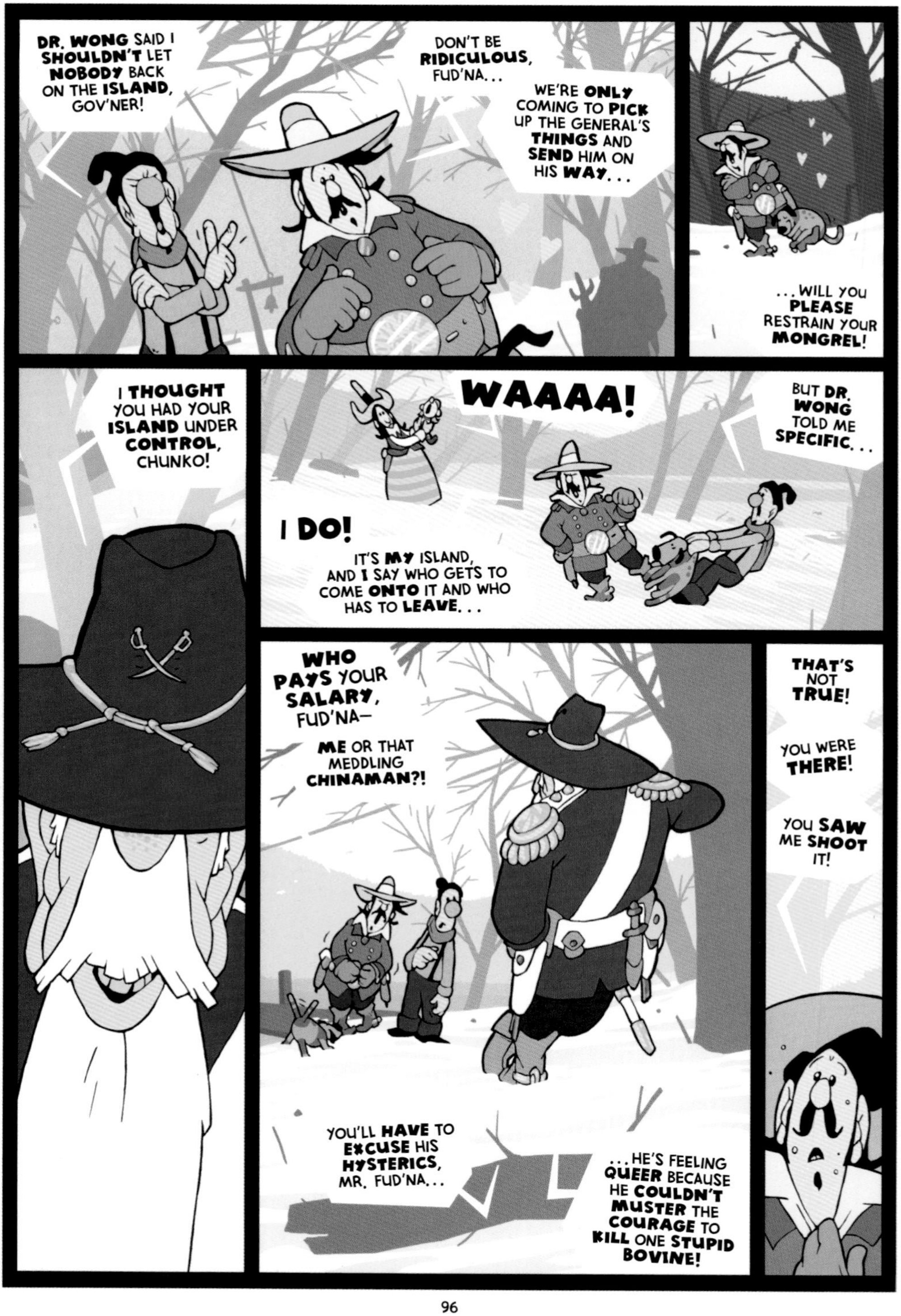

DR. WONG SAID I SHOULDN'T LET NOBODY BACK ON THE ISLAND, GOV'NER!
DON'T BE RIDICULOUS, FUD'NA...
WE'RE ONLY COMING TO PICK UP THE GENERAL'S THINGS AND SEND HIM ON HIS WAY...
...WILL YOU PLEASE RESTRAIN YOUR MONGREL!
I THOUGHT YOU HAD YOUR ISLAND UNDER CONTROL, CHUNKO!
WAAAA!
BUT DR. WONG TOLD ME SPECIFIC...
I DO!
IT'S MY ISLAND, AND I SAY WHO GETS TO COME ONTO IT AND WHO HAS TO LEAVE...
WHO PAYS YOUR SALARY, FUD'NA–
ME OR THAT MEDDLING CHINAMAN?!
YOU'LL HAVE TO EXCUSE HIS HYSTERICS, MR. FUD'NA...
...HE'S FEELING QUEER BECAUSE HE COULDN'T MUSTER THE COURAGE TO KILL ONE STUPID BOVINE!
THAT'S NOT TRUE!
YOU WERE THERE!
YOU SAW ME SHOOT IT!

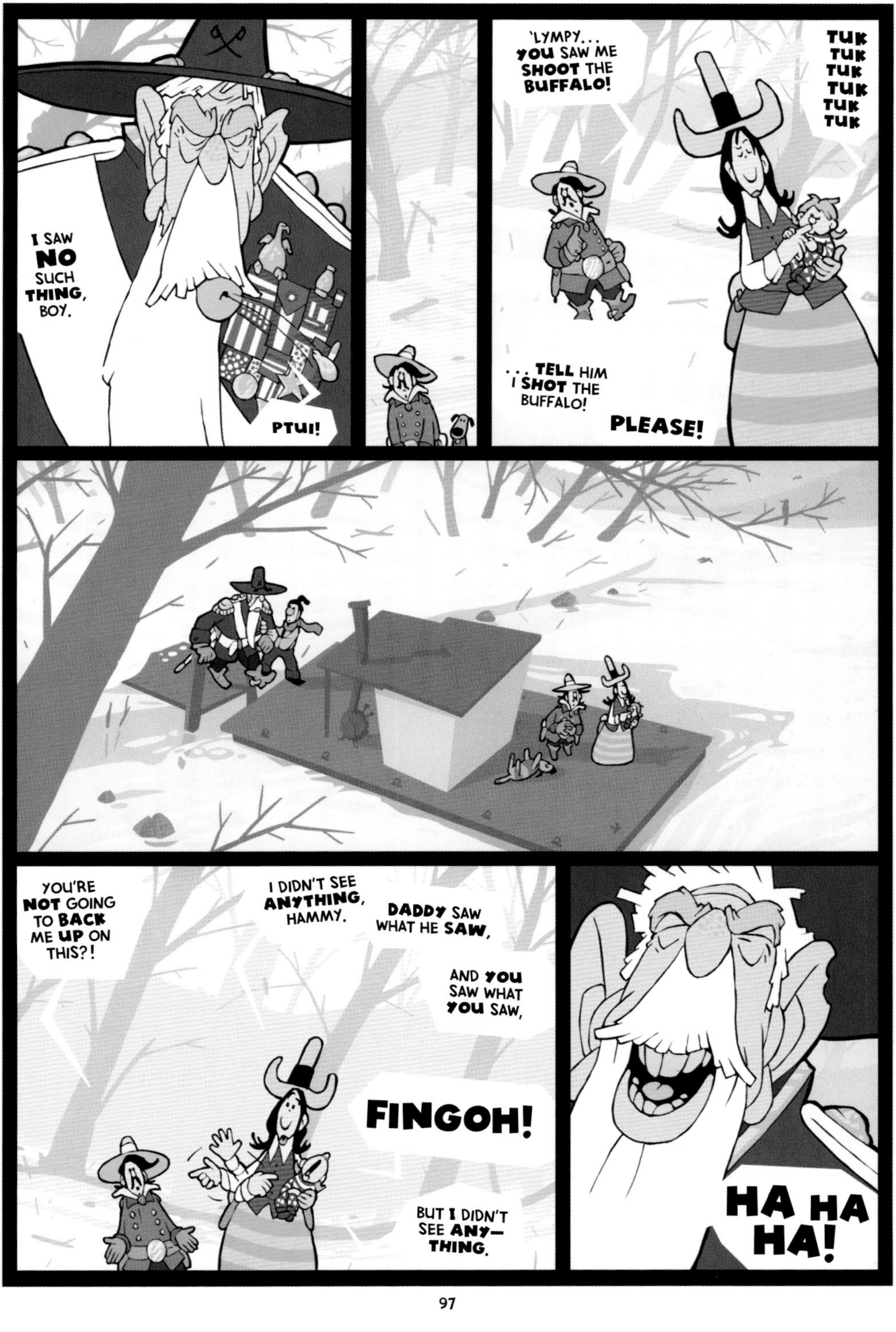

I SAW NO SUCH THING, BOY.
PTUI!
'LYMPY... YOU SAW ME SHOOT THE BUFFALO!
TUK TUK TUK TUK TUK TUK
...TELL HIM I SHOT THE BUFFALO!
PLEASE!
YOU'RE NOT GOING TO BACK ME UP ON THIS?!
I DIDN'T SEE ANYTHING, HAMMY.
DADDY SAW WHAT HE SAW,
AND YOU SAW WHAT YOU SAW,
FINGOH!
BUT I DIDN'T SEE ANY-THING.
HA HA HA!

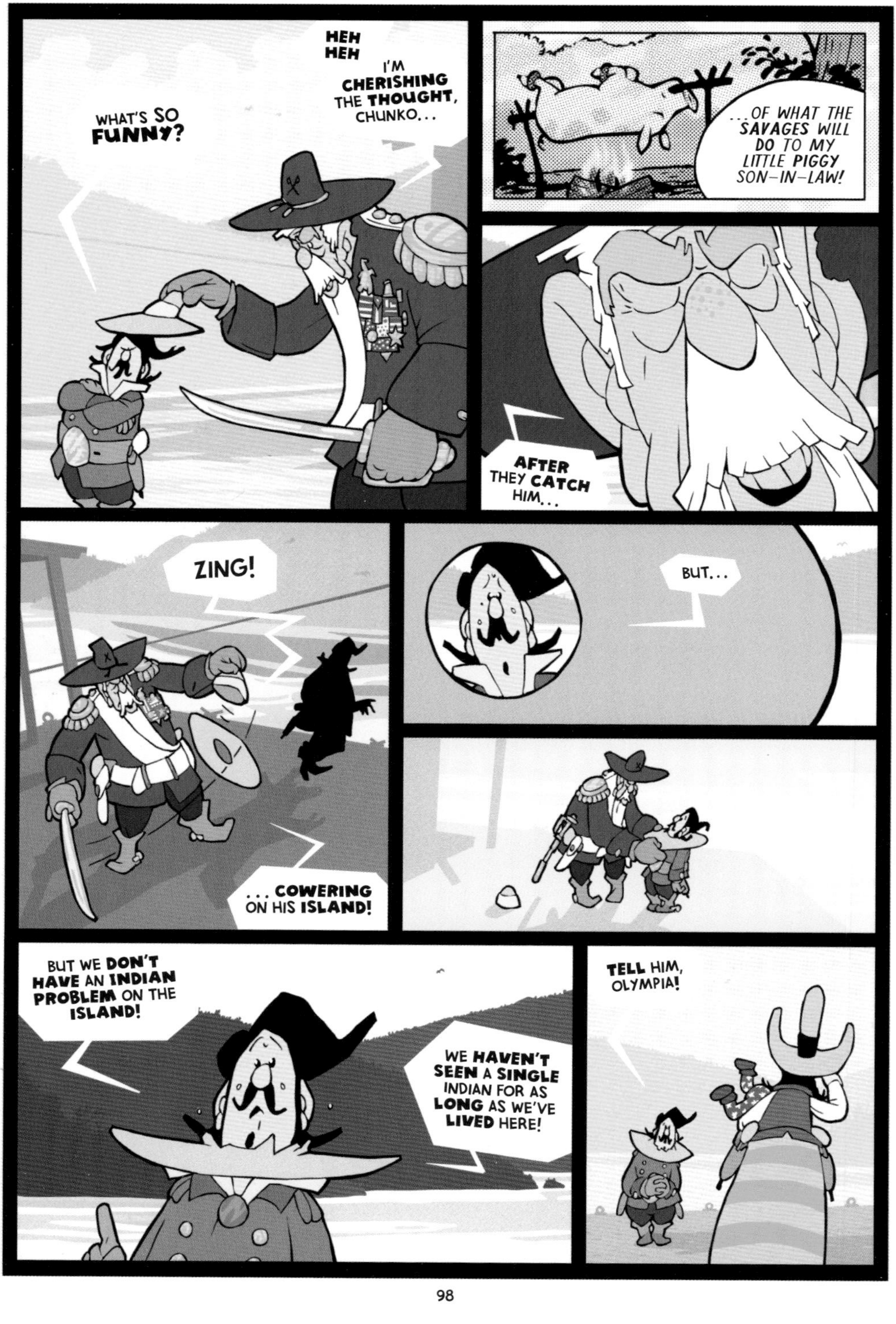
WHAT'S SO FUNNY?
HEH HEH
I'M CHERISHING THE THOUGHT, CHUNKO...
...OF WHAT THE SAVAGES WILL DO TO MY LITTLE PIGGY SON-IN-LAW!
AFTER THEY CATCH HIM...
ZING!
...COWERING ON HIS ISLAND!
BUT...
BUT WE DON'T HAVE AN INDIAN PROBLEM ON THE ISLAND!
WE HAVEN'T SEEN A SINGLE INDIAN FOR AS LONG AS WE'VE LIVED HERE!
TELL HIM, OLYMPIA!

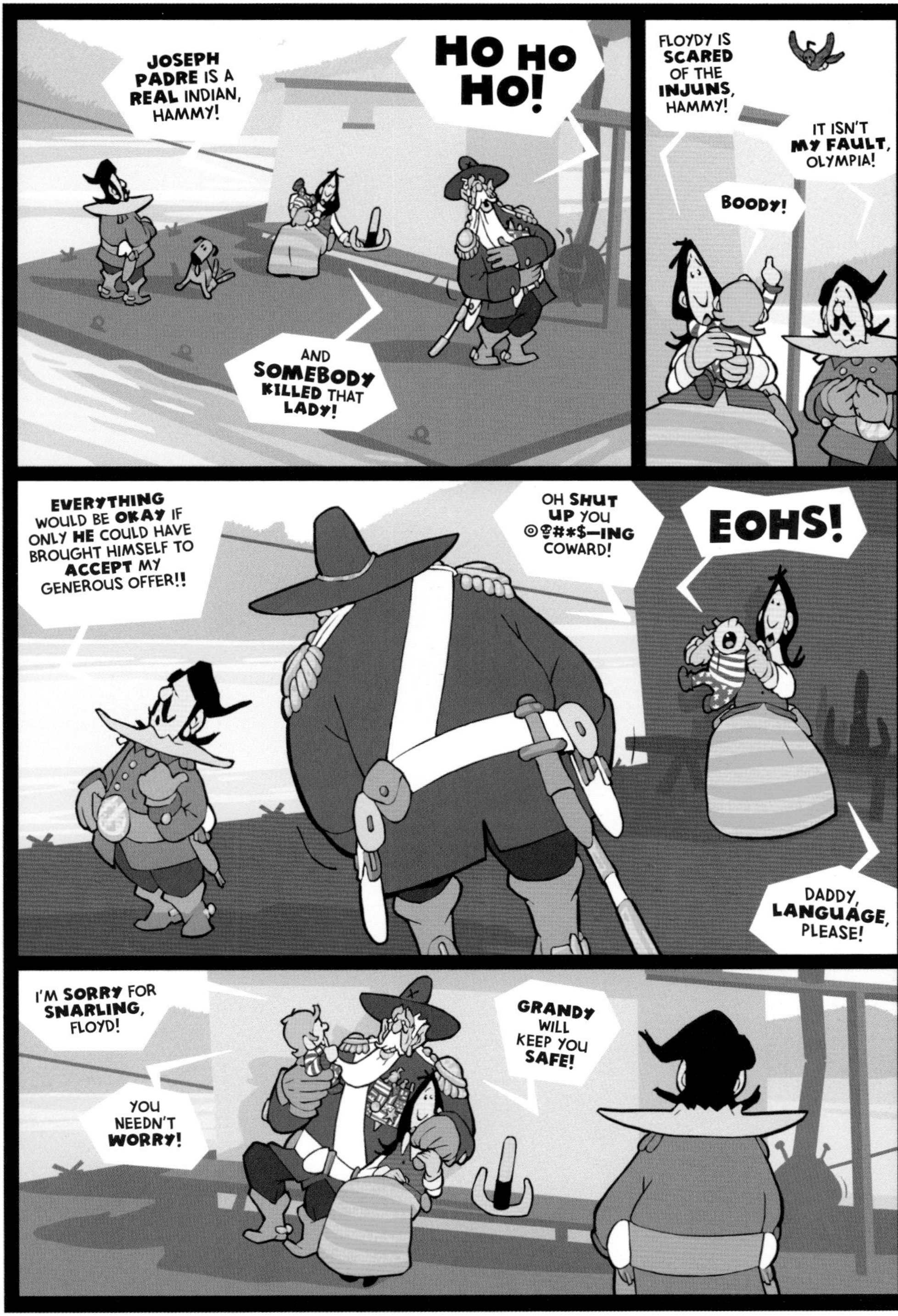

JOSEPH PADRE IS A REAL INDIAN, HAMMY!
HO HO HO!
AND SOMEBODY KILLED THAT LADY!
FLOYDY IS SCARED OF THE INJUNS, HAMMY!
IT ISN'T MY FAULT, OLYMPIA!
BOODY!
EVERYTHING WOULD BE OKAY IF ONLY HE COULD HAVE BROUGHT HIMSELF TO ACCEPT MY GENEROUS OFFER!!
OH SHUT UP YOU @☠#*$—ING COWARD!
EOHS!
DADDY, LANGUAGE, PLEASE!
I'M SORRY FOR SNARLING, FLOYD!
YOU NEEDN'T WORRY!
GRANDY WILL KEEP YOU SAFE!

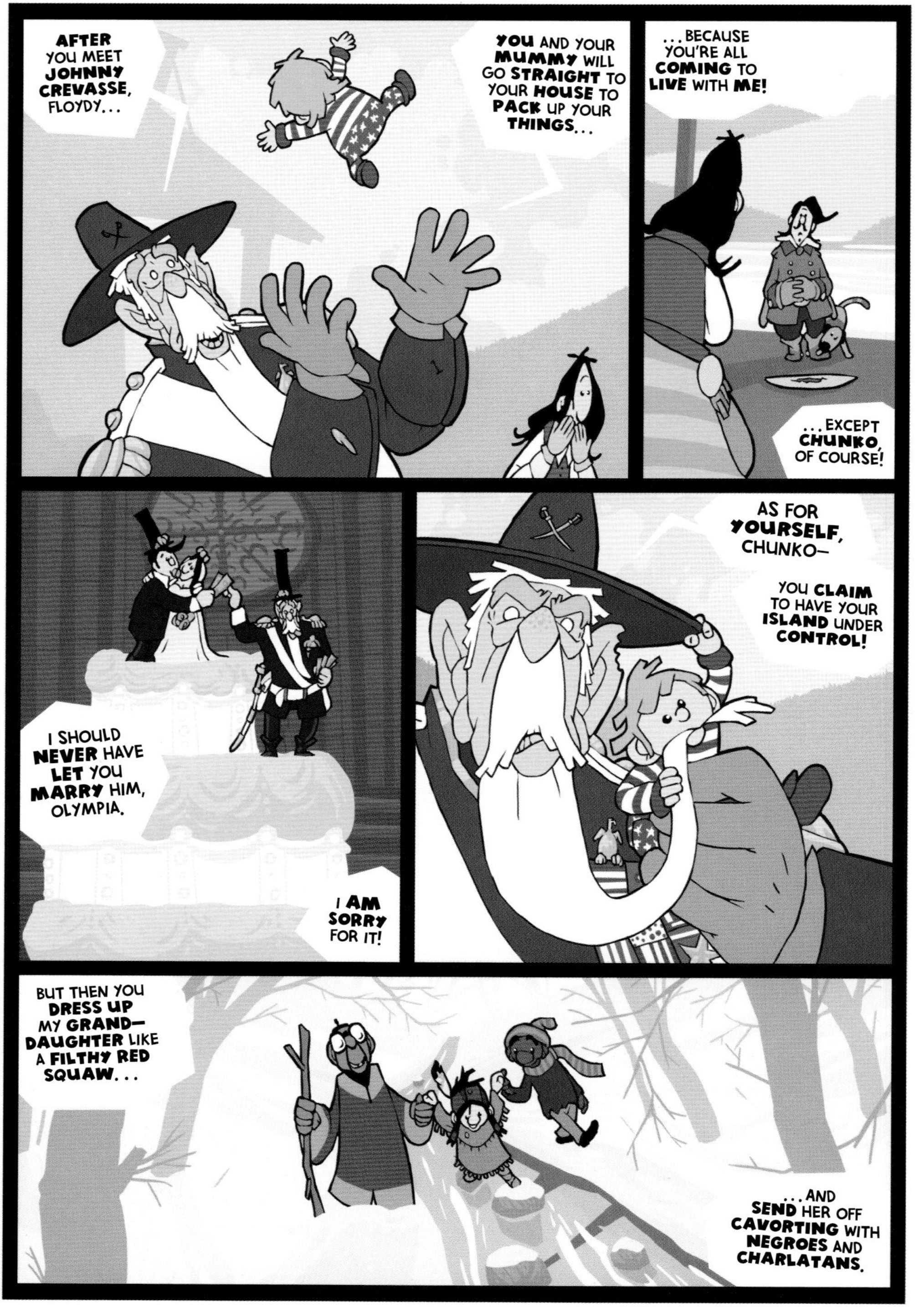
AFTER YOU MEET JOHNNY CREVASSE, FLOYDY...
YOU AND YOUR MUMMY WILL GO STRAIGHT TO YOUR HOUSE TO PACK UP YOUR THINGS...
...BECAUSE YOU'RE ALL COMING TO LIVE WITH ME!
...EXCEPT CHUNKO, OF COURSE!
I SHOULD NEVER HAVE LET YOU MARRY HIM, OLYMPIA.
I AM SORRY FOR IT!
AS FOR YOURSELF, CHUNKO—
YOU CLAIM TO HAVE YOUR ISLAND UNDER CONTROL!
BUT THEN YOU DRESS UP MY GRAND-DAUGHTER LIKE A FILTHY RED SQUAW...
...AND SEND HER OFF CAVORTING WITH NEGROES AND CHARLATANS.

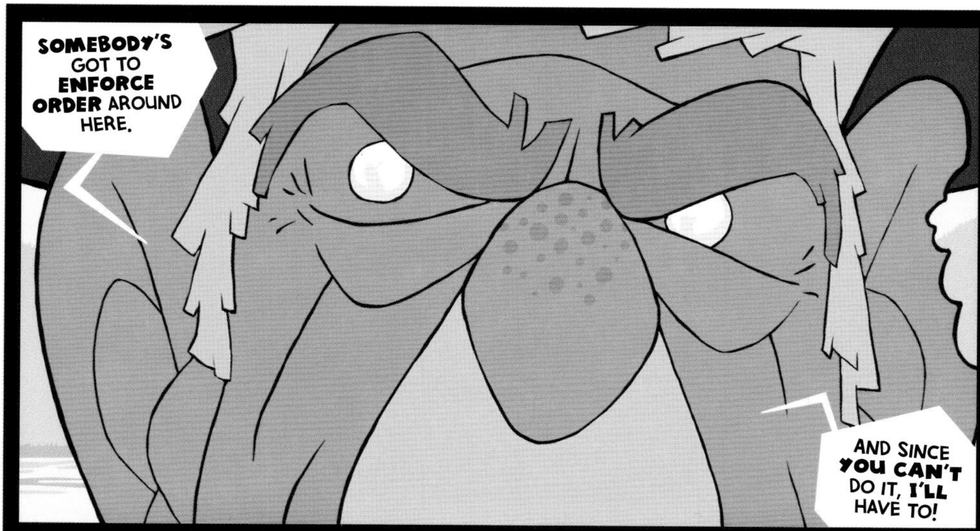
SOMEBODY'S GOT TO ENFORCE ORDER AROUND HERE.
AND SINCE YOU CAN'T DO IT, I'LL HAVE TO!

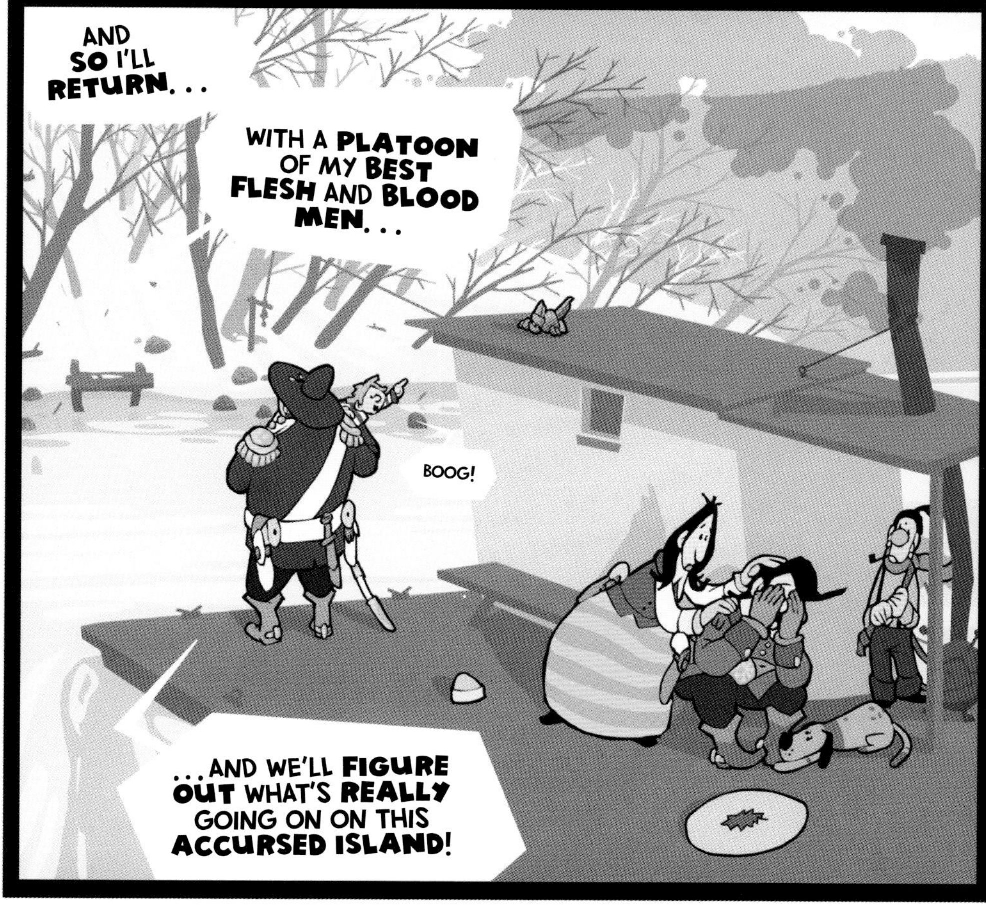
AND SO I'LL RETURN...
WITH A PLATOON OF MY BEST FLESH AND BLOOD MEN...
BOOG!
...AND WE'LL FIGURE OUT WHAT'S REALLY GOING ON ON THIS ACCURSED ISLAND!

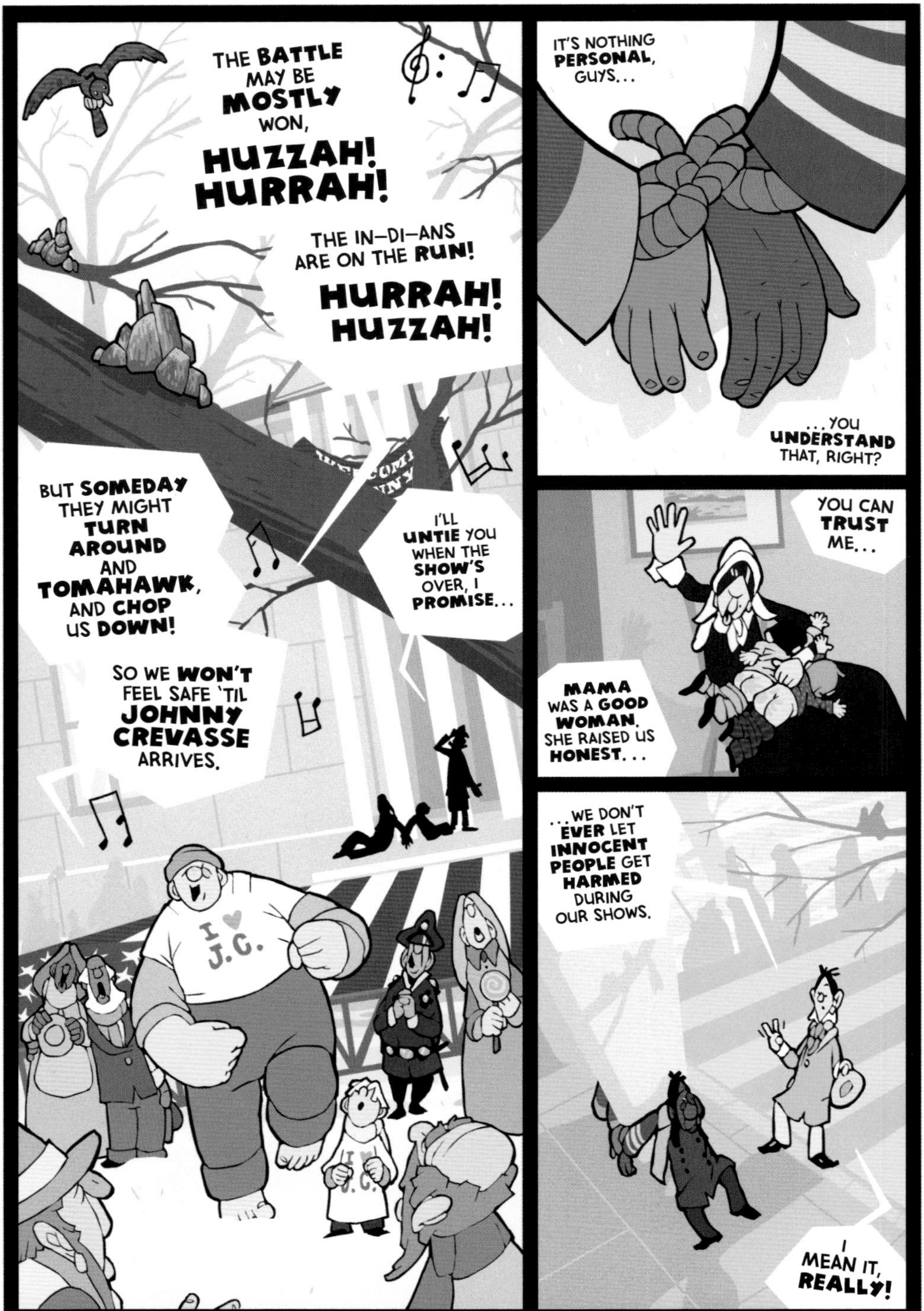
THE BATTLE MAY BE MOSTLY WON, HUZZAH! HURRAH!
THE IN-DI-ANS ARE ON THE RUN! HURRAH! HUZZAH!
BUT SOMEDAY THEY MIGHT TURN AROUND AND TOMAHAWK, AND CHOP US DOWN!
I'LL UNTIE YOU WHEN THE SHOW'S OVER, I PROMISE...
SO WE WON'T FEEL SAFE 'TIL JOHNNY CREVASSE ARRIVES.
I ♥ J.C.
I ♥ J.C.
IT'S NOTHING PERSONAL, GUYS...
...YOU UNDERSTAND THAT, RIGHT?
YOU CAN TRUST ME...
MAMA WAS A GOOD WOMAN. SHE RAISED US HONEST...
...WE DON'T EVER LET INNOCENT PEOPLE GET HARMED DURING OUR SHOWS.
I MEAN IT, REALLY!

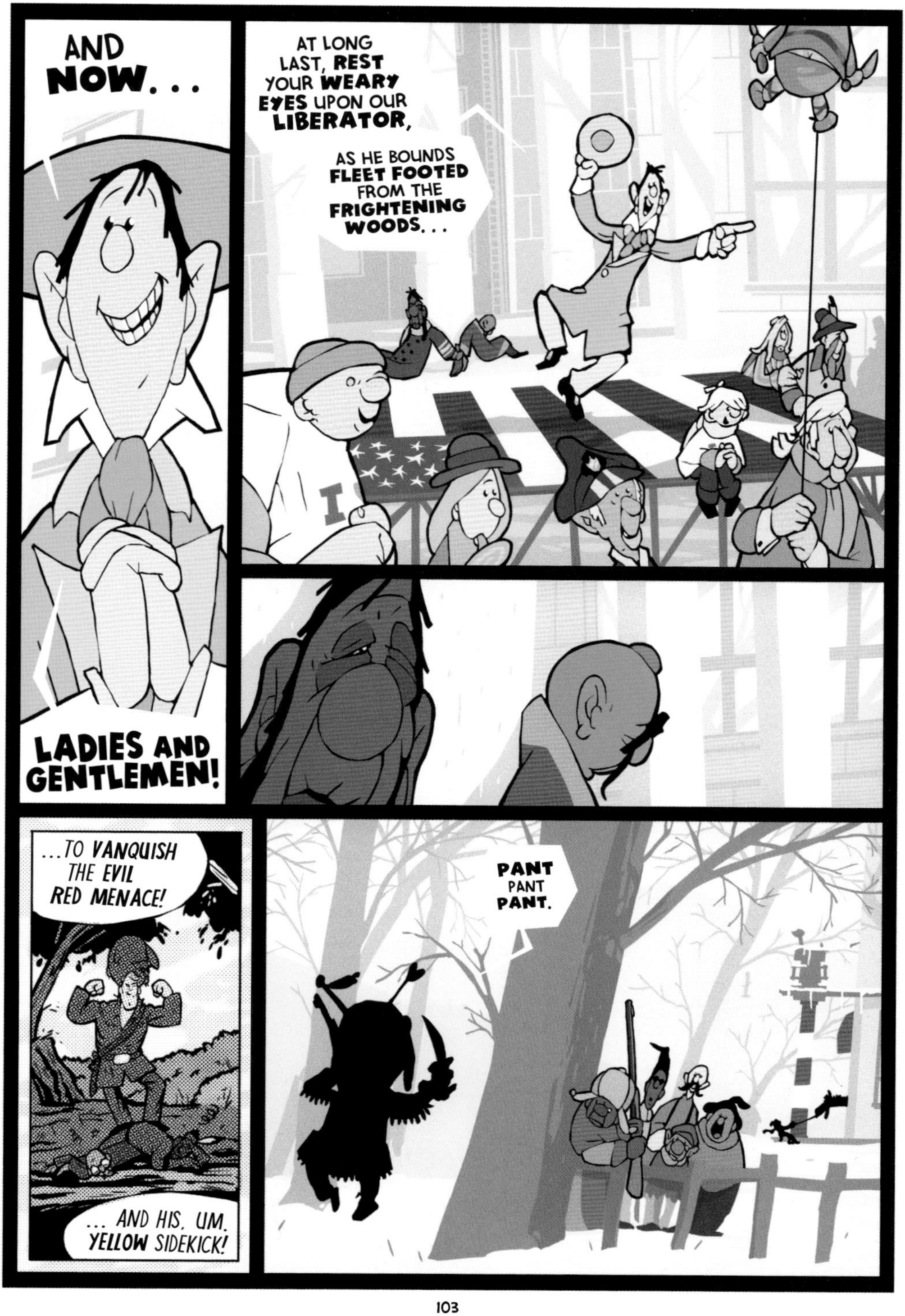
AND NOW. . .
LADIES AND GENTLEMEN!
AT LONG LAST, REST YOUR WEARY EYES UPON OUR LIBERATOR,
AS HE BOUNDS FLEET FOOTED FROM THE FRIGHTENING WOODS. . .
. . .TO VANQUISH THE EVIL RED MENACE!
. . . AND HIS, UM. YELLOW SIDEKICK!
PANT PANT PANT.

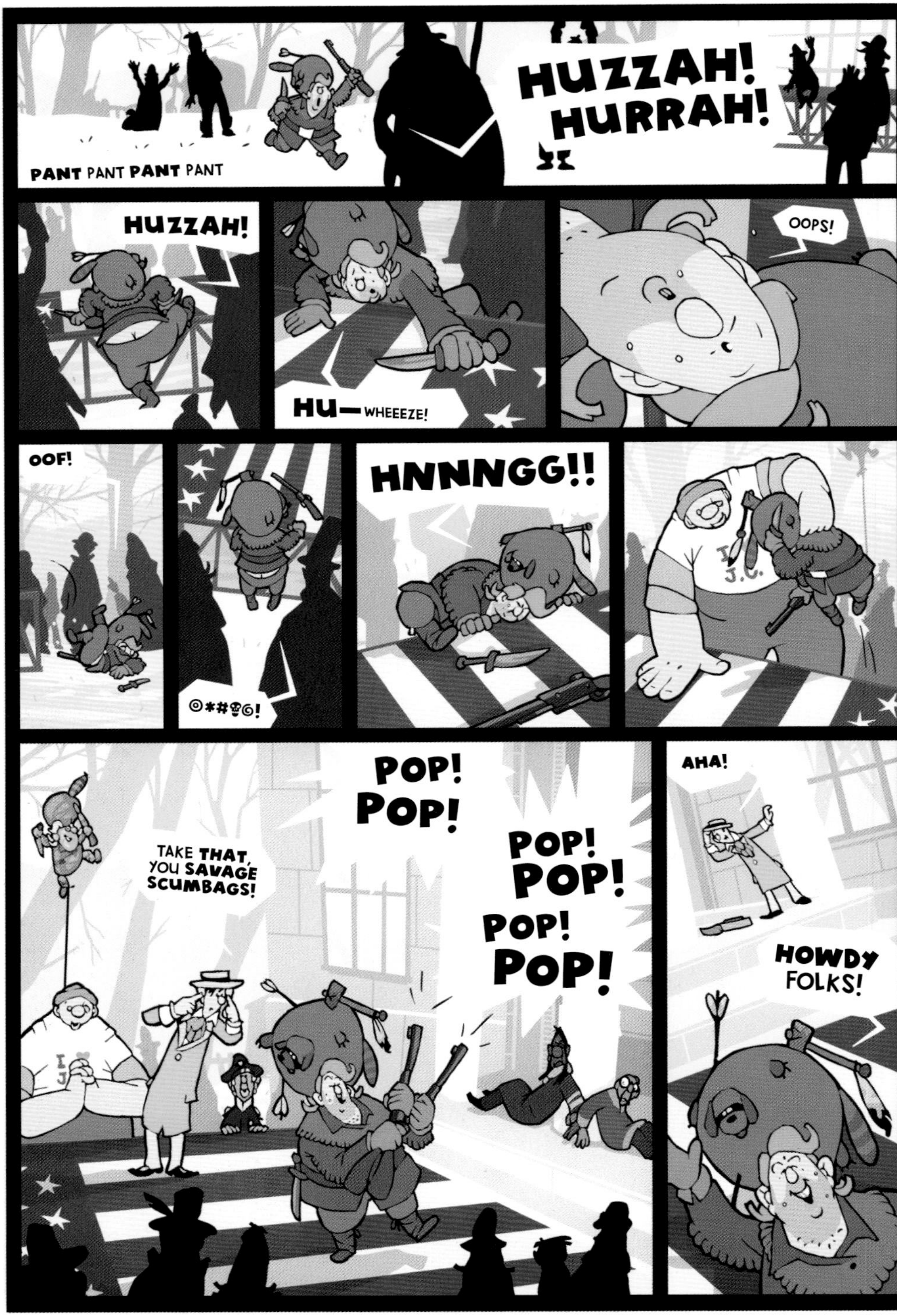
PANT PANT PANT PANT
HUZZAH! HURRAH!
HUZZAH!
HU— WHEEEZE!
OOPS!
OOF!
@*#☠@!
HNNNGG!!
TAKE THAT, YOU SAVAGE SCUMBAGS!
POP! POP!
POP! POP!
POP! POP!
AHA!
HOWDY FOLKS!

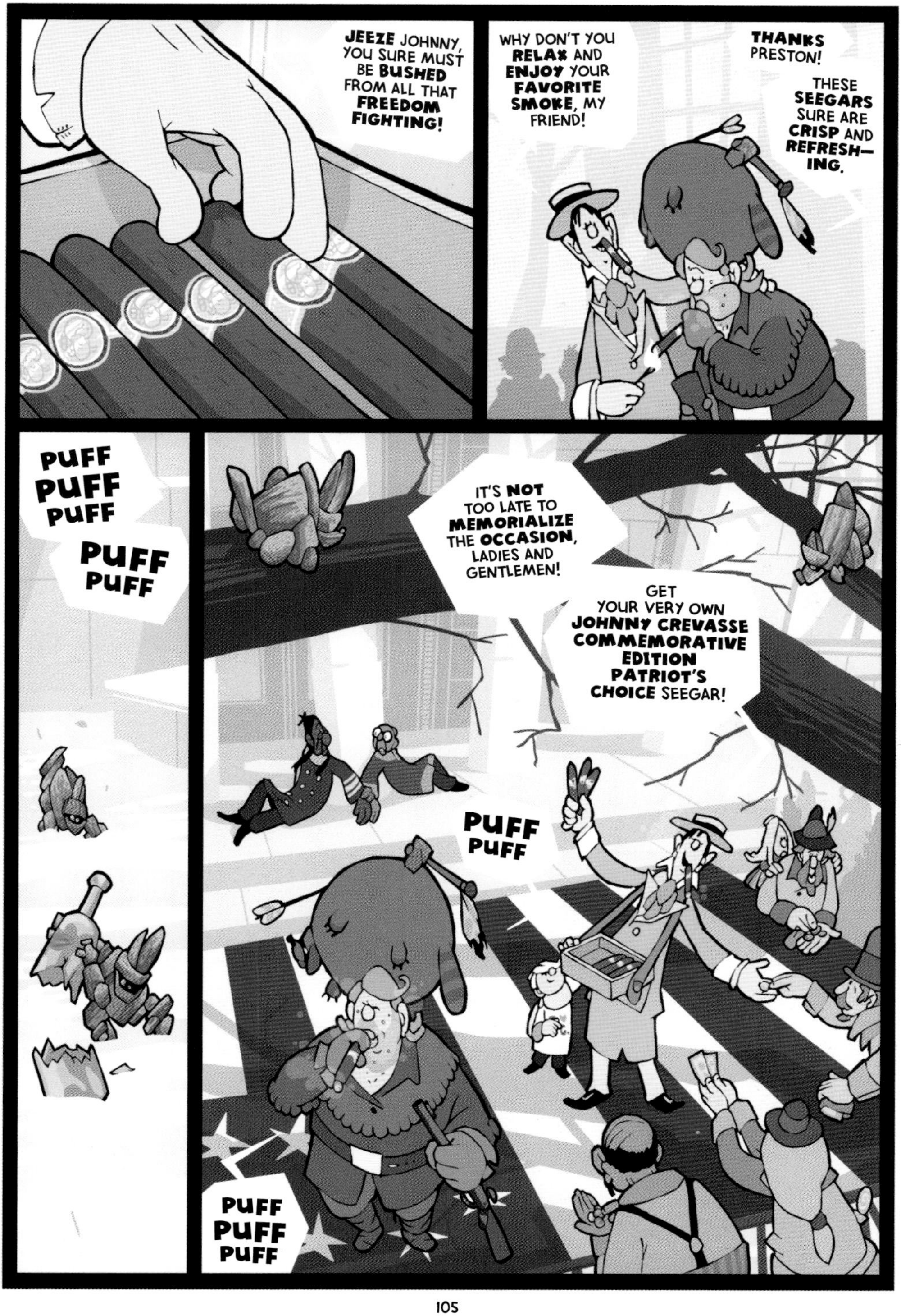
JEEZE JOHNNY, YOU SURE MUST BE BUSHED FROM ALL THAT FREEDOM FIGHTING!
WHY DON'T YOU RELAX AND ENJOY YOUR FAVORITE SMOKE, MY FRIEND!
THANKS PRESTON!
THESE SEEGARS SURE ARE CRISP AND REFRESH- ING.
PUFF PUFF PUFF
PUFF PUFF
IT'S NOT TOO LATE TO MEMORIALIZE THE OCCASION, LADIES AND GENTLEMEN!
GET YOUR VERY OWN JOHNNY CREVASSE COMMEMORATIVE EDITION PATRIOT'S CHOICE SEEGAR!
PUFF PUFF
PUFF PUFF PUFF

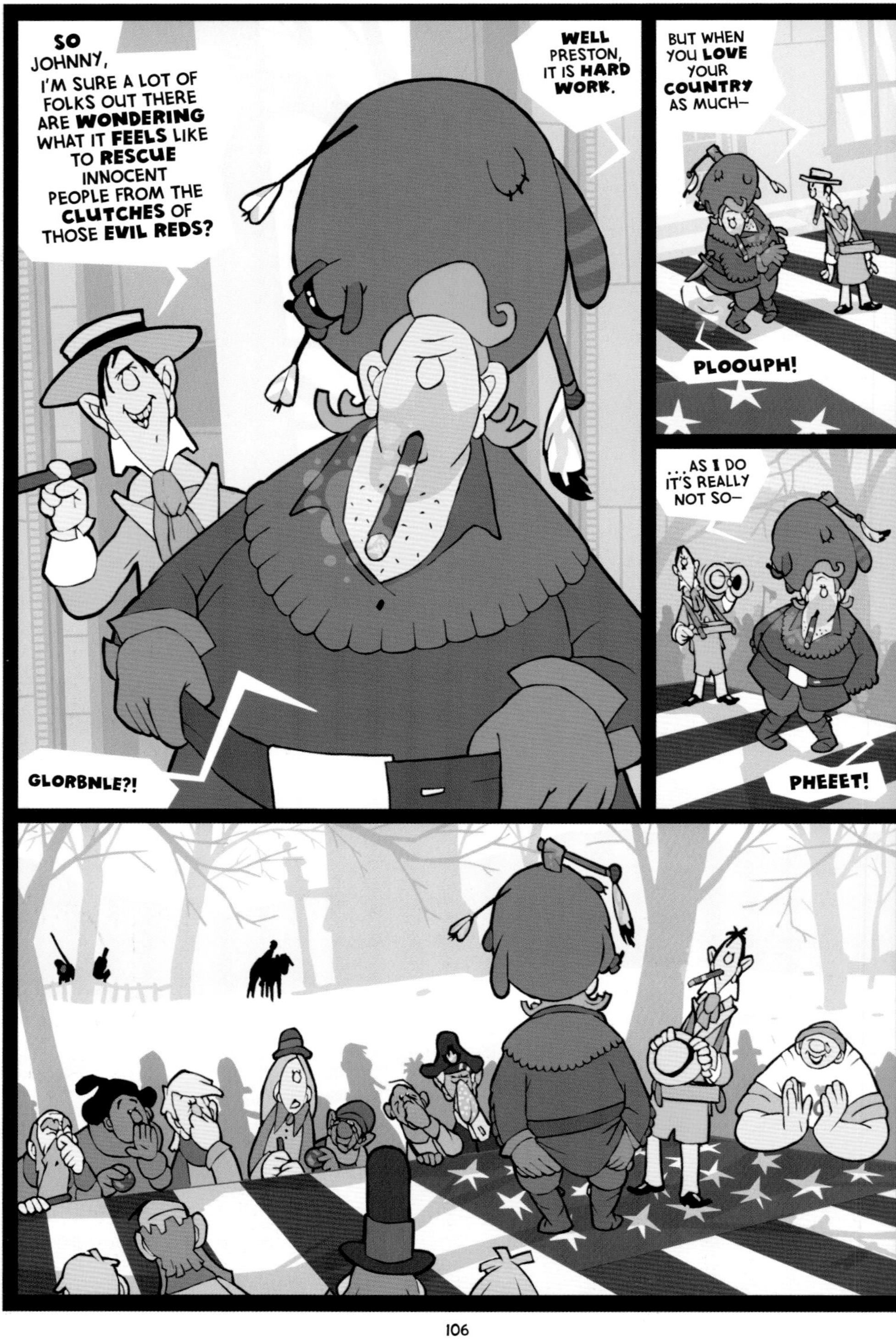
SO JOHNNY, I'M SURE A LOT OF FOLKS OUT THERE ARE WONDERING WHAT IT FEELS LIKE TO RESCUE INNOCENT PEOPLE FROM THE CLUTCHES OF THOSE EVIL REDS?
WELL PRESTON, IT IS HARD WORK.
GLORBNLE?!
BUT WHEN YOU LOVE YOUR COUNTRY AS MUCH–
PLOOUPH!
...AS I DO IT'S REALLY NOT SO–
PHEEET!

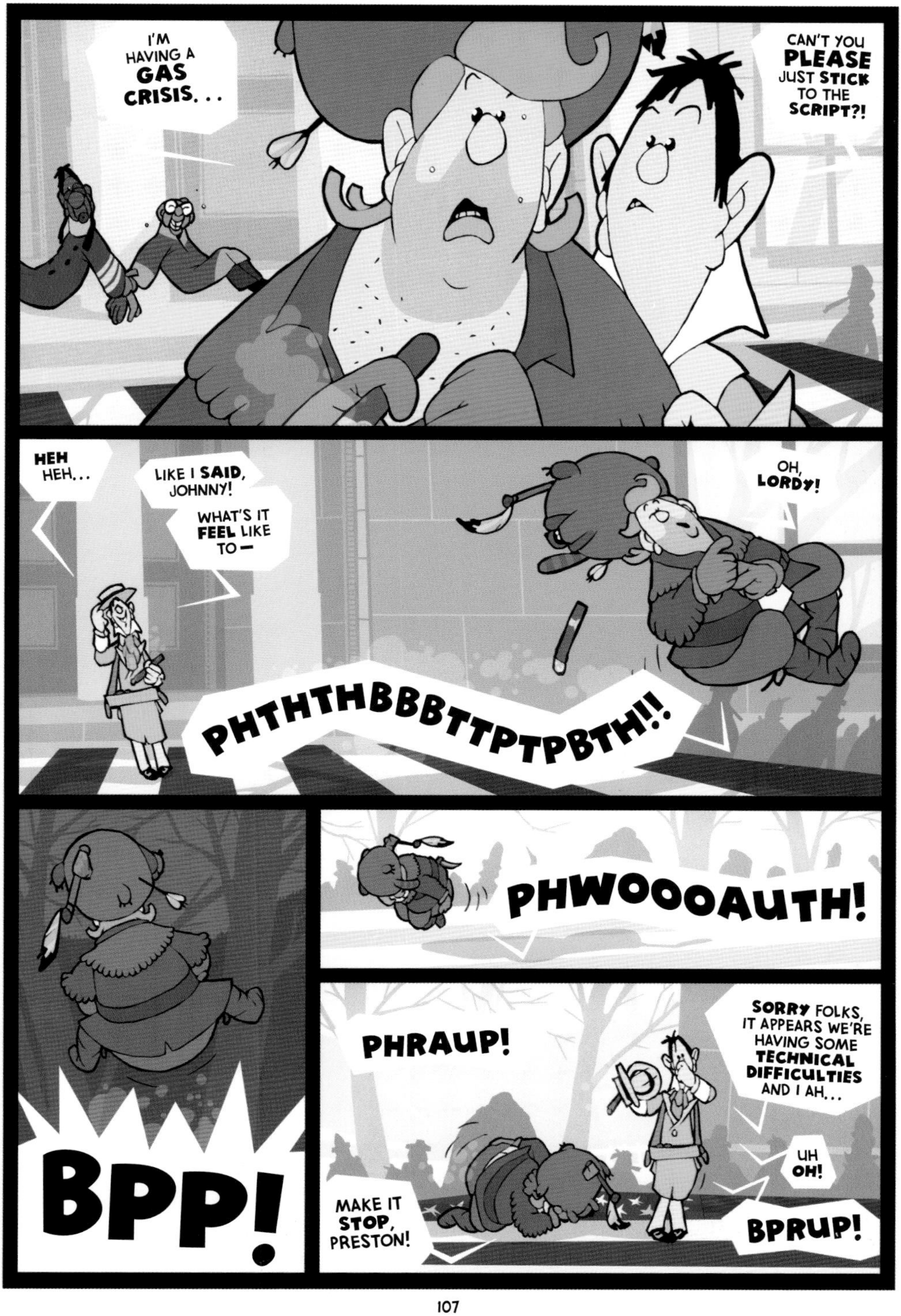
I'M HAVING A GAS CRISIS. . .
CAN'T YOU PLEASE JUST STICK TO THE SCRIPT?!
HEH HEH. . .
LIKE I SAID, JOHNNY!
WHAT'S IT FEEL LIKE TO—
OH, LORDY!
PHTHTHBBBTTPTPBTH!!
BPP!
PHWOOOAUTH!
PHRAUP!
SORRY FOLKS, IT APPEARS WE'RE HAVING SOME TECHNICAL DIFFICULTIES AND I AH. . .
UH OH!
MAKE IT STOP, PRESTON!
BPRUP!

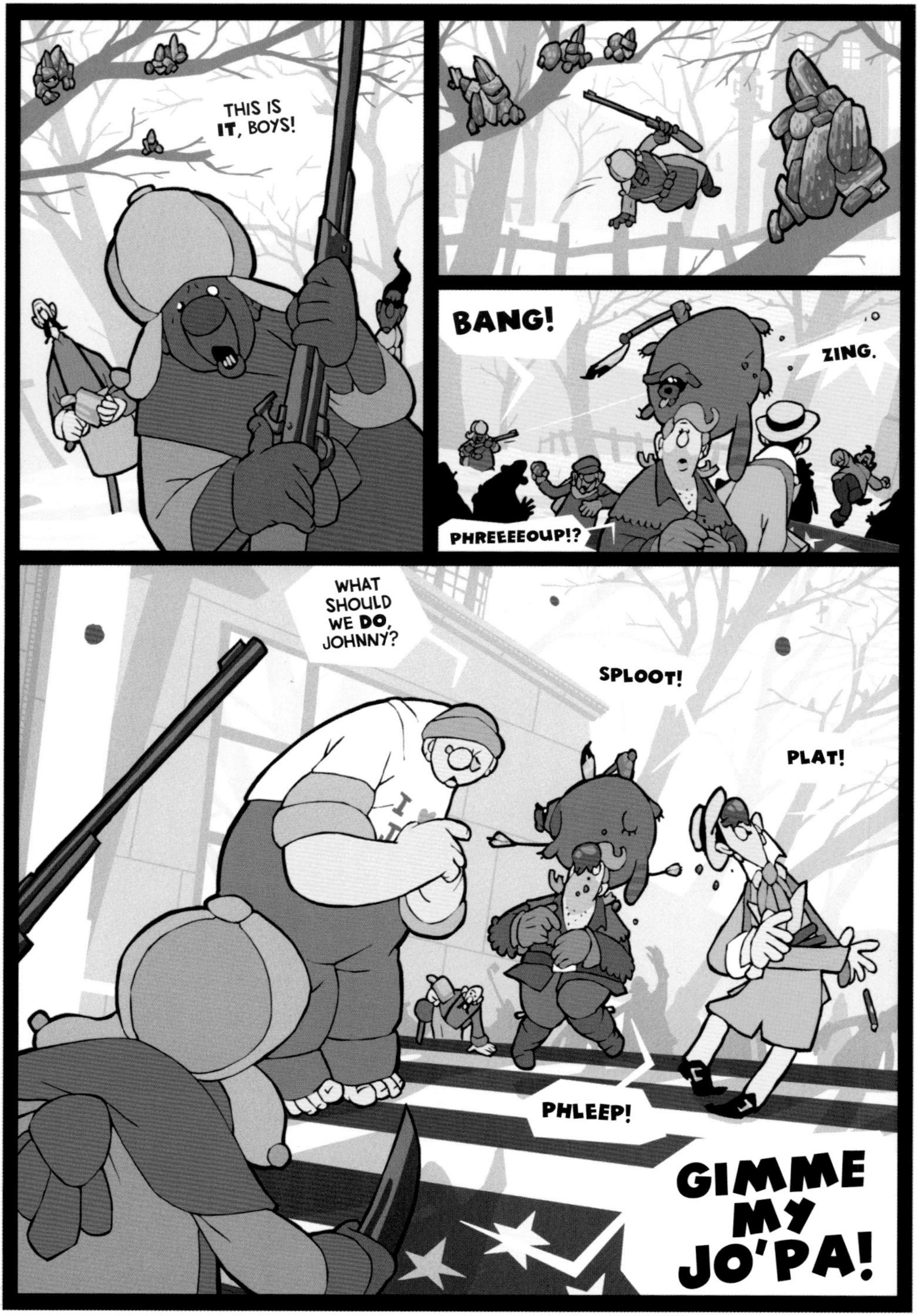
THIS IS IT, BOYS!
BANG!
ZING.
PHREEEEOUP!?
WHAT SHOULD WE DO, JOHNNY?
SPLOOT!
PLAT!
PHLEEP!
GIMME MY JO'PA!

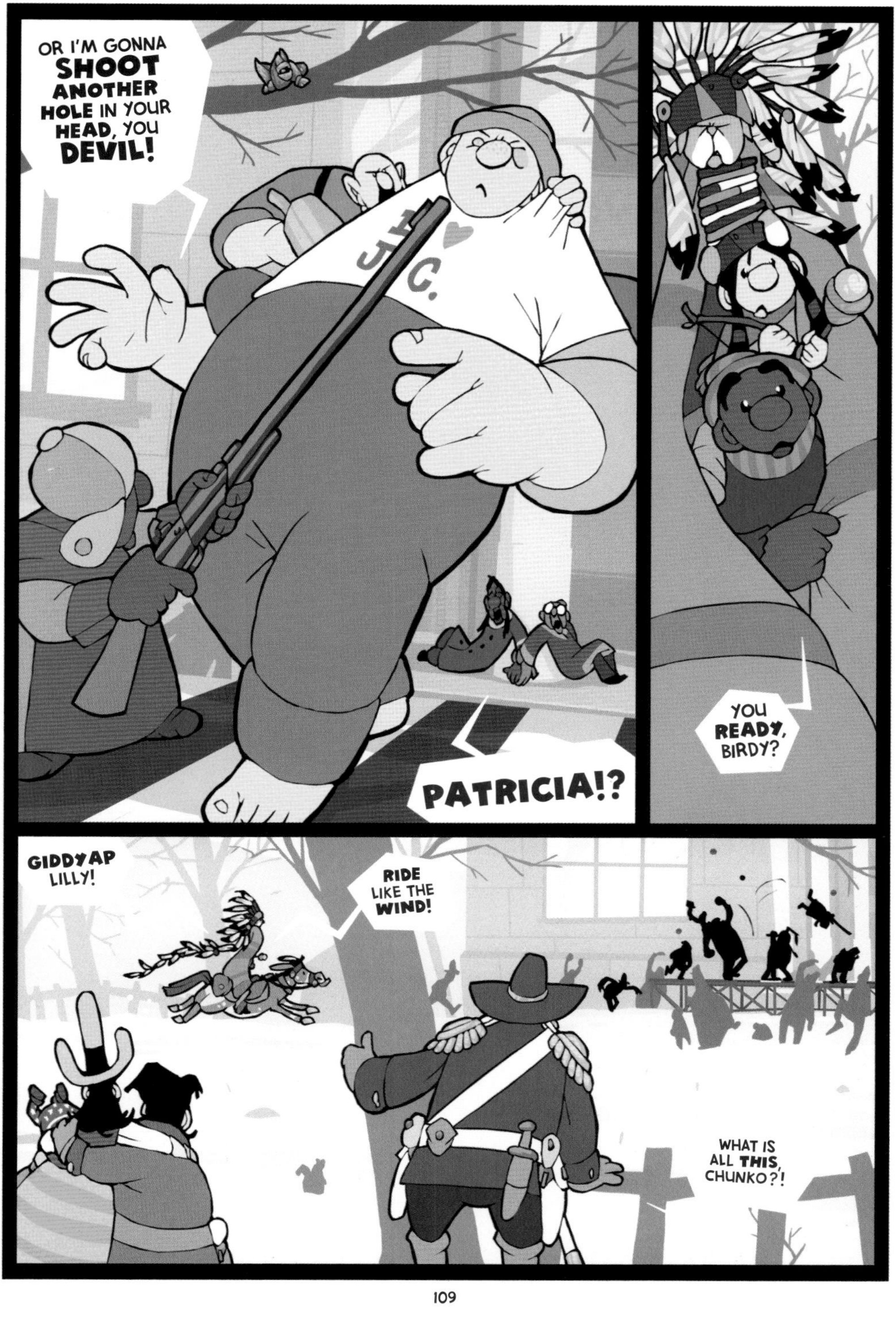
OR I'M GONNA SHOOT ANOTHER HOLE IN YOUR HEAD, YOU DEVIL!
PATRICIA!?
YOU READY, BIRDY?
GIDDYAP LILLY!
RIDE LIKE THE WIND!
WHAT IS ALL THIS, CHUNKO?!

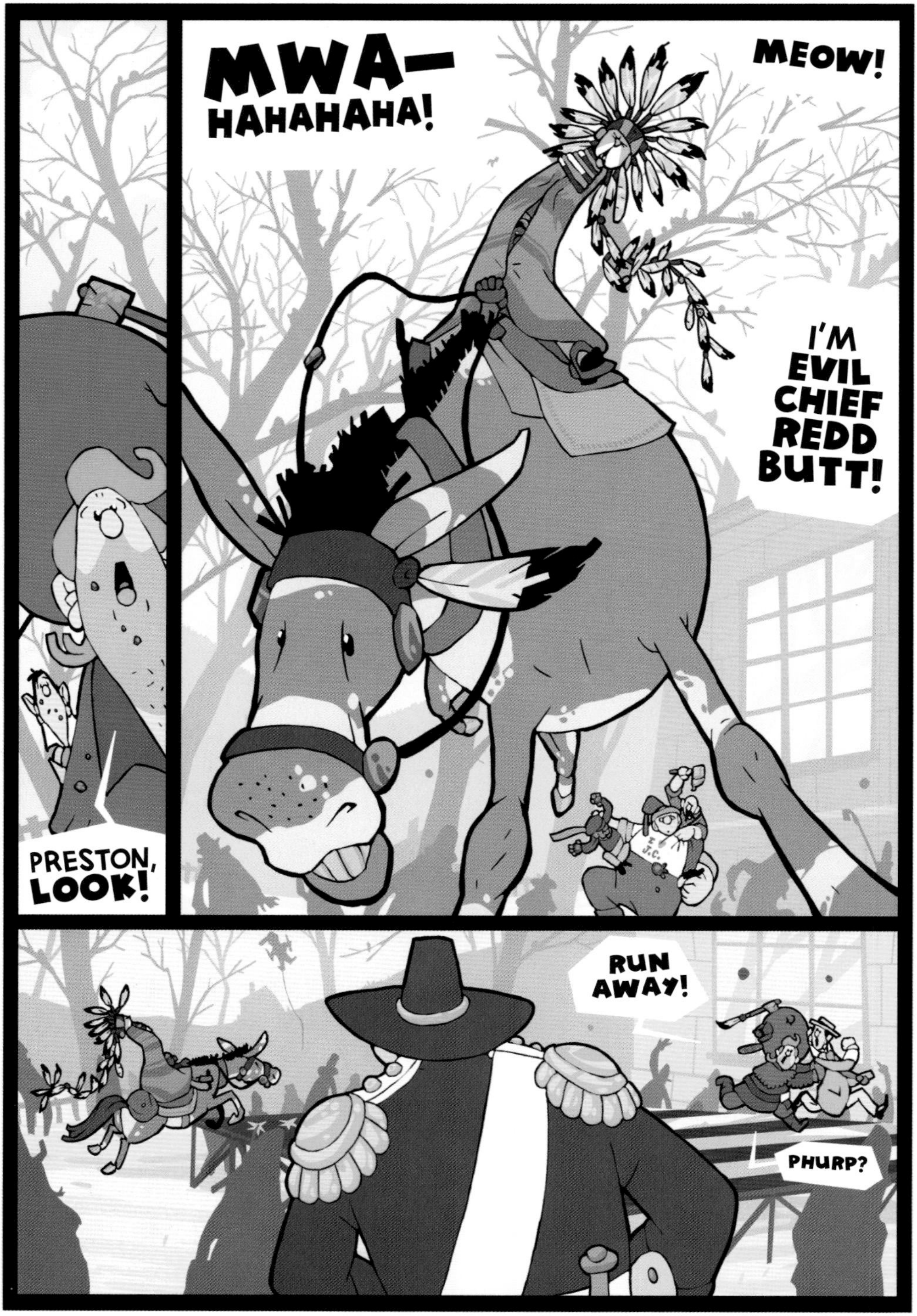
PRESTON, LOOK!
MWA-HAHAHAHA!
MEOW!
I'M EVIL CHIEF REDD BUTT!
RUN AWAY!
PHURP?

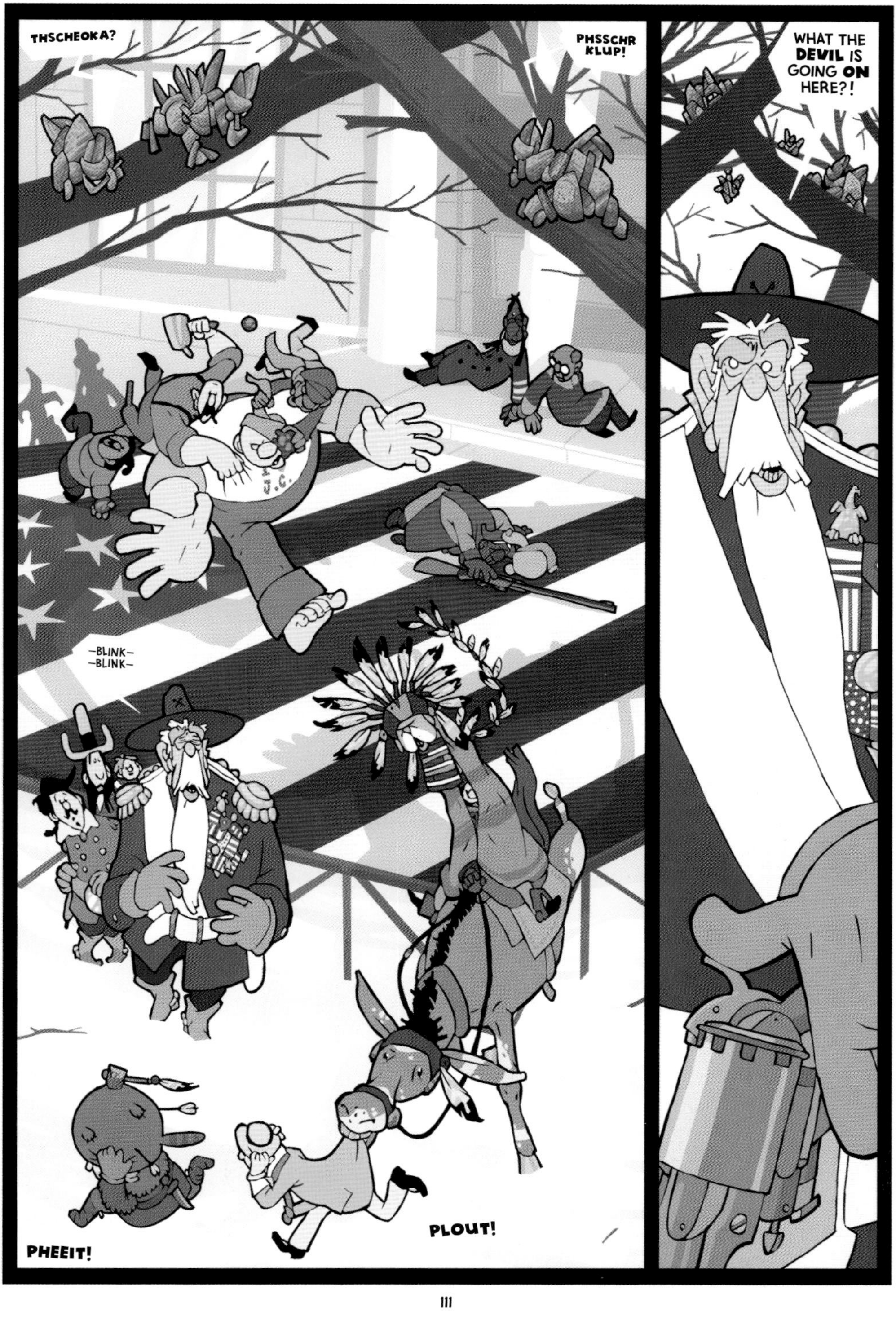
THSCHEOKA?
PHSSCHR KLUP!
-BLINK-
-BLINK-
PHEEIT!
PLOUT!
WHAT THE DEVIL IS GOING ON HERE?!

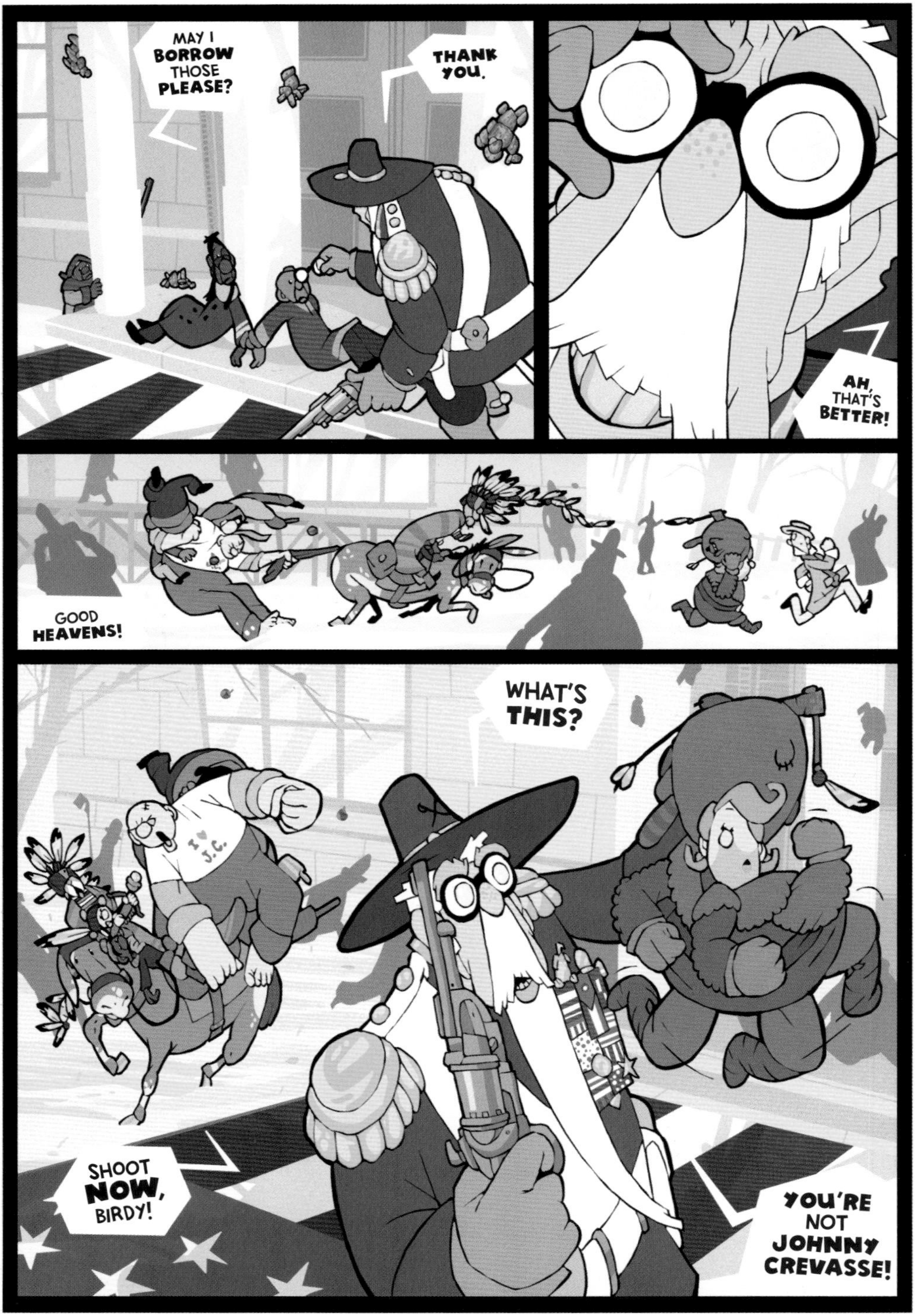
MAY I BORROW THOSE PLEASE?
THANK YOU.
AH, THAT'S BETTER!
GOOD HEAVENS!
WHAT'S THIS?
SHOOT NOW, BIRDY!
YOU'RE NOT JOHNNY CREVASSE!

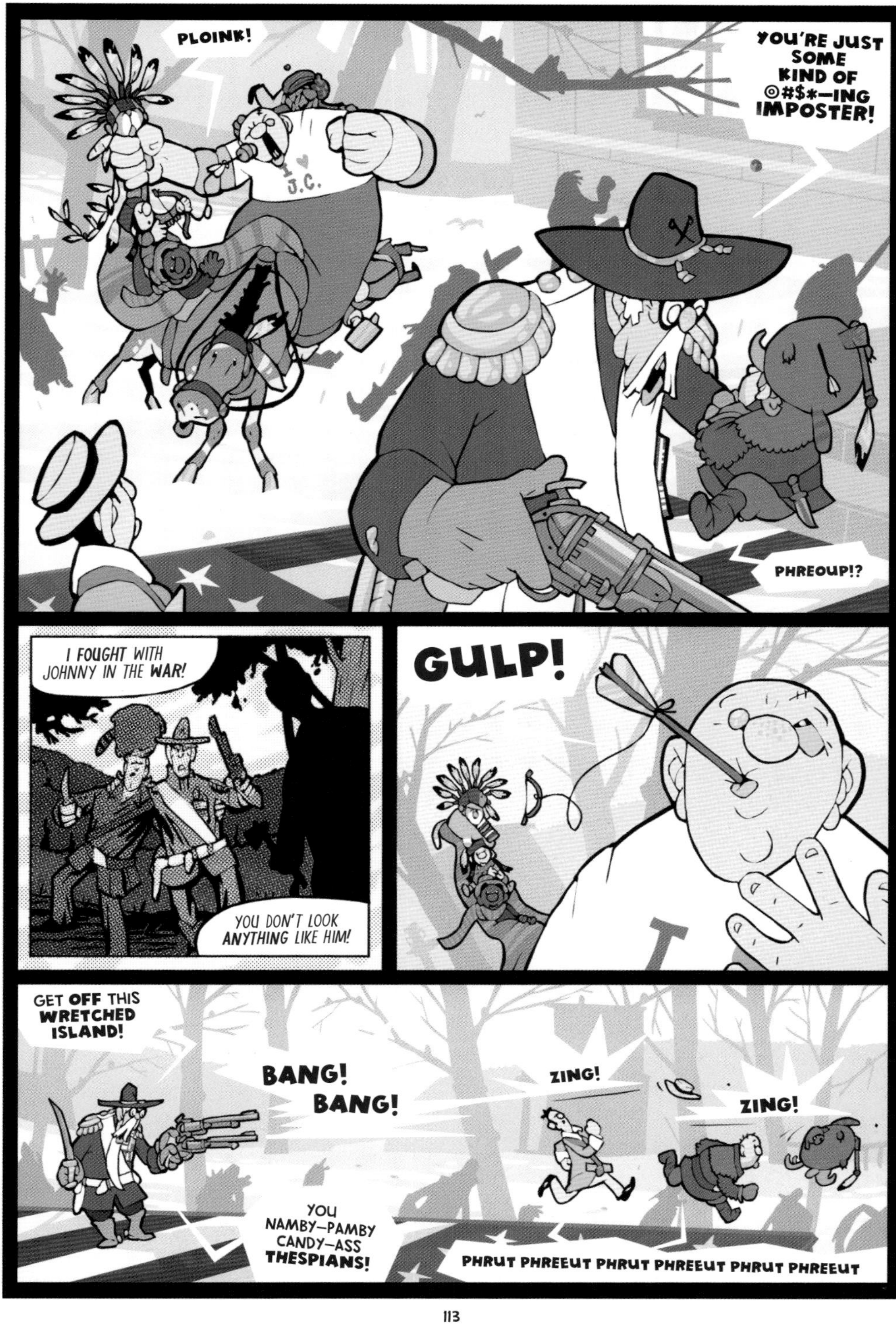

PLOINK!
YOU'RE JUST SOME KIND OF @#$*-ING IMPOSTER!
PHREOUP!?
I FOUGHT WITH JOHNNY IN THE WAR!
YOU DON'T LOOK ANYTHING LIKE HIM!
GULP!
GET OFF THIS WRETCHED ISLAND!
BANG! BANG!
ZING!
ZING!
YOU NAMBY-PAMBY CANDY-ASS THESPIANS!
PHRUT PHREEUT PHRUT PHREEUT PHRUT PHREEUT

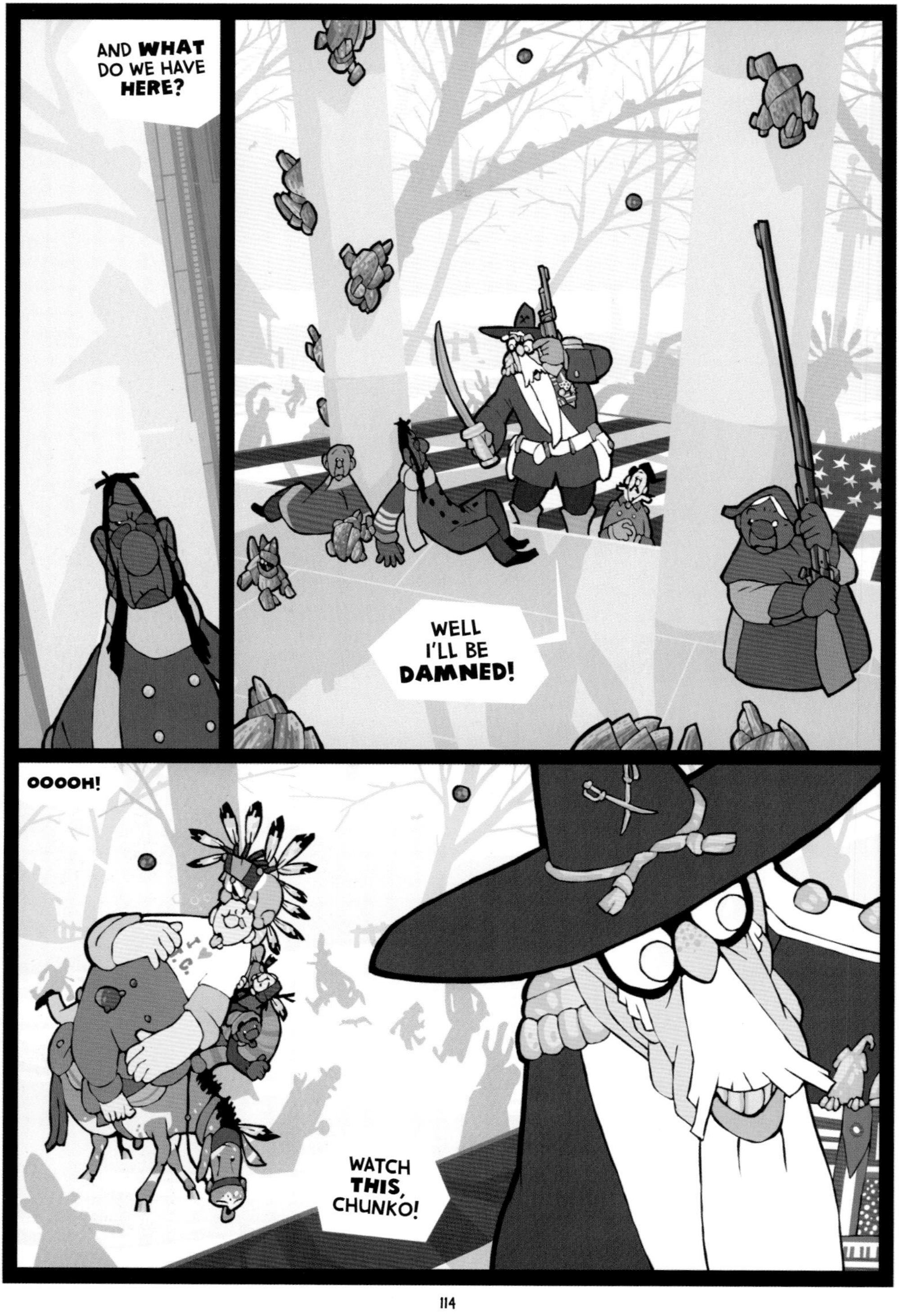
AND **WHAT** DO WE HAVE **HERE?**
WELL I'LL BE **DAMNED!**
OOOOH!
WATCH **THIS,** CHUNKO!

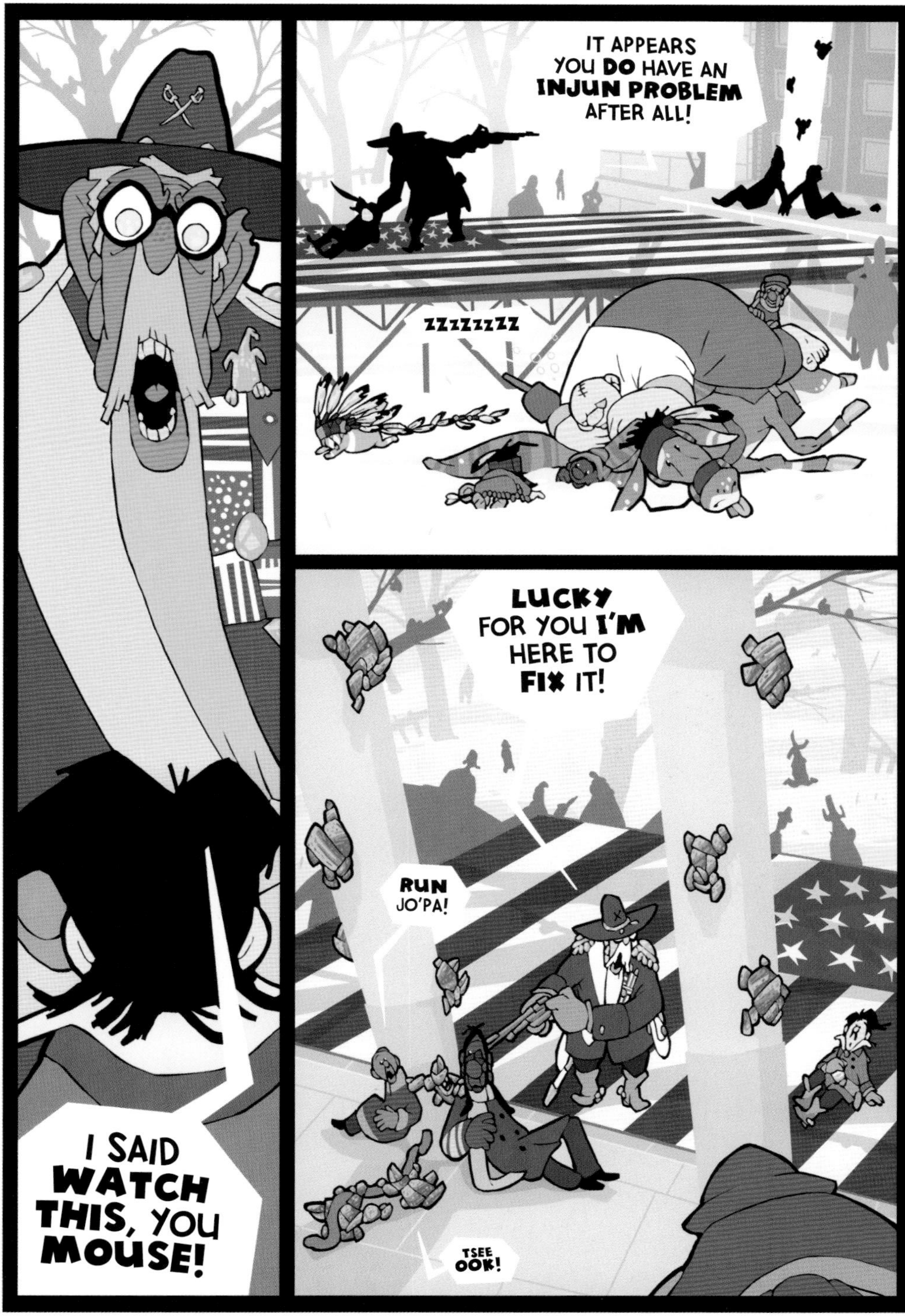

I SAID WATCH THIS, YOU MOUSE!
IT APPEARS YOU DO HAVE AN INJUN PROBLEM AFTER ALL!
ZZZZZZZZ
LUCKY FOR YOU I'M HERE TO FIX IT!
RUN JO'PA!
TSEE OOK!

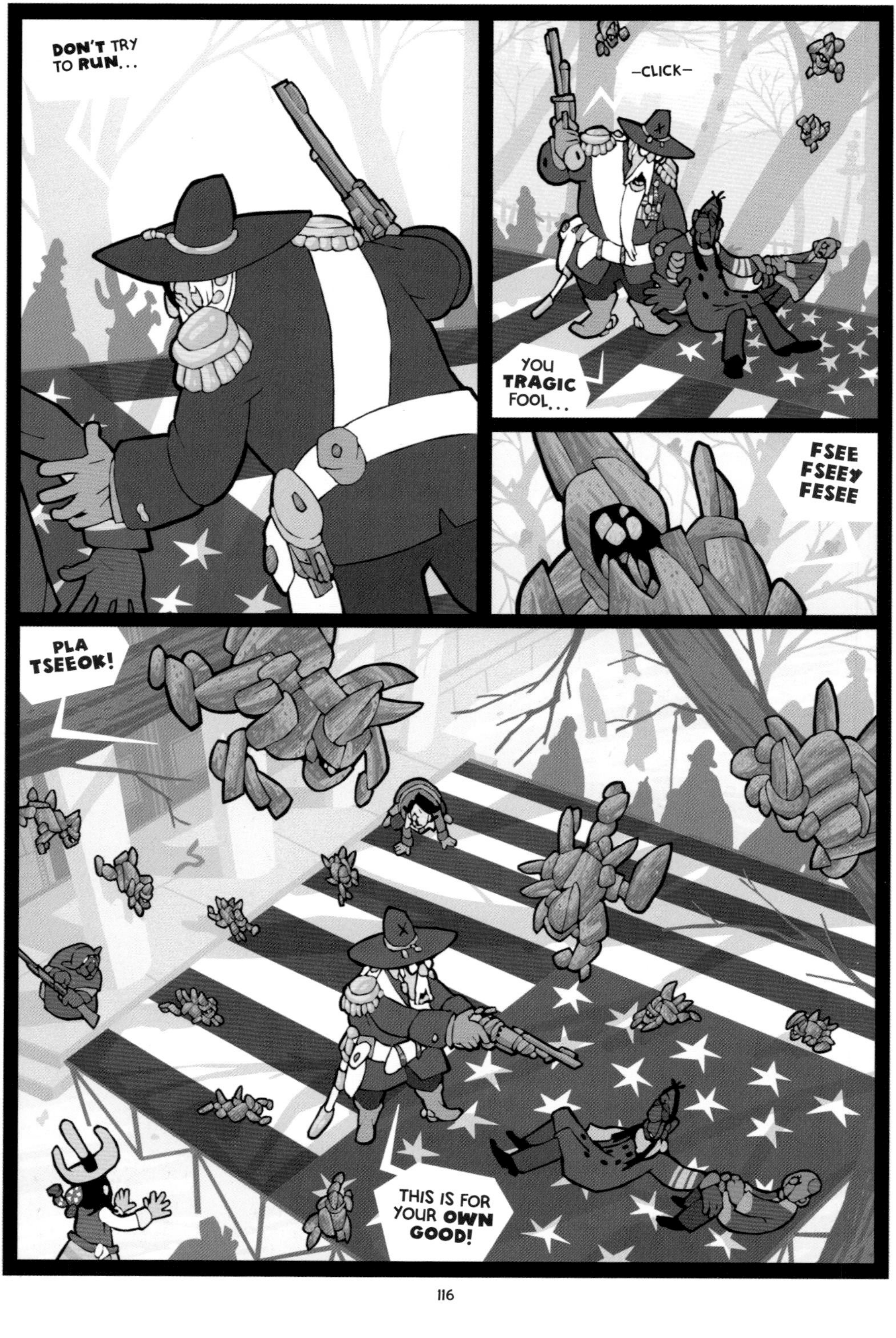
DON'T TRY TO RUN...
—CLICK—
YOU TRAGIC FOOL...
FSEE FSEEY FESEE
PLA TSEEOK!
THIS IS FOR YOUR OWN GOOD!

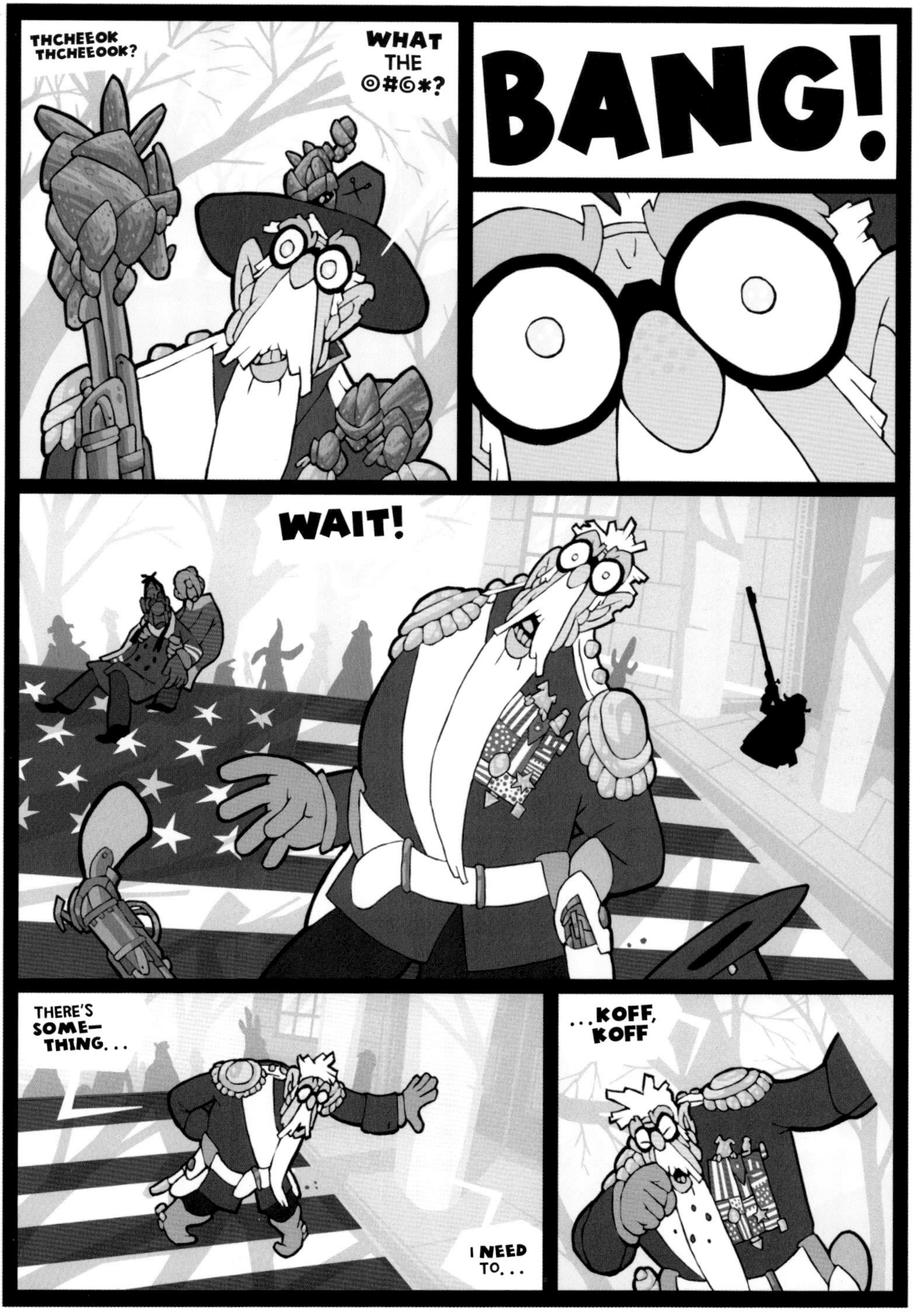

THCHEEOK THCHEEOOK?
WHAT THE ◎#⑥*?
BANG!
WAIT!
THERE'S SOME—THING...
I NEED TO...
...KOFF, KOFF

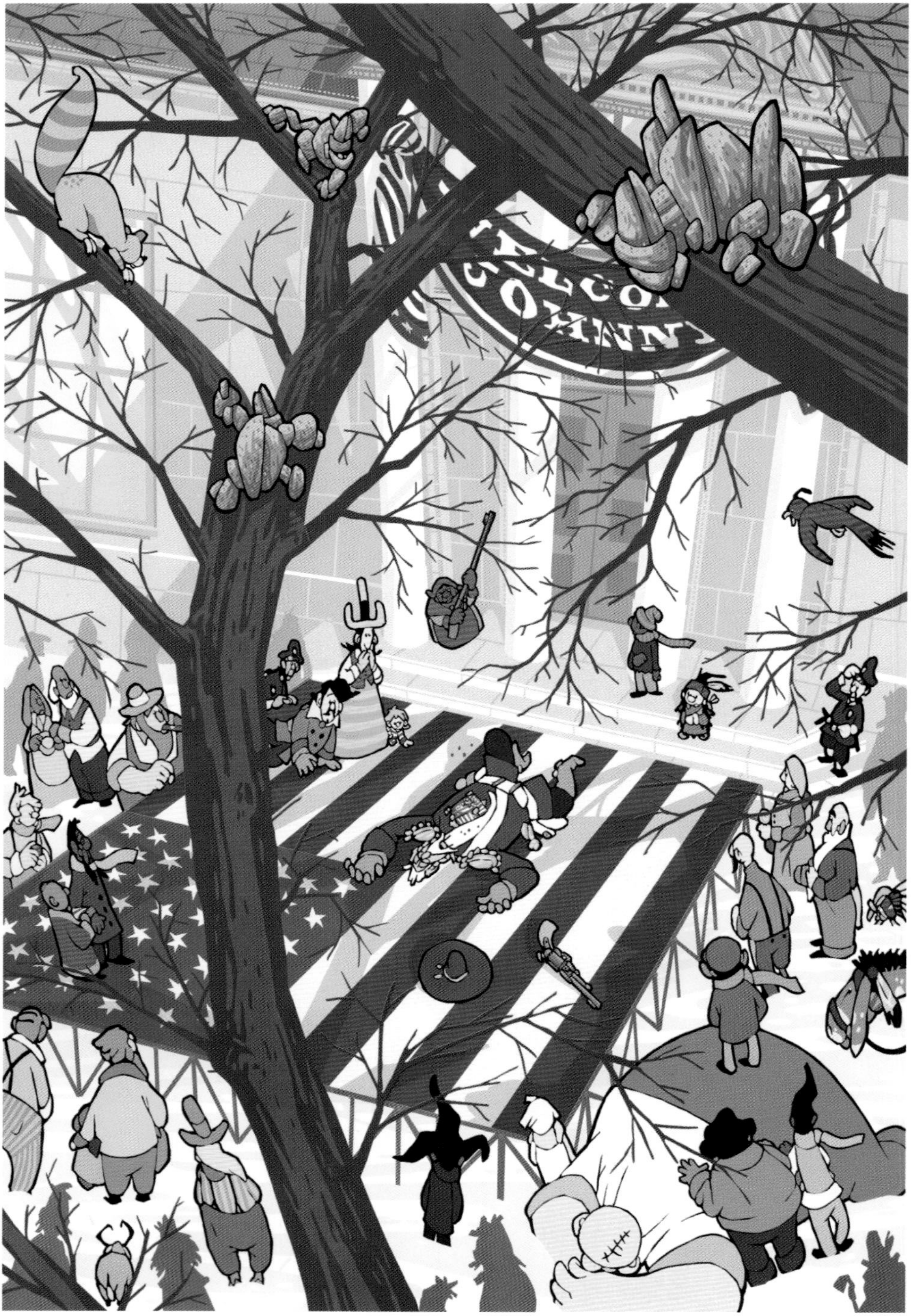

To be CONTINUED...

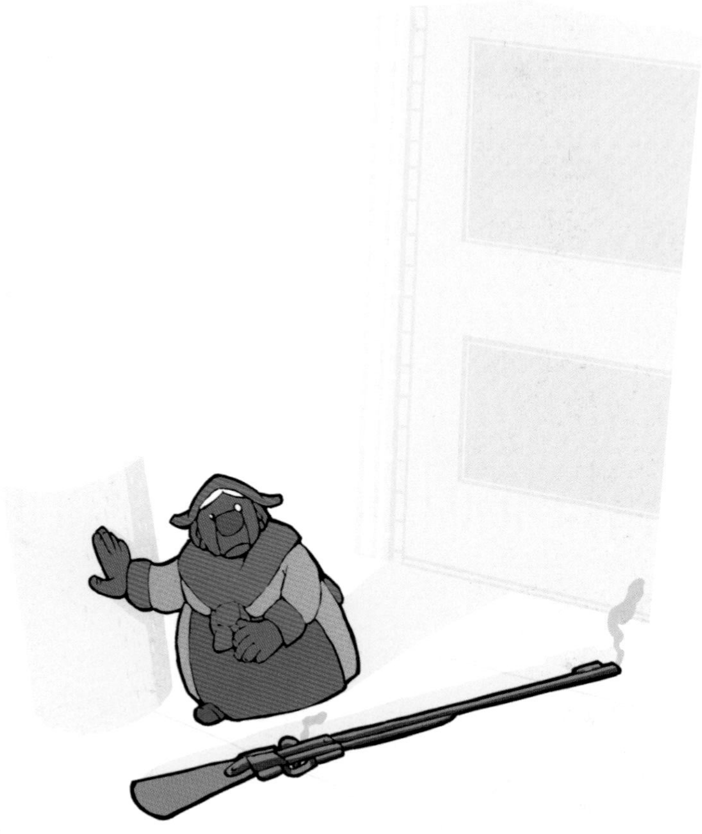

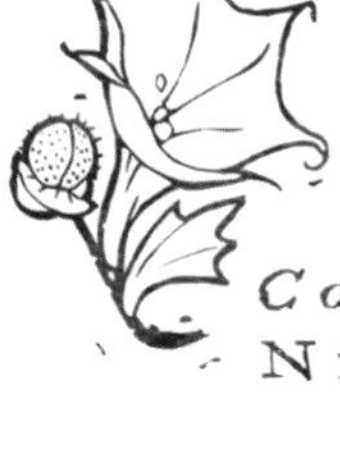

Coming NEXT Season:

THE LOST COLONY

BOOK NO. 3

Last RIGHTS

First Second

New York & London

Copyright © 2007 by Grady Klein

Published by First Second
First Second is an imprint of Roaring Brook Press, a division of Holtzbrinck
Publishing Holdings Limited Partnership
175 Fifth Avenue, New York, NY 10010

Distributed in Canada by H. B. Fenn and Company Ltd.
Distributed in the United Kingdom by Macmillan Children's Books,
a division of Pan Macmillan.

Cataloging-in-Publication Data is on file at the Library of Congress.

ISBN-13: 978-1-59643-098-3
ISBN-10: 1-59643-098-2

First Second books are available for special promotions and premiums.
For details, contact: Director of Special Markets, Holtzbrinck Publishers.

First Edition June 2007

Printed in China

10 9 8 7 6 5 4 3 2 1